NEW LANARK
IN SEARCH OF UTOPIA

C A Hope

D1422229

Marluc Publishing

First published in Great Britain as a paperback original in
2015 by
Marluc Publishing

www.completely-novel.com

ISBN 978 184914 7972

Printed and bound by Lightning Source International
Front cover produced by ronindreamer
All rights reserved
Front cover Artwork by Lane Brown
Back cover photograph of New Lanark by C.A. Hope

For my beloved sons with all my love.

New Lanark In Search of Utopia the Third Book in The New Lanark Trilogy

Introduction

In January 1814, Robert Owen made a triumphant return to the New Lanark Mills, bringing with him new business partners who were sympathetic to his plans. This was his opportunity to put his philosophy into practice and provide a practical example of how to achieve a peaceful and happy society.

The United Kingdom was still heavily embroiled in wars with both France and America. Blockaded to the east and west, the island nation was facing starvation, merchants crippled by rising taxes and a frightening scarcity of jobs due to the industrial revolution. With food riots, organised gangs breaking machinery and calls for rebellion against the government, Lord Liverpool and his Cabinet were struggling against a tide of discontent.

Owen firmly believed that he held the answer and with his new found fame he embarked on standing up for the working class and spreading his 'New View of Society'.

Told through the lives of the people who lived there, this is the unfolding story of the social enlightenment which took place in New Lanark in the early years of the nineteenth century.

All the true events have been meticulously researched, as have the lives of Owen, his family and contemporaries. A full list of the real characters can be found at the end of this book.

Chapter One

"I know that society may be formed so as to exist without crime, without poverty, with health greatly improved, with little, if any misery and with intelligence and happiness increased a hundredfold."
Robert Owen

1814

The icy flakes falling on the afternoon of Robert Owen's euphoric return to New Lanark were the forerunners of weeks of prolonged snowfall.

After many months away from the factory, Owen plunged straight into handling a potentially catastrophic situation. The entire British Isles lay paralysed and shivering beneath severe frosts and heavy snowstorms. Roads were hazardous and tales abounded of even the mighty mail coaches floundering or overturning. Efforts to clear the drifts were thwarted by north winds blowing blizzards of snow over layers of impacted ice.

The New Lanark mills were frequently cut off from the ports of either Glasgow or Leith. Raw materials ran low and orders mounded up in the basement storerooms awaiting collection. Even the sea froze in sheltered harbours, smothering the lapping waves and threatening to crush boats between groaning blocks of ice.

Silent and eerily still between frost whitened cliffs, Corra Linn waterfall displayed a static spectacle of glistening icicles. Water ran under the Clyde's snow covered surface, but there was rarely sufficient to power all the waterwheels, forcing two, sometimes three, of the four mills to stand idle. By organising shifts, Owen kept Mill One working night and day, determined to keep all his workers employed and production maintained.

It was well into March before the thaw set in properly, bringing the welcome clatter of laden wagons and the return of sightseers to view the pioneering village. Despite the daily struggles of going about their chores in such harsh weather, the residents of New Lanark were in good spirits. After all the uncertainty of the last

1

year, they were deeply relieved to have their old master back in charge.

One Sunday, as the congregation of the Old Scotch Independents Church flowed out from the service in New Buildings, the dainty cloaked figure of Anne Caroline Owen detached from the crowd. Picking her way cautiously between mounds of deflated snow and slushy puddles, she wished to visit their village house, concerned by reports of the housekeeper having been struck down with apoplexy.

The gravity of her servant's condition was clear the moment Anne Caroline looked on Mrs Cooper's pale face. Cruelly lit by a shaft of stark daylight from the skylight, her pointed features were exaggerated, protruding from deeply lined skin, her eyes sunk in black shadows, one side of her mouth drooping, dribbling.

The invalid was embarrassed by her predicament and could not bring herself to meet her employer's gaze.

'Good evening, Cooper, I hope you are warm enough?' Anne Caroline cast an assessing eye around the attic bedroom noting yellow flames licking over black coal, the chill of damp air against her face. 'Keep the fire in at all times,' she instructed the gawky young maid, 'and close the door, the draught from the stairwell is strong. I sent word of my visit, requesting a nourishing broth to be prepared for the patient. Has she taken a dish?'

'No, ma'am.'

'Have you offered her a dish?'

'No' yit, ma'am, it's no ready yit.'

Exasperated, Anne Caroline prayed for patience. She sat down on the edge of the bed, there being no chair in the room, and pulled at the fingers of her gloves; peeling them off and laying them on her lap.

Movement under Cooper's papery eyelids showed she was awake. Occasionally, her sparse grey lashes flickered apart to glance towards her visitor before closing again.

Anne Caroline turned her attention to the servant girl.

'You are Lorna, are you not?' the maid nodded, bobbing a curtsey and nervously rubbing the end of her wet nose. 'Lorna, bring up whatever is ready. Now! How can Mrs Cooper recover if she is starving? And bring more blankets.'

2

After an awkward start and a few kind words, sounding trite even to her own ears, Anne Caroline opened her Bible. She suggested the chapter the Reverend had chosen that day, Deuteronomy 13, already marked by a frayed pink silk ribbon. The two women shared little in common except the Scriptures and the silence was more easily filled if they did not have to converse on a topic.

The only relevant topic, of which they were both well aware, was what to do with Cooper until she died. She certainly could not run a household or cook a meal. The sudden collapse of her strength, especially down her right side, rendered her incapable of even the smallest task.

To the accompanying tick of a little wooden carriage clock on the mantelpiece, Anne Caroline completed her reading, with Cooper joining her in the last line. The old woman's words were slurred and indistinct, like a distorted echo, 'to do that which is right in the eyes of the Lord thy God'.

Then, taking Cooper's mottled, blue veined hand in hers, they prayed.

Immediately upon her return to Braxfield House, Anne Caroline sought out her husband in his study and relayed the episode.

'I was with the poor woman for barely thirty minutes and I fear they may have been the only minutes of the entire day when she had company. Oh, it was cheerless and so cold! I am sure the fire was lit just minutes before my arrival. That maid will have to go.'

Robert Owen gave her his full attention, laying down his quill. It joined a pile of others on a brass tray housing a candelabra, glass inkwells, stubs of sealing wax and a blotting roller: an arrangement Owen found the most practical. He had been engrossed in paperwork for hours, his dark hair tousled and falling over his forehead, shirt open at the neck, sleeves rolled up. Neat stacks of correspondence and ledgers covered the surface of his desk, allowing only sufficient space for his current letter, half written and placed precisely in the pool of light.

'You say she was taken ill some days ago?' He asked. 'Our physician has seen her?'

'Yes, it was he who sent word to me and I know he has arranged for two of the village women to attend to her ... personal requirements. She is completely debilitated and will not recover, but, Robert, she has nobody.'

'No one in this community is alone. We must all take care of those who have fallen ill or are suffering hard times.'

'That is all very well to say, my dear, but you must understand that our housekeeper was not well liked. Indeed, her difficult temperament is known to many and I had a great deal of trouble hiring a maid to work under her at all. It is an unchristian thing for me to say but I'm afraid Cooper may well have been harsh with Lorna and it is unfortunate that she must now rely upon her for sustenance. In turn, this must make it hard for the child to show charity.'

'Hard it may be, but it serves no purpose to either party to simply dismiss the maid. Besides, there is yet snow upon the ground and no other work to be found in the county, I cannot turn the girl away. Perhaps she has never nursed anyone before and having been subjected to Cooper's criticism in the past, is at a loss as to what to do?'

'Perhaps.'

'Caroline, you are a kind person, you know instinctively how to make a patient comfortable, but that is because you were fortunate in having a loving childhood. All around you, you were given examples of how to relieve suffering. It would seem obvious that our young maid has not had this experience; she needs to be taught what to do. This is easily remedied!' Owen's lean features exuded satisfaction. 'We have many capable housewives who can show her how to care for an invalid, I will ask Clegg to enquire of the Committees in the village. Then we shall not only alleviate Cooper's sad situation but also provide Lorna with a useful lesson which she can apply throughout her life.'

'Well, if you believe this can be done.' Anne Caroline moved restlessly around the room, she was not convinced. 'However, we still have the problem of hiring a new housekeeper which I will discuss with Miss Wilson and, of course, Cooper cannot stay in the house indefinitely.'

'We will find suitable accommodation where she can be cared for in more comfort.' Owen sat forward again, charging his quill with ink and proceeding to write a list of requirements. 'My plans for the youngest members of society may be receiving the most

4

attention at present but it is equally important ...' the quill scratched noisily across the paper, 'to care for our elderly and infirm.'

Much as she disapproved of him working on the Lord's day, the day of rest, she left Owen to his papers. Retiring to her bedroom to change for the evening, she lingered on the staircase to enjoy the peaceful sounds of her home.

It gave her a warm, secure feeling to have her husband with them again. His long visits to London throughout the previous year had been made all the more harrowing because of Robert Dale's terrible illness. However, it was not just in times of trouble that she needed his presence, it was to share their lives together, the little moments.

The house was unusually quiet. The children were down in the basement, in the old part of the building, taking their weekly tea with Miss Wilson in her sitting room.

Anne Caroline allowed this little ritual, despite initial misgivings of such an indulgence on the Sabbath. Wafts of warm baking aromas filtered past the green baize door when Sheddon, the butler, and a young footman moved to and fro, quietly lighting candles and lamps, replenishing coal scuttles, bolting shutters, drawing curtains, sharing hushed conversations with the maids as they prepared the large house for the night.

The threat of losing the mills at New Lanark and her husband's immense effort to retain them, made their present life all the more precious. Recalling the day he returned from Glasgow with his new partners, a smile tugged at her lips.

Oh what a day!

The pipe band swaggering in time to the pounding drum beat, music bellowing amongst the thronged streets, fiddlers dancing as they bowed lively jigs: she could almost hear it now. Everyone joined in, from the stooped elderly residents leaning on their canes to little boys and girls jumping in exhilaration at the spectacle, all shouting and waving their congratulations. She was deeply affected by the boisterous and obviously heartfelt affection showered upon her husband. It also brought home to her the strong sense of responsibility he felt for their welfare, causing her to become much more involved with the village and its people.

During the months leading up to that memorable day, when the shadow of losing all he had worked for was at its darkest, she was embarrassed to realise her thoughts had been primarily on her own and her family's welfare. If they lost New Lanark, where would they live? The shame of telling her sisters and wider society that her husband had been dispensed with, sacked from the mills, and was virtually penniless.

It made her flush with mortification to look back on her selfishness.

Robert had no such thoughts, he never concerned himself in how other people viewed him, a quality she envied. He was utterly driven by his desire to implement his plans to better society and with every passing day he became more passionate about his ideals. As he told her, back in the worst moments of their dilemma, if he lost New Lanark he would just start again, somewhere else. She did not doubt him but her prayers were filled with pleas for their safe deliverance from the impending loss of their home and livelihood. Sometimes, she admitted to herself, dear Robert's optimistic, confident attitude seemed to border on naivety.

She smoothed her fingertips over the oak banister, enjoying the warm scent of polish, a reminder of her childhood in Charlotte Street which in turn brought memories of her beloved father.

'These are happy times,' she told herself, catching at her skirt to continue up the staircase, 'I thank you, Lord, for blessing us with these happy days.'

***

Fiona threw the plaid shawl around her eldest daughter's shoulders and adjusted the ribbons on the girl's bonnet. Her two youngest sons were already buttoning their own jackets, jostling with other lads as they passed, joking and throwing playful punches at friends. It was the end of the school day and over a hundred children were streaming noisily down the stairs in Mill Four, pulling on warm clothing and racing out the door.

At thirteen years, Sionaidh was unable to tie a bow or have the inclination to dress warmly before going outside. She lived each day in her own world, rarely speaking except to repeat back the words spoken to her and paid little attention to classes during

6

school time, preferring to hum tunelessly, grimacing or smiling at thoughts only known to her. At first glance, there was nothing to distinguish her from the other girls of her age: slender build, her dark wavy auburn hair pulled back in a plait showing a clear brow and plain features and always neatly dressed in the regulation tunic. However, as teachers and fellow pupils soon discovered, she was so engrossed within her own mind that her gaze, sliding over their enquiring faces, seemed vacant.

There were several other children in the school like Sionaidh, incapable of understanding or taking part in the lessons. Their families worked in the mills and neighbours either did not know how to cope with them or in some cases professed to be frightened of them, so they were deposited at the classroom door every morning.

'Och they're jist different,' Fiona would say when the other class assistants declared they did not like looking after 'the Dafties'.

It hurt her to hear the cruel name-calling, causing many a tear when she was alone in the evening. Had it not been for Mr Owen's strict rules to be kind and understanding to the children at all times, she dreaded to think of the spiteful treatment her daughter might have endured. Then the fits started, mercifully few and far between but nevertheless, a constant worry.

'Fiona! there ye are!' Sarah hurried across the crowded hall of Mill Four, 'Weel, Ah've done it, whit ye esked.' She held up a small wooden box. 'Spectacles!'

'An' dae they help? Can ye see?'

'It wis like a miracle! Oh, an' sae funny ...' Sarah started to laugh. 'Ah've alis been able tae see things far awa' like, but the last few years everything near tae me wis blurry. Sae there Ah wis sitting on a wee stool wi' ma eyes tight shut, wi' him bending o'er me pushing the wires aroond ma ears an' pressin' on ma neb. He stands back an' says, 'open your eyes woman!' The giggles erupted again, 'Ah let oot this whoop! Honest tae guidness, Ah could nae haud it in! Weel, he sort o' staggered back, startled, and doesn't he knock into a table wi' jars? Sent them crashing tae the flair!'

Fiona was laughing too, picturing the scene. 'Why did ye scream?'

'It were sich a shock! His face seemed tae be jist inches awa', his fine dark eyes and lang lashes ... an' sae clear an' sharp! Ah have nae seen a man's face that clear since ... Ah cannae mind when! Aw, it were braw!'

'D'ye ken ye can see weel enough tae sew ma new outfit?'

'Oh aye. An' Ah've bin thinking on it and have an idea of whit would look bonnie. Is it in the evening or the day?'

'Three o'clock. Ah've bin gi'en permission tae leave ma work early. Och, it maks me sick wi' nerves tae think on it!'

Fiona took Sionaidh's hand and they walked out together, the boys running ahead with their little cousin, Lily. Sarah's face was alight with enthusiasm as she described her design and when they reached the far side of the lade she insisted they go straight to the store and look at material.

At that moment, Cal was walking home from the Forge and caught sight of them disappearing through the shop door. Through the dusk he noticed his nephews, Tom and Alex, running off towards the steps leading out of the village: the girls must be intending to take their time.

He picked up his pace again: he did not want his family to know where he was going.

After days of turning the matter over and over in his head, he decided to pay a call on Mrs Cooper. He knew where she was because of Rosie's love of showing off her knowledge of village business. Walking slowly up Braxfield Road he noted the numbers over the doorways until he came to the right one.

What would he say? Maybe she was too ill to accept visitors?

He glanced at the house again, catching sight of a thin, dishevelled man staring at him from the window. With a sharp intake of breath, he recognised the face: grimy from a day's work, horse hair stuck to his torn jacket, lank curls straggling over his collar from under a cap.

It was his own reflection.

Whatever had he been thinking? He could not enter the house of the woman who had once been the Owen's housekeeper while stinking of stables, sweat and coal smoke. Wiping at his arms, he walked away shedding wisps of hay and showers of horse hair, cursing the time of year for them casting their coats. He would

8

wash and change before going back, but maybe not this evening, maybe tomorrow.

It was three days later, having completed an errand for Kyle MacInnes, before he spurred up his courage, purchased a sugared biscuit from the store and returned to Mrs Cooper's lodgings. His tentative knock on the door brought no response and reasoning the woman was probably alone and incapable of opening the door herself, he knocked again, politely removed his cap, and entered.

In contrast to the bright Spring day outside, the room was dark and it took a few moments for his sight to adjust.

Approaching the bedside warily, he whispered, 'Mistress Cooper?'

There was no movement in the form under the tightly tucked blankets and his pulse began to race; was she dead? Was he too late? He leaned in closer, relieved to hear the gentle rhythm of shallow breathing.

For a long time he stood in silence, not knowing what to do or say, just watching the old woman sleeping. Although she had always been gaunt, she was considerably more haggard than he recalled; her features frail and suddenly aged. Someone had combed her grey hair to fall around her shoulders and dressed her in a white cap and high collared nightgown. The soft frills of lace encircling her wizened face were out of character for the stern, puritanical housekeeper he once knew. This upset him. She would abhor the thought of being seen with her hair loose, decorated with ribbons and lace. A wave of pity made him hope she had lost her senses and did not know what was happening to her.

He laid the paper bag with the biscuit on a wooden stool near her bed which held her Bible and an unlit oil lamp.

'Mistress Cooper, ye may remember me, Calum Scott? Sarah's brither?'

Her jaw moved, the tip of her tongue attempting to moisten the thin puckered lips, eyelids fluttering but not opening.

'Ah dinnae ken if ye hear me, but Ah came tae say ... thank ye. Thank ye fur saving me. T'were a lang time ago, but ye did a fine thing an' weel ... there's those who say ye didnae care fur ithers, but ye stopped me frae daen something terrible an', weel, ye cared enough tae save ma life.' He watched for signs of understanding.

9

'Ah ne'er showed ye ma gratitude an' fur tha' Ah'm sorry but Ah hope ... an' wid esk ye ... forgive me?'

She swallowed, trying to form words, her breathing becoming laboured and rapid.

'Ah dinnae want tae upset ye, Ah'll leave noo.'

Then her eyes opened; cloudy, struggling to focus as she murmured, 'Bless you.'

Her left hand grasped feebly towards him and involuntarily he covered it with his own, pressing reassuringly, his thumb stroking across her fingers to give comfort as he would to an injured animal.

Again she whispered and he strained to hear.

'Your sister ... I pray for her ... tell her ... sorry.'

There was a sharp rap on the door and Cal released Cooper's hand in an instant, swinging round to find the corpulent black frock-coated figure of a minister of the Kirk entering the room.

'Ye have a visitor this day!' Reverend Grieve's cheery voice boomed into the silent scene but on seeing Cal standing at the bed side, his eyes narrowed. 'What business d'ye have here? This lady is gravely ill.'

'Ah wis jist awa'.' Cal edged past the chubby figure.

'Aye, I would think that best.' There was no dismissing the suspicious tone nor the quick glance at Cal's hands and towards his pockets.

Cooper tried to turn her head towards the commotion, seeing Cal's silhouette moving past the bright window towards the door.

'Stay!' she begged, but no voice would form, leaving the sound of her cry ringing in her mind.

'Now, Mrs Cooper,' the reverend levered his large backside onto the end of her bed. The patient was clearly asleep but he felt it his duty to spend some time with her so opened his Prayer book, 'Let us share the glories of the Lord our God.'

He spotted the paper bag and on exploring its contents, rationalised that it would only go to waste if he did not eat it. Biscuits became soft so quickly and this was fresh and crisp.

Crumbs fell across his black clericals as he launched into the prayers between bites, imbuing the words with feeling, enjoying the sound of his own voice and the taste of sugar.

Unnoticed, tears escaped from Cooper's eyes, trickling down to soak the lacy folds of her night cap.

***

By the beginning of April, although snow still lay in the lee of stone walls and in deep gullies, fresh shoots began to spread colour across Clydesdale. Freed from the frozen hillside, water sparkled in silver ribbons, streaming down the hills into the river Clyde and rushing through the gorge. It created such a roar pounding over Corra and Bonnington Linn's waterfalls that it could be heard for miles. The brimming, swirling water filled the mill lade to full capacity, powering all four of New Lanark's mills with ease.

Owen was relieved.

The protracted wars were grinding down markets, making trade almost impossible especially as it was driving up prices for the raw materials. Cotton manufacturers throughout the United Kingdom were suffering the consequences, facing falling income and in too many cases, closures.

Now that he was back at the helm, Owen was exploring every avenue to keep his mills afloat. His new partners agreed to forego profits for the first few years, allowing the money to be ploughed into his plans for the school and the new Institute for the Formation of Character.

The stone and mortar buildings might stand boldly within the village but they were empty shells until sufficient funds could be found to complete the interiors. By persuasive discussions in the loud, smoky Tontine Rooms or during hasty introductions in corridors or even seeking out merchants in their city haunts, Owen brought in orders and signed new contracts at every opportunity.

Driven by his desire to put into practice his vision for creating the new, better society outlined in his essays, Owen spent hours analysing his managers' reports. It was vital to not only seek new business but to find ways to cut waste, increase out-put and create the much needed profit.

Russia was proving to be a fruitful market and his agent was hopeful of expanding his customers in the coming year: the war permitting.

11

While Mrs Cooper was slipping slowly away from Life amidst the relentless routine of mill bells ringing and workers hurrying to and fro along New Lanark's streets, the great war machine in Europe was churning to a peak.

With cautious hopes, Owen scanned news reports telling of the victories against Napoleon's armies. By the end of March the Allies were entering Paris but the beleaguered Emperor fought on until finally, on April 6th, realising all was lost, he abdicated.

Throughout Great Britain, Town Criers clattered their bells and declared the end of the war with France.

After nearly six million deaths, the bloodshed from the battlefields in Europe appeared to be coming to an end. It was hard to grasp and was greeted by apprehension and disbelief. The indomitable Napoleon Bonaparte was no longer a threat? What would happen now? Those who remembered the French Revolution and the bloody excesses and tyranny which caused it, shook their heads and sucked their teeth.

For the merchants throughout the land, Owen included, it was a cause for rejoicing.

'I must journey to London next week,' he announced at dinner, glancing around excitedly at his wife and their two eldest sons. 'There is much to be done and people to see. All the latest news will be in the capital.'

Anne Caroline was about to take a mouthful of sponge and egg custard; she laid the spoon down again.

'So soon?'

'The roads are clear and the weather milder so why delay? Mr Bentham has expressed an interest in meeting with me to discuss my plans and I am eager to oblige.'

Having not confirmed his intentions to invest in New Lanark until a few weeks after the dramatic auction, Jeremy Bentham was a late addition to the new partnership.

Robert Dale and William were immediately full of questions: could they go with him? would he meet the Prime Minister? or go to the Palace? Anne Caroline watched their animated faces, heard her husband's responses and attempted to finish her plate of cooling dessert.

'How long will you be away?' she heard herself ask, even as the words formed she wished she could retract them.

'No more than a week or so.'

She laid her serviette on the table and prepared to offer thanks to God for the meal, her sons immediately bowing their heads. As soon as the short prayer was over, Owen excused himself, eager to return to his study but as he passed her chair he laid a hand on her shoulder, warm, reassuring, then, with a light caress to her cheek, he was gone.

How easily he affected her mood, she mused. It was only to be expected that he would have to go to London from time to time, but then he would come home again and they could do things together, as a family.

The next morning, while Ramsay was styling Anne Caroline's hair, Miss Wilson came to the bedroom door to say Peggy would be grateful if the mistress could come to the nursery before going out that morning.

The reason for the summons was obvious the moment Anne Caroline saw her eldest son.

On Monday, he was fine. She remembered watching him at morning prayers and thinking how well he looked. On Tuesday, he kept squeezing his eyes shut, saying his vision was blurring, last night he was rubbing them and now she looked in dismay upon his bloodshot pupils and swollen lids.

'Are you in pain, my dearest?' she laid her palm against his forehead, relieved to feel it cool and dry, his dark locks springing back into a thick fringe. He was sitting on the edge of his bed and she knelt before him, peering into his face. 'Robert, can you see me?'

'Yes, I can see you, Mama, but as if through a mist and tears keep escaping but I am not crying.' He said the last quite adamantly. 'It is not exactly *painful*. Hot, my eyes feel hot.'

Peggy's usually cheerful face was a picture of concern as she hovered at her mistress' side.

'He's been sae much better these past weeks an' noo this! Ah wis askin' if he was playing wi' the dogs,' she said, anxiously, 'ye mind how sore his eyes were that time he hadnae washed his hands and got dirt all o'er his self? But, he had nae.'

Anne Caroline stood up, tightening the satin sash of her housecoat as if to gain control of the situation. Robert Dale had been such a strong, healthy boy until he was struck by the measles.

Since then, for over a year now, he struggled with weakness and fell victim to every chill and digestive complaint which presented itself. Not only was he physically unwell, he was abnormally sensitive emotionally, being moved to tears on hearing a tune played in the minor key, reading a poignant piece of prose or any show of affection towards him.

'I am sure it will pass,' she said firmly, forcing a smile. 'However, stay in bed for this morning and I will send for McGibbon, just to ease our minds.'

The physician arrived within the hour and Anne Caroline met him in the hallway. Outwardly, she appeared composed, demurely dressed in a high necked day dress, her hair swept up under an unadorned cap. She had prayed that the days of calling the doctor would not return and strove to remain calm.

After a thorough examination, McGibbon was no nearer a diagnosis.

'Keep him away from bright light, draw the curtains closed in this room throughout the day. I would suggest bed rest and no reading or straining of the eyes in any form. We will see how he is in a day or two.'

When no improvement could be seen after several days, McGibbon recommended the services of an oculist in Hamilton who he knew by good reputation.

'It is very concerning,' Anne Caroline told her husband after the eye specialist's visit. 'He suggests our son takes the fresh air of the sea-side, apparently it works wonders for these sorts of conditions. Yet, here in Lanark we are as far from the coast as one can be in this country.'

'I shall make enquiries,' Owen comforted. 'I believe there are places near Edinburgh, on the east coast, where the air is considered purest.'

'Poor dear, he has suffered so much, it pains me to look on his sweet face and yet he remains quiet and stoic. I am praying for his recovery.'

Downstairs in the kitchen, Miss Wilson was sharing a pot of tea with Cook and Ramsay, relaying the latest news of Master Robert's condition and Sheddon, passing the doorway, joined them. He did not enter into gossip but was as anxious as any in the house to hear about the child.

14

'Och, it's a cryin' shame,' Cook pursed her mouth. 'That lad was ne'er happier than running aboot the woods or awa' on his pony, an' noo he's up there in his bed. But we must jist be thankful it's no' a fever he has! They say the pox is bad in Glasgie ...'

'Well, there is no fever here, Cook,' Sheddon said gravely. 'If it is an affliction to the eyes and the physician believes salty sea air will cure it, then I have no doubt the Master will make the required arrangements.'

Cook folded her arms and looked doubtful but said no more.

'As you know,' Sheddon continued, 'Mr Owen will be travelling to London next week and Murdoch will be accompanying him. Mrs Owen will have a great deal on her mind with Master Robert ill again and we must do all we can to make her time here alone as smooth as possible.'

Miss Wilson straightened her shoulders, 'You can be sure of that. The other children are all hale and hearty and with the lighter days upon us now no doubt she will be kept busy with matters in the village.'

Sheddon was about to withdraw to his office when he turned back, 'Has a replacement been found for Mrs Cooper yet?'

Miss Wilson gave a rueful sigh. 'There is one applicant who may be suitable. I discussed her letter with Mrs Owen and have written to invite her for an interview.' Her gaze wondered over the game birds and smoked hams strung from the ceiling hooks, interspersed with bunches of rosemary, thyme and plaits of onions. 'One would think there would be many people after the position and, in truth, we had a good few enquiries, but they will be expecting to come to a household like this. Most were giving references from good addresses where there are at least a dozen indoor servants. It is different in the village house and for all her unfortunate traits, Mrs Cooper did her duty well with only a maid or two to hand.'

'It is a peculiar job,' Sheddon agreed. 'If there are as many visitors to the mills this year as last, the important ones, and certainly the acquaintances of the Master who have travelled a distance, require refreshments after the tours and sometimes beds for the night. Yet, to all intents and purposes, the house is empty.'

'With long days of solitude to contend with,' Ramsay nodded, knowingly, 'that was Cooper's problem.'

15

'She had mair problems than that,' Cook laughed, tapping her temple and rolling her eyes. 'A mair miserable auld bisom it would be hard tae find.'

Sheddon tut-tutted, 'Now, that's unkind. The poor woman is on her death bed.'

'May the Lord forgive me, but she wis as bitter as the north wind in winter.' Cook waited until the butler was out of ear shot before muttering, 'Snapped at me, she did, many's the time! Bit ma heid aff! And fer somethin' as small as sittin' in the wrang seat at the Sunday service! No wonder she needed tae pray sae hard. Ah hope He taks her intae Heaven or she'll be muckle disappointed!'

Miss Wilson's conscience pricked. 'I should go and see her,' she said quietly. 'Oh, I know she was a difficult woman but ...'

Cook's button eyes glistened, 'Noo ye make me feel bad but ye ken whit they say? Ye reap whit ye sow.'

Down the corridor from the kitchen, the back door opened and maids carried baskets of folded washing in from the line, their giggles echoing around the flagstones and tiled walls.

'I'd best get on,' Cook pushed herself up from her seat, 'It's guid tae hear the lassies in high spirits. Laugh when ye can, that's whit Ah say!'

In Cooper's room in Braxfield Road, there was no laughter.

Curled up on her side, mouth open, eyes closed to the world, the old lady's erratic, rattling breaths slowly gave way to other sounds in the room. Neighbours took turns to sit with her and on that afternoon Mrs Lambie's clicking knitting needles added a staccato rhythm to the ticking clock and coals hissing in a crimson mound in the grate.

It was only on changing over her needles and tucking the free one securely under her arm to count her stitches, that Mrs Lambie became aware of a change and looked across the shadowy room to the patient.

It was quiet. She immediately laid her handiwork to one side and went over to the bed, already knowing what she would find.

'God bless ye and grant ye everlasting salvation,' she whispered.

For several minutes, she stood respectfully beside the corpse, murmuring the Lord's Prayer. Since Dale's time, she and the housekeeper attended the same Old Scotch Independents Church

16

services in the village yet apart from a few pleasantries at the doorway, she knew little of the woman whose life had just ceased.

'A merciful release,' she said to the empty room, laying her wool and the half finished baby shawl neatly into her basket.

Other thoughts were already crowding her mind. If she hurried up the street she could tell Isa of Mrs Cooper's passing so she would no longer be needed and could see to her daughter's baby instead. Then there was the doctor to tell ... or should she see the Reverend first? And Mrs Jacob, who was only a few doors away, she would want to lay out the body as soon as possible. A quick glance at the clock told her she might also have time to visit her sister for a while and still have her husband's meal on the table before the Mill Bell released him from the factory for the night.

Chapter Two

"O, wad some power the giftie gie us
To see oursels as others see us"
Robert Burns

To hide her trembling fingers, Fiona tucked her arm under Joe's, relaxed her tense shoulders and walked into the Mayor's reception at the Town Hall. She was breathless, her heart racing; never had she felt so uncomfortable about the thought of meeting people.

'Dinnae leave me alane,' she begged Joe. 'Whit will Ah say tae them?'

'Ah'll no' leave ye, lass.' He paused at the doorway, removing his hat and smoothing his thick, ruffled, fair hair into place. He was looking around for a familiar face. 'There's Mr Ewing. Come, ye've met him afore and Melanie, his dochter.'

He stepped forward into the crowd, a tall figure in his black tail coat and newly washed cream breeches. Fiona clung to his arm as unobtrusively as possible, fixing a smile on her lips. She nodded thanks to the chattering men and women moving out of their way and gazed around at the scene, finding Sarah's words, 'you'll be mixing with the toffs,' to be true.

A small bewigged, formally dressed chamber orchestra played in one corner, competing with the rumbling chatter of guests. In waves, guests swarmed around several long tables draped to the floor in white cloths. Arranged at intervals between platters of food, tall vases of vividly coloured hot-house flowers trailed strands of ivy to sweep down, encircling gilt-edged dishes.

To Fiona's left, the loud English tones of a matronly lady cut through the general swell of conversation, beseeching her husband to find her a seat. To her right stood a cluster of earnest youths in spotless white breeches and cutaway velvet jackets. They were in a lively exchange about the war with America, talking over each other and jabbing the air to force home their points of view.

'Mrs Scott,' Melanie Ewing cried, her chubby cheeks dimpling with pleasure between the bows of her straw bonnet. 'Ah have known of you fae sae lang, I feel you're already a friend!'

'And Ah've heard much of you, Miss Ewing.' Fiona paid particular care in pronouncing each word. 'D'ye always come tae these affairs? Ma heid's spinning wi' the noise!' She was going to add that she hadn't felt so overwhelmed by sound since working the jennies in Mill One. However, in the company of the county gentry, town councillors and a good sprinkling of Lords, she thought better of drawing attention to herself as having been a mill worker.

'Mrs Scott,' Mr Ewing's grey head nodded courteously.

So long her husband's employer, Fiona found it hard to meet him socially and found herself blushing: should she bob a curtsy or bow her head?

Beneath his bushy grey brows, his eyes twinkled appreciatively. For his part, he recalled seeing Joe's wife fleetingly over the years and while noting her pleasing face, as all men did, seeing her dressed up for an occasion took him by surprise.

'Ye'll soon get used tae the din,' he assured her.

Fiona treated him to a wide smile, aware of his gaze straying to her bosom and feeling immense gratitude to Sarah for the modesty of her dress.

The current fashion was for low cut bodices and short puff sleeves but Fiona was horrified by the amount of flesh this revealed. With more than four decades behind her, not to mention seven children, she would not have people thinking Joe's wife was a floosie. After a good deal of laughter, Sarah reached a compromise and found gauze to match the pale yellow background of the green sprigged material for the dress. When this was stitched along the entire neckline and drawn up to form a soft frill around the throat, Fiona felt far more comfortable.

The effect was elegant and simple, embellished with frills on the hemline and, an inspired addition, a matching reticule. Even Fiona's poke bonnet, which had seen better days, was transformed by Sarah's skill in making use of left over gauze and the careful placement of wide satin ribbons tied into a flourishing bow.

Joe introduced her to several people of whom she had often heard him speak and was delighted to put the faces to the names.

'Mr Scott, how lovely to see you here!'

Fiona swung round to find the neat figure of Anne Caroline Owen smiling up at Joe. Seeing the mill owner's wife at such close

19

quarters, her resemblance to her late father was obvious. Although not a beauty, Mrs Owen's kindly features, porcelain complexion and perfectly styled brown hair exuded an attractive, unpretentious charm.

'Mrs Owen,' Joe gave a polite bow. 'May Ah present my wife?' Joe's arm went proudly around Fiona's waist, drawing her into the conversation.

'Oh, but we have met before,' Anne Caroline's brown eyes searched Fiona's face. 'As an impressionable child, I witnessed the day of your marriage and it is engraved on my memory. You were such a beautiful bride and I must say you look just as lovely today! It is hard to believe so many years have passed.'

Fiona was overcome with nerves.

'We were honoured, Ma'am,' she blurted out, 'tae be wed by yer faither, Mr Dale.'

'It was his pleasure, I'm sure,' Anne Caroline smiled warmly but there was a wistful tone to her words; 'God rest his soul.'

An awkward silence threatened until, adroit in social chitchat, Anne Caroline enquired after their children, easing the conversation into an area of mutual interest. On learning of Fiona's role in the classroom, they talked of the new improvements in the School and around the village.

'And your sister,' Anne Caroline addressed Joe. She was so small and her hat's brim so wide that he had to bend forward to engage eye contact. 'I have not seen nor heard of her for years,' she continued. 'Did she move from Glasgow?'

'Aye,' Joe answered, hesitantly, 'she left Glasgie. Unfortunately, her husband died.'

'Oh gracious! I am so sorry to hear that. How is she faring?'

'She is well... now, Ma'am. Thank ye. She's in New Lanark again, in the mills.'

Anne Caroline was aghast. 'The mills! How long has she been in the village?'

'Oh, some years. Her youngest daughter is now ...' Joe turned enquiring eyes to Fiona.

'Lily will be seven years now, Mrs Owen, an' she wis born jist efter Sarah returned.'

'Why ever is she working in the factory? She has great talent as a dressmaker, surely she would be better suited to that industry?'

'Oh aye, there's nae doubt o' that,' Fiona smoothed her hand down the skirt of her dress. 'Ah persuaded her to mak this fer me.'

'It is charming!' Anne Caroline looked more closely at the details around the cuffs. 'You say, you *persuaded* her. Tell me, does she wish to be in the mills? By that I mean, does she *not* wish to sew?'

'Oh no, Ma'am, she wid much raither be sewin'. She hates the mill work ... Oh, Ah beg yer pardon, it's no' that she disnae appreciate havin' a joab, she does ... very much.' Fiona paused to gather her thoughts, startled by her own foolishness in saying anything against Mr Owen's mills.

'It wis her eyes, Mrs Owen,' Joe said simply. 'She could nae see tae use a needle but now, and in no small part due to Mr Owen's arrangements in New Lanark, she has recently acquired spectacles.'

'Well, I am delighted to know this! Do you think she would come up to Braxfield and see me? I would be very grateful if you would ask her.'

'Ah'll be sure tae tell her. Thank ye.'

The music suddenly died away, replaced by a commotion at the head of the hall; the Mayor was preparing to speak.

Anne Caroline rose on her toes and looked around. 'Please excuse me, I must find my husband and make sure we leave as soon as the speech is over. He is going to London tomorrow and there is much to be done but he insisted we attend this function.' She patted Fiona on the arm, 'I am so glad we did!'

Watching her wend her way towards the unmistakable dapper figure of Robert Owen, Joe turned to Fiona, murmuring 'No' half as pleased as Sarah.'

There was another reason for Anne Caroline's sudden departure to her husband's side. Owen was engaged in conversation with Lord Armadale, but the wiry figure of Reverend Menzies, known for his hostility towards the changes at New Lanark, was edging towards them, a glowering expression creasing his whiskered face.

Menzies' grievance was with Owen's lack of Christian belief and she felt that if she stood beside her husband both her feminine presence and her own devotion to the Scriptures would defuse any argument before it even began.

Fortunately, at that moment a councillor tapped loudly on his glass and called for silence, forcing the cleric to change course and face the Mayor.

The speech was short but enthusiastic, embracing both the main reason for the reception, the start of the horse racing season at the town's famous course, and the triumphant news of the cease of hostilities with France.

At the end, everyone joined in a toast to Peace and the orchestra struck up again to accompany the party's hearty rendition of the national anthem.

'Weel,' Fiona sighed with relief as they wandered home along the Wellgate. 'Ah did nae think Ah wid, but ye ken, Joe, Ah fair enjoyed mesel'!'

'Aye, it wis a grand do.'

'Ye ken sae many o' the folk in Auld Lanark! An' seeing Mr and Mrs Owen there ... Ah alis thocht they were jist at Braxfield Hoose or in the village.'

'Naw, he's well kent noo and liked an' all. Mind the cheerin' an' carry oan when he bought back the mills?'

'Aye, but that wis doon at the mills.'

'Lass! It wis all through the toun! Ye see the visitors walking aroond the mills an' takin' a toor o' the school room? Those same people are stayin' at the inns, spending their money an' fillin' the pockets o' businesses up an' doon the High Street. The Mayor's fair made up wi' Mr Owen. An' he's a Justice o' the Peace here too.'

They walked on, slowly, Fiona leaning her head tentatively against his shoulder, mindful of crumpling the bows decorating her bonnet.

'Ah'm sae prood o' ye,' she whispered. 'Ah wis thinkin', when the Mayor was talking, his chain flashing an' all those posh folk aroond us ... it wis like a dream, like Ah wis watching mesel' frae the doorway.'

'Yer a funny lass, it wis real enough and noo we ha'e tae be hame ...' he chuckled, 'if ye din nae walk a bit faster we'll niver get there.'

'Ah cannae! These pointy shoes Sarah loaned me are squishing up ma toes!'

'D'ye want tae wait here while Ah fetch up Rusty and ye can ride hame?'

'Away! In this dress?' she glanced around. The town was now behind them, in front lay the road towards New Lanark bordered by hedgerows and pastures grazed by lazy eyed cows. 'There's no yin tae see ... an' ma hems lang.'

With a quick movement she pulled off the offending shoes, turning coyly away to untie the ribbons on her stockings and roll them off.

Joe held out his hand to steady her as she picked her steps over soft spring grass and budding dandelions, deftly avoiding thistles. Seeing her swinging along barefoot, laughing and talking about the afternoon, it brought to mind their early trysts when time was short and she was ruled by the Mill bells.

She was still ruled by the bells. The town clock was tolling six and in the next hour Fiona needed to ready herself for work and hurry down to the school room.

'It wis grand tae ha'e ye wi' me,' he broke into his wife's stream of words. 'Ye were the bonniest lass there.'

She squeezed his hand, 'Noo, that's gie nice tae hear but it's no' true! Those lassies, the ones wi' the feathers in their hats near the musicians? They were bonnie! But did ye e'er see sich daring dresses?'

He laughed, 'Ah doubt there wis a man there who did nae! They were frae London, stayin' at Bonnington fur the racing.'

'Aw, Ah wid love tae see the horse racin'! It's no' far oot o' toun, is it?'

'Jist alang fae Ewing's place.'

She gave him a mischievous look from under her lashes. 'Tak me tae the races, Joe? Tae see the winning o' the Silver Bell?'

They both knew this was very unlikely but he went along with her, 'Oh aye, why no'?'

'Ah've got the dress noo, an' all!'

'Weel, mak sure ye buy a pair o' shoes ye can walk in!'

The merry mood stayed with them and on reaching the cottage and realising they were afforded the rare luxury of being alone, a quick glance passed between them.

Whispering like lovers, they hurried upstairs.

23

***

'Ah'm here tae see, Mistress Owen.'

The footman gave a quizzical look at the middle-aged woman in front of him, recognising her as a mill worker from the shawl, muslin cap and the dusty clogs showing below her gathered skirt. He opened the back door wider and gestured for her to enter the servants' hall.

'Whit's yer name?'

Such a simple question but it was the first stumbling block.

'Mrs Rafferty, but ... perhaps ye should say, Mr Scott's sister? Ah'm a seamstress and she asked me tae call.'

The lad relaxed a little under his smart blue livery. 'Seamstress, Mr Scott's sister. Wait here.'

There were numerous obstacles to be overcome before Sarah even arrived at Braxfield House: how to ask for time off work? What to wear? Although it soon became obvious that she would not have time to change from her mill clothes, and when best to present herself to Mrs Owen?

She was not even sure why she was being summoned. If, as seemed the most likely, it was to make clothes, Sarah was at a loss as to how she could manage to find the time. Sewing Fiona's dress was only made possible because Cathy looked after the household chores and cared for Lily.

Now, she was here, drawn by the lure of earning additional money as well as the opportunity to break the monotony of her life, even if just for one afternoon.

She braced herself for what lay ahead.

The footman's sharp footsteps echoed away down the corridor, then came exchanges of words with another male voice, the background murmur of activities in the kitchen, pans clattering, snatches of conversation and a boot boy whistling while brushing rhythmically from a nearby room.

Eventually, after a long wait, the housekeeper rustled into the room.

'I do apologise for keeping you waiting,' Miss Wilson smiled. 'Mrs Owen is pleased you have come to the house. Please wait here and I will take you upstairs when it is convenient.'

24

Left alone again, Sarah drew out a chair from the long dining table and sat down. Her Overseer had granted her two hours away from the factory floor and he would not be at all pleased if she was any longer. It would mean her Silent Monitor being turned to blue, a disappointment after weeks of keeping it to yellow or white for good attendance and high productivity. Losing two hours of wages could be borne, but three?

Upstairs in her study, Anne Caroline read over the letter she was penning to a boarding house in Portobello, close to Edinburgh. She was enquiring about the possibility of Robert Dale and William staying there for several months through the summer to aid in his recovery from the inflammation in his eyes. The establishment came with high recommendations and with her husband now away in London she was dealing with the arrangements.

Satisfied with the contents, she folded the sheet of paper and sealed it, reaching for the bell cord to summon the footman. It would be hard to send her two eldest children away for such a long time but something had to be done about Robert's ill health and this seemed to be the best option available to them.

For the last few days she was plagued by low spirits and a lethargy draining her desire to do anything. The days dragged and she sought solace in visiting the nursery or reading her Bible. Without Owen's energetic presence around the house there was a sudden void. His study door remained shut, his place at the head of the table lay bare and the untouched pillows beside her in bed were cold reminders of his absence.

When the footman answered her bell, she handed him the letter and instructed the seamstress to be brought upstairs.

'Thank you for coming to see me,' she greeted Sarah. 'I understand from your brother that your husband passed away, please accept my condolences.'

Sarah bobbed a curtsey, 'Ma'am.'

Anne Caroline returned to her chair at the writing desk, taking her time to arrange a cushion at her back in an effort to disguise her shock at the change in the woman's appearance.

She remembered Sarah as a cheerful housemaid in the early days of staying at New Lanark and then later, in Glasgow, when she was employed by Holroyd's, the eminent city outfitters. At that time, the young seamstress's poise, immaculately styled blond hair and pleasing clear features set her apart from the other tradeswomen. Although still recognisable as the same person, she was a pallid shadow of her former self. Her pale eyes were dull, ringed with dark shadows, lines creased around her lips and there was a dejected, defeated slope to her shoulders.

However, the main reason for Anne Caroline's discomfort was the pathetic hopefulness in Sarah's questioning gaze.

'I was not aware of your presence at the mills until your brother informed me.' Anne Caroline paused, collecting her thoughts. 'Since then, I have spoken with Mr Owen. It is obvious from your fine work in creating the beautiful outfit for Mrs Scott that you have not lost your talent with a needle. Am I correct in understanding, you were troubled with your eyes and that is the reason you are employed in the factory?'

'Aye, Ma'am.'

'And this shortness of sight has been remedied by the prescription of spectacles from our good doctor, Mr McGibbon?'

'Aye, Ma'am.'

'Tell me, my husband has asked me to enquire, would you return to needlework? Or are you satisfied to earn from the mills?'

Sarah was thrown into a quandary. Was Mr Owen considering throwing her out of the mills?

'Ah need tae earn a wage. Ah'm skilled at the carding jennies ... Mr Owen can see Ah dae ma joab weel.'

'I have no doubt you do but, if you could earn a wage as a seamstress or in the mills, which would you prefer?'

Panicked, Sarah blurted out. 'Ah dinnae want tae leave New Lanark, Ma'am! Ma eldest is in the twisting room an' wee Lily is in the school room ...'

Anne Caroline raised her hand, 'Forgive me, I am not explaining myself. Mr Owen and I are in agreement that someone with a talent such as yours should be encouraged. There is a position in the village shop for a skilled seamstress and also, occasionally, as a teacher of needlework to the girls in the classroom. He feels, as do I, that you would be better suited to these pursuits. What do you say?'

'Oh may the Lord bless ye, Mrs Owen! Whit wid Ah say? Oh aye!' a frown suddenly dashed the smile from her face. 'But, Ah wid be paid ... aye?'

'Yes, there would be a wage for both appointments.' Anne Caroline reached for a sheet of folded paper on her desk. 'I thought you would accept this proposal but Mr Owen insisted I speak with you directly to hear your views before giving you this note. However, we are both concerned that there appears to be no record of you in the mills? Mr Owen did not have time to pursue this matter but he informed me there was no Mrs Hendry in New Lanark.'

'Ah'm Mrs Rafferty, in Mill Three.'

'Rafferty?' For a moment, a suspicious tone crept into Anne Caroline's voice, 'I was sure your name was Hendry?'

'Aye, it wis ... when Ah wis in Glesgie, but when ma man died an' Ah came back tae the village, Ah went back tae Rafferty.'

Anne Caroline looked perplexed. 'Your name appears to change with startling regularity. You are Joseph Scott's sister, Sarah, and yet I recall some difference in your Christian name when we first met in Charlotte Street ... and now you tell me your name is Rafferty. Have you married again?'

'Naw.' Sarah's eyes rippled with tears. Was this wonderful chance to leave the mills going to be forbidden because of her past sins? Hadn't she been punished enough for colluding with Sean?

'Mr Rafferty wis ma first husband,' she stuttered, desperately trying to salvage the situation, 'the faither o' ma bairns ...'

'Oh, I am so sorry,' Anne Caroline cut in. 'You have been bereaved twice and I am upsetting you with my prying.'

'I swear oan the Bible, Mrs Owen,' Sarah cried, 'ma name is Sarah Rafferty and Ah've bin in the mills fer the past six years.'

'Please do not distress yourself,' Anne Caroline plucked her quill from its holder, dipped it in the ink well and scored out the name Hendry, inserting Rafferty on the top of the sheet of paper, then she held it towards Sarah. 'Mr Owen prepared this before he left. Take this to the manager's office and they will do whatever is necessary.'

'Oh, Ah cannae thank ye enough.' Sarah took the note, not bothering to look at it because the words would be indecipherable. 'God bless ye, Ma'am and Mr Owen.'

'I pray this will be the start of a happier time for you and your family. I am personally delighted for a very selfish reason. I urgently require new items for my wardrobe and would be grateful

27

for your services.' Anne Caroline stood up, 'I shall discuss these in more detail when you are settled at the shop.'

Repeating her effusive thanks, Sarah backed out into Braxfield's hall where the footman was waiting to escort her downstairs.

'Well, ye look cheery!' he commented. 'A change frae the dour face ye brought in wi' ye.'

'Ye ken when a dream comes true? That feelin' when ye wake frae a nightmare an' find the sun shinin'?'

'Naw ...'

She wasn't listening to him, caught up in her own euphoria.

'Ah cannae believe it!' she clutched Mr Owen's note tight to her breast. 'Och, this is a braw day!'

'It wis spittin' an gie breezy last time Ah looked.'

'It can rain all it wants, son, it's the best day Ah've known in mony, mony years!'

Arranging her shawl to cover her head, the precious paper hugged against her, Sarah barely noticed the rain. Tripping along avoiding the puddles on the driveway, her smile gave way to a chuckle from time to time when she shook her head in wonder and sucked in the sweet damp air, releasing it in long satisfied sighs. Outside the manager's office, she hesitated, steadying herself. This could be the start of a new life. She longed to know what Mr Owen had written but everyone who could have read it to her was working: she cursed her ignorance.

The clerk in the front office looked up from behind a stack of ledgers, his unruly curls flopping over his eyes.

'Ah've tae gie ye this,' Sarah proffered the folded paper.

A flick of the hair indicated a table laden with papers. 'Pit it oan there.'

'It's important!'

'Oh, aye.' The tone was sardonic.

'Whit's that supposed tae mean?' Sarah's hackles were rising. 'This is frae Mr Owen! Ah've jist bin up wi' Mrs Owen ... an' ye can mak sure the manager sees it richt awa'!'

Startled, but trying to remain superior, the clerk reached for the paper, checking for himself if it was indeed from his employer.

'Manager's oot ... an' won't be seeing this until the end o' the day so, get back tae yer werk.' He gave a pointed nod towards the clock.

Sarah bit back a retort. What had she expected? To be ushered immediately into the Village Shop and plied with a welcoming dish of tea? No, for now, little was changed and she must endure four hours of tedious, deafening work on the carding machine.

But soon, very soon, she could leave the mills behind and this time, she promised herself, it would be for good.

***

The war with France may have been declared over but as the weeks rolled on and the Scotts received no word from Sam, they began to have serious concerns. It was years since they last heard from their brother and, at that time, he was to leave Britain and join the large contingent of troops in the Iberian Peninsula. Only Gerry followed the war reports, having regular access to newspapers in the office. He carefully distinguished between the alarming ones, which went in the fire, and those which he could take home for his wife to read.

They were despairing for Sam's safety, with Rosie already shedding tears at the very mention of his name, when a letter arrived.

'It's frae Sam! Ah ken his seal an' his writing ...' Fiona thrust the letter at Joe as soon as he came through the door. Ailsa and the two younger boys were jumping up and down excitedly, imploring their father to hurry up, taking his hat and helping him shrug off his heavy top coat.

'Mrs McLaren next door paid the postie,' Fiona continued over the din, 'fur she thocht it must be important which wis gie nice o' her ... dinnae fear, Ah've paid her bak ... an' its been fair killin' me no' tae read it but it's addressed tae ye.'

Joe tore open the red seal.

'He's alive ...' Joe's eyes prickled with tears. 'He's in Gibraltar ... safe and well. He sends his love tae a' the family an' hopes tae be comin' hame soon.'

'Run and tell yer aunties,' Fiona told the children. 'An' stoap in at Tam's an' tell yer big brithers. Aw, this is grand news!'

Donnie, Davey and Robert spent a lot of time with Tam these days. After finishing the renovation work on the house Tam inherited from his father, they fell into the habit of going round in

29

the evenings, sometimes staying the night on makeshift mattresses in the empty room upstairs.

Eager to share their good news, Ailsa took Sionaidh by the hand and ran down the hill with her brothers, wondering which aunt to visit first.

They chose their Aunt Rose, which turned out to be opportune for Sarah and Calum were in the middle of a blistering argument.

It had started with a knock at the door and the delivery of a small brown paper parcel with 'Sarah' scrawled in stylish script across the top.

Her name was one of the few words she could recognise and she pulled off the string and paper in puzzlement.

'It's a Bible. An auld, thumbed Bible?' There was a square of card tucked between the first pages. 'Read this fur me, will ye, Cal?'

Cal was half asleep beside the fire, his feet propped up on the stool, a jar of warm ale in his hand.

He stared at the note, seeing the signature first. 'It's frae Reverend Grieve an' says, 'This Bible was be ... bequeathed to you by my recently deceased parishioner ...' a shock went down his spine, 'Mrs Cooper.'

'Whit!' Sarah's eyes blazed, 'that auld bisom thocht Ah wis nae heeding the word o' the Lord! That Ah needed tae be mair God fearing ...' She threw the little bible onto the floor boards, sending it skittering under the nearest wheelie bed.

'Naw, Ah'm sure she didnae mean it like tha'!' Taken unawares, Cal leapt to the old lady's defence. 'She said she wid pray fur ye ... that she wis sorry.'

He stopped, the words hanging in the suddenly silent room.

'Whit did ye say?' Sarah stared at him, incredulous. 'How d'ye ken that? Whit's Mrs Cooper an' her business tae dae wi' ye?'

Cal's jaw set in a determined line, his eyes downcast.

'Ah'm sent a Bible by a mean auld bat who threw me oot ma joab an' had nae an ounce o' Christian forgiveness in her hairt an' ye tell me she wis *sorry*? Dinnae gae all silent an' closed up wi' me, Callum Scott!' Sarah's voice was rising, 'How d'ye ken she wis gaun tae pray fur me? tell me that?'

'She telt me, jist afore she died.'

'Och, she wis struck doon fur weeks afore she passed ... how could ye see her, she wis in her bed!'

Cal squirmed in his chair. 'Ah went tae see her.'

'You? Why, in the name o' the wee man, wid ye visit that dying auld witch?'

'Dinnae call her that!' Cal jumped up, his face distorted with fury. 'She helped me ... a lang time ago. It wis Mrs Cooper who found me yon joab wi' the MacInnes brithers ... she unnerstood.'

Sarah was speechless: Cal rarely lost his temper.

'Whit did she unnerstaund?' she asked, gently, 'Ye niver said onythin'? Not aboot how ye came tae to be taken oan at the forge or ... visiting Mrs Cooper,' her tone became softer, sisterly. 'We all kent ye were in a bad way afore ye stairted wi' Macinnes, whit happened? Tell me, Cal? Ye ken all aboot ma life, the mistakes, the sins ... but ye niver speak o' yersel'. Tell me?'

He started to tell her about the day when he decided life was not worth living and she saw how desperate he must have been. The anguish returned to his voice, etched in the pinched lines on his face and bowed shoulders.

'After that day, we niver spoke o' it again, me an' Mrs Cooper. Ah wis ashamed. Joe ... an' all o' ye, were all sae kind tae me. Fur a lang time, well, e'er since, Ah've alis thocht it wis sich an insult tae ye, ma *family*, if ye found oot Ah wis jist gonnae leave ... Ye have tae see, Sarah, Ah wis tha' caught up wi' masel efter the cruel time awa' frae the village, hurtin' ... in ma heid. Bad thochts churnin' aroond, makin' me mad ... Ah felt useless.'

He sat quietly for several minutes with Sarah kneeling beside him, one hand laid comfortingly on his knee, saying nothing.

'It all came back tae me,' he murmured, clearing his throat, 'when Ah heard she wis dying. Ah went tae thank her fer helping me.' He raised his head and met his sister's serious gaze. 'She wis ill, weak, but kent who Ah wis an' remembered ye, said she wid pray fer ye and tha' she wis sorry. Every yin wis saying how bad she wis, how mean an' crotchety ... but she wis guid tae me. She saved ma life.'

'When were ye gaun tae tell me? That she wis sorry?'

He shrugged, 'Ah could nae find the words. Where tae stairt?'

'Aw Cal,' Sarah took him in her arms, pressing her cheek to his. 'Weel, ye have noo.'

31

Running footsteps pounded up the stairwell and at the sharp knock on their door Sarah pushed herself to her feet. Cal ran his fingers through his dirty blond hair, pulling his distracted thoughts back to the present.

'Ye'll niver guess?' Ailsa burst into the room, Rosie hurrying behind her, a shawl hastily thrown over her night clothes, her hair bouncing with curling rags.

'Sam's alive!'

***

'It is such a pleasure to have you here, I have missed our talks!' Rosemary Pemberley gushed, breaking off another piece of ginger biscuit and popping it into her almost toothless mouth.

Anne Caroline sipped her tea. It was a long time since she visited Glasgow and while her husband was steeped in business meetings, she was enjoying visits with her city friends.

She was also a little surprised to find Rosemary in such good spirits: Mr Pemberley having passed away less than a month before.

'My sisters entreated me to pass their love and condolences to you.'

'So sweet of the dear girls, I received their thoughtful letters, as I did yours. So kind. But, my dear, I can speak candidly with you, one of my oldest friends? My husband's death has not caused me distress, I am no grief-stricken widow. Our marriage became one of convenience. These last three years he was confined to bed, as I'm sure I related tediously in my letters, and his mind wandered so that I hardly think he knew me from the maid!'

'Do not joke of these things, Rosemary.'

''Tis the truth! I have nothing to regret, while he had his wits about him I made him happy, I believe. I was a good wife and mother to his children. He, in return, has left me well accounted for in this lovely house with adequate finances to live in comfort, if not luxury.'

An uneasy pause followed; Anne Caroline struggling to understand her friend's unemotional reaction to the loss of her husband.

32

'I hear your Mr Owen is becoming famous?' Rosemary enquired, sucking at another morsel of biscuit.

'Indeed, that appears to be so. Ever since his pamphlets were published there is a lot of attention on his work at the mills and there are now even more visitors arriving every day to see his 'New View of Society' for themselves.'

'Such a clever man, I could see that straight away. He has a charm, a quiet charm.'

Anne Caroline smiled. 'His calm appearance belies his passion. He is ardent in his pursuit to stop the suffering and hardships of the poor and has great plans to bring education to all children, even the poorest. I pray his new business partners are of the same mind for he has been bitterly disappointed in the past.'

'And how are your own children?' Rosemary cared little for politics or business. 'When last you wrote, you were concerned for little Robert's eyes?'

'He and his brother are taking the sea air in Portobello and William writes regularly that the treatment is working and the inflammation is clearing. It is a blessed relief.'

'They are alone?'

'They are under the supervision of a kindly lady who keeps a boarding house for this purpose. William informs me mainly of their walks on the beach and the excellent meals. They are having quite an adventure!'

Rosemary was keen to relate her own sons' achievements at Hutchesons, where they were both considered fine scholars, destined for university and careers in the sciences. Her daughter was becoming a proficient, if not naturally talented, pianist.

It was soon time for Anne Caroline to take her leave and while walking to the door, Rosemary asked if she had seen Mary MacIntosh.

'We are dining with them at Dunchattan tomorrow and Mary has invited Charles and Margaret Tennant to join us.'

Disappointment flickered in Rosemary's eyes, 'Please pass them my love.'

'Oh, I shall. I am sure you would have received an invitation had you not been in mourning, dear Rosemary. I hope you will visit me at Lanark this summer? Shall I ask Mary and Margaret as well and perhaps you could all travel down together?'

33

This cheered her friend and they parted with warm embraces; the scent of Rosemary's unique perfume bringing back poignant memories.

A sadness for the loss of past happiness shrouded Anne Caroline during the short drive back to Charlotte Street. She did not notice the crowded Glasgow streets nor hear the clatter of metal wheels and horses hooves on the cobbles. She was swept back to a moment at Rosebank at the end of a luncheon party celebrating her first wedding anniversary.

The perfume awakened her father's genial laughter, tinkling music from her sisters on the drawing room piano, her own feeling of light hearted anticipation, all caught in the instant of kissing her friend farewell. She was in the last months of carrying her first born, naively believing the act of giving birth to be the great hurdle before future happiness, blissfully unaware of the tragedy lying ahead.

The horses slowed to a walk through the gates to Charlotte Street and Anne Caroline looked wistfully to her right, shading her eyes to see figures promenading in the sunshine on Glasgow Green.

She was no sooner through the front door and talking with Renwick, who was now very stooped and heavily reliant on a polished cane, when the footman opened the door to Owen.

'My dear!' Owen called, his voice conveying his usual vigour. 'I am so pleased you have returned from visiting your friend. I chanced to have a time free from appointments and propose we take the children out and show them our early haunts? Does that suit? It is a fine warm day, hardly a breeze.'

The veil of melancholy lifted.

'A lovely idea!' she cried, rustling towards the staircase. 'I shall inform Peggy and change my shoes ... '

On hearing of the walk, Jean and her sisters immediately wished to be included, hurrying to their rooms for pelisses, bonnets and parasols.

'My word, we have a party!' Owen laughed, watching the stream of colourful, chattering figures filing out of the front door: four of his children accompanied by Peggy, his sisters in law and Anne Caroline, leaving only little Mary in the nursery. He offered his arm to his wife and led the way towards the Green, raising his hand in acknowledgment to the man swinging open the heavy wrought iron street gate. 'How I enjoyed our walks all those years ago and now, here we are treading the same paths with our own little family.'

'Dear Robert,' Jean exclaimed, walking briskly to reach his side at the head of the troop, 'this is exactly what we all needed.'

'Spending time among nature is very therapeutic.' Owen agreed. 'It has often been noted by scholars and physicians that a person's feeling of well being can be greatly enhanced by taking the air and looking around at the views. Even those struck with chronic despair have been relieved of the symptoms when rambling by a river or through woodland.'

'God has given us all we need to raise our spirits. It is here, all around us!' Julia said sweetly. 'His Creations are a marvel, from every tiny bee or crawling insect to those majestic chestnut trees! May we all be truly thankful for His work.'

'Amen,' cried Margaret, linking her arm with Julia's and using her white frilled parasol as a walking stick. 'Let us walk to the river?'

Anne Caroline glanced at her husband, trying to gauge his reaction to her sisters' words but his bland, genial expression told her nothing of his thoughts, neither disapproval nor exasperation. If he found it trying to be surrounded by a devoutly Christian family, he did not show it, but sometimes she wondered how she might feel if the roles were reversed. Would she wish to contradict or cause a disagreement? or would she remain composed and keep her views to herself? They shared so much already, yet she dearly wished he would share her devotion to Christ.

'Look, Papa! Mama!' David's high-pitched child's voice cut through her thoughts. 'Do I like butter?'

He was holding a buttercup flower beneath his chin.

Owen made a show of examining the bright yellow reflection of the shiny petals on his skin. 'My goodness! Yes, you do!'

Jane and Anne ran to gather flowers to try this for themselves, their aunts joining in the game.

Owen winked at Anne Caroline, whispering playfully, 'On such a sunny day, I wager everyone will like butter!'

The family's last two days in the city were filled with social and business appointments. Anne Caroline especially enjoyed the hospitality shown by Mary MacIntosh whose lively sense of humour in the drawing room after dinner was as entertaining as always. In contrast, the evening reception with Sir John and Lady Hannah Maxwell at Pollok House was a more formal affair. Their hosts were ardent Whigs, causing eyebrows to raise amongst the more conservative guests.

After several weeks away in London and necessary time spent in Glasgow, Owen was eager to return to his mills. There was a change to his demeanour, evident to even himself. Whilst he had been confident and self reliant his entire life, the acceptance of his ideals was inspiring an even deeper conviction in his own abilities.

His business acumen was producing the desired results at New Lanark to allow it to survive these years of recession. This had never been in question, whereas he had always met opposition to his plans for improving the lives of the paupers on which the cotton industry relied upon.

Having met like-minded men, social philosophers of repute in London, he was encouraged to find them excited by his essays. They grasped his urgency for a change in the Law to force factory owners to treat their workforce with more responsibility for their health. His adoption of Joseph Lancaster's principles for teaching was heartily congratulated by his new enlightened friends, unlike the indifference he met from his previous partners.

There were some in Glasgow who read his essays and knew of his vision but considered it, out of hand, as unworkable. Shorter working days, education for everyone and, in Owen's view the most important aspect, treating children with respect and kindness during their formative years, did not add profit to their balance sheets. These men were not interested in the long term benefits of raising future generations to be educated, healthy, rational members of society.

If there was no money to be gained from such a scheme then it was of no interest to them.

This did not daunt Owen's enthusiasm. Emboldened by support from respected intellectuals, he was fired up and determined to carry out his experiment at New Lanark.

He wondered sometimes, of the two main barriers to the betterment of the human condition which was worse, indoctrinated religion or money?

Chapter Three

"It is forbidden to kill; therefore all murderers are punished unless they kill in large numbers and to the sound of trumpets." Voltaire

On their journey back to New Lanark, Anne Caroline and her children were treated to the beauty of the Clyde valley in her Spring glory. A warm spell was breathing life into the landscape, unfurling thickly blossomed fruit trees and studding meadows with brilliant green shoots.

The rutted, winding road followed the riverbed upstream through flood plains grazed by cattle and sheep, some with calves and lambs gambolling at their sides. Beyond Hamilton, the banks drew closer, cutting a deep valley into the rising hills and forcing the road to cling to the hillside above the sparkling water gurgling and splashing far below.

Unrecognisable as the same filthy, sluggish body of water pushing its way through Glasgow to reach the Atlantic, the upper reaches of the River Clyde revealed her youthful, wild side. When the carriage came to a rocking halt outside Braxfield House its occupants climbed out; stretching and yawning amidst long, dew-laden evening shadows.

Owen, who had ridden on ahead, was already engrossed in business at the mills.

He was pleased to note steady attendance and generally good behaviour in the workforce and relieved to find the accounts showing a marginal profit. While in London, he heard of many cotton barons struggling to keep their mills open, severely hit by the loss of orders from the military after Napoleon's defeat. Even the hoped for recovery of markets within Europe could not guarantee their survival.

Louis XVIII had spent the last few years of his long exile living graciously at Hartwell House in Buckinghamshire. The beautiful, rented country mansion was also home to his niece, the daughter of the unfortunate Marie Antoinette, nearly two hundred staff and dozens of émigrés. The latter turned the extensive roof into a miniature farm, complete with rabbits and chickens in cages and vegetables grown in pots, also using the outhouses as shops in an effort to raise money. Louis' brother, Charles, Count of Artois, visited occasionally but preferred the faster life of London's high society in company with the Prince Regent.

When negotiations were successfully completed to restore Louis to the French throne, he found himself temporarily confined to a wheelchair with a severe bout of gout. It was Charles who was sent to Paris to rule the kingdom, briefly, as Lieutenant General under his brother's instructions,

This time, however, the Bourbon king returning to the French throne would be a constitutional monarch under conditions imposed by the senate, established by Napoleon. The French were determined to maintain the rights they fought so bitterly to achieve. When Louis finally arrived and took up residency in the Tuileries, he was presented with a constitution ensuring freedom of religion, freedom of the press and equality before the law. Unfortunately, the king opposed the senate's constitution and unrest rippled through the country once more.

Great Britain was also suffering disturbances amongst her people. From Perth to Bristol food riots were becoming more frequent, jobs scarce, taxes rising by the month and merchants and bankers alike scuttled about their business with anxious faces, deeply apprehensive. The war with America, entailing vast expense and manpower, was haemorrhaging money out of a country already bled dry by France.

Weeks of warm dry weather brought more problems.

Crops were not growing in the dusty fields and the parched land sucked up any rainfall before it could reach the rivers. The great shale and sandstone ledges of the Corra and Bonnington Linns lay pale between trickles of water, pooling among prominent rocks.

Owen watched with a heavy heart as the river bed beside the village became almost completely dry. Any water upstream was being corralled by the weir and sent to feed the mill lade. By June there was only sufficient power to turn the wheels in Mill One and he took the decision to run it continuously, changing shifts of operatives to maintain production throughout the night.

The Misses Edmonstone at Corehouse were not happy. They instructed their agent to advise Owen of the terms of their agreement which expressly forbade all night use of the weir unless in extreme circumstances.

These *were* extreme circumstances: Owen forged on with his strategy.

Early each morning he awoke with the hope of drawing back the curtains in his dressing room to find a droplet spattered window pane and banks of cloud showering the garden with rain. He desperately needed to fulfil orders and keep income flowing into the company, not only to pay his workers, but for his own salary.

To an onlooker, Owen appeared successful, optimistic, master of one of the largest cotton mills in Great Britain. They saw him travelling up and down the country, dining with leading merchants, socialising in the private circles of the most influential educationalists and philosophers and conducting enthusiastic tours of the village for scores of visitors every week. Everyone he spoke to was appraised of his grand plan to open his Institute for the Formation of Character, his desire to set an example of how to improve the lives of working people.

Yet, behind his professional life, his personal finances were in dire straits. Saved from bankruptcy by the good will and financial guarantees of his sisters in law, he still required thousands of pounds to repay the original debt to Campbell. If this were not enough, Robert Humphreys, his one time partner and senior manager at New Lanark for many years, was suing him for loss of earnings. This came as a double blow to Owen who had considered him a friend since they first worked together some twenty years before at Peter Drinkwater's mill in Manchester.

He was dealing with correspondence in the peace and quiet of his house in the village when he received the legal notice of Humphreys' intent. Throwing the letter onto his desk, he strode over to the window; deeply disappointed.

Owen was barely twenty one years old when he took up the position of manager at Bank Top Mill, renowned for its production of very fine yarn due to the modern steam-driven machinery. It was there, in the workrooms of the bulky four story building in Auburn Street that he first put into practice his belief that every one of the employees, down to the smallest pauper child, should be treated fairly and with respect. He found Humphreys to be sympathetic to these values, working with him to achieve a stable workforce and, from that, high productivity. It was these qualities which made him an obvious choice to invite to work with him again at New Lanark.

Owen looked out at the lawn sloping downhill towards the mill lade, subconsciously noting how much larger the yellow patches of dry grass were becoming and the wilted, dust laden foliage on the surrounding bushes.

The special arrangement he made with Humphreys to pay him a higher wage in lieu of an annual return on his shares, was designed to alleviate the man's concerns over any lack of money. It would not have arisen if Humphreys had shared Owen's confidence in the future profits of the mills. Now, due to backing the wrong side and throwing his cards in with Dennistoun and Campbell in trying to buy Owen out, it had backfired. Humphreys was now without employment and no longer held shares in a lucrative business.

Turning away from the bright scene outside, Owen felt calmer.

It was greed again; Humphreys and his demanding wife were victims of that corruptive urge to obtain and accumulate money by whichever means came to hand.

Owen dashed off a response to his solicitor, stating clearly that he would defend his case in court, if necessary. He sincerely believed he owed Humphreys no more than the considerable sum already paid in settlement of his shares on the sale of the mills. On sealing the letter, he tried to ease the unpleasant feeling of being treated unjustly. Retying his cravat, loosened while busy in the stifling office, he plucked his hat from the stand and headed outside.

He was barely a dozen steps from his door when he met a party of visitors viewing the stark stonework of the village, exclaiming at the way it appeared to be carved from the rocky sides of the valley. Owen immediately introduced himself, welcoming them to his mills and falling easily into conversation regarding his proposals for the imposing Institute building.

For now, Humphreys was forgotten.

Every day, during the summer months, dozens of carriages negotiated the country roads to see 'Mr Owen's Mills', the men enthusing about the immaculate workrooms and well-kept machinery, the ladies charmed by the romantic setting and the sight of so many healthy, clean, factory children.

Lying in a drawer in his study at Braxfield were tradesmen's estimates for completing the interior of the Institute. Owen knew exactly what he wanted to achieve and only required the money to fund it. This did not stop him from implementing any changes to the factory and school which did not need additional finance.

Using Joseph Lancaster's Monitorial method of teaching, once the older pupils were taught by the tutor, they then passed their knowledge on to the younger ones. This allowed the instruction of hundreds of students under one qualified school master. Arithmetic, reading and writing were predominant, however, now there was more time devoted to dancing, singing and playing musical instruments.

On fine days, the children were taken out in parties of up to thirty and encouraged to explore the countryside belonging to the mills. There they discovered flowers, insects, birds or interesting rocks, whatever caught their eye. Down at the riverside, they delighted in spotting holes in the sandbanks where flashing turquoise and orange kingfishers nested or the patches of close cropped grass where watervoles gnawed on a juicy stalk. There was often stifled laughter when the little creature saw them and plopped into the water.

After several hours of rambling in the fresh air, they would return to the classroom to learn about their finds from a small library supplied for their use by Owen. Maps were brought in and poured over, geography taught and for the older children, discussion and questions encouraged.

The children's enjoyment of their lessons was infectious and easily transferred to the curious visitors who were invited to inspect the schoolroom.

In August, William Allen, one of Owen's most attentive partners, travelled north from London to pay a visit to his newest investment. This was his second visit, his first being on the freezing January day eight months previously, following the auction in Glasgow.

Fortunately, the Scottish weather returned to normal a few weeks before his arrival, filling the Clyde and allowing all the mills to show themselves at their best. Every spinning jenny, twister and carding machine was thrashing away at full production.

'My, it looks a different place from when last I was here!' Allen cried, climbing from his carriage in front of New Buildings.

At forty-four years of age, he was barely a year older than Owen but whether it was his greying sideburns or his formal brown jacket, breeches and hose, he presented a much more mature figure.

Owen raised his hat in greeting, neither expecting nor receiving this courtesy to be reciprocated by his Quaker partner.

'That was a splendid day!' Allen recalled. 'My word, the bagpipes and cheering rang in my head for days afterwards. To see the streets empty, as it is now, and barely a sound except the birds and ...' he paused, listening, 'perhaps the rushing of the river beyond ... the water wheels? Why, it is a joy to behold!'

They set off briskly through the village and down onto the lowest road beside the riverbank. Dwarfed by the towering stone structures, they were forced to shout above the roar of water spurting back into the river from the mill wheels.

'Such power!' Allen beamed, pushing back his wide brimmed hat to rub the sweat from his receding hairline. 'This little idyll is a strange marriage of pastoral beauty and blatant industry.'

Owen laughed, agreeing. 'It is the best of both. Allow me to show you where the real business takes place.'

Allen was a quick witted, busy man, whose deeply held Quaker beliefs shaped all his endeavours. He was a pharmacist of great repute, having his own business in Plough Court, London, and close ties with most of the leading scientists and researchers in the city but he was also tireless in pursuing his philanthropic ventures. As an ardent Abolitionist, for the last ten years he had served as a member of the Society for the Abolition of the Slave Trade.

Another passionate concern of Allen's was free education for the working classes which was his main reason for investing in New Lanark. He had long been a supporter of Lancaster's

42

methods but was appalled to find the educator, a fellow Quaker, seriously lacking in financial sense. Never one to hold himself back, Allen co-founded the British and Foreign School Society to promote the monitorial system and provide schools for the poor of all denominations.

After inspecting the mills, they took seats at the side of the classroom to watch children performing both precise cotillions and energetic Scottish reels. Accompanied by fiddle music there were upwards of a hundred little bodies dancing and swaying, clapping and pirouetting, each knowing their positions or giggling and squealing on taking a wrong step. Their bare feet added a muffled, rhythmic drumming to the scene, reverberating through the floorboards.

'Notice their pink cheeks and sparkling eyes?' Owen asked, ushering Allen to the door. 'I think you will agree, this is excellent for their well being.'

'It is a joy to see so many smiling faces, I grant you, but this is a school not, as the Scots would have it, a ceilidh.'

'They are learning at the same time,' Owen said, seriously, as the men made their way down the stairs to the main hall. 'They have to work together, keep in time, allow for each other's mistakes and share the sense of success on arriving at the end of the set piece of music, not only at the right moment but in the correct positions.'

'And when do they study the Bible? I hope the nature rambles and musical interludes are the exceptions and studying the Scriptures takes priority.'

'Oh, it is included in the curriculum,' Owen nodded, reassuringly, 'have no worries on that score. Now, may I join you in your carriage and we can ride the short distance to Braxfield where my wife has arranged a meal for us?'

Clearly, Allen did have concerns about the apparent lack of religious education for it became the recurring topic of conversation during the remainder of his visit.

'My goodness,' Anne Caroline declared, her hand still raised in farewell to Allen's retreating coach. 'He is a very energetic man, is he not? I mean, in his love of organisation. So many ventures! It was certainly refreshing to be asked my opinions on matters, for few business men entertain the notion of a female having views worth relating.'

'It is one of the most attractive aspects of his faith.' Owen put his arm around her shoulders and they walked back inside the house to the drawing room fireside. 'Believing all men and women to be equal. They have many ladies who become ministers, business proprietors or scientists. It is as it should be. The male of the human species can count as many fools amongst its numbers as the female!'

They relaxed into their seats on either side of the hearth, the fire having been freshly stoked while they waved their guest away.

'Mr Allen seemed very interested in the allotments you give to the workers,' Anne Caroline mused. 'He knows a great deal about nutrition. I had no idea he opened soup kitchens for the poor in London! Admirable.'

'Sadly, they are in high demand. I see the starving beggars for myself on every trip to the capital. It is an outrage and he is providing a much needed service. The trouble is he is attending to the symptoms of a way of life which should not exist. What is required is a complete overhaul of the policies and the very basics of the way we live. Only that will bring an end to our citizens dying from malnutrition.'

'May the Lord have mercy on those poor souls. Surely the Church administers to the poor?'

'Indeed it does, as do religious orders of every persuasion across London and up and down the country. The Poor Relief doles out meagre supplies but the demand is high and will grow alarmingly with the return of our soldiers from Europe. But again, they are dealing with the effects rather than grasping and resolving the cause.'

She looked directly at him, saying candidly. 'You believe you have the solution.'

'I have. My essays both state, as clearly as I am able, how to ameliorate the suffering of the poor and create a new reasonable social order. They are now in the hands of men who have the power to make the necessary changes. I have openly requested their thoughts and views on my work, asked them to scrutinise it and determine its truth for themselves. If I can but convince

44

these leaders of my views and their practical application, we could banish the evils of society and replace them with contentment and happiness.'

'May I read your most recent essay?'

'Of course! You will find the principles the same, reiterating the fact that man's character is formed for him, not by him ... by his surroundings and the treatment meted out to him by his parents or those ideologies held by those closest to him.' He sighed. 'Once it is understood that a man committing a crime should be understood and the rotten influences of his past taken into consideration, then, and *only* then, will it be seen that it is not his fault. He should not be banished to Botany Bay for stealing a loaf to feed his children or hung by the neck for breaking into a property to steal items he can sell to maintain his family.'

'These acts cannot go unpunished?'

'At present we lock him up, hang him, deport him to the other side of the world! In other words, we put him out of sight, get rid of him. Society must change, gradually, fundamentally, so our thief would not become a victim of an unjust system in the first place. He would be treated kindly and fairly from childhood, attend school and be given the tools to be self sufficient. He would be a useful member of his community and in so doing be able to provide for his family without resorting to criminal methods.'

'That would take many years ...'

'Yes, it is not intended as a quick remedy. It is a long term strategy, taking several generations but eventually achieving the greatest of benefits for happiness and prosperity. Caroline,' there was a tremble in his voice, his chin crumbling with the emotional force of his goal. 'Would it not be wonderful if by the time our own dear children were parents themselves, there was a rational, kinder society in this world?'

She agreed, breathlessly, moved to tears by his show of compassion, 'It is what we all pray for, my dearest.'

***

On the 24ᵗʰ of August, a Wednesday, the New Lanark residents toiled at the mills, cared for their families and, for the most part, retired to bed for a sound sleep. Bats flittered between the buildings and through the surrounding trees, owls hooted, the flowing water of the river rippled smoothly through the valley with only a light breeze to disturb the night air.

In America, Major General Robert Ross, a hardened, experienced British army officer, was leading four thousand British troops towards Washington.

Attending an early morning meeting, President James Madison was advised of the enemy's approach but was assured that British troops would not be interested in attacking the capital; it was not yet formed as a proper city. Baltimore was far more likely to be their target. By noon, the situation took a serious turn: the British were in Bladensberg, only six miles from Washington.

Caught off guard, a very flustered Brigadier General Winder mobilised his motley collection of militia men and rode off to stop the enemy crossing the Potomac River and invading the capital. It was immediately apparent that the State War department had underestimated the threat to the region. Although over four thousand men were galvanised, they were virtually all ill-prepared farmers rushing to fight in haphazard clothing, without flints for their rifles nor training for battle.

Shocked by the unfolding emergency, the President borrowed two pistols and galloped towards Bladensberg. Despite his racing heart and the wind in his ears as he spurred on his horse, he could hear the ominous roar of thousands of marching feet, horses' hooves, bugles and drums.

Suddenly, on cresting a small hill, he was almost amongst them! Wheeling around, he sought a vantage point and stared out upon a sea of red coats with flags flying beneath a cloud of rising dust, relentlessly advancing in disciplined lines. Rockets, the new British weapon, flared overhead: this was a formidable army.

In the ensuing chaos, Ross's horse was shot from beneath him. The Irishman, only just recovered from a serious wound to his neck six months before, leapt to his feet and commandeered another horse. Within moments, he was back in the thick of it.

The battle was a fiasco for the Americans.

Ross's advisor, Rear Admiral George Cockburn, recognised and seized upon his enemy's disarray and sent troops streaming across the river by way of the bridge, inadvertently left intact: Winder's army scattered to the hills.

Dolley Madison, the President's wife, was known for her superb entertaining and was preparing to receive forty guests for a formal dinner when she received urgent instructions to vacate the White House.

Determined to salvage all she could of the life they knew, she even called for the red velvet curtains in the Oval Room to be taken down and packed with the silverware. In the middle of this turmoil, with her carriage at the door and a friend urging her to leave straight away, she ran to the East Room, beseeching young Sioussat, a Frenchman who knew about art, to advise her slaves how to take down the massive portrait of George Washington. The heavy frame was bolted to the wall but fearing it would fall into British hands, she insisted the canvas be cut out. Every moment was precious but she stayed until the cumbersome painting was released and handed over to two gentlemen for safe keeping.

By mid afternoon, with the sun beating down on their backs, the red coats of Major General Ross's troops marched past straggling houses, stone yards, brick kilns and shacks until they reached the centre of Washington. In their ranks were the dark, glistening faces of freed African slaves. They were gathered from across the Chesapeake region with the promise of release from bondage, keen to join forces with the British to fight their oppressors.

Before long, a Union Jack was flying over the Capitol building and Cockburn gathered one hundred and fifty soldiers and marched directly on to the White House.

To their astonishment, on racing up the steps and entering the magnificent President's residence, they found a crowd of vagrants already ransacking the lower rooms. The soldiers threw them out: looting or harm to civilians or their property was not tolerated. However, on finding Dolley Madison's grand banquet laid out in the dining room they took off their hats, drew out the chairs and sat down to enjoy the feast.

Then, throwing the chairs up on the tables and sprinkling them with gunpowder they set it alight before moving back through Washington, systematically setting fire to all the government state department buildings. Soon, only the great corn cob pillars and thick stone walls remained standing, scorched by the intense blaze devouring everything flammable. Even the famous glass skylights in the Capitol became molten, dripping to the ground and adding to the ferocity of the flames.

Just hours after arriving, Rear Admiral Cockburn and Major General Robert Ross pulled their troops together and marched away from the burning city. Behind the columns of desperately weary soldiers, the horizon was filled with flames leaping high into billowing black smoke.

***

When the news of the 'Burning of Washington' appeared in the British newspapers many thought it signalled the end of the war with America. Unfortunately, these reports were quickly followed by depressing accounts of further battles where the Americans were the victors.

Anne Caroline preferred not to read these stories. She was sickened by the violence and sheer waste of lives and prayed for all those suffering the horrors of war.

Robert Dale and William returned home from their seaside adventure in good health, their skins tanned golden and, she was sure, several inches taller than when they left. Robert's eyes were completely cured and even his sensitive emotions were improved. He was not the bold, strong little chap he was before his illness, but she could see a return of spirit she once feared lost.

In late September, they received another visit from William Allen, this time accompanied by a fellow business partner, Joseph Fox. As on the occasion of Allen's inspection of the mills the previous month, the cotton producing side of the enterprise was considered excellent. However, in the privacy of Owen's study in Braxfield, the two Quakers told him in no uncertain terms that there was not enough attention paid to the spiritual needs of the children under his supervision. They were particularly alarmed at Owen's own lack of belief in Christianity.

After listening politely, Owen told them that he considered spiritual beliefs to be a very individual and private subject and he stressed the importance of religious tolerance amongst all his employees and their families.

'I am proud to say that we have Papists and Protestants working side by side, their children playing together happily.' Owen looked intently from Fox to Allen. 'It was not always so. When I came here, there was a great deal of fighting, name calling and unpleasant, violent behaviour, much arising from religious bigotry. It is neither helpful on the factory floor nor in the community.'

'They must learn the Gospel!' Fox cried, 'Hear the words of the Lord! How else will they attain good Christian values?'

In great detail, Owen told them of the company's arrangements for worship within the village. It covered a diverse population of over two thousand souls, predominantly Scottish Presbyterian or David Dale's Old Scotch Independents and, particularly favoured by the Irish, Roman Catholicism.

The other smaller groups like the Baptists and Methodists were catered for with allocated times in the meeting rooms. He was detailed in his answers, supplying the names of the ministers who attended the village, the times of the services and the provision of Gaelic speaking ministers to give sermons to the Highlanders whenever possible. There was, he assured them, daily Bible reading in the classroom and many hours engaged in singing hymns and psalms.

Eventually, the London gentlemen appeared to be placated and by the time Sheddon was summoned and a tray of refreshments ordered, a congenial atmosphere was restored.

A few weeks later, Owen declared he was returning to London. This time, Anne Caroline was more resigned about being left alone at Braxfield. Her husband was making quite a name for himself in the upper circles of society and she should be proud of his achievements and take pleasure from his growing success.

Owen's servants were also proud of their master. Although remaining discreet, Clegg and Murdoch relayed snippets about some of the well known people and places Owen visited,

49

especially his growing relationships with Members of both Houses of Parliament.

'How lang will ye be awa' this time?' Peggy asked Murdoch during their main meal of the day.

The servants' hall purred with conversation and scraping cutlery. Sheddon sat at the head, a large starched serviette spread across his chest while spooning his soup.

'He telt me tae pack fur a month, but he's alis longer. There are two formal engagements so Ah'm takin' twa pairs o' his white hose. The streets are like middens, much worse than Glesgie. There's all these wee bairns wi' brooms takin' pennies aff the ladies tae sweep paths fur them in the muck across the road. Horse dung stains like the de'il.'

'Murdoch, I hardly think discussion of that kind is called for at the table,' Sheddon admonished.

'Yer richt, Ah apologise, Mr Sheddon.'

'While you are away,' Miss Wilson said pleasantly, smiling at the valet, 'we will be having guests at Braxfield. Mrs Pemberley and her daughter are coming with the Miss Dales.'

Cook was pleased. 'Now there's a fine chance to make some fancier food! Ah ken the master is no' sae keen on ma spicy sauces but Ah'm sure he'd be happy fur his ladies tae enjoy them.'

A murmur of approval rumbled round the table. Owen's penchant for plain food meant a simple menu for the entire household. No one complained, they knew they were better provided for than most in the country but welcomed the thought of tasting the leftovers from Cook's more adventurous dishes.

'Ah mind way back in the early days,' Peggy said loudly, sitting back in her chair and smiling wistfully, 'when auld Mr Dale wis still wi' us. We wid stiy at his big hoose in Glesgie an' yon rambling place oot at Cambuslang an' Oh! what food there would be in the pantry. His cook wis gie strict wi'us wee maids but if the food had nae bin eaten by the second day, well, it wis dished up fer us. My, it were grand. Wine sauces, jellies, fish mousses ...'

Miss Wilson saw a huffy expression flit across Cook's face, and said quickly, 'In that case I am sure you are in for a treat, Peggy, as are all of us.'

'Oh aye, that'll be like it, Cook,' Duncan laughed. 'Ye'll all be livin' the high life here while Ah'm makin' Mr Owen his porridge in the city.'

***

Anne Caroline allowed herself a little self-congratulation.

'I am proud of myself,' she told her lady's maid while dressing for dinner. 'My sisters and Mrs Pemberley are enjoying their stay at Braxfield and I admit that I, too, am finding a great deal of pleasure in their company.'

'Aye, ma'am, the party is in rare high spirits.' Ramsay pushed the last mother of pearl button into place and smoothed the fabric. 'Such a bonnie dress.'

'I am especially pleased with it because I can show it off this evening and claim, quite rightly, it is the work of our new seamstress in the village.'

Ramsay angled the ornate oak cheval mirror to show the full effect.

Turning this way and that, Anne Caroline admired Sarah Rafferty's needlework. Invisible stitching created a virtually seamless fall of pale pink muslin over a white satin underskirt, a flounce around the hem was caught up into posies of tiny appliquéd deep pink and white silk flowers with embroidered green leaves, repeated on the scooped neckline and cuffs of the puff sleeves.

The design was more elaborate than she would normally choose for an evening at home with no gentlemen present so, not wishing to seem ostentatious, she turned it into an amusement.

Telling her house guests she had a surprise for them, she suggested they all dress formally and gather in the drawing room as the grandfather clock in the hall struck four.

Cold October winds gusted against the windows, rattling doors and flickering candles but inside there was a homely excitement to the afternoon.

When the children's tutors left for the day, the rain was teeming down and, under instructions to leave their mother and aunts undisturbed, they turned to playing in the nursery wing. The older boys dashed up the splintery staircase for a game of

51

hide and seek in the attic, making the girls squeal at the mention of cobwebs and mice. Peggy pulled out boxes of watercolours and sheets of paper, encouraging them to paint or draw, or to take orderly turns on the old piano in the corridor.

It fell to Dora, the nursery maid, to care for little Richard and Mary. She enjoyed these kind of days, spending most of her time on her hands and knees on the hearth rug, singing nursery rhymes or building bricks with them, always making sure the boisterous toddlers stayed away from the fire.

In the kitchen and up and down the servants' stairs, maids and footmen bustled about their duties. Occasionally, Cook and Peggy managed to take a few minutes off when a pot of tea was deemed necessary. Clearing a space amidst the mixing bowls and chopping boards, they sampled sugary lemon biscuits or whatever else was cooling on the baking trays.

Miss Wilson glided from room to room, keys jangling from her belt, ensuring the ladies upstairs were attended to while keeping a close eye on the house maids. She did not usually follow Senga or Alice, they were very capable, but she was avoiding Mrs Pemberley's personal maid.

The poor girl was not accustomed to travelling with her employer and barely said a word at servant meal times. With hindsight, Miss Wilson realised she should have put her under Alice's guidance, instead she took it upon herself to show her the scullery and downstairs facilities. Now, the maid was making a regular habit of appearing at the housekeeper's office asking for assistance. From requiring soft soap, a needle and thread or a pair of scissors, to more duck-down filled cushions for Mrs Pemberley's bed and hot boiled water for her mistress's peppermint tea, it seemed she could find nothing for herself.

Unaware of Miss Wilson's trials, Sheddon prepared for the dinner party in his usual exacting manner. By a quarter to four the last silver fork was tweaked into perfect symmetry with the rest of the table settings, a flower drawn fractionally further out of its crystal bowl to balance the bouquet, judged from several angles then readjusted until found to be satisfactory. Apart from the candles to be lit, the dining room was ready.

As arranged, the party of ladies were assembled in the drawing room when Anne Caroline joined them at four o'clock.

52

'What a lovely sight!' she cried, admiring their sleek hairstyles and elegant evening wear, their perfumed throats and wrists adorned with jewellery. These sophisticated ladies, and she included herself in this thought, bore little resemblance to the ones returning from walking with her sisters' dogs just a few hours earlier; all wind-ruffled hair, pinched noses and pink cheeks. 'Thank you for humouring me.'

'You mentioned a surprise?' Margaret asked.

Rather self consciously, Anne Caroline turned a small circle, displaying her dress with its flowing hem.

'Rosemary, do you remember Mrs Hendry who you introduced me to ... at Holroyd's outfitters?'

'Of course! I rue the day she left Glasgow. Rumour has it, she was poached by a firm in London and now sews exclusively for Royalty.'

'I'm afraid the rumour is incorrect,' Anne Caroline shook her head, an enigmatic smile curving her lips, 'but it is my great good fortune to know where this talented needlewoman is now working and this,' she twirled again, 'is one of her creations!'

'Oh, let me see!' Rosemary hauled herself up from her chair, a manoeuvre which was becoming difficult due to problems with her hips and the considerable weight she carried.

'So, where is she working?' Julia cried, scrutinising the embroidery.

'She can be found in our village, here ... at New Lanark!' There was a gratifying gasp of astonishment. 'Sadly, she has been forced to bear the loss of not one but two husbands and now goes by the name of Mrs Rafferty. Suffice to say, she once worked in our father's mills as a child and has now returned. Not to mill work, I am pleased to say, for she is employed in the haberdashery at the Village Store. She is to be congratulated, I believe.'

'Bereaved twice! As you say, truly tragic. Oh, what a romantic story ...' Julia returned to her seat at the piano, running her fingers over the keys and lapsing into a soft melody in a minor key.

Rosemary gave a humourless laugh, murmuring, 'There is nothing romantic about tragedy.'

Jean nodded, sympathetically, 'Well, I am thankful the Lord has given this Mrs *Rafferty* the strength to carry on through her troubles. We must pray He has delivered her to happier times. That is a fine surprise,' she smiled at Anne Caroline. 'How well the gown befits you! I am pleased you are having the opportunity to wear it this evening.'

'Ah, but that is only part of my surprise. Very soon a carriage will arrive at the door and we will have company.'

Julia's recital came to an abrupt end, the others glancing swiftly at their hostess.

'I have invited a close neighbour of mine who, like you, dear Rosemary, is recently widowed.'

'Who is she?'

'Lady Mary Lockhart Ross from Bonnington House.'

'We visited her when we were children!' Jean recalled. 'On the occasion of viewing the Falls of Clyde!'

'She wore a towering wig on that day,' Margaret giggled, moving the fire screen to a better angle to protect her face from the scorching flames.

'That was a memorable day, indeed! But it is the previous Lady Lockhart Ross you remember,' Anne Caroline told her. 'This is her daughter in law who I would submit must be of similar age to myself, perhaps a year or so younger? Her late husband, Sir Charles, was much older...'

'Goodness me, I can empathise with the poor lady,' Rosemary cut in, 'older husbands are all very well when first they woo you, but then they just become *elderly* husbands ... and die.'

'Oh dear! Please be gentle with Lady Mary, I beg you, for I understand she misses him sorely. He was a Member of Parliament and they own land in Perthshire but I know little more. Robert is a trustee for their children because he knew Sir Charles quite well, but, as I say, he sadly died in February.'

'And her family?' Rosemary enquired; these things were important to her.

'Her father was the 2nd Duke of Leinster and her brother, Augustus, now carries the title. They are Fitzgeralds? Irish, from Kildare, I believe.'

Rosemary pondered on the name, unable to find a connection in her circle of friends but nevertheless excited at this unexpected opportunity to meet a member of the aristocracy. She patted the curls at the nape of her neck, happy to know she would look her best at their introduction.

Just moments later a commotion in the hall heralded the arrival of the Lady in question. There was a flurry of smoothing hair, tweaking lace cuffs and adjusting positions, with Margaret and Jean hastily calling their little spaniels and scooping them up on to their laps.

Announced to the room by Sheddon, Lady Mary Ross entered at a brisk pace; a dark haired, willowy figure in a copper taffeta gown, a paisley shawl draped around her broad shoulders. She was greeted by Anne Caroline and formally introduced to the party before being offered a seat.

It was instantly clear that she was a confident woman but her genial expression and frank smile softened the force of her very inquisitive eyes.

After only a few minutes, she was engaged in easy conversation, her words sounding all the more interesting for their attractive Irish inflection. Petting the dogs and relaxing back into the cushions, she soon casually removed her shawl and commented on the 'welcome warmth' of the fire.

Activity in the kitchen was reaching a crescendo in a haze of steam, filled with the pungent aromas of fried bacon and ginger.

Cook hurried to and fro between the ferocious heat of the range to the table, calling on her kitchen and scullery maids to pull down bunches of rosemary and thyme from the ceiling hooks, wash spinach, drain potatoes, chop onions, fetch more ice, grate more sugar, stoke the fire .... Finally, testing the roast pheasants with a skewer and seeing the juices run clear, she sighed with relief.

'Weel, praise the Lord fur tha'!Noo they need tae rest awhile ... like masel!' She flopped down onto a chair, mopping the sweat from her flushed face.

The rest of the dishes were ready, sitting in their elaborate china tureens, half immersed in trays of hot water. After much deliberation and discussion with Miss Wilson and Mrs Owen, Cook felt the meal was a triumph. Of course, they would start with soup, a game consommé, followed by the main dishes of roast pheasant, fish pie with puff pastry, pigeon breasts with

55

ginger and sour plums and veal scallops. The sauce for the scallops was a favourite recipe of Cook's, using plenty cream, white wine and mushrooms, the flavour sharpened with anchovies and nutmeg and decorated symmetrically with bright green parsley and lemon slices.

Waiting in the cool larder were individual vanilla custards in crystal bowls, bramble and apple cake, meringues and lemon biscuits.

'My, it's grand tae be using ma spices again,' she muttered, more to herself than the maids scurrying around clearing up, 'but Ah'll admit it's a mercy the master has a preference fur plain veggies and unfettered meat. Ah'm trauchled! '

***

Unaware of the passing of time, Sarah was so engrossed in sewing and deep, personal thoughts that she did not notice the room growing dark around her. Her attention was focused within the pool of light from her candles, her mind on Bessie, regretting not making the effort to make more visits to the old lady she had grown to love as a mother.

Bessie had died a few days ago, slipping peacefully away in her sleep at her daughter's home in Lanark. Her passing seemed to underline the changes they were all experiencing; the end of an era.

Lamp light glowed from the stairway and the tall figure of a man followed its own shadow into the room.

'Mrs Rafferty?'

She jumped. 'Och! Whit a fright ye gave me, Mr Grant.'

'We did nae ken ye were still here but saw the licht frae the road after locking up.'

'Ye locked me in?'

'Aye. Come awa' noo, lass. It's time tae gae hame.'

She took off her spectacles, rubbing a hand over her tired eyes. It was a long time since someone called her a lass; it made her smile.

While she readied herself to leave, the sound of a carriage trotting through the village drew the shopkeeper to the window.

Sarah joined him, looking out through the rain and gloom towards the mills.

'That's the Bonnington coach,' he observed, recognising the four grey horses and large black cab clattering below them, its lamps reflecting off the wet cobbles. 'It's not often Lady Ross passes through the village, Ah daresay she's bin up at Braxfield House.'

'An' noo she's gaun hame. It's the end o' the day fur us, an' a lang day at that, but Ah'm fair made up wi' this joab, Mr Grant. It disnae feel like werk tae me. See o'er there, at the mills? All the windaes blazin' wi' light, a' the wee black shapes o' people still gaun hard aboot their werk? Sometimes, Ah feel Ah should nae stoap an' gae hame if ma sister an' dochter are still oan the jennies.'

'Weel, I'm no' keepin' the shop open jist for you, Mistress Rafferty.' The candlelight showed the creases of amusement around his eyes. 'Let's be awa'!'

He held his light high and she moved in front of him, feeling her way carefully down the stairs and through the front rooms of the store. Having known the village shop for many years, Sarah was still not used to seeing it from the inside, not as a customer. She was relieved to have been accepted by Mr Grant and the other staff and determined to repay Mrs Owen's faith in giving her this position.

Her only concern being that it seemed too good to be true.

Chapter Four

*"Two things fill the mind with ever new and increasing
wonder and awe - the starry heavens above me and the
moral law within me." Immanuel Kant*

On Christmas Eve, in the Flemish city of Ghent, the long awaited
end to the war with America was finally agreed. The news reached
Britain just before Hogmanay. Every broadsheet in the country
started the New Year by reporting the occasion of the Prince
Regent signing it into law in Parliament.

'So,' Kirkman Finlay raised his glass to the men clustered round
his table in the stuffy, overheated Tontine Rooms, 'to the end of
the war with America! God Save the King and the Prince of
Wales!'

'And God save *us*,' a fellow merchant shouted over the clashing
of tumblers and goblets.

Owen joined them, his brow furrowed.

'On the day the Peace was signed,' he murmured, 'the great
customer of the producers has died.'

It was difficult enough for the textile trade in this long financial
depression but at least the War Office had required uniforms,
ships' sails and all manner of cotton supplies which kept the order
books filled.

'The taxes are killing us!' a young bank clerk cried, comically
gripping his throat and gurgling.

'Aye!' Finlay swigged back the last of his whisky and thumped
the glass on the table. 'If ye're lucky to make a profit at all, the
Treasury has it in its fist afore ye can use it.'

'With the cease of fighting on both fronts, Parliament has lost its
excuse to tax the life out of the markets.'

Listening to his colleagues and the rumbles of despondency
around the crowded coffee house, Owen waited for a pause in the
conversation.

'I believe this a great opportunity,' he said, quietly, drawing their
attention. 'We should be rejoicing there is an end to the needless
bloodshed ...'

58

'America should never have waged war at all!' A man called out. 'No-one's won: the territories gained by either side have all been returned to their pre-war state. It's ended in stalemate!'

'Same as Europe!' shouted another.

'Indeed it has,' Owen continued, 'but we are now entering a time of peace. After two tumultuous decades of funding wars around the world and having the strongest men removed from our workforce, we can start again. At present, we have unrest. The Luddites are smashing machinery in the north of England, there are food riots in market places and subversive meetings amongst the working class who are driven to starvation. Ask yourselves this, gentlemen, it may be a dire situation now but what will happen when thousands, nay, *tens of thousands* of men return home? Yes, we must have reduced taxes so we can grow our industries and give employment, but this is a very different country to the one before the French revolution. It is essential we also implement changes to improve the lives of the workers, particularly those in our new factories.'

'It is true,' McNaughton frowned, stroking his moustache. 'I grant you, that where there were jobs for ten men, there is now one woman but I, for one, cannot take anymore on the pay roll. Anyway, what would they do?'

'Jobs can be found, useful, productive jobs,' Owen put in passionately. 'Our country has been neglected out of necessity while we fought abroad. There is much to be done. New roads, houses ... agriculture is on its knees ... there *will* be employment but it will be different from those the men left behind. This will be a time of change and massive opportunity! We must strive to find an alternative for them because they will be horrified to find their wives and daughters working machines where they and twenty other men once stood.'

Finlay grinned benignly, 'Ever the optimist, Mr Owen!'

Owen leaned forward, being careful to avoid catching his sleeve in a pool of claret on the table.

He looked earnestly into the faces of his audience.

'Let us call a meeting of manufacturers where we can agree a proposal to be sent to Westminster?' He caught the glint of interest in Finlay's eye, knowing the others would follow suit. 'I shall speak to the assembly, as I did a dozen years ago, insisting the import taxes are reduced. With our markets no longer restricted either to the east or the west, we would see growth, more money in the country ... and the rest will follow. We will gather names and support ... and *this* time the government is in no position to ignore our voices.'

Energised by this decision, Owen left the Tontine in high spirits, declining an invitation to dine with Finlay and setting off on foot along the frosty streets of Glasgow.

Winter in the country was pleasing to the eye, in the city it was offensive.

Here and there, in the alleyways and warehouse doorways, figures crouched around smoky fires, creeping back and forth to makeshift timber hovels, crudely covered by tarpaulins or old ship's sails salvaged from the river. Shrewd dogs ran from group to group, fighting over any white, boiled bones thrown in their direction, turning their hungry eyes on rats competing for the prize.

Dusk was falling, frost stiffening the muddy roads into uneven rough tracks causing a passing carriage to slow to a walk, bouncing its occupants almost out of their seats. Owen watched the laughing faces of a middle aged couple, grappling at one another for support in the orange lamp light within their coach.

Drawing out a handkerchief, Owen wiped his freezing nose and walked on towards Charlotte Street, his mind busy with ideas and opinions.

He did not disagree with nor resent the affluent merchants in the city, after all, he was one of them. It was the injustice that grated. If a person, man or woman, worked hard and applied their intelligence or physical energy, then why should they not profit from their labours? Like the gentleman and his wife in the carriage; there was nothing wrong with enjoying life and taking advantage of the comforts they could afford. The fault with society was the acceptance of extreme poverty living as a close neighbour to wealth.

His late father in law often spoke out about this unfairness, sharing his abhorrence of this inequality. For all their differences in age, background and religious beliefs, they were of one mind in desiring to better the lives of those worse off.

Thinking of David Dale brought up memories of Robert Scott Moncrieff. This sincerely good-hearted man, Dale's partner in the Royal Bank of Scotland's Glasgow office, had been very good to

Owen in the early years. His generosity in sharing valuable business acumen in long chats beside the coal fire would never be forgotten, nor could they be repeated. Since retiring, Scott Moncrieff moved to Edinburgh and they saw little of each other. Then, while in London in November, Owen received a letter from Ann Scott Moncrieff, informing him of her husband's death.

A cat dashed across his path, jolting him out of his thoughts.

Lamplighters were moving down the street, creating glowing pools in the gloom, the jagged, towering roofline looming black against the clear night sky.

'Everyone should have a safe place to sleep,' he thought, almost tripping over a vagrant sleeping in a doorway whose spread eagled legs were bound in sack cloth for want of boots. 'Enough food and clothing to fend off the chill, enough schooling to allow them to make the best of themselves ... let them grab opportunities. Not trapped in these cheerless, squalid lives, surviving on bread hand-outs from the Poor Relief, unable to read or understand the wonders and possibilities this world holds for everyone. This *must* be changed.'

A thrill of anticipation caused him to raise his head, push his top hat more firmly into place and pick up his pace.

'My essays are being read by the men who can make the changes.' He told himself. 'They cannot fail to see the sense in my arguments ... there *can* be a better society. They will act when they realise my new system will cure the very foundations of Man's unhappiness.'

He passed the opening to a narrow vennel where several dishevelled men were engaged in oath-spattered discussions, some slumped against the walls, too drunk to participate. High above them, leaning from open windows and accompanied by the wails of hungry infants, women called to each other across the gap: hoarse, tired voices.

Owen walked smartly on, his long coat swinging around his ankles, the leather tassels of his boots rattling in time to his footsteps. Leaving the slums behind, he skirted the edge of Glasgow Green, where the caped figures of two City Constables ambled ahead of him.

His mind turned to the recent reports on the conditions in textile factories, fuelling him with indignation and repulsion. Beatings

61

and sixteen hour shifts were witnessed, not as an occasional outrage but as a regular practice. Many of the children employed were not even eight years of age, far too young for their fragile bodies to endure this unremitting labour.

He gritted his teeth in frustration, 'If we all worked together and cared for each other from the earliest days of our lives, we simply would not tolerate the existence of this suffering.'

On reaching Charlotte Street, Renwick informed him the Miss Dales were in the drawing room.

'Ah, Robert!' Jean greeted him, laying her embroidery hoop to one side. 'I'm afraid to say we have already dined. Shall I have Cook prepare you something?'

'Please forgive me for staying so late in the city,' Owen leaned down to pat the spaniels sniffing round his feet. 'I intended to be with you much earlier. I do not wish to inconvenience you but must confess I am indeed hungry. Perhaps some broth?'

'Of course,' Margaret nodded to Renwick, still standing at the doorway.

Owen warmed his hands at the fire, smiling ruefully at the young ladies he looked upon as sisters. 'Can I beg your indulgence and ask to take it in the library? There is much I should be doing and also, I do not wish to interrupt this peaceful scene.'

'Dear Robert, you are always so busy,' Julia patted the cushions at her side. 'Sit with us and tell us a little of your day and then you may attend to your work.'

Owen was happy to comply but as soon as Renwick informed him the food was prepared, he excused himself and hurried across the hall.

A stoked fire shone from the grate and a pair of silver candelabra, each holding three newly lit candles, was placed on the desk. Renwick was well acquainted with Owen's habits: the large room had been warming for him since the middle of the afternoon.

Left alone, Owen's attention became quickly focused on his plan to address a meeting of cotton merchants and the demands they needed to make of the government. Spreading a napkin across his knees, he supped the broth, occasionally tearing off chunks of bread and chewing methodically, gazing in front of him, unseeing, all the time composing the speech.

As well as demanding a reduction in taxes, this was the opportunity to garner support for reforms in the mills. It was vitally important to choose his words carefully for the greatest impact.

His meagre meal finished, he set to work.

***

Joe pushed more hay into Rusty's hayrack and patted the pony on the neck, smoothing his hand down her thick winter coat. She was a great wee cob for pulling the cart but he needed something bigger, a horse he could ride. He left her munching contentedly and bolted the barn door, standing back to eye the building with a view to adding a stable on the side.

The truth was, in every respect he needed a larger place.

The children were growing up, the oldest lads already adults and the cottage was proving to be too cramped. Besides that, he didn't feel he could entertain his Brothers from the Lodge or the acquaintances he and Fiona were making at the occasional receptions they attended in Lanark.

He shook his head at his own pride, pushing away thoughts of inferiority. Wasn't he content with having left the rented room in New Lanark?

No, he wasn't, but he also admitted to himself the real reason for this growing dissatisfaction with his home: the plot of land for sale not five hundred yards up the hill.

One day it was a piece of rough pasture, the next, a notice was nailed to one of the mature trees by the road, declaring, 'For Sale' and the details of where to enquire. Reining Rusty in, he had looked more closely at the patch of level ground and beyond to the hills on the other side of the Clyde. It was a splendid view, a fine sight to wake up to in the morning and see from your bedroom window. He wondered who would buy it and if they were proposing to build a house, whether he should tender for the contract.

The thought had stayed with him, working away in his mind: the memory of the view and the horse chestnut trees.

At the end of the day, he went back and looked at it again.

63

There was no denying it, *he* wanted to buy it. He wanted to build a house on it and *he* wanted to live there with Fiona and his family.

'Joe!'

Ripped from his thoughts, Joe saw a narrow, frock coated figure standing at the corner of the cottage staring at him.

'Tam. How lang ha'e' ye bin there?'

'Nae lang, ye seemed awfy caught up wi' sumat? Is the roof a'richt?'

'Dinnae mind me,' Joe slapped his friend on the back. 'Jist dreamin'. Come awa' in, **Ah did**nae see ye at Ewing's the past few days an' need tae ask ye aboot yon costings fur the back wall on Mr Combe's hoose.'

'Aye, weel,' Tam followed him indoors, waiting for a candle to be lit before he continued. 'Ah'll no' be gaun back tae Mr Ewing's. Ah've resigned.'

'Whit! Tam, are ye aff yer heid?'

The flame was growing stronger and Joe saw Tam's features more clearly, showing swollen eyelids and a gaunt, anxious expression.

'Melanie is betrothed tae Jim Calder. It's all official, ken. There's nae hope fur me an Mel ... she's bin sae dear tae me fur sae lang but noo ... it's o'er.'

'Whit dis Mel say?'

'Whit can she say?' Tam's voice was full of bitterness. 'Her Da's telt her tae dae her duty an' marry a man who'll tak o'er the business an' look efter her an' her aunt ... as weel as him when he's too auld. She's sich a guid lass, ye ken? She telt him she wants tae be merrit tae me but ...' Tam swiped at his eyes with his cuff, 'he will nae have it.'

'Och, that's a blow,' Joe wished he could find words of comfort but none would come and the silence hung between them.

'Anyhoo,' Tam sniffed, 'Ah cannae gae back up there sae Ah wis wonderin' if ye could dae wi' takin' me oan, full time?'

Joe took a deep breath, he was already supporting a family of seven, was he now to commit to employing someone he didn't need?

'Let me fix the fire an' we can talk ...'

As the evening wore on, Donnie and Davey came back and were soon drawn into the conversation. They carried through a pot of barley and leek soup their mother had set aside in the scullery and put it to heat over the fire.

The men were still talking when Fiona came home and realising straight away there was something wrong, she chivvied the younger children through their meal and followed them up to bed.

'Whit wis tha' aboot, wi' Tam?' she asked Joe when he finally came up to the bedroom.

She was not surprised when he told her, but it did not lessen the sympathy she felt.

'He'll be gie sore,' she whispered, 'broken hairted.'

'Aye, an' nae joab. Ah've sed Ah can gie him a bit mair wurk an' Ah'll ask aroond among the Brothers.' Joe pulled the heavy nightshirt over his head, shivering in the winter air. 'By, it's cauld...' he clambered quickly into bed. 'It's the best Ah can dae.'

Fiona wrapped herself tightly against him, rubbing his back and tucking the blankets firmly over his shoulders.

'Ye cannae solve every yins problems, ma darlin'. Yer a guid friend tae him an' that's worth mair than ony thing. If there's ony thing Ah can dae, tell me?'

He hugged her close, enjoying her warmth as they drifted towards sleep, then his eyes flickered open.

'There is yin thing ye could dae?'

'An' whit's tha'?' she asked softly, nuzzling his neck.

'Blaw oot the caunel!'

***

Robert Owen's public speaking skills were greatly improved from his first hesitant days as a youth in Manchester. As a teenager, the evenings of debating philosophical questions with Dr Dalton and Mr Winstanley had acquired him the name 'the reasoning machine'. When this led to his introduction into the Literary and Philosophical Society of Manchester, his first stammering, blushing speeches had been on cotton manufacturing, but he had learned a valuable lesson from those days.

The difference in his now assured delivery, even since addressing the Scottish cotton barons in 1803, was evident to all when he took the podium in the Tontine.

The bustling meeting room was filled with merchants and bankers, their top hats perched upon their knees, gold watch chains flashing, the younger men sporting jackets of richly coloured brocade or velvet and shot silk cravats. The country might be on its knees, but the rich were still rich. All eyes turned to Owen and after a few coughs and creaking chairs, they settled back to hear him speak.

His notes lay before him but he knew his subject so well he barely referred to them.

His first point was to state the need for a reduction in the taxes upon cotton coming into the country. The raw material was already proving expensive but with the Government's taxes added to the imports, it was becoming almost impossible to achieve a profit. Loud calls of support and banging of canes on the floor applauded his words and he moved on to the demand for changes to the Factory Reform Laws to protect children on the factory floor.

Stressing the differences brought about in the manufacturing industry over the last twenty five years, he hammered home the detrimental effects to the working population of Britain.

'Before factories and machinery, the majority of people worked in agriculture. They lived in small, close knit social communities and while they laboured hard, they could converse with one another, the children could play or rest when they wished and at the end of the day the crops or livestock they raised was theirs to eat or take to market. Now, not only do they not see the product of their toil, they are encased in man-made structures under extreme conditions of noise and a filthy atmosphere throughout long ... intolerably long, shifts.'

'I know there are those amongst us who strive to take better care of our employees, provide schooling and weather tight homes, but, gentlemen, there is an endemic problem in our industry which must be addressed. Mill owners must be made to give their workers better conditions. It is not enough to rely on goodwill. We all know the profits which can be made, but they do not need to be made by driving our workers to the point of exhaustion and in some cases death. I speak especially of the children.'

At the end of his speech, he asked for votes in favour of formally putting forward his demands to the government. On the reduction of tax, the vote was unanimous. On the second point, laws for shorter hours and a minimum age for child workers, very few raised their hands, most preferring to talk among themselves or ostentatiously prepare to leave the meeting.

'It was a disappointing show of support for the factory reform,' his clerk, Clegg, ventured on their drive back to Charlotte Street.

Owen sat opposite him, quiet and thoughtful, his eyes directed to the passing scenes outside the carriage window.

'Yes,' he darted a glance at Clegg. 'Disappointing. That it is, certainly.' He looked out the window again, his lips set in a firm line, accentuating his angular features, the constantly shifting light catching his high cheekbones.

Clegg regretted mentioning the second vote. 'However, sir, good news concerning the need to cut the taxes!'

Owen shifted his position on the upholstered seat and fixed Clegg with a defiant look.

'The need for laws to protect the youngsters in British factories is of vital importance! If these businessmen are not interested in raising this issue then I shall take up the matter, personally!'

Clegg returned a wavering smile, 'Indeed. Very well, sir.'

'The wars with overseas enemies are over, but if we are to pursue business by way of our new factory system we must address the evils within our own society. I shall make it my utmost priority to take this to the House.'

A few days later, on the 26th of February, an unforeseen obstacle arose.

A portly middle-aged gentleman rose early, shaved and paid particular attention to smoothing his once black hair until it lay as he wished. With the aid of his manservant, he set about dressing in immaculate white breeches, a cutaway, long-tailed navy blue uniform jacket and brass buttoned waistcoat. After a short struggle to draw on his boots, he sucked in his paunch and admired his reflection.

His actions were undertaken in silence, his breathing a little nervous.

Solemnly, his servant handed him his bicorn hat and cloak, saluted him and went to squint out between the slats of the window shutters into the grey dawn.

For nine months, the exiled Emperor Napoleon had lived on the tiny island of Elba, ruling its twelve thousand inhabitants in a benign, paternal manner. Now, he was escaping.

Over the time of his enforced stay on Elba he was not secluded. Through thousands of letters, visits and a regular supply of the leading national newspapers, he gauged the time was right to return to France. There were serious concerns that Louis XVIII was eroding the liberties of the people.

Napoleon could see his great Empire was shrinking, land being returned to nobles and the revolutionary ideals were being lost. He was determined to return and lead his country back to the path of freedom of speech, equality and brotherhood.

Trusted colleagues reassured him that plans were in place on the mainland with thousands of soldiers ready to be mobilised under his command. The four hundred troops stationed with him, rigorously drilled over the past months, were already gathering at the harbour. Usually, the billowing sails of French and Austrian ships could be seen patrolling his exit, but today he knew they would be absent.

Now was the time.

Evading a couple of Austrian guards who were chatting and admiring the rising sun from a bench on the terrace, Napoleon kissed his mother and sister goodbye. He received their good wishes with a confident smile and strode down to the waiting ship.

He, Emperor Napoleon 1, would take his countrymen and fellow Imperialists back to war and lead them to victory.

***

Rosie made her way slowly behind Fiona, plucking at her skirts to raise them above her little boots, keeping her pink cotton hem well away from the undergrowth. They were taking a short cut through the woods to the allotments on the hillside above the mills. Spring bird song rang out all around them, lazy tortoiseshell butterflies fluttered aimlessly in patches of sun, roused from their winter slumber too early to find flowers.

The unseasonably warm day was a welcome surprise, coaxing them out after their Sunday meal to pay a visit to Cal's pride and joy. He had foregone the weekly family gathering to work on his piece of ground so Fiona packed him a picnic and suggested they all take it down to him.

Sarah and Cathy excused themselves; the luxury of a whole afternoon of doing nothing appealed to them far more than going for a walk.

The younger children pleaded to be allowed to stay, enthralled by the new occupant sharing Rusty's barn. Calling on Cal's expertise before making the decision, Joe had bought a big dappled grey mare. High withered and deep chested, with cob somewhere in her breeding, she stood sixteen hands high and her name was Bluebell but, with a snort of derision, Joe declared he would call the beast Bluey.

Rosie was pleased the horse was an exciting novelty for the children, finding she could only bear a couple of hours of their constant chatter and boisterous games. Seeing the men take out the Dominoes, she donned her bonnet and joined her sister in law.

Since being given an allotment, the whole family heard little else from Cal: what he would grow, how often he could attend the plot, his plans for making a hut for chickens, or possibly geese, and all the herbs he was going to plant to sell to Auld Bel for her medicines.

Not wishing to leave her at home, Fiona brought Sionaidh with them. The girl skipped along in her long tunic like a child half her age, picking up twigs and snapping them, then tossing them away before snatching up another one. Some were fringed with woolly grey lichen causing her to stop and inspect it minutely, before it too would be broken and thrown into the air.

'Sae whit dae ye think?' Cal beamed at them, pushing his long hair behind his ears.

Flat terraces were carved into the hillside, each level marked out with posts or low willow hurdles to divide the areas into separate spaces. Owen's managers allocated the plots to anyone in the village who wanted one, but the demand soon took up all the available land.

'Ah wis gie lucky tae get this yin. Ah've dug it a' twice, heavy work! Ah thocht ma hairt wid stoap at times!' they were laughing

69

but he was not exaggerating. The task was almost too much for him but, little by little, pacing himself, it was done. The sense of achievement was immense. 'There's no' a weed or root left but, see here?' he scooped up a handful of soil, 'see yon wee stanes? Ye leave them, it stoaps the soil frae clogging up wi' watter. Ah learnt tha' frae big Cuthbert, he has his bit o'er there.' He waved towards a lower terrace. 'He kens a lot aboot plants an' that.' He dropped the clod of earth and rubbed his hands together. 'O' course, fur carrots, ye cannae ha'e ony stanes. Naw. Sand's the best fer them ... an' sieved soil.'

Fiona walked up and down the side of the neatly turned rectangle of earth, pulling at her bonnet brim to shade her eyes against the low afternoon sun.

'We'll eat like kings!' she cried. 'An' if this war is as lang as the last, it will nae matter tae us.'

'Ma Gerry says there's fightin' gaun oan in the cities fur want o' food. Och, it's a cryin' shame yon Frenchies are at it again, can they no' gi'e us a bit o' peace?'

Cal put his hands on his hips, adding more dirt to his heavily stained smock. He loved being in the open air. The fragrance of fresh vegetation and the breeze's soft caress soothed his soul, cleared his mind and lifted his usual cloud of anxiety. From spotting the different russet furred squirrels, some with blond tails, some almost black, long ear tufts, no ear tufts, to the tracks of animals crossing his plot at night, polecats, foxes and deer, he revelled in the Nature all around him.

'Weel, ye've done a braw joab, Cal,' Rosie said sweetly, trying to find something nice to say about a bare stretch of dirt. 'Ah'll leave ye tae it. Cheery the noo!'

Knowing his fastidious sister, Cal laughed at her retreating figure, 'Ye'll like the veggies Ah drap at yer door.'

'Aye, that'll be fine.' Her face was hidden by the poke bonnet but Rosie's smile could be heard in her voice, 'Mind an' wash them afore ye bring them tae ma hoose!'

A robin flew down to within a few yards of them, its beady black eyes blinking, head jerking to one side inquisitively.

'He comes a lot,' Cal whispered, taking his spade and digging it into the ground. 'Sionaidh ...watch!'

70

He flicked the earth in a scattering shower towards the little bird and within moments it hopped forward and seized a worm in its beak.

Sionaidh shrieked with delight, clapping her hands excitedly, sending it swooping away into the bushes.

'Och, darlin',' Fiona said quietly, putting her finger to her lips, 'ye ha'e tae be quiet. Ye've scared the wee soul.'

'He'll be back,' Cal told her, 'dinnae fret.'

After several minutes the bird had still not appeared and Fiona tried to encourage her daughter to give up waiting.

'We need tae be gettin' hame.'

'Ye gae hame, Ah'll bring her up later,' Cal said, genially. 'She's nae bother.'

For a moment, Fiona hesitated. Cal knew about Sionaidh's fits but had never witnessed one and they could look very frightening. She looked at the two of them, their heads close together, sifting through a pile of dead undergrowth, pulling out lacey skeleton leaves.

'Ah'll see ye afore it's dark, then?' she called. 'Keep an eye on her, mind?'

Cal looked up, shaking his hair away from his eyes. 'Away! We'll be jist grand.'

'Where's Sionaidh?' Joe asked, the moment she walked through the door. There was rising panic in his voice. 'Ah thocht she wis wi' ye?'

'Aye, she wis, but dinnae worry, she's doon wi' Cal, grubbin' aboot in the dirt. She's enjoying hersel'.' She looked around the empty cottage. 'Ha'e they gaun doon the hill a'ready?'

'The weans are oot the back an' the lads are aff tae Tam's.' Joe threw another log on the fire. 'Come, sit wi' me. This peace wulnae last long, ye can be sure.'

They talked of how well Sarah looked, how pleased they were Mrs Owen had arranged the position for her in the shop. The worry of more years of war and whether Sam was still in Gibralter, both hoping he would not be caught up in the new battles.

'At least the bairns are weel.' Superstitiously, Fiona tapped the wooden arm of her chair. 'Ailsa's happy enough in the mills.'

'Robbie wis telling me he's bin moved tae a big new loom,' Joe told her, 'and promoted. He's fair chuffed.'

'He's a guid lad. Weaving was whit he wanted fae the stairt an' noo he's gettin' oan weel. Oor Tom is a clever lad, with his letters an' reading. His number work is better than ony o' the ithers!' Fiona patted her chest. 'Ah'm sae prood o' whit the teacher says aboot him. He's a Monitor, ye ken, mind Ah tell ye at the back o' the year?'

'Weel, he's aulder than most ...'

'He could be a scholar, Joe.' Fiona's almond eyes glowed. 'In a' ma years at the school, Ah've no' seen a bairn sae keen tae learn.'

Joe gave her a long, questioning look. 'And ...?'

'Nuthin!' She smothered a laugh. 'But ...'

'Ah!'

'He should be gaun intae the mills this year, he's ten year auld noo. It wid be a shame, d'ye no' think? Mr Owen says ony o' the children can stiy in the classroom longer, if that's whit their Da' wants.'

Joe considered the problem for a long time, mulling over how fair it would be to the rest of his children.

'All oor bairns ha'e worked fur the family, we cannae treat Tom ony different.'

'An' why no'?' Fiona demanded. 'Each yin is as different frae his brither as the next! Donnie wi' his stane work, Davey joinering, Robbie at his weaving ... they're a' wurkin', but at different things. Like Ah said, Ailsa's content in the mills, Ah'm sure she wid be happy fer her wee brither tae learn his books.'

'It's guid fer them tae work, bring in money fur the hoose an' unnerstaun whit hard work is.'

'But dae we need it? Aye, we've struggled an' counted every penny through the door but noo, do we need a few mair shillings a week?'

There was a feisty side to his wife and he could see it in the line of her shoulders, her resolutely pursed lips. He wondered why she even asked his opinion on this matter for it was clear she was set on Tom staying longer at school.

'Let him stay fur anither year.'

'Och, yer a darlin'!' she rose from her chair and planted a smacking kiss on his forehead.

'A year, mind? An' we'll see how it goes.'

She disappeared through to the scullery, singing a cheery ballad he knew to be her favourite.

Stretching his arms above his head, he yawned then relaxed, crossing his legs and gazing into the fire's embers.

No, they did not need a few more shillings a week. What was more, he was in the comfortable position of preparing to offer on the land up the lane. He would say nothing for now, but was enjoying the feeling of satisfaction that came with a healthy bank account and two lucrative contracts agreed for the coming months.

Tam was proving himself to be far more than just a clerk. Bringing years of experience from his time with Ewing, he was full of good advice for making savings, finding more reliable suppliers and keeping a track on materials.

So long as his customers didn't take fright at the news of the war, the next six months looked promising.

***

Owen paced backwards and forwards between the two tall drawing room windows overlooking Bedford Square, eager for the arrival of the carriage to take him to his appointment.

He was staying as the guest of one of his business partners, John Walker, who had kindly placed his coach at his disposal. Walker and his large family were at their glorious country house, Arnos Grove at Southgate. That enchanting place held fond memories for Owen of strolling beside a brook under a canopy of mature beech trees, learning of Walker's pauper boys' school on the estate, the family's deep interest in entomology and, most treasured of all, finding a true friendship.

In the four weeks since arriving in London, Owen organised the printing and circulating of his newly published pamphlet, *Observations of the Effects of the Manufacturing System*, which included the draft of a Bill he wanted to have presented to the House of Commons. His London friends and acquaintances helpfully advised on the best people to approach, all of which culminated in a meeting with Nicholas Vansittart, the Chancellor of the Exchequer.

It was a difficult time for Vansittart, he was under a great deal of strain due to Napoleon's unexpected return to France and the ensuing expenditure for another war. He was, however, sympathetic to Owen's cause and gave him a long interview to discuss the implications of reducing taxes on imported goods.

Then, listening to his demands for better factory working conditions, he scratched at the few remaining strands of grey hair on his head.

'Mr Owen, you make a good case for at least reviewing the current Factory Reform Law, ye need to find someone to act for you.'

Calling his clerk, he gave instructions to issue letters for Owen to meet with several leading lights in both the House of Commons and the Lords.

Immediately, Owen set to work lobbying everyone who would grant him an audience. It soon became clear, if anyone was going to take up his demands for improvements in factories, the best man to approach was Sir Robert Peel.

Glimpsing Walker's carriage, Owen hurried downstairs and out into the fresh spring morning. Bedford Square's magnificent, symmetrical six story buildings surrounded a large oval garden. On that morning, the young pine trees and low growing shrubs were shining with dew, allowing glimpses of pastel shades where ladies walked, arm in arm, taking the air.

Although his mind was full of the coming meeting, Owen took in the pleasant scene almost subconsciously, thinking how much the greenery and beauty of nature aided a feeling of well being amidst the rumble of the capital. It was just one of the many contrasts in life which divided the urban wealthy from the poor. In the slums, dockyards and factory areas there were no flowers and shady dells, just unremitting dirt, stench, noise and industry.

For the rest of his journey, he tried to concentrate on the subject in hand while Walker's coachman skilfully handled the coach and pair to make slow progress through the city's crowded streets. All around, sometimes peering in the windows, there were hawkers, ragged urchins, flocks of geese, smart liveried carriages with haughty footmen steering gleaming horses between hand carts and rustic wagons; these piled high with sacks of vegetables or caged chickens destined for market stalls.

Sir Robert Peel was a big personality in politics, not least due to his blunt northern ways. He was believed to be the richest cotton

74

master in Britain, with vast mills in Lancashire employing thousands of workers, many of them children from the Poor Houses. It was Peel who presented, and succeeded in seeing through Parliament, the Health and Morals of Apprentices Bill a decade earlier. This was the Law which both Owen and Dale were deeply disappointed to find was watered down to the point of being useless.

Clearly, Peel had a vested interest in making good profits from the factory system but it was also evident that he was aware of the poor working conditions and the need to bring in more rigorous regulations.

The meeting started warily, both men sizing up the other while Owen was invited to take a seat and the necessary social pleasantries were exchanged. They were in a small oak panelled study, one of several set aside for Ministers to engage in private meetings. The only show of hospitality being a coal fire struggling to keep the damp at bay and a tray of cut crystal decanters and glasses placed on a card table by the window.

'We have much in common, Mr Owen,' Peel stated affably, 'Both self-made men. There's too damn few of us down this way. It is good to hear a man speak with his local tongue. You have an odd turn to your words, mind, London with a bit of Welsh but ... Manchester tae boot?'

Owen laughed, the older man's deep northern vowels had not been softened by Westminster society.

'This is true! My first experience in mills was in Manchester. So long as I can be understood, that is all I desire.'

'I knew your late father-in -law, ye knaw.' Peel sat back in his chair, his thick curling grey hair, square shoulders and muscular legs, encased in formal black breeches and hose, gave the appearance of a man much younger than his sixty five years. 'We exchanged many letters and views. David Dale was a giant of a man in the cotton industry. Him and Arkwright. Bye, what men! Leaders in their field and wise, good men too. God rest their souls.

'My grandfather was a farmer, ye knaw,' Peel continued with pride, not allowing space for Owen to speak. 'My father too, afore he took up the weaving business. I knew the toil of the land, the sleet in my eyes, digging ewes out from snow drifts, picking frozen turnips until my fingers were blue! Blue and numb! When I were a lad we were putting out work to dozens of homes and many's the day I drove a cart full of yarn from valley to valley ... in all weathers. Oh aye, I know the textile trade as well as the best o' them. I took my father's cottage industry to the heights it is today! I make no apology for my wealth, Mr Owen, nor should I! Likewise, ye have Mr Dale's renowned Scottish mills at New Lanark, ye understand the process and the importance of manufacturing to this country.'

'I certainly do, Sir. The importance to the wealth of the country is evident. We cannot return to putting out work to villages or farm steads, that is clear. However, the seriously injurious conditions of this new method of manufacturing are also unambiguous. You have read my pamphlet?

'Aye, and your New View of Society. It is on many of the Members' desks.'

'And they are reading it!' Owen said, with quiet satisfaction. 'I have been stopped by several in these corridors who tell me it is enlightening. Once it is grasped, the fact that a person's character is formed *for* them, not *by* them, *then* we can progress. That is why it is vital that Britain's main employer, namely manufacturers, treat their workforce in a humane manner.'

The content of Owen's essays was discussed for a while then, mindful his allotted time was nearly over, he brought the subject back to his proposed Bill.

Peel rubbed his chin, as if coming to a decision. 'I am of a mind to recommend it for deliberation in the House. It needs careful discussion. We are all aware of Ned Ludd and his cronies, tempers are running high and we cannot be seen to be backing down on mechanising our factories. They are the way forward.'

'It is the conditions *inside* these factories which must be addressed.' Owen sighed, 'Sir, you know the dangers of greed and the overriding desire to accumulate more wealth. While a gentleman like yourself has the intelligence and ethics to instruct your overseers to act responsibly, you do not know what happens while you are in London.'

'Exactly why I was compelled to put forward the Act of 1802.'

'With respect, Sir, these atrocities have not stopped. You will have read, as I have, reports from inspectors at mills across Britain?'

Peel nodded, gravely, and Owen carried on.

'Small children working in foul air until they can barely stand, then being flogged for failing to do their job. Young women abused by men who hold a position of power over them, fearful to lose their means of a wage. We must curb these desperately long hours which drive the unfortunate worker to physical collapse and when they cannot rise from their bed to attend the mill, they are sacked and merely replaced.'

'I agree with you, Mr Owen. In our excitement of creating such wealth, many do not know the boundaries of decency towards their human beings.'

'Then we must have a Law which can enforce wholesome behaviour in the workplace, cease the practice of infant labour and regulate the hours allowed for one pair of hands to continuously operate machinery.'

'It will not be popular,' Peel gave an ironic smile.

Owen's lips also curved, his eyes shining with innocent charm. 'No doubt, Sir Robert, with your considerable influence and reputation as a cotton master, those who fear any loss in earnings will soon be persuaded to do the *right* thing.'

Chapter Five

"My own mind is my own church."
Thomas Paine (1794)

On returning to New Lanark in early June, Owen lost no time in checking the mill's balance sheets and launching into further plans to improve the village. He was filled with enthusiasm and a confidence born of the welcoming reception received by his essays: from merchants and philosophers to members of political parties on both sides of the House of Commons.

The loss shown in the accounts at the end of the previous year, 1814, was mainly due to the closure of Stanley Mills in February of that year.

Having leased them to the Glasgow merchant Stewart Douglas in 1811, their poor performance had forced Douglas to withdraw from the business and they had been put up for sale just two years later. The hoped for proceeds from the sale did not materialise and, indeed, there were still no interested parties. As well as the Manager's house, a grand residence, there were two mills containing sixteen thousand mule and water spindles, outhouses and gardens.

It was a terrible waste, he acknowledged that, but with Mr Craig, the previous manager, racking up nearly £24,000 in debt to Dale's estate, and a further £16,000 invested to try to make it work, Owen knew it was better to leave it empty than pour more good money after bad.

However, the New Lanark accounts in the first quarter of the current year were promising and the second quarter looked to be bringing a fair profit. Bolstered by this financial success but determined to continue raising the income, he pressed his foreign agents for more overseas orders and despite the war, set about engaging the tradesmen required to complete the new Institute.

Then, he turned his attention to the school children.

The lowlands of Scotland were enjoying settled warm weather, encouraging scores of visitors to view the mills every week. A highlight of the tour was the schoolroom and, in particular, the choir and dancing classes. The sight of dozens of happy children

78

providing their own music and giving a fine display on the dance floor drew Owen's thoughts to their uniform.

'We're tae ha'e new cla'es,' Fiona told Joe one evening.

'Ma cla'es are fine...' he replied, engrossed in the piece he was learning for the Lodge: a new apprentice was being entered.

'Naw, no' fur ye, at the school. Mr Owen says the bairns are needing different cla'es. He wants them tae be free tae move aroond an' dance an' leap!' She giggled to herself. 'Och, the wee souls, they look sae bonny but yin wee lad ripped his troosers doon the back the ither day. His wee face!'

'Weel, Mr Owen can dae whit he likes. Donnie an' Davey will be workin' fur weeks doon there on Owen's money, sae Ah'm weel pleased.'

'Aye, it's aboot time those big buildings were finished aff,' she dropped a kiss on the top of his head as she passed by, nudging his shoulder with the laundry basket 'Ah'm peggin' these oot fur a blaw afore the dew comes doon an' then Ah'll fetch Sionaidh up frae Cal.'

'Will ye spare a few minutes wi' me?' Joe asked, reaching for her arm. 'Ah want tae show ye sumat?'

'Aye. Noo?'

'Efter ye've pegged the washing.'

The Lanark clock was peeling nine when Joe and Fiona walked up towards the old town. Insisting on tying on her bonnet in case they met anyone, Fiona kept pausing to take in the splendour of the glorious sunlit evening. Swallows swooped around their heads, little brown sparrows, yellow headed yellowhammers and flocks of chaffinches chattered in the hedgerows, sometimes flitting along the lane ahead of them before diving for cover amidst the thick foliage.

On coming to the group of horse chestnut trees and the open plot of ground facing the valley, Joe came to a standstill and squeezed Fiona's hand.

'Here,' he pointed south to the faraway wooded hills of Corehouse estate, 'whit dae ye think o' that fur a view?'

Fiona's expressive face gave him the reply; she was struck by the beauty of the scene.

'Whit a braw place! *Brèagha*! An' it's sae open, ye can see the sun frae rising until its last moments o' the day.'

They walked off the lane, between the trees and out onto the pasture.

'Forget-me-nots ...' she plucked a stalk of the dainty bright blue blooms from a host of other flowers. 'Ma favourite.'

'Ah wanted tae see whit ye thocht o' this place fur, weel ... Ah think it's grand.'

'An' who widnae like it?'

'Ye might no' have, fur whitever reason a woman sometimes conjures frae nuthin,' he winked, cheekily, 'an' Ah didnae want tae buy it an' have ye angry wi' me.'

'Buy it?'

'Aye.'

'Joe!' she spun round, noticing the large open area and the posts denoting the edge of the plot. 'It's a huge place? Whit wid ye dae wi' it?

'Ah saw it fur sale some time past, but they're asking a lot o' money. Then, on talkin' wi' a brother frae the Lodge, he knew of a Glesgie man who wants tae build a hoose in Lanark, sae Ah brought him here. It's a gie big piece o' grun ... an' Ah fancy the site as much as he. Weel, efter a lot o' havering we struck a deal which means Ah build twa hooses, side by side, an' he wid ha'e yin an' we wid ha'e the ither.'

Realisation slowly dawned on Fiona.

'We wid ha'e oor ane hoose? Here?'

'If ye like it.'

'Oh, aye, Joe. I like it jist fine. Whither Ah will believe it until it's built, Ah cannae say,' tears were tripping her.

'It could be years afore it's ready,' he wiped her tears, cuddling her against him. 'Ah wish Ah could ha'e done this fur ye a lang time ago ... ye deserve a guid hoose.'

'As dae ye, ma sweethairt. Aw, darlin', oor ane hoose!''

He shrugged, pleased with his plans. 'Let's hope Ah git the walls up afore Ah'm too auld tae enjoy it.'

***

Peel intended to present the Bill to the House of Commons in early June but the unfolding drama in France was taking up so

80

much time that Owen became frustrated when it was postponed, again and again.

Then, news arrived of the Duke of Wellington's victory over Napoleon at a hard fought battle at Waterloo, and Owen laid the newspaper flat on his desk at Braxfield, sat back and folded his arms.

Napoleon was capitulating and expected to surrender at any time, bringing this expensive, short lived war to an end.

Britain, as a member of the hastily arranged Seventh Coalition, now had a great deal of work to undertake and he knew his Bill would rank low in the order of matters to be attended to in Parliament. True enough, a few days later, he received a letter from Sir Robert, regretting he would not be in a position to present the Bill in the foreseeable future.

'This set back in London will not prevent you from opening the new Institute, though, will it, dear?'Anne Caroline comforted her husband.

He was standing at the drawing room window, gazing out over the lawns where the children were playing.

'Not at all. New Lanark is proving itself many fold, I am just keen to spread its success to other mills and find the delay extremely provoking.'

'When I was in the village this morning, I heard several very pleasant comments regarding the new roman style tunics the children are wearing in the school. The edging of tartan was much admired.'

'They are practical as well.'

'Pure white is hardly practical!' Anne Caroline wrinkled her nose. 'Perhaps for attending church or taking tea with an aunt but you expect them to be running freely in the woods.'

'They will be washed every two or three days so they always appear fresh. I think the children like wearing them, they were pleased to have something so bright.'

Anne Caroline shook her head, 'I am sure the mothers of these children will not be so happy while attending to the laundry! '

'Oh, I would not burden them with that task. The village laundry will take care of the washing, it is all in hand.'

'You think of everything. Goodness, dearest, I don't know where you find the time. Letters and visitors ... and travelling up and down the country roads to Glasgow ... or all the way to London! I rarely leave Lanark and yet I am tired by the end of the day.'

'There is much to be done and I never tire of doing it, perhaps that's why I find only a few hours of sleep is sufficient.' He came over to where she was sitting at her little writing bureau. 'You do a great deal for the villagers. Just yesterday, Mrs Simmons came out her door and stopped me as I passed, eager to tell me you visited her daughter after her baby died and how much it was appreciated.' He caressed his wife's cheek, 'I hope it did not cause you too much distress? Such a tender subject.'

She reached up for his hand. 'We prayed together and, I admit, my sadness was not confined to the young woman's recent loss. My grief for Daniel will never leave, but I thank God for giving us those precious months with him before taking him up to Heaven.'

'He will be forever in our memories, dear Caroline.'

'There are women in the village who have lost several babies. Their pain and bravery in overcoming such intense personal grief is no less tragic for being a common occurrence. Why, when the King's daughter died it drove him to madness, his high birth did not save him.'

'We are all the same, we do not suddenly acquire higher sensibilities when we acquire money. Your father used to preach on the matter. I recall him being incensed on occasion by the dismissive behaviour of fellow merchants, wrongly believing the paupers did not suffer pain and heartache to the same degree as those from noble birth.'

'We must pray for their forgiveness and Our Lord's guidance to show them Christian kindness.'

Owen withdrew his hand from between hers, softening the movement with a smile.

'Kindness,' he said firmly, 'and behaving with compassion is not exclusive to Christians. It is the basic tenet of the world's main religions and if practised wholeheartedly by all followers would extinguish suffering in a blink. Sadly, as we can see with our own eyes, this is not the case.'

Anne Caroline fell silent.

'It is not the fault of anyone alive today,' Owen said with feeling, 'it is generation upon generation of indoctrination from the families and social groups that have formed the population. Down the years, Man's character has been trained to accept taking up arms against perceived enemies, the highest achievement is deemed to be holding an accumulation of wealth and power. And the result? Misery. The pattern *must* be changed!

'If the young generation is raised within a rational, caring environment, at home as well as at school, they will pass this to their children ... and so forth.' He went back to the window, 'I can see it so clearly, Caroline. It *is* achievable. A New System to drive out ignorance and selfishness, where religious tolerance is the accepted behaviour and achieving happiness for oneself and one's community is the goal to be held in the highest regard. This would allow true freedom of personal belief and remove bigotry and greed.'

'You sound like the revolutionaries in France,' Anne Caroline murmured.

'Liberty, equality, fraternity. Sound ideas. I agree entirely with these ideals and vision, however, I strongly oppose the violent way it was enacted.' He glanced back at her in the shadows of the room, his eyes still dazzled from the bright scene outside. 'You know, I sent Emperor Napoleon a copy of my first essay, A New View of Society.'

'Gracious!'

'He read it while on Elba and found it very interesting. For all his ego, he brought about a welcome change to the French people.'

'My dear, you are alarming me, do you agree with Bonaparte's actions?'

'No. However, I can see the merit of his ideals. The revolution created a new enlightened era to Europe and he took up the lead in carrying out the wishes of his countrymen. The simple beauty of my New System is that there would be no fighting, no bloodshed, no killing. It is a way of *being*, educating, a way of living our lives without brutality or causing suffering. Lords and Ladies would remain in their mansions and prayers would be said in Churches of all denominations without fear for their safety, for they would not be oppressing anyone.'

A knock came at the door and Sheddon took his customary two steps slowly into the room, hand still on the door knob.

'Sir, there is a clerk from the Court Office to see you. He says you were expecting him?'

Owen hurried away to meet his visitor, leaving Anne Caroline to the sudden silence.

She turned back to the letter she was writing, shaking her head in reluctant admiration. His apparent disregard for the Lord's word caused her discomfort, but, like her father, she knew that in all but name, Owen behaved in every way as a disciple of God's teachings. He was determined to do the right thing for his fellow man; on a mission. Owen's presence caused a frisson of energy, it burned like a delicious secret behind his eyes, emanating from his earnest features and genial smile.

'At least, I have him here, at home for a while,' she told herself, inspecting the nib of her quill and removing a speck of fluff. 'I can enjoy his company all summer.'

Owen had other ideas. Within a few days of hearing about the delay in Parliament from Sir Robert, Owen decided to conduct a tour of the largest manufacturing mills across Britain.

'This way I can make a report,' he declared to his wife and eldest sons at the dining table. 'An accurate, up to date report of the current conditions endured by the workers.'

'Which mills are you intending to visit?' young Robert asked, tucking into his mutton and a pile of plain root vegetables.

'As many as possible,' his father told him. 'Why don't you accompany me? William, you are yet too young to witness such a gruelling adventure, but you can aid us in planning our route.'

The boys were delighted. Not wishing to dampen their lively exchange throughout the rest of the meal, Anne Caroline restricted her comments to purely practical matters.

Inside, she felt a growing coldness. Despite the warm Paisley shawl around her shoulders, she shivered, recalling her old lady's maid, Toshie, who would have said, 'someone's walked o'er ma grave'.

***

The Owen carriage left Braxfield early on a drizzling morning, the smothering clouds showing a pale halo where the rising midsummer sun was hiding. The party on board were in good spirits despite the weather, with Owen pointing out landmarks to Robert Dale along the way, a map spread across their knees.

In the mills and school room, wicks were turned up in the lamps, as they did on dark winter days and when the bell rang out for the end of the day, few villagers chose to climb the hill to their allotments.

'Git oot o' yur wet school frock, Sionaidh,' Fiona cried, urging her daughter into the cottage. 'All o' ye!' she called to her younger children, 'let me set the fire ablaze and we can dry oot.'

Ailsa obediently mounted the stairs, Tom hard on her heels with little Alex roaring and pretending to scamper on all fours like a lion. Tired though she was, Fiona had to laugh; the last lesson of the afternoon was about animals of the jungle.

Fetching more dry twigs for kindling from the basket in the scullery, she returned to the front room and was about to drop to her knees at the hearth when it struck her that the room was empty.

'Sionaidh?' she called up the steps, 'Is Sionaidh wi' ye?'

'Naw!' Tom squealed above the banging and shouting of a play fight with his little brother.

A glance at the front door showed it was ajar: Fiona rushed outside.

Everything was still and quiet, the higher branches of the trees lost in a fine mist, a steady dripping of rain running off the thatched roof. She ran round the cottage and peered into the barn, calling her daughter's name, checking the privy, even opening the stable to make sure she wasn't playing hide and seek and cowering among the straw.

'Where is she, ma?' Ailsa shouted from the front door.

'Ah dinnae ken, but she's no' here. The door wis open sae she must ave come ootside ....'

'Och,' Ailsa said, exasperated, 'whit d'ye bet she's doon at Uncle Cal's veggie patch?'

Relief flowed through Fiona, 'O' course! Chap Mrs Mclaren's door on passin' jist incase she's wi' her? But, yer richt, she'll be doon at the allotments. Be a guid lass an' run doon an' fetch her back. Yer uncle may no' be gaun there this day. Pull ma auld cloak o'er ye or that's mair cla'es that'll be wet through.'

The flames were starting to spread some warmth when Ailsa returned.

'She's no' next door nor doon the hill, Ma,' she cried breathlessly, brushing away raindrops running off her hair and down her face, 'nor Uncle Cal. That auld man, Cuthbert, he telt me Uncle Cal has nae bin up this eve at a' ... an' ... he has nae seen oor Sionaidh either, but he wis busy makin' hurdles tae keep the deer aff his plot, sae mibbee he didnae see her pass?'

Tom and Alex were listening, eyes wide with worry.

'She cannae be far awa',' Fiona's tone was calm, reassuring, though her heart was racing. 'Tom, run up tae where yur Da' an' brithers are workin', ye ken? Top o' the brae? They said they wid be clearing brash frae the new land efter work. Tell them whit's happened.'

Having been barefoot all day, Tom pushed his grimy feet into a pair of boots, muttering they would help him run faster in the slippery mud. He laced them up, grabbed his cap and tore out the door.

'Ailsa, stay here, tak care o' Alex ... and tell yur Da' Ah'm gaun doon tae the mills. She *cannae* be far awa'...'

Running through the rain, Fiona was soon out of breath, forced to stand still for a few moments, pulling her shawl tightly around her shivering body. It was not cold, the air was warm, but her wet hands were shaking uncontrollably. If it was any of her other children she would be slightly concerned, angry perhaps, but it was Sionaidh.

The shining slate tiles and grey bulk of the mill village came into view, half hidden in smoke from the hundreds of chimneys mingling with the mist caught in the bottom of the valley. Of the few figures discernible to Fiona, none were in white school tunics, but she hurried between them, asking if they had seen her daughter.

'Mrs Young!' she knocked on the door of her old tenement, rapidly explaining her plight.

'Naw, dear, she's no' bin here. Ah'll get ma lads tae look ...'

Hitching up her skirts, Fiona pounded up the stairs to Sarah and Cal.

Cal was eating at the table but on hearing the news, dropped his spoon and rushed out, saying he would look down by the river.

'An' Ah'll leave Lily wi' Mrs Young and we'll help ye look ...' Sarah tied on her bonnet, handing a cloak to Cathy.

The word spread and dozens turned out, joining Joe and the rest of the Scotts to scour the streets and up through the hillside.

'Where wid she gae?' Rosie asked, sensibly, walking beside Fiona on the road to Bonnington House. 'Does she like ony place, special like?'

'She likes the woods an' the wee burns.'

A horseman appeared out of the gloom, splashing through the puddles.

The rider doffed his hat, reining in to a halt. 'Mrs Scott, Mrs MacAllister, a dreich nicht tae tak a walk?'

Fiona squinted through the rain, 'Mr McInnes ...'

He saw how distraught she was, asking, 'Whit's wrang?'

Rosie launched into the story but, hearing the predicament, Kyle held up his hand.

'Wid she ha'e bin wearing white, frae the school room?'

'Aye!'

'Ah saw a pale shape by the river, through by ...' he pointed towards the river. 'There's a white deer in these parts, mind, it could ha'e bin the deer.'

Without another word, Fiona was pushing her way through the marshy woodland, eyes scanning the silhouettes of the distant tree trunks showing dark against the light waters of the Clyde.

A movement caught her attention: a small herd of roe deer. Weak with disappointment, she stopped and leaned against a tree for support, watching the animals while they watched her. None of them are white, she thought, and at that moment a figure moved from beyond some shrubs, close by the riverside. Sionaidh.

The next moments were filled with confusion.

The deer suddenly took fright, spinning away and bolting directly towards the child. Sionaidh's screams of alarm sent them careering in all directions, kicking up turf and leaping through the bracken.

In horror, her feet refusing to move fast enough, Fiona saw the little girl stagger backwards, arms flailing, losing her balance and sliding, slipping, falling into the fast flowing river.

Downstream, Cal heard the commotion. He was at a rocky outcrop, scanning the banks for any sign of his niece and then his stomach churned: there was something in the water. Like a pale rag doll, dark hair waving about its head, pulled and pushed by the currents, rising and falling over submerged boulders, he could make out Sionaidh's prone body.

Fiona's cries of raw distress came over the rushing water and in a flash he was stumbling down the rocks. He knew this stretch, a few yards downstream the water would swirl towards the bank.

Bracing himself for the impact, arms outstretched, he had one chance of catching her when she swept past.

The force of her weight thudding against him threw him off balance but he wound his fingers into a strong hold on her clothes and clung on, her legs swinging in an arc, dragging him into the flow.

For a second, they were both pulled under. Kicking desperately at the riverbed, he jammed his feet against two large rocks and broke the surface. Spluttering and gasping, he couldn't move for fear of losing his footing but knew he had to turn her face out of the water. Gritting his teeth to shut out the pain of his thundering heart, he summoned all his strength and managed to roll her over, face up.

The effort took the last of his breath.

Dark speckled shadows swam over his vision and he felt his knees buckling, his feet lifting away from the riverbed and then the icy chill of water covering his head.

Joe was with the village folk shouting from the bank, joining a group wading out, desperately grappling under the water.

'We've got them!' a man shouted.

A hush fell on the scene, all eyes on the two limp bodies dragged out onto the land.

'Turn them o'er, Ah've seen it done, let the water run oot ...'

Fiona fell to her knees between them.

'Naw ... naw ... ma darlin'...' she pulled the child into her arms, rocking and stroking her. 'Ah cannae bear it ...'

It started slowly with a shudder then Sionaidh's whole body began to wretch, taking long struggling breaths before gagging and coughing.

'She's alive!' Having been utterly absorbed in her daughter, Fiona now looked around, seeking and finding Joe. She saw a moment of relief on his face but there was something else in his expression, he looked lost, bereft. Then she understood.

Cal lay motionless, eyes half open, his usually lined and anxious forehead smooth beneath his sister's caress.

Choked with grief, Rosie's words were barely audible, 'Ye saved her, Cal, she's alive. Be at peace, ma fine ... *brave* wee brither ... '

***

Joe had no recollection of the hours following Cal's death. He knew he took charge, but only because others told him afterwards.

He had immediately sent Donnie and Davey away from the distressing scene, instructing them to take their mother and Sionaidh home and Rosie back to the village. Accepting Kyle Macinnes' offer of a cart, he organised the harrowing process of carrying his brother's body from the riverbank, through the boggy wood, and up to the road. Every step was hindered by reeds and slippery clumps of wild garlic, thick moss disguising fallen branches. Saplings growing closely among the larger tree trunks forced the men to weave a meandering path with their dripping burden before reaching the waiting wagon.

In dim lamplight, Joe worked with the others to erect a makeshift trestle in the tack room beside the forge, the very place where Cal worked for nearly twenty years. Mr McGibbon visited briefly, confirming for himself that the man was deceased and offering Joe his condolences before leaving the group of villagers to continue their preparations for the wake.

When Auld Bel arrived to tend to the corpse, Joe was encouraged by Kyle and several others to go home for the night. They would arrange for the body to be watched, they urged, he should be with his wife.

It was only when he was walking home, alone, that he became suddenly aware of the rain drops on his face and the strong smell of soaked earth. As if waking from a nightmare, he was struck by strange, disjointed thoughts: where was Cal's cap? he always wore his cap, he shouldn't be without it ... it was in the river ...

A spark of memory jumped into view, breaking through the wall of traumatic disbelief, shaking him to the core.

It really happened. Cal was gone.

Shaking with sobs, Joe paused in the shelter of some overhanging beech branches. He was broken by the sudden onslaught of grief and knew he could not return to the cottage until he gave vent to this overwhelming sadness. Only the woodland creatures witnessed his distress, allowing him the indulgence of weeping unselfconsciously until, eventually, the storm of emotion lost its grip.

Looking out over the valley, now shrouded in darkness, he traced the curves of the river where the lighter grey of the sky's reflection turned the waters into flowing silver. It looked no different from the night before but everything had changed for Joe. Cal might have been his brother but he also loved him with the fierce protective love of a father.

Sionaidh was alive. He should feel relief, but instead a nasty feeling crept over him and he shook his head, rejecting it violently. No, she was innocent, she did not mean to cause harm ... she was as much a victim of this dreadful day as Cal.

'No,' he muttered aloud, 'I must *not* blame her.'

***

Lady Mary Ross sampled a shortbread finger, found its crumbly texture to her liking and nodded her approval.

'You have a fine pastry chef, Mrs Owen.'

'We are blessed with an excellent cook, she can turn her hand to any dish.'

'As I can vouch, after the delicious meal you served a few months ago.'

They were taking refreshments together in Braxfield's drawing room, Anne Caroline having received a note from Bonnington House, saying Lady Mary wished to call on her that afternoon.

'I apologise for giving such short notice before imposing on your hospitality,' Lady Mary said, seriously, 'but I was not aware your husband was away. I have always found it is so much easier to speak of difficult matters rather than write them in a letter.'

'Oh dear, difficult matters?'

'Again, I must apologise for bringing up this unpalatable subject with you, it was intended for Mr Owen. I refer to the drowning of a man in the Clyde two days ago. He was one of your husband's employees, I understand.'

'God rest is soul. Yes, indeed he was.'

'My gamekeeper tells me he was on our land, several hundred yards upstream of the weir, a considerable distance from Dundaff Linn and the mills.'

Anne Caroline had been deeply shocked when she first heard the news, the more so on discovering the identity of the victim. Sarah Rafferty was, quite understandably, absent from her work the day after her brother's death, so she had sought her out at home to offer sympathy and comfort.

'It was a tragedy,' she told Lady Mary, recollecting the grief-stricken family. 'A heart-rending accident.'

'The loss of a life is always lamentable, but on hearing there were perhaps a dozen of your villagers on Bonnington Estate at the time, I felt I should be given an explanation for their presence.'

'You are not aware of the appalling sequence of events which led to this man's death?'

Lady Mary tilted her head on one side, 'I understand the man was a labourer from the mills,' she noticed Anne Caroline's trembling lips and averted eyes. 'Although he was never caught my bailiffs believed him to be a habitual poacher.'

'I know nothing of that,' Anne Caroline stated, firmly, stemming a rush of compassion and regaining her composure. 'However, I do know he gave the ultimate sacrifice of his own life to rescue his young niece from certain death.'

'I see,' Lady Mary was moved. 'This was not mentioned to me. However, please, bear with me, Mrs Owen, in the absence of your husband, are *you* able to explain why he ... and this unfortunate child ... were on my land? Or, indeed, the presence of so many other workers from the mills?'

As briefly as she could, Anne Caroline related the tale, choosing her words carefully to avoid another surge of unbecoming emotion.

'Please understand,' she ended, 'these villagers were not wantonly trespassing on Bonnington land. Calum Scott came to the mills as a child many years ago, more than I care to remember for I was but a child myself at the time. Lady Mary, New Lanark may look like a factory but it is a community, as closely woven as any village. There are generations of neighbours, friends and families,

91

often intermarried, and the Scotts are well known to all but a few. On hearing of a missing child, they turned out to help, so if they strayed onto your land, there was no malice in their action.'

'I am glad we have spoken,' Lady Mary reached for another slice of shortbread. 'My agent was intending to prosecute those he could identify, but I shall instruct him to leave the matter alone. Instead, I would be grateful if all your husband's employees were reminded to remain respectful of the boundaries. Times are hard, poaching of deer, fowl and fish are rampant across the countryside and I must make it clear, it will not be tolerated.'

Anne Caroline was relieved; had the incident taken place on the far bank, owned by the Edmonstone sisters, they may not have been so considerate.

While dozens of villagers made their way down to the forge to join the drinking and dancing at the wake for Calum Scott, Robert Owen and his eldest son were settling into an inn at Matlock in Derbyshire.

'This valley is very beautiful,' Robert Dale cried, throwing open the small paned window to gaze out on the view. 'Green rolling hills dotted with sheep, hedgerows, clusters of ancient oaks. It is more like Clydesdale than I would have imagined, but gentler.'

Murdoch and a lad from the inn carried in their trunks and then left the father and son alone.

'And a pleasant enough room for us,' Owen declared, waving his arm towards the two beds, their frames filled with plump mattresses. He lifted the jug on the wash stand and sniffed at the contents. 'Fresh water. Although we would be wise to drink only the weak beer, at least it has been through one boiling.'

The previous few days of their journey had already set a pattern. On arriving in a market town they found a hostelry, ordered food to be brought to their room, slept as soundly as the conditions allowed and then rose to inspect the nearest mill. Sometimes there were two or three large mills within walking distance and now, on the Derwent River, they would find many just an easy ride away.

'We are now in the county where some of the largest factories are at work,' Owen said, laying out his writing case on a table. 'I fear we must brace ourselves, for up until now we have been seeing mills where there are less than fifty or so operatives, not long evolved from the cottage industries.'

Robert was still looking out the window. 'There are always so many women and children in the mills. What do the men do?'

'Aha! You have hit the nail on the head! Yes, the rise of the machines has come at a time when the country has been at war, its men folk away from home. It will be in the coming years that we see this imbalance in its true light.'

'But, when the soldiers come home, can they not enter the factories too?'

'The neat, quick actions performed by the hand of a child or woman are much more suited to the processes required in a cotton or silk mill. If one were to take the viewpoint of social *advantages* of this factory system, then it could be considered a glorious coincidence that mechanisation came at a time when women were forced to earn for their families. In the past, in a household where the man, the usual breadwinner, was called to fight, they would have struggled to survive, but a woman with, say, five children, can all find employment in mills.'

'At New Lanark, we have men working, don't we? I've seen them.'

'They make up but a third of our workforce,' Owen knew the figures by heart. 'Our employees number one thousand, four hundred and eighty, of which only four hundred and sixty six are male, some of those children.'

'Don't they want to work in factories?'

'I'm sure they would take the work, if they could.' He joined the boy by the window. 'There are a few youths, nimble with their fingers and sharp-sighted, who can be trained to the carding or spinning machines. However, in practice it is mainly children in the picking rooms and women spinning, reeling and sorting. For perhaps seven men in the sorting room, you will find forty women. It is the nature of the work. Of course, the managers, shop keepers and those who carry out the engineering or heavy labouring work are all men.'

Knowing his father's preference to attend to letters and reports before ordering food to eat in their room, Robert took advantage of the dry evening and went out to explore.

The familiar rippling sound of a large river attracted him to the banks of the Derwent and he wandered along until finding his way barred by a fast rushing stream.

93

An old man, bearded and dressed in a patched red coat and pig skin breeches, called out from where he was leaning against a tree smoking his pipe.

'Ye'll have been to the waterfall, lad?

'No?' Robert approached the stranger. 'Is there a waterfall nearby? I should very much like to see it.'

'Aye, Lumsden Falls, up the bank ...' he pointed with his pipe. 'Wouldn't take a young nipper like you any time at all. Just follow the Lums, it'll take you there.'

'It was a fine waterfall, Papa,' he related over their meal. 'Small compared to the Clyde's mighty Corra Linn but picturesque and it appears to be serving several mills. In places the cliff drops are sheer!' His eyes shone with his achievement, 'but I was not at all frightened. In its quieter parts I saw a kingfisher ... and dragonflies hovering over pools where the rocks were green with moss, hanging with ferns and the water as clear as I ever saw at home.'

'We will be visiting Garton Mill in the morning, the largest on the Lums. It was a cotton spinning factory, built at the same time your grandfather built New Lanark, but it failed a year or so ago and is now given over entirely to bleaching. I am keen to see the conditions.'

Robert Dale sliced the very fatty ham on his plate into tiny pieces, finding it disgusting unless smothered in pickle and hastily swallowed with a chunk of bread.

'What about the other mills?' he asked.

'They are mainly grinding mills: bones, minerals like baryte which are found round here in the limestone and also grains, corn and such.'

'Why do we need to grind baryte?'

'It is white and used in the manufacture of paint, but for any further information I'm afraid you would need to ask a chemist.'

They finished their supper in companionable discussion and Owen looked fondly on his son, thoroughly enjoying his company.

The next day saw them set out early with a list of three mills to visit, all conveniently close to their lodgings. The sun was setting in a milky sky when they returned to their room and sat down to supper. The atmosphere was despondent, both deeply affected by what they had seen.

'We believe ourselves to be civilised,' Owen pondered, pushing potatoes around on his plate. 'The great speeches of Wilberforce against slavery and barbaric conditions on plantations could so easily apply to those poor wretches we witnessed today.'

'The children,' Robert raised sad eyes to his father, 'some were as young as David and Richard.'

'And yet the owners state blithely that they do not employ children under eight years old! Pah! How do they live with themselves? These workers have no voice, not just the orphans from the Poor Houses but the men and women who are driven by poverty and lack of education to take any means to earn a living. This is why I am doing all I can to make their plight known.'

Robert Dale was very quiet, his mind streaming with a flow of images he wished he had not seen. The tiny bodies running and crawling between the machines, all wizened and bruised under scruffy smocks and filthy, tangled hair, Whether they were girls or boys, he could not tell, but the fear and exhaustion on their faces was clear enough.

The air, especially in the last factory, was putrid, causing him to gag and put his hand over his nose. He knew from New Lanark that the temperature must be moist and high, over seventy degrees, to keep the cotton running smoothly, but with the cobweb ridden windows stuck closed and cotton dust misting the work room, every breath was suffocating.

Worst of all were the ominous leather thongs carried by the Overseers. Even during the few minutes they were shown around the factory, he saw two infants and a youth being shouted at and lashed.

Owen was late to bed that night, finally laying down his quill when the last candle guttered in its death throes.

Like his son, he was revolted by what he was seeing. Even the harshest inspection reports did not adequately describe the daily suffering of thousands upon thousands of British people every day; day upon day, year upon year.

The problem lay in ignorance, Owen was convinced of it.

If the government knew the true horror of life on the factory floor, they would pass laws to change it. If people in power took up his New System, as laid out in his essays, the effects of hardship, cruelty and disrespect would be swept away.

If the well bred ladies sipping tea and admiring fabrics knew the human cost of their latest table cloths or day dresses, they would be sickened.

'If', Owen mused to himself, 'if must be changed to 'when'.

He sank down into the straw mattress and drew the blanket over his shoulders. It was a warm night and the window was propped open allowing distant voices to drift in, but beneath the combed ceiling of the bedroom only his son's gentle breathing disturbed the silence.

Feeling the tension of the day seeping away towards sleep, Owen turned on his side, relaxing, watching the shadows dancing in the dwindling candlelight until, with a final flicker, darkness fell and he closed his eyes.

When they were preparing to leave the next morning, Owen noticed the pensive expression clouding his son's face, the slight frown and general reluctance in his movements.

Seeing his father's gaze, Robert gave him a long soulful look.

'Papa, I imagined all the mills would be like New Lanark. These ... the last one ... it was dark, at least, in my memories it is dark. There was a feeling of dread which despite its high windows and it being summer, well, it seemed clouded by despair.'

Knowing his son was an avid reader of poetry, and many of the subjects melancholy, Owen was not surprised by his words.

'You feel things acutely, others have a thicker skin, or choose to ignore any feelings of empathy. It is right to feel upset when faced with despicable acts, only then will you act to correct them.'

'I know I am more sensitive since my illness, Papa, but I cannot be alone in being unable to understand how those brutes with whips could beat a small child?'

'They have been conditioned and trained to be like that from early childhood.' Owen picked up his jacket, 'it is ingrained in them. Only by breaking this vicious circle of bad behaviour and replacing it with kindness can we bring about a happier, better society.' He touched his son fondly on the cheek, smiling, 'Now, it is a sunny morning so let's be about our business.'

For the next few days, the Owen carriage journeyed through the rolling hills and dales of the Peak District.

Making the most of the summer months, the fields were busy with men and women pulling weeds, banking up earth on potatoes,

96

picking beans and peas: little children running between them with baskets and casks of ale to slake their thirst.

Market squares in even the smallest towns were a lively affair, offering everything from fresh fruit and game to music and puppet shows. Larks sang above the moorland, ducks and geese swam on village ponds, swallows chattered and swooped between barns and houses, bee-keepers, their straw hats swathed with fine netting, tended their hives.

The contrast between the country villages and the factories soon became startling. From a distance, many of the mills' stark brick walls stuck out from the pastures and, needing to be close to the water for power, they were often set on the shadowy floor of the valley. Even on the sunniest day, they looked foreboding, the rear walls strangled by unkempt nettles and bramble thickets, dank, green stained stone latrines squatting at their sides. On entering, the wall of noise and hot, polluted air swamped the senses, instantly removing any resemblance to the summer day outside.

Worse was to come when, on countless occasions, they saw children with injuries being forced to continue at their positions, their cries ignored and being beaten or shaken into submission. Owen was aware that his presence was restraining further violence and made a point of acquiring the names of the physicians who attended the mills.

Before leaving the area, he called on these doctors and took statements to back up his own reports.

There was relief from the gloom at Cromford Mill and Owen was relieved to find the benevolence of its creator, the late Richard Arkwright, was continuing.

'It was much better here,' Robert commented under his breath when he climbed back into their carriage. 'Even though we are deep in this valley, it is altogether less miserable ... and the workers as well, they did not appear so glum, nor thin.'

'It is clean,' Owen agreed. 'And they have schooling and good discipline.' He had already told his son how Arkwright was his grandfather's first partner in New Lanark. 'It depends so much on the leadership and management of a mill, doesn't it? Do you see the importance of that?'

The coach lurched forward and began the steady pull up the hill.

'I think so.' Robert's attention was on a group of labourers, stripped to the waist, dredging the mill lade.

'It only takes a strong individual to set the standard. Never underestimate the strength of one man. We acknowledge this fact when it comes to wars, look at the changes Emperor Napoleon brought about? The same can be done for factories. It can seem a daunting task, but it just takes the leaders of the industry to embrace new systems and the rest will fall into place.'

'And the new Law you want passed, it would do this?'

'It would help, of course it would. What I want and will pursue with all my might, is for my New System to be taken up. It is being considered by the highest in the country at this very moment.'

Robert beamed, trusting his father implicitly.

'You must come to London with me, my son, when I next go there. You can meet these great men, fine philosophers and true philanthropists. You would enjoy it.'

From Cromford they set off further south, taking in William Strutt's magnificent new 'fire proof' mill at Belper, built on the foundation's of his late father's mill which had burned to the ground a dozen years before. The massive scale of this modern, iron framed structure was almost outshone when they came to the Silk Mill in Derby.

Taylor's Silk Mill rose to five storeys, taking raw silk through every process to produce superb silk thread. Owen was acquainted with the famous mill through colleagues and pamphlets and expected to be impressed. He was not.

A clerk escorted them over the three top floors in stifling heat, roughly pushing aside barefoot women and children and shouting with self importance over the din of dozens of Italian designed winding machines. Moving lower, down a blessedly cool stairway, an evident culture of pervasive brutality accompanied the stench and oppressive conditions. Many of the four hundred strong work force showed pallid, feverish complexions and signs of physical abuse.

After weeks of gruelling inspections, Robert woke one morning to hear his father speaking to Murdoch. He was giving him instructions to pass to their coachman: they were heading north, back to Braxfield.

***

Autumn was upon them, shrinking the hours of daylight and filling the evening skies with flocks of spiralling rooks and starlings. Soon, the morning frosts would bring an end to the easy days of running barefoot.

Fiona bustled around her cramped scullery, scrubbing pans, sweeping the floor, folding clothes from the pulley; muttering to herself, frowning with an inner disquiet. Heaving the basket onto the table, she inspected bruised windfalls the children gathered from under the apple tree. Choosing the best to peel and core, she set them to simmer, their sharp, sweet scent rising in the steam.

The shelves of untidy boots kept drawing her attention but her eyes would slide away to seize on a different subject; refilling the oil lamps or emptying ash from the range.

Over the last few months the family were coming to terms with losing Cal, allowing the mention of his name without fear of provoking fresh tears. The grief was still raw, but individually they were finding ways to cope. Sionaidh felt his death as keenly as any of them, screaming and lashing out in frustration when she could no longer find her Uncle Cal.

It was no use explaining, the child's wandering attention gave no indication of listening, let alone knowing what the words meant. Time and again, she would slip past them and try to escape to the allotment.

Returning from throwing out the peelings, Fiona mopped energetically around the dusty hearth, aware she was running out of excuses to avoid the boot rack.

Her tongue probed a throbbing tooth. There was no denying it hurt viciously and was loose, moving in her gum. The clove oil barely gave relief and even trying to chew food on the other side of her mouth was becoming unbearable. It had to come out.

'Och, git oan wi' it,' she told herself, not thinking of her tooth but of the boots.

Jammed between various sizes of men's footwear sat a pair of dainty ankle boots. Mud spattered, the embroidered canvas torn and the sole gaping from the toes, these were the little boots she was wearing on that fateful day.

Wincing, her eyes smarting, she drew them off the shelf, awakening the same panic and horror she felt the evening they were thrust away. She turned them in her hands, tears trickling down her cheeks as she rubbed at the dried mud and shrivelled brown shreds of grass. The welling pain of grief far exceeded the ache in her jaw: when the tooth was drawn, the gum would heal.

As if the accident itself had not been bad enough, the effect on Joe chilled her to the bone.

He tried to disguise it, sometimes forcing himself to show affection towards Sionaidh, but she knew he blamed his eldest daughter. Having always believed they could speak to each other about anything, Fiona found herself unable to broach the subject, lying to herself that she was imagining what lay behind the cold look in his eyes. Slowly, it began to melt. It wasn't until he found Sionadh crying, curled up in the grass beside Cal's vegetable patch, that she saw a change in him, an understanding.

Decisively, she threw the boots on the fire: the terrible circumstances of his death should not be how Cal was remembered. Piling on more sticks and coal, she used the bellows to make a blaze. She would recall him laughing when he won at Dominoes, flashing his cheeky grin when complimented on a glistening trout, patiently kneeling beside Sionaidh throwing worms to the birds. That was the real Cal and, as they all agreed, he was at his happiest in the last years of his life.

She was laying the table when she glimpsed Ailsa leading Rusty past the window; plumes of purple willowherb adorning the girl's head and the pony's bridle. Her family's voices, muffled and boisterous beyond the stout stone walls, brought a tender sensation to replace her grief.

'My, tha' smells braw,' Joe cried, striding through the door, the others running behind him. 'We've cleared all the tatties frae Cal's patch an' sacked them up.' He leaned towards Fiona, planting a fleeting kiss on her lips. 'He'd ha'e bin fair pleased!'

'He wid that,' she picked up the newly boiled kettle and followed him into the scullery. 'Yer hauns are black! Here, Ah'll gie ye some warm watter ...'

'Ye all richt, love?' Joe was looking at his wife's flushed cheeks; her eye-lashes wet and spiky.

'Aye, bu' a cuddle widnae gang amiss.'

He reached for her, 'E'en wi' black hauns?'

Her answer came by hugging him tightly and burying her head against his rough jacket, inhaling traces of fresh air, autumn leaves and soil.

Beside them in the cramped room, Davey flicked back his long fringe and rolled his eyes in jest, 'Jeezo, Ma, can ye no' dae tha' in the ither room ... gie us room tae wash!'

'We'll ha'e plenty o' room soon,' Donnie said, leaning against the door jamb, arms folded, uncannily like his father at the same age. 'Ye ken, Da, oor wurk doon at the Institute is nearly done sae we can pit mair time intae oor ane hoose.'

'We've tae feenish Baxter's first, mind,' Joe released Fiona and began scrubbing his hands, 'but it's comin' oan weel, we'll be topping oot next week if the weather holds.'

'Mr Owen wants tae ha'e a grand opening on the first o' January,' Donnie told them, a rye smile on his lips.'There'll be mony a sair heid amangst the crowd efter Hogmanay but he's set on the date, sae, we'll see. Ye ken, he wants the whole village tae be there?'

'Aye, an' music tae.' Fiona squeezed between her tall sons to tend to the meal. 'The bairns are rehearsing their pieces a'ready. It'll be a bonnie show.'

The best of the day was past, a brisk wind rushing clouds across the darkening sky, hastening the onset of evening.

While the Scotts were gathering around the table in lamp light, pure white sunlight glared down on the south coast of Spain.

Sam Scott lounged back in his chair and gazed across the Piazza. It was a scene he knew well, indeed, he knew every inch of Gibraltar: it would be hard to leave. The opportunity had arisen several times but it was too easy to stay, keep to the routine, take each day as it came.

He watched Pablo, the owner of the cafe, pouring cardamom spiced coffee into tiny cups, sharing a joke with his customers. This swarthy, curly haired Genoese man was probably his closest friend, outside the barracks.

Beyond the shady interior, the main square was a glorious mass of sunlit colour. He could see ebony skinned Moors with their startling eyes and flashing white teeth, resplendent in coloured silk turbans and flowing djallabas. Amongst them, the British soldiers'

101

red uniforms appeared cumbersome, stuffy, the ladies on their arms adding a more frivolous note to the picture with their poke bonnets, fluttering ribbons and lacy dresses.

As the crowds browsed the market stalls, light fingered, barefoot urchins darted here and there. The dark figures of Jews lingered by the shady walls, draped in gabardines, their heads crowned with skull caps.

Finishing the dregs of his sherry, Sam prepared to leave, embracing Pablo with brotherly bravado and murmuring good wishes to him and his family. Outside in the bright daylight, he donned his bicorn and raised a hand in farewell to local men sitting cross legged in the shade of a palm tree. They nodded, watching him from between black lashes, sucking on their sebsi pipes in a haze of smoky cannabis.

This was the place he would remember: the noise of street musicians and wailing songs, monkeys riding on men's shoulders and bowed old women gossiping in the narrow, ramshackle side streets.

Yes, his years of service at the garrison were etched on his mind, the last three under the able command of Lt Col Guy l'Estrange.

Since serving in battles in Spain and the Low Countries, including the disastrous tour in Walcheren, the Cameronian's last few years had been blessedly free of the bloodshed and horror of the battlefield. That was not to say life had been easy. He had suffered typhoid fever, seen the ravages of yellow fever, lost good men, friends, to disease and festering wounds.

Hour upon hour, day upon day of drilling, marching, witnessing floggings ... the brutality was as much a part of his life as the comradeship and ceremonial duties.

Every ghastly discomfort known to man was lurking amongst the filth on this God forsaken lump of rock, but things were changing. General George Don, the new acting Governor of the British Colony, was tackling the vital issues of decent sanitation and the supply of clean water.

Sam chuckled to himself: Don was a Scotsman. It seemed apt to leave the place in a fellow countryman's hands.

The wars were over, the port no longer crammed with warships and supply ships. Sam's regiment, the 26th Rifles, was now swollen by two hundred and seventy five men, drafted from the 2nd Battalion before it was disbanded.

Making his way across the busy square, he breathed the musky air and felt the warmth of the sun; more conscious of his surroundings than ever before. This evening, he was dining in the Garrison Library followed by a long night of drinking and then, tomorrow, he would set sail for England.

Chapter Six

"... the character of man is, without a single exception, always formed for him; and that it may be, and is, chiefly created by his predecessors that they give him, or may give him, his ideas and habits" Robert Owen

The rising sun glimmered like a silver coin through a thin layer of cloud on the first morning of 1816 but within hours the sky was clear and the air promisingly mild. Owen had been working in his study since six o'clock, the curtains drawn aside to reveal the first lightening of dawn.

This was a great day: the day he would unveil his long awaited Institute for the Formation of Character.

Anne Caroline finished with her breakfast tray much earlier than usual, ensuring plenty of time to dress for the occasion.

'I will need the woollen stockings,' she told Ramsay, 'and perhaps, also the new woollen pantaloons which my sister Jean recommended?'

It was cold in the lofty bedroom despite a screen placed to ward off draughts from the door and her chair being positioned close to the fire. Shivering in her short corset, she pulled on her stockings, tying them off above the knee before Ramsay helped her step into each leg of the pantaloons.

'These really are the strangest pieces of clothing?' she exclaimed. 'I hope there is no breeze or they will show around my ankles.'

'Your skirt is heavy, Ma'am, and weighted in the hem. It will look bonnie ... as well as keepin' ye warm.'

'Mmn, I will need my cape as well, the red one. You know, my first winter coat was of bright red wool. Dale's red, they call the dye, because it came from my father's dyeworks.'

The lady's maid smiled politely, Mr Dale was a revered name in the household, although she had never met the gentleman.

When Anne Caroline descended the stairs, the grandfather clock was striking half past the hour of nine and Owen was pacing in the hall, papers tucked under his arm.

'I hope you have not been waiting, my dear?'

'No, Caroline, you are perfectly punctual but we will leave straight away ... the carriage is at the door.'

As soon as they passed the lodge and descended Braxfield Road, it became evident that most, if not all, of the villagers were turning out. The streets were filled with a moving mass of bodies mingling with each other to gather on the slope between the towering tenement block of Nursery Buildings and, on a lower level, the new Institute.

'I've closed the mills for the day,' Owen told her, his voice loud with excitement while raising his hand in acknowledgement of cheerful smiles and waves. 'I see they are dressed in their Sabbath best.'

At exactly ten o'clock, Owen called for quiet. Around him stood the mill managers, all attired formally in top hats and dark jackets, only differing in their choice of waistcoats.

Owen cut a slender figure in his double breasted dark blue wool coat and tall hat, unremarkable, until he turned to face the crowd and stepped forward. Immediately, everyone's attention was drawn by his direct manner, his lean, intelligent features set in an earnest expression while surveying the assembly.

The doors of the Institute were opened and Owen, with Anne Caroline on his arm, led the crowd inside and up the stairs to the largest schoolroom. When the space was filled, he took up a position on a raised platform at one end where a podium was placed. Within moments, the rowdy shouts and chatter fell away, leaving only a barely discernible rustle amongst twelve hundred men, women and children standing silently, expectantly.

'We have met today,' he called out, 'with the purpose of opening this Institution: and it is my intention to explain to you the objects for which it has been founded. These objects are most important.'

He paused for emphasis, keen to see their reaction.

'The first relates to the immediate comfort and benefit of all the inhabitants of this village.

'The second, to the welfare and advantage to the neighbourhood.

'The third, to extensive amelioration throughout the British dominions.

'The last, to the gradual improvement of every nation in the world.'

This was the first time Anne Caroline was hearing her husband speaking publicly and her heart was racing with nerves on his behalf. She need not have worried. His speech was eloquent, passionate and yet delivered without haste, relating his hopes and his vision: his New View of Society.

From beneath her feathered hat, she watched the faces of his employees as he explained his long held views for bettering their lives, telling them he had been working towards this hour for more than twenty five years. She saw expressions of awe, puzzlement over some of his vocabulary, delight at his revelations, pensive frowns on older residents, but all were absorbed in his words.

'It is a delightful thought ...' he expounded, 'to be instrumental in introducing a practical system into society, the complete establishment of which shall give happiness to every human being through all succeeding generations. And such, I declare, was the sole motive that gave rise to this Institution and to all my proceedings.'

Joe was at the back of the crowd, in the gallery, with Fiona, his sisters and their older children. They were all struck by the profoundness of Owen's words, hanging on every sentence and closely following his explanations. His belief that Man's character was formed for him by his surroundings and home life made sense and when he stated clearly that to convey his philosophy properly, he knew he had to *act* not just *speak*, there was a general murmur of agreement.

All the changes he brought into the village which so many railed against were now taken as normal daily life. Their lives were improved by cleaner homes, better food, the reduction in thieving, fighting and drunkenness in the village and the silent monitors quietly brought about a smooth running factory. Yet, as he pointed out, not once had he punished them physically or abused them vocally. There had been no recourse to the courts: all his actions were taken reasonably and without anger.

'The Institution has been devised to afford the means of receiving your children at an early age, as soon, almost, as they can walk. By this means, many of you, mothers of families,' he looked specifically towards various female mill workers in the later stages of pregnancy, several already holding babies. 'You will be able to earn a better maintenance or support for your children; you will have less care and anxiety about them; while the children will be prevented from acquiring any bad habits and gradually prepared to learn the best.'

Fiona and Sarah exchanged meaningful looks.

Sarah whispered, 'there's many a time Ah wished some yin wid tak ma bairns aff ma hauns ...'

In detail, he explained the different rooms and classes there would be inside the building, allowing the little ones to play or rest, should they wish, and the older children to learn through games and exploration. He did not want them bothered by books until in the upper classes, but all would be taught geography and natural sciences as well as reading, writing and arithmetic.

Not only was the Institute to be for the children, but it would have several rooms open in the evenings for adults wishing to expand their education or to simply socialise.

As he went on, it also became clear Owen intended dancing and singing to be a major part of the curriculum. Then, surprising many of the older residents, he declared he was making the school available to all children in the market town of Lanark and the surrounding area.

The very name of the Institute for the Formation of Character took on a new meaning. Unlike other visionaries who wrote and spoke of a world of harmony, equality in education and respect, their master was physically carrying it out into practice.

'Do we not learn from history,' he asked, extending his voice to the back of the crowd, 'that all infants through all past ages have been taught the language, habits and sentiments of those by whom they have been surrounded? That they had no means whatever of giving to themselves the power to acquire any others? That every generation has thought and acted like preceding generations? with such changes as only the events around it, from which experience is derived, may have forced upon it?'

With every question he cast an enquiring glance around the villagers, engaging their interest.

'... the faith or belief which he possesses has been given to him by causes over which he had no control.

'Experience, my friends, now makes these conclusions as clear as the sun at noonday. Why then shall we not instantly act upon them?

'In short, my friends, the new system is founded on principles which will enable mankind to prevent, in the rising generation, almost all, if not all, of the evils and miseries which we and our forefathers have experienced.

'If it should be asked, whence, then, have wickedness proceeded? I reply, *soley from the ignorance of our forefathers!* It is this ignorance, my friends, that has been, and continues to be, the only cause of all the miseries which men have experienced.

'Will it not, then, tend to the welfare and advantage of this neighbourhood, to introduce into it such a practical system as shall gradually withdraw the causes of anger, hatred, discord, and every evil passion and substitute true and genuine principles of universal charity and of never varying kindness, of love without dissimulation, and of an ever active desire to benefit to the full extent of our faculties all our fellow- creatures, whatever may be their sentiments and their habits.'

After nearly two hours, Owen paused to consult one of his managers.

'And now, there will be a short interlude to hear music from our pupils.'

Over two dozen children marched in from the hallway behind the music master. All immaculately dressed in white and plaid tunics, they lined up in rows with drums, bugles and fifes before bursting into an enthusiastic medley of Scottish ballads.

'Ah'm that prood o' ma Gerry,' Rosie cried, 'did ye see him there? Wi' the Master?'

'Naw,' Sarah teased, 'wis he there?'

'Aye! richt aside Mr Owen ...' Rosie caught her sister's smile and gave her a playful push. 'Weel, ye wid be fair made up if ye'd spent oors steaming yon hat an' brushin' his jaikit.'

'Ah didnae unnerstaun some o' whit he said,' Sarah admitted, 'he uses awfy lang wurds.'

Fiona laughed, 'Weel, did ye no' hear the bit aboot the lessons fur aulder folk in the evenings? Ye'll have tae come tae yon classes.'

Sarah passed the comment off with a shrug but found the thought appealing. Maybe, if it was free, she could at last learn to read and write.

While the music competed against bubbling conversation and much coming and going in the crowd, Anne Caroline mused on the scene. The Institute had been built in the same place where her father spoke to the first mill employees when Mill One burnt to the ground.

On that occasion, David Dale stood a little higher on the hill, reassuring the devastated families that their jobs were safe, the mill would be rebuilt. Then, the villagers were in the open air, choked with smoke, loud with crackling, splintering destruction.

Now, their numbers were swollen to ten times. This was a brightly clothed, cheerful group of people. Shining white frills of gathered caps showed beneath the women's bonnets, their faces washed to a sheen.

What a difference the intervening twenty eight years had made to the village. She was not alone in drawing the comparison: her glance roamed over mature faces she once knew as children. Her own life was as bound to New Lanark as any of those gathered to celebrate her husband's plans.

A group near the front drew her attention. The women and children were struggling unsuccessfully to suppress their laughter while watching the musicians, intently. One of the smaller fife players kept waving to his parents, sometimes missing the beat when he joined in again, but carrying his mistakes off with a confident swing of his hips.

Anne Caroline watched the little boy with affection. She remembered his mother's delight at his birth and the surprise arrival of a curly haired little sister a year later. She also knew of the anguish endured in their tenement home when his grandfather died.

She prayed with and for every single one of them, but perhaps most of all for her husband.

The interlude over, Owen resumed his monologue.

'What think you know, my friends, is the reason why you believe and act as you do? I will tell you. It is solely and merely because you were born, and have lived, in this period of the world, in Europe, in the island of Great Britain, and more especially in this northern part of it. With the shadow of a doubt had everyone of you been born in other times or other places, you might have been the very reverse of that which the present time and place have

109

made you. You might have been, at this moment, sacrificing yourselves under the wheels of the great idol Juggernaut or preparing a victim for a cannibal feast. This, upon reflection, will be found to be a truth as certain as that you now hear my voice!

'Will you not, then, have charity for the habits and opinions of all men, of even the very worst human beings that your imaginations can conceive? Will you not, then, be sincerely kind to them, and actively endeavour to do them good? Will you not patiently bear with, and commiserate, their defects and infirmities and consider them as your relatives and friends?

'If you will not, if you cannot do this, and persevere to the end of your days in doing it, you have not charity; you cannot have religion; you possess not even common justice; you are ignorant of yourselves, and destitute of every particle of useful and valuable knowledge respecting human nature.

'Until you act after this manner, it is impossible that you can ever enjoy full happiness yourselves, or make others happy.

'Herein consists the essence of philosophy; of sound morality; of true and genuine Christianity, freed from the errors that have been attached to it; of pure and undefiled religion.'

'With regard to myself, I have not anything to ask of you, which I have not long experienced. I wish you merely to think that I am ardently engaged in endeavouring to benefit you and your children, and, through you and them, to render to mankind at large great and permanent advantages.

'I ask not for your gratitude, your love, your respect; for on you these do not depend. Neither do I seek or wish for praise or distinction of any kind; for to these upon the clearest conviction, I am not entitled, and to me, therefore, they could be of no value. My desire is only to be considered as one of yourselves, as a cotton spinner going about his daily and necessary avocations.

'But for you I have other wishes. On this day a new era opens to our view. Let it then commence by a full and sincere dismissal from your minds of every unpleasant feeling which you may entertain towards each other, or towards any of your fellow-men. When you feel these injurious dispositions beginning to arise, for, as you have been trained and are now circumstanced, they will arise again and again, instantly call to your recollection how the minds of such individuals have been formed, whence have

110

originated all their habits and sentiments: your anger will then be appeased; you will calmly investigate the cause of your differences and you will learn to love them and to do them good.

'A little perserverance in this simple and easily acquired practice will rapidly prepare the way for you and everyone around you, to be truly happy'.

He paused to allow his last words to take effect then raised his hand to quell a rising swell of clapping and conversation.

'Before you disperse! I have a further announcement to make. Listen up! From tomorrow, the hours of the working day will be decreased! You will report for work as usual, you will carry out your duties ... as usual ... and take the meal times ... as usual. However, the mill bell will ring the end of the day one hour earlier. From now on, these mills will work ten and three quarter hours, no more!'

Voices rumbled from the assembly, the tone perplexed.

Owen recognised their concern and immediately called out:

'Fear not, my friends! Your wages will remain the same.'

A deafening cheer roared from hundreds of gaping mouths. Men's caps flew up into the air, children joined hands and jumped up and down in wild circles, women turned to each other dislodging hats and trailing shawls while hugging each other and praising the Lord for this wonderful news.

The senior mill manager turned to Gerry MacAllister as they joined the applause for Owen.

'Tis a sight fur sore eyes, it must be admitted.'

'Aye, and a brave move to cut the hours.' Gerry knew his wife would be more than pleased. 'The country is on her knees frae the war an' tales o' riots fur lack of food and joabs, spinning jennies being smashed ... an' yet ye'd ne'er believe it fae these well fed bodies and joyful cries.'

'Mr Owen's gie set on his course,' the older man leaned close to Gerry's ear, muttering, 'Ah pray he's richt aboot this route across unchartered waters. This grand building disnae produce a penny o' profit an' noo we ha'e less time tae mak mair thread ... God help us all if he's wrang.'

Gerry wondered as much himself. 'Weel, he's done us prood sae far. Only time will tell.'

111

There were further changes and surprises over the next few days, passed on through managers and Overseers to the workforce. To the delight and pride of her family, Molly Young was made the chief assistant to John Buchanan, the new teacher in the school room.

Young Mr Buchanan was a New Lanark man, already working in the mills and living with his wife in the village. He was barely literate himself but chosen by Owen for his patient, kind nature.

Sarah also received a formal 'letter of engagement', read to her by Rosie, to provide four hours of sewing instruction to the older female pupils for five days of the week.

Before the Village Shop opened its doors for the day, Sarah sought out Mr Grant, the most senior of the store keepers, only to be told he was not available.

'Can I be of assistance?' asked Mr Dudley, who, of all the managers, she knew the least.

'Mr Dudley,' she ventured, Owen's instructions in her hand, 'may Ah shew ye this?'

'Ah, yes,' he handed the paper back to her, 'the master informed us yesterday, as he did you. Why did you not present this immediately?'

'Ah cannae read, sir. Ma sister telt me whit it said efter wurk.'

'Ye cover it well, Mrs Rafferty. I was not aware.'

'Och, Ah ken a few wurds ... an' ma name. An' all the numbers fur measurements an' the like ... it disnae hairm ma joab ...'

'That much is clear.' His features softened, allowing a warmer expression to reach his eyes.

For her age, Sarah Rafferty was a fine looking woman. He was no young lad himself, his first four decades were now behind him, along with memories of his deceased wife. Until the arrival of this impressive needlewoman with her stylish walk and memorable blue eyes, he had successfully kept loneliness at bay by immersing himself in the store and attending church.

His shy nature did not allow for conversations with the female members of staff but he noticed Sarah more than any of the others: he noticed her every move.

He knew when she was happy, the quick, wide smile and her infectious laugh, the many days when she was preoccupied, intent on her work and a little short-tempered but then apologising to the other girls for any hurt she might have caused. When she was tired, he caught the slope of her shoulders, her light gold hair escaping the fashionable combs to float in tendrils at her cheeks and the terrible days after her brother drowned when she was bowed with grief.

Oh, how he wished he could have eased her sorrow, instead, he admired her relentless hard work, understanding her need to keep busy and stem emotion.

'I wish you well over at the school, Mrs Rafferty,' he said, evenly, 'and trust you will continue in your position here at all other times to make up the ten hours for which you are employed.'

'O' course! Ah mean, aye, sir. Thank ye, sir.'

'They could not ask for a better teacher.'

Sarah blushed, bowing her head, 'It's sumat Ah've alis bin taken wi'. Mr Dudley, dinnae fash yersel aboot me no' keepin' ma oors, ye'll see, Ah'm true tae ma wurd, sae help me God!'

Surprised by her vehemence, he just nodded, 'Very well, be sure to tell me when you leave for the school and report to me when you return.'

She gave a quick curtsey and hurried away up the stairs, leaving the storekeeper in a quandary. Why had he not used softer words, complimented her, reassured her that he knew she could be relied upon? He turned back to his duties, pulling cheeses out of boxes packed with straw, wiping them off and laying them on display.

At least he would see her every time she came and went to the school.

Chapter Seven

"Every man is a creature of the age in which he lives and few are able to raise themselves above the ideas of the time." — *Voltaire*

On a warm spring evening, Fiona and Sarah left the Institute together with their younger children running round them. They were all tired but content from a satisfying day's work in the school room.

The streets were flowing with mill workers released for the day, loud with shouting and whistling, snatches of laughter mingling with coughs. In front of Nursery Buildings, the milk wagon was surrounded by children bearing jugs to be filled, and the last groups of straggling visitors were boarding carriages after touring the factory. It was one thing to view the looms in action and admire pauper children performing in the school, quite another to be surrounded by them *en masse*.

'Are ye wi' us again the morra?' Fiona asked when they passed through the gates, preparing to go their separate ways.

'Aye, in the mornin'.' Sarah looked for Lily's bouncing curls in the crowd. 'An' Cathy an' Ah are gaun tae the lessons again t'morra eve. This readin' an' writin' is no' as hard tae learn as we feart!'

'It's ne'er too late tae learn.'

'Och, an' Ah fair enjoy masel' showin' the bairns how tae sew. It disnae feel like wurk ...' she snorted back a laugh, 'ye ken, Ah've said tha' aboot ma joab in the shop, an' all.'

'Weel, we're the lucky yins. It's no' like in the mills when yer oan yer feet a' day and wrapped in yon clatterin' din. Ailsa feels the benefit o' the shorter oors but she's still worn oot.' Fiona's eyes kept straying to a man standing by the steps leading up the hill; he was watching them.

'C'mon, Ma!' Alex tugged at her skirt, 'Ah'm hungry!'

'Aye, in a meenit, son.' She nudged Sarah,'Who's tha'? O'er there ... the man in the dark cape and cocked hat?'

Seeing the women staring at him, the figure began to make his way towards them, a raven haired boy following at his heels.

114

Just yards away, he pulled off his hat and flung his arms wide.

'Sarah! Fiona! By! Ye're looking grand, the pair o' ye!'

'Sam!' Sarah rushed into his embrace. 'Whit a surprise!'

Releasing his sister, Sam hugged Fiona, smiling at Sionaidh who shied away from his outstretched hand.

'She's wary,' Fiona explained before turning to the boy standing silently beside them. 'An' this must be Connor!'

'Aye,' Sam ruffled his son's hair affectionately. 'He disnae remember being here afore. An' here's Tom, my you've grown! But who's this?'

'Oor youngest, Alexander!'

'Every time, anither wean!' Sam bellowed with laughter.

He was looking well, Fiona thought, perhaps stockier and heavier around his chin, the short cropped fair hair now sandy and grey at his temples. It was strange to see him without the crimson and gleaming brass of the Cameronian uniform. The yellow wool waistcoat and cream breeches gave him the appearance of a country gentleman. His resemblance to Joe was still there but less obvious, the intervening years of war having taken their toll.

'The village looks mighty changed from whit Ah remember,' he was saying. 'That muckle buildin' wis nae there nor the one across the lade. Whitiver are they? mair mills?'

'Naw,' Sarah's sunny expression clouded, 'we'll tell ye later ...'

There was an uneasy pause before Fiona took hold of Sionaidh's hand, asking too quickly, 'Ha'e ye seen Joe yit?'

'He's no' at yer hoose sae we came doon here,' he looked questioningly from one to the other of the women. 'Is Joe all richt?'

'Och, aye, ye ken yer brither, he's alis busy,' Fiona noticed tears welling in Sarah's eyes despite her valiant attempts to remain composed. 'There's much tae tell ye Sam, an' we all want tae hear yer ane news, sae ... Sarah, ye come up tae oor hoose wi' Rosie ... we cannae staun here blethering when we could be roond a table.'

Sam was not fooled for a second. 'Whit's happened?'

'No' here ... Sam ...' Sarah whispered, 'We cannae talk here.'

'Cal?' He persisted, 'is Cal all richt?'

'Uncle Cal drowned,' Lily said innocently, too young to realise the deluge of grief she was unleashing. 'He wis very brave, he saved oor Sionaidh.'

115

Sarah put her hand over her mouth to stifle a sob.

'Ah didnae mean ye tae hear it like that, Sam.' she whispered, the floodgates opening, her voice high, distorted. 'Ah'll fetch Rosie ...' she turned away, wiping at her wet cheeks, 'we'll be up wi' ye at the back o' seven.'

No words passed between Sam and Fiona until they were almost at the top of the hill, then he cleared his throat and asked what had happened.

Choosing her words carefully, she related the whole incident. He was entitled to know, he needed to know. When they reached the cottage she suggested Sam might like to walk up to where Joe was working and meet him there.

'Tell him Ah've told ye? It's bin gie hard fur him ... ye ken how close he wis tae his wee brither.'

'Aye, Ah'll tell him. Where will Ah find him?'

'He's up at oor new hoose ...'

'Ye have anither hoose?'

'He's buildin' it ...' she smiled, feeling a twinge of guilt to be pleased about her future home so soon after telling him of Cal's death. 'Ye'll see it fer yersel', it's jist stairtin' but he has grand plans.'

For several seconds Sam seemed lost. His gaze wandered past her to the children then locked with her eyes, filled with different emotions as if he was about to speak, ask her something, confide in her? Then he bowed his head, the point of his hat's brim obscuring his face, just standing still on the doorstep staring at the ground.

Perplexed, Fiona laid a caring hand on his shoulder. 'Ah can send yin o' the bairns tae call him hame, if ye wid rather wait here?'

'Naw, lass,' there was a gentle tone to his voice. 'Tell me where tae gae an' Connor an' Ah'll walk up.'

Calling back directions, she hurried through to the scullery and drew a tankard of weak ale from the cask and, as an afterthought, half filled a second one

'Ha'e this,' she thrust them at Sam and his son, suddenly matter of fact. 'An' mind an' tell him tha' his sisters will be up the hill within the oor.'

When the door closed behind him, she crumpled into silent tears, slowly untying the ribbons and removing her bonnet with shaking hands. The look in Sam's eyes was the same as Joe's after the accident: he blamed Sionaidh. Like Joe, he also knew the poor girl was innocent and there lay the sickening, heartbreaking dilemma.

On following Fiona's directions, Sam soon came to an opening between tall trees where a track split to each side of a long barn, its pale, clean roof timbers still bare to the weather. To the left stood a squat stone building with three windows in the upper floor and one on either side of an imposing front door. To the right, where the sound of hammering was loudest, low walls showed the footprint of a second house.

Sam prepared to give his apologies if he was trespassing then glimpsed a figure crouching beside the stonework.

'Aye, this is yer Uncle Joe's place,' he nodded to Connor, 'let's gie him a surprise!'

Joe was thrilled to see his brother again and very relieved when, almost immediately, Sam blurted out how grieved he was to hear from Fiona of Calum's accident.

Neither wanted to dwell on it, there would be a time for reminiscing but not at that moment and by mutual, unspoken agreement, they turned to admire the plan of the house.

'Ye see the view?' Joe clapped his hand on Sam's back, swinging him round to look out, far over the valley and off to the hills beyond.

'Guid Lord, brither, ye've chosen a splendid place tae live! Whit a sicht!'

Even Connor was moved to cry out and run to the top of the slope, shading his eyes to scan the rolling countryside.

Mr Baxter's smart sandstone house, taking up more than half of the plot of land, stood clean and symmetrical amid churned up mud and piles of building materials. It was nearly ready for the painters to finish the interior and Joe insisted on giving Sam a tour.

'Oor's will be smaller, but mair or less the same wi' wee changes Fiona was keen tae have.' Joe led him into a good sized flag stoned hall where a staircase curved up the wall on one side and doors opened off to left and right. Wood shavings littered the floorboards of the main rooms, the air cold with the strong, sharp smell of new plaster.

'It's no' a grand affair but there's twa big rooms at the front and twa at the back,' there was pride in Joe's voice, 'wi' four

117

bedrooms of a good size up the stairs an' twa mair wee yins in the attic. An' there's a scullery an' store room leadin' aff frae here.' He marched into the kitchen which was fitted with a new cast iron range set into the brickwork of the chimney opening. 'Whit d'ye say tae this fur a hame!'

'Whit can Ah say? Ah'm stuck fur wurds,' The look of undisguised amazement said it all. 'Ye've built this yersel'?'

'Aye, richt!' Joe's eyes crinkled, a grin spreading over his face. 'Me an' ma sons ... an' half a dozen ither lads! Ah've three guid teams o' men tae call on noo. Ah cannae complain, business is pickin' up since the war ended an' there's mair on ma books.'

Sam shook his head, 'Ah tak ma hat aff tae ye,' he reinforced his words by raising his tricorn. 'Ye've done weel, very weel.'

Connor was running from room to room, exploring upstairs and opening and closing doors and shutters.

Joe ran his finger down a pliable strip of putty on a pane of glass, linseed oil glistening on his fingers. 'The windaes were pit in no' lang ago, the crown glass wis costly but these sash windaes are sae easy tae open it wis worth it. Davey's still tae fit a few shutters but it's nearly done.'

'Your Davey? He made this?'

'He's a hard worker, an' skilled. Come ...' Joe walked through to the hall, his boots echoing in the empty rooms. 'See yon banister? Curved and carved tae mak a feature? That's ma lad's handiwurk.'

Sam caressed the polished oak, 'How auld's Davey noo?'

'Turned twenty one a few weeks back.'

'We're all growing aulder.'

An awkward silence yawned between them: Cal would not be growing older.

Connor's appearance at the top of the stairs broke the tension.

'Come doon, laddie,' Joe called, 'an' Ah'll show ye the stables.'

They wandered outside, Joe rubbing his chin, proud yet embarrassed in case he was thought to be showing off.

'Fiona's made up wi' the thocht o' living up here,' he told Sam. 'Ah jist wish Ah could ha'e gi'en her a hame like this sooner.'

'She's a guid wumman, bonnie and wi' brains, teachin' at the school, an' that.'

'An' tell me, how's Roisin? Is she at the cottage wi' Fiona?'

Sam shot a look towards Connor, checking he was out of earshot. He was nimbly climbing a sturdy oak tree.

'Roisin died while Ah wis awa'.'

Joe was stunned. 'Aw Sam, that's a tragedy. Wis it the pox?'

'Naw,' again the anxious glance to make sure his son was not listening. 'It wisnae frae disease ... although, that's whit Ah tell ithers. Joe, swear ye'll no' tell anither living soul?'

'Aye, Ah swear.'

It was still a struggle but he needed to confide in someone and of all the people in the world, Sam trusted Joe.

'She died in childbirth, the bairn too. Her mither wis wi' her ... an' her daughter's shame took that paur wumman tae an early grave an' all.'

'Shame?'

'It wis nae mine, the babbie. Ah'd bin awa' nigh on twa year afore she fell pregnant. They couldnae bring themsels tae tell me, an' o' course, Roisin could nae write nor read, not that she wid ha'e telt me, anyhow. Ah knew they were gettin' the money Ah arranged frae the regiment an' her Da' wid sometimes write back tellin' me ma son wis well ... no' often, mind, but enough tae mak me believe there wis nuthin wrang.'

'When did ye hear aboot Roisin?'

'When Ah reached their door, aboot twa months ago, Ah found Connor wi' his Grandfaither. Aw, the state o' that paur auld man. His mind wandering, all grey whiskers an' spittle ... grievin' fur his wife an' daughter. The wee lad wis takin' care o' him, no' the ither way aroond.' Sam wiped a hand over his face, pushing the memories away.

'Where's the auld man noo?'

'Taken in by the nuns. He disnae ken who he is, or where he is, but they'll care fur him ... feed him ... pray fur him. May the Lord bless them.' The sound of Connor jumping down from the tree prompted Sam to grasp Joe's arm, his blue eyes unusually dark, profoundly serious. 'No' a wurd tae a soul! The boy kens his Ma' died frae an illness an' that's the way it's tae stay.'

Joe briefly clasped his hand over his brother's; 'Aye, ye have ma wurd.'

'We should be getting back tae the lassies,' Sam released his grip as his son drew closer. 'Yer wife will be efter me fur no' telling ye

119

sooner ... Sarah's awa' tae tell Rosie Ah'm here, an' they're baith comin' up tae yer hoose.'

'When?'

Sam reached for the watch hanging from his belt, flicking it open and wrinkling his nose apologetically, 'The noo?'

'Then let's no' tarry. There's much tae speak of and not all of it bad. It's bin too mony years, brither! By Christ, it's guid tae see ye again!'

***

While Sam and Connor tackled nettles and buttercups on Cal's overgrown vegetable patch, Owen and his eldest son set out on their travels again, this time for London.

After months of inaction, a Committee was being set up to explore the implications raised by the Bill which Peel was presenting to the House.

Their journey south included more visits to mills, notably Sedgewick's large establishment at Newcastle.

With echoes of the previous summer's inspections, they viewed bruised and stunted women and children toiling for up to sixteen hours, sustained on nothing more than bowls of oatmeal, ladled from filthy cauldrons. The bulky red brick factories merged as one, the workrooms uniformly stiflingly hot, the workers, even the Overseers, sharing the same weary expressions of oppression.

Young Robert Dale left New Lanark in high spirits, set for a grand adventure, but seeing, once again, the grey, bitter face of desperate poverty and exhaustion, a cloud of futility settled on his shoulders.

The weather did not help his mood.

Day after day of low cloud shielded the sun from spreading any warmth to the bleak countryside. This dull monotony was only broken by soaking showers of rain, filling the uneven roads with puddles and swelling the rivers. As their carriage rattled past brown fields and mud choked farm yards, the occupants strained to see through the dribbling, streaking rain drops on the windows. Livestock stood in desultory groups pulling at piles of the remnants of last year's hay, labourers with sacks over their shoulders, caps pulled low, plodded about their business.

It was April, green shoots should be showing, fruit trees budding and the air full of nesting birds and busy insects, yet Nature was still displaying her winter face.

Since the previous autumn, the national newspapers had been reporting dismal harvests, lack of grain for flour, potatoes rotting in the ground and milking cows being killed for meat for want of winter fodder.

Market places were patrolled by soldiers to stop fighting, neighbours elbowing each other out the way, coming to blows over the last cabbage on a stall: all frantic to feed their families. Although he had read the figures of those sent before the magistrates for stealing and violent assault, young Robert found it difficult to believe the scale of the problem until he saw it for himself.

'If the worn down mill workers were not enough to plunge me into a depression,' he confided to his father one evening, 'the sight of so many anxious faces in the towns, tales at every inn of shortages and men fighting over the sparse supply of jobs ... and then there is this infernal drab weather which seems to be determined to prolong winter for the entire year!'

They were within two day's travel of London, having pulled up early to spend the night in a coaching house while the horses were re-shod.

'I can do nothing about the weather,' Owen smiled, pushing a pile of fatty meat to the side of his plate and loading his fork with the only edible thing on the plate, mashed potatoes. 'I *can* do something about the wretches on the factory floors. We are not onlookers on the misery of others, we understand the causes of their unhappy state and, moreover, we have a solution. Do not be downcast, my son! The sun will rise tomorrow and in due time Spring will bear blossoms and the grass will grow.'

Looking at his father's persuasive smile with the distinctive sparkle of vitality gleaming in his eyes, the boy could not prevent his lips from curving in agreement. Like so many who met Owen, even his own son was not immune to the man's forceful, optimistic charm.

To Murdoch's delight, although John Walker and his family were abroad, Owen was once again staying at 49 Bedford Square. The valet found the male servants' quarters comfortable and also the meals and laundry facilities were excellent, as would be expected for such a wealthy gentleman's residence. His main pleasure, however, was in renewing his acquaintance with Emily, the senior parlour maid. Throughout the intervening months, memories of her limpid grey eyes and throaty laugh were never far away. On this visit, he hoped romance might be in the air.

While his father was engaged in pressing for his reforms, young Robert made good use of his time. He was thrilled by London and guided by Owen's friends to see the famous sights and meet them for walks in the pleasure gardens. A favourite pastime was booking a horse for the afternoon at Philip Astley's magnificent amphitheatre. The great circus entertainer had died the year before but his son, John Astley, was a mutual friend of one of Owen's colleagues, who made the necessary introductions. Riding around the indoor performance area, thirty six feet in circumference, overlooked by the stage at one side and lavishly decorated chandeliers, theatre boxes and seating on the other, Robert allowed himself to dream of being a performer.

On one evening, he found himself dining alone at Plough Court with a Quaker friend of William Allen's; both his father and Allen being otherwise engaged. To his astonishment, the guest was Thomas Clarkson. Having read Clarkson's 'History of the Abolition of the Slave Trade', Robert was an avid admirer and the unlikely pair talked late into the night.

While on visits to Scotland to further the cause, Clarkson had met with David Dale, a staunch Abolitionist, and regaled Robert with anecdotes about his much loved grandfather. He also related recollections of meetings with William Pitt, the then Prime Minister, to discuss the need to end this abominable trade. His words were painful to hear but made a deep and lasting impression on the young man.

Owen was the main witness to be called before the Committee and he was eager to progress the Bill's passage into Law. A respected young lawyer, Henry Brougham, was presiding and a gathering of Members of Parliament and businessmen made up the numbers.

Tall and darkly handsome with wildly expansive hand gestures, Brougham was sympathetic to Owen's views for the need for reform in the factory system. With years of experience in the courts, he was a good choice and kept the proceedings moving and on topic through the day, ensuring they started and ended the meetings punctually.

Robert accompanied his father, taking a seat at the back of the room. He grew to know the peculiarities of the men facing him, their veined or hawk-like noses, bald heads or thick with curls, chubby with double chins or lean, dandified or ruggedly masculine. He noted their preferred positions of slouching or stretching and cracking their knuckles if gearing up to ask a question: playing with their beards or fiddling with snuff boxes. Often, they would reach to take an unnecessary gulp from their glass to punctuate the end of their words.

The backs of the heads of those infront of him, with their high starched collars or shoulders snowy with dandruff, became as familiar as the low ceilinged, dimly lit room; lamps and candles being required throughout the later afternoon proceedings. Pigeons strutted on the ledges beyond fly-speckled mullioned windows, cobwebs clustered white in the corners.

All the details were absorbed by Robert along with the odours of stale perspiration, colognes and a musty aroma of damp wood.

Owen was required to remain standing at the front during hour upon hour of questioning. Insidiously at first, but then quite obviously, it became clear that there was a great deal of opposition towards any measures which might harm the income of the mill owners.

Sarcasm and belittling comments were common place, some of the committee playing for the attention of their colleagues with barbed jokes, enjoying the ripples of laughter at their puns rather than concerning themselves with the serious matter at hand.

On the third day of giving evidence, Owen was subjected to increasingly personal questions. He quietly and firmly deflected them, replying with his reasons for insisting on better ventilation in the spinning rooms and shorter working hours.

'So, Mr Owen, we are to pass a law forcing cotton barons up and down the country to expend funds on fangled new practices to clean the air, run their machines for fewer hours ... and still expect them to return profits?'

'Properly managed, there would be no loss of profits, sir.'

'Properly managed! Are you saying your fellow masters are inept?'

'As you are all aware, I run my own mills. I know by experience that a tired, unhealthy operator causes delays in production with broken thread, jamming machinery and accidents. When the same employee is clear headed, their efficiency is vastly increased. In the long run, it is in the interest of the mill owner to ensure his operatives are as well cared for as the mechanical elements of his factory.'

'Aha, New Lanark! If we are to follow your example, should we also pass a law to enforce the provision of expensive dancing and sewing tuition for paupers?' Chuckles and groans met his words, but the speaker continued, 'And yet, you are not so keen on teaching the word of Our Lord? What are your views in that direction, eh?'

Owen would not be drawn. Standing his ground, he reiterated the need for allowing the workforce enough hours away from the factory floor to restore their health and attend to the care of their families and, in younger children, their education.

Again and again, he was attacked from different angles about his stance on attending the Established Church or, indeed, any church

Robert listened with rising horror. How could they be so cruel? These men with their jewelled fingers and embroidered jackets, hissing and jeering, poking fun at his father's replies. Their frustration grew as Owen remained composed, pressing on with his proposals. So they turned to pulling words out of context and throwing them back in his face.

Twice Brougham intervened, reminding certain members of their duty and the purpose of the Committee, chastising them for contemptuous remarks. Then, after a particularly vitriolic attack on Owen's personal religious beliefs, Brougham hammered his fist on his desk and demanded the questioning be stopped.

'These last remarks shall be struck from the record!' He swung his arm dramatically as if throwing them away himself. 'Gentlemen! I will not condone this boorish behaviour! We will break now and reconvene tomorrow at the usual hour.'

Unable to control his tears, Robert sought his handkerchief and wiped his eyes. He blamed the lingering effects of illness for his sensitive nerves, leaving his emotions too close to the surface to be suppressed. Although, in truth, he believed any loving son would be distressed by this hateful scene.

'How could you restrain yourself from rising to temper, Papa?' he asked when they were alone, walking through the city streets.

'I felt no anger.' Owen said, simply. 'Those men showed themselves to be so entrenched in habits that they cannot reason. For generations they have been trained to desire money, it is made the goal above all things. They call themselves Christians, but they do not practice the most basic tenets of every true religion, goodwill to all men.'

'Would they lose money, a lot of money, if your Bill became Law?'

'In the beginning, there would be certain expenditure and a small loss in production, that is a fact but it would be the same for all the factories so no-one would be disadvantaged in the market place. However, it need not be so. As we have seen at New Lanark, with the shorter hours, our workers are producing almost as much as before and why? Because they are more alert, more content and have the opportunity of following pursuits or enjoying leisure out-with the factory.'

'Surely, if you explain all that to the committee they cannot object.

Owen laughed, 'My dear boy, they can and they *will* object. There will be a lot of noise, I am expecting that, for that is always the forerunner of change, but it will only be a temporary bother because in the end the Law *will* be passed.'

***

The swallows arrived full of joyful chattering, gobbling flies as they swooped and dived between the buildings, busily repairing their nests from the previous year. Unlike south of the border, the sun shone on bursting buds, covering the ploughed fields and pale heath land with a haze of promising green.

Rosie , Cathy and Sarah met in the street after work to share the chore of dragging down their mattresses, dumping the old stuffing and refilling them.

After emptying the contents, the dirty but easy part of the chore, they stood patiently in line beside the new delivery of straw and

125

bushy heather. Mrs Young's hefty sons were stuffing four palliasses: there were two other batches to go before their turn.

'Sam would ha'e this done in a blink,' Sarah sighed. 'Ah wonder if he's up at Cal's patch? Lily, run up an' see if he's there, esk him tae gie us a haun?'

'He's makin' a rare joab wi' the plants,' Rosie said warmly. 'It's braw tae ha'e him wi' us fur a while.'

'Sad aboot his wife,' said Cathy. 'Ah cannae bring her face tae mind but she came wi' him last time, did she no'?'

'Ah didnae tak tae her,' Rosie sniffed. 'Snooty lookin', kept keekin' oot the side o' her eye at Fiona. Naw, Ah didnae tak tae her.' Adding swiftly, 'God rest her soul.'

'Ye cannae speak bad o' the deid, Auntie Rose,' Cathy cried, her words hushed.

'Weel, she cannae hear me, lass, she's in Ireland ... buried, deid.'

'God can hear ye,' Cathy whispered, but a smile played on her lips.

'Then He knows whit Ah mean,' Rosie sounded righteous. 'It's a crying shame fur the bairn. Nice wee lad, an a'. Ah hope they stay a while.'

'Ye ken whit Sam telt Joe aboot that?' Sarah asked brightly.

'Aboot stayin? Naw ... d'ye ken he'll live here noo?'

Sarah shook her head, enjoying the rarity of knowing more gossip than her sister. 'Sam's lookin'fur a wife. A mither fur his boy.'

'Aye,' Rosie mulled it over, 'that wid be a guid thing.'

'Then he's awa', like he alis said he wid when he left the army. Awa' tae New South Wales tae buy some land.'

'Weel, that'll be a shame,' Cathy put in, 'why wid he want tae gae sae far fae his folks?'

'He's a restless yin, oor Sam,' her mother told her, folding her arms, a breeze was picking up, whisking wisps of straw around the street. 'He's sailed the seas an' walked on foreign soil, seen sights we only hear aboot in the school room. He wis in Egypt, near the Holy Land an' o'er in North America.'

'An' Spain,' added Rosie, 'although he rarely speaks o' it, Fiona says he telt Joe it wis 'hell on earth'.'

Cathy chewed at the side of her fingernail, 'whit's sae special aboot New South Wales?'

126

'Dinnae ken, lass.' Rosie shivered. 'That's where they send the prisoners. All the bad yins that dinnae git the noose. Who'd want tae gae an' live wi' that shower o' thieves?'

'Och, this is takin' a time!' Cathy scowled at two old women picking over the bedding pile, their helpful grandsons gathering up the particular bunches indicated. 'Ah wanted tae gae doon tae the Institute this eve an' there'll be nae time tae dress.'

Sarah raised her eyebrows, 'That'll be Ross Marshall ye'll be wantin' tae impress?'

'Aye, an whit o' it?'

'Nuthin'! If Ah had twenty years less in ma bones, Ah wid be thinkin' him a fine lad.'

'Weel,' Cathy gave an impish grin, 'yer Mr Dudley wis askin' if ye were gaun tae the dancin'?'

Rosie's ears pricked up, her eyes darting to Sarah, 'Ye ha'e a follower?'

Sarah covered her embarrassment with a giggle, 'No' a *follower,* he's jist a kind man, a nice man from the shop.'

'Oh, Ah ken who Mr Dudley is,' Rosie was intrigued by the blush rising on her sister's cheeks. 'Ah jist didnae ken he wis sweet oan ye.'

'Och, Rosie, dinnae gae makin' a muckle oot a mickle! We work t'gether every day, 'tis all.'

After a pause, Rosie said kindly, 'He's had a sad time, ma Gerry kens him weel enough. His wife died some years back, an' a wee while ago his only son wis killed in the war.'

'Aye, Ah've heard this an' that frae the lassies at the store. They say that's why he's sae quiet.' Sarah thought of his hopeful eyes when he asked if she would be going to the Institute. 'He's a guid man.'

Rosie snorted, 'Weel, nae offence tae yer faither Cathy, may the Lord grant him peace, but it wid be a change fer yer mither tae take up wi' a guid man.'

Cathy shrugged, hurt but not surprised. Rosie had always made it clear she never liked Sean Rafferty.

Lily eventually returned with Sam when the mattresses were ready to be carried upstairs, a task he happily undertook.

'Whit a difference in this room!' he declared to Sarah, admiring the neat table with a jug foaming with sprigs of white hawthorn. 'Ah niver took ye fur a keen hoosewife.'

She was not offended, 'Ah'm no'! Ah'm a lazy bisom, if truth be telt but the past years o' fearing the weekly inspection has made me keep it richt.'

'Weel, ye've made it a hame tae be prood o'.' He wondered how his sisters felt about Joe's grand house but held his tongue.

'How d'ye manage at Joe's?' she was asking, throwing blankets over the beds, 'it must be crampit?'

'The three aulder lads are stayin' wi' Tam Murdoch. They tell me it's no' on ma account. Ah hope that's true?'

'If they say it is. Ah ken Donnie an' Davey ha'e bin sleepin' there a while. Och, they're young, they dinnae want their Ma knowin' whit they git up tae of an eve!'

Cathy came hurrying into the room, a dress draped over her arm.

'Cathy's awa' tae the dancin',' Sarah gave Sam a pointed look. 'She'll be wantin' tae change ...'

'Yer gaun aff on yer ane?' Sam was shocked. 'Up in toon?'

'Naw,' Sarah scoffed, 'there'll be a crowd o' them an' it's at the Institute sae they'll be weel looked efter.'

'Ye should come,' Cathy cried, pleased with the idea. 'If ye want tae find a wife ye'll surely find yin in the village for there's many mair lassies than lads.'

'Ah'm no' whit ye'd call a lad!'

'An some o' them are no wee lassies ... aw, Mam disnae want tae, but will ye come wi' me, uncle?'

'Why no', eh?' Sam glanced down at his dirty jerkin, aware of the musky smell of sweat when he lifted his arms. 'Ah'd better dae sumat aboot mesel' an' all!' he headed for the door, swinging back with a cheeky wink at Sarah, 'Come wi' us?'

She smiled, 'Next time.'

And next time she would mention to Mr Dudley she was thinking of going along with her brother. Yes, it was a pleasant, almost exciting, prospect.

Owen's plans to hold regular evenings of dancing and singing, open to all the villagers and their guests, was slowly gathering momentum. On the first occasion barely a dozen people attended, nervous as to what was expected of them.

Sometimes, the more sedate dances or recitals by trained musicians were replaced by local fiddlers, persuaded by Kyle Mcinnes to supply lively tunes to encourage a few reels.

Tales of the little ceilidhs spread through the tenements. Young and old, residents decided to 'look in' at the next one and within a few months they were becoming a popular entertainment for several hundred.

When Sam and Cathy entered, climbing the stairs to the second floor with a trickle of others, they were met with a loud, colourful scene. Fiddlers pranced and played on the upper gallery with their friends dancing beside them, while the centre of the main room was filled with many sets of eight figures, whirling, whooping and swaying in the practiced steps of a reel.

They joined the crowd of bystanders, clapping with the rhythm and watching the display of flushed dancers.

Sam mused to himself on some of the carefree, almost wild, gestures and movements. Crossing arms and grasping their partners' hands to swing around, some of the young men took a pride in lifting the girls' feet clear off the floor. Skilfully judging the moment, they pulled her safely back into a close hold, a moment of stolen intimacy, before spinning her away again.

It was a far cry from the stilted dances of the regimental balls in Gibralter or high society drawing rooms.

The music came to a stop amidst a round of enthusiastic applause and whistles and for a few minutes the dance floor lost its clear formations: tired couples leaving, new couples taking their places. Cathy's young man whisked her away to take up positions at the head of a group, ready for the next reel to begin.

'Uncle!' Davey punched Sam playfully on the shoulder. 'You awa' in a wee dwam?'

'Aye! Grand tae see ye, lad.'

Sam found his nephew's appearance a little strange. With his swarthy colouring, Davey would have been more in-keeping with some of the Native American braves he saw near Niagara. There were leather laces plaited into his long hair, strings of polished stones, feathers and even an eagle's talon on a string around his neck.

'Ah'm here tae play ...' Davey held up his fiddle, 'in a while, when Kyle's worn oot!' his eyes were searching the moving figures, 'Ah!' he waved, 'wait til ye see yin o'the bonniest wee maids in a' o' Clydesdale.'

The girl making her way eagerly towards them was very young, perhaps no more than fourteen or fifteen years old. Sam smiled benevolently, but his eye was drawn to the woman at her side. Both were petite and shared pale complexions and the fairest of flaxen hair, but while the girl's full lips and wide eyes clearly held a youthful beauty, he was captivated by the features of the more mature woman.

'*Feasgar math!* Mrs McInnes an' her bonnie dochter, Marie,' Davey introduced them, 'Ma brither, Sam Scott.'

'Madam.' Out of habit, Sam saluted.

Freya Mcinnes regarded him with cool appraisal before directing her attention to Davey with a torrent of Gaelic.

To Sam's amazement, Davey replied, also in Gaelic, as fluent as if it was his native tongue. Then, with a smile shining from her blue eyes, Freya nodded to Sam and turned away, hustling Marie towards the door.

Watching them leave, Sam said,'Sae, ye ken the Gaelic.'

'Oh aye, we heard it fae Ma' when we were bairns but the ithers lost maist o' it. Me, weel, Ah alis felt mair like a Highlander. The folk, their ways ... the boy who taught me tae fiddle, he wis frae the Highlands an' didnae or *wid nae* learn the English.'

'Mairi's a braw wee lass, yer richt,' Sam wondered if he was stepping out of line, 'but she's jist a chield yet?'

'Och, Ah'm no' efter the bairn!' Davey shook his head, laughing, sending the thin plaits swinging amongst his long dark locks. 'Kyle Mcinnes, up there playin' the noo,' he pointed to the upper gallery, 'he's Mairi's faither, an' treats her like a princess. Naw, Mrs Mcinnes wis telling me tae gae up an stairt tae play. She wants her husband hame.'

'An' she looks like a wuman ye widnae cross!' Sam felt a jab of disappointment. So much for the fleeting hope that Mrs Mcinnes was a widow. No, the lovely golden haired creature's husband was very much alive.

'Fur all her fragile, winsome ways, Ah've heard the woman's a richt harridan indoors.' Davey gave a resigned sigh, taking a last look around the room.

'Ye lookin' fur someone?'

'Aye, she wis here last month, dochter o' a weaver an' as sweet as ye like. We spoke of meeting again, here, but ... weel, Ah'd best be up the stairs.'

'Dinnae mind,' Sam winked, 'Ah'm sure yer never at a loss fer a lassie.'

Davey shrugged, 'But it's finding the richt lassie, no' jist ony lassie ... that's the tricky bit, eh?'

Sam agreed, staying to watch Davey playing for the next dance and then deciding to pack it in for the evening.

Half way up the hill out of the village he heard his name called and saw Joe and another man walking up behind him.

'How wis the dancin'?' Joe asked, after acquainting his brother with his companion, Philip Norton, a fellow mason.

'Braw! Davey's playin' an' he's a crackin' fiddler.'

'D'ye play, Mr Scott?' Norton asked Joe.

'Away! Not a note. An', as ma wife will tell ye, Ah cannae sing, neither. An' did ye meet ony yin, Sam?'

'Cathy's lad, an' passed some wurds with a few folk an' Ah met a Mrs Mcinnes, a beauty.'

'Oh, the Fair Freya!' Norton snorted, 'once met, ne'er forgot.'

'She wis tellin Davey tae get up an' take over frae her husband wi' the music for she wanted him hame.'

'Sounds like Mrs Mcinnes,' Joe murmured with a rye smile.

'Ye cannae blame her,' Norton puffed, finding it an effort to talk while climbing the steep steps. He stopped, turning to look down on the roofs of New Lanark. 'He wis an awfy man.'

'Aye,' Joe agreed, waiting for his friend to catch his breath. 'gamblin' wis his game ... mibbee still is?'

'Cards an' women.' Norton waved his hand at the tenements, 'He's bin forced tae change his ways with Fair Freya roond his neck but there's a few wee Kyle Mcinnes' running aboot doon there carryin' ither men's names.'

'Ah, so that's why she wanted him hame!' Sam began walking again. 'Weel, if there's a comely spinster or widow doon there, Ah'll mak it ma business tae sweep her aff her feet an' save him frae temptation!'

***

131

Across Clydesdale, the season flowed on into summer. Raised strips of bushy green potato plants grew up beside kale and cabbages, pink and white blossoms of cherry, apple, plum and damson trees faded into foliage and budding fruit. Perhaps the growth was not as vigorous as other years and it was certainly cooler than previous summers, but those who kept abreast of news from further south sent thankful prayers to the Lord for looking favourably upon them.

South of the border and all across Europe, the sun was rarely seen, the cloud laden sky bringing low temperatures and days of misty rain. Newspapers carried dismal reports of snow in Spain in July, blighted crops from France to Switzerland and even on the east coast of America.

When Owen returned to Braxfield he could hardly believe the lush countryside and, just minutes after arriving, insisted on taking a stroll around his garden with Anne Caroline and the children.

'Robert will bear me out when I say we could count on one hand the days of sun while on our trip. It was quite the most dreary weather I have ever experienced. Nothing is growing as it should, neither in the countryside nor in the London pleasure gardens. They are usually a riot of colour but now rotting in the ground. It is deeply concerning.'

'Well, dear, as you can see, our flowers are blooming.'

The children were playing tag on the lawns, their high voices and laughter clear on the late afternoon air. Around them, in the tall beech trees cocooning the garden, red squirrels scurried in the canopy, sending the leaves whispering with the bird calls.

'I have undertaken another project,' he told her casually. 'I was breakfasting one morning with Bathurst, the Bishop of Norwich, and he asked me to do him a favour. It seemed simple enough at the time, merely to attend a gathering in his place and lodge his subscription to the cause.'

'The Bishop of Norwich ...' Anne Caroline murmured, pleased.

'The meeting turned out to be exceedingly interesting. It was to appoint a committee to consider practical measures to provide relief to the manufacturing poor.'

'An interest close to your heart, my dear!'

'As it turned out, the following day I attended their first meeting and was invited to speak! Well, I was not prepared with any notes and followed several economists and public men to the podium. I gave them my views in a broad context and ... the upshot is, I consented to write a full report.'

'My goodness, as if you did not have enough to fill your time!'

'There is always time if one wishes to find it.'

They adjourned to the drawing room before the dew settled and much to Anne Caroline's delight, the whole family spent time together. If Owen was disappointed that his proposed Bill was still no further forward, he made no mention of it. Instead, he knelt on the hearth rug and played with Richard and Mary, pushing their little wooden horses and helping to straighten the sails on a carved ship.

Through letters, Anne Caroline knew a great deal about their stay under Walker's roof and the important politicians and lawyers her husband now counted as friends. In her son's letters, she heard of the hospitality they enjoyed at Plough Court with Mr Allen, the fine roast beef served in a club and the grandeur of Westminster.

What neither her husband nor Robert described was the appalling ordeal of the cross examination at the Committee.

Owen looked tired, she thought, drawn, but that was completely understandable having completed a four hundred mile journey.

When the children went upstairs with Peggy, Owen rested back into his chair, looking fondly at his wife.

'Richard is becoming so grown up! He has a forthright manner to him already, such a frank look in his blue eyes.'

It was pleasant to share their pride as parents, noticing things in their children which no-one else would see, or even care to mention. After months apart, they slipped easily into conversation, moving from topic to topic, interested in one another's opinions and, for Owen, catching up with family news.

'My sisters are much taken up with Mary's forthcoming marriage. All the arrangements are made and they are expecting us at Charlotte Street the day before the ceremony.'

'They are exchanging vows in the drawing room, as we did?' Owen asked.

'Yes, it is fitting, do you not think? It was what Papa wished for me, so there is every reason to believe he would be content to have the same for all his daughters.'

Noises from beyond the hall told of Sheddon's preparations in the dining room, a light supper was being laid out.

Unconsciously, Anne Caroline smoothed the silk panels of her bodice, her fingers moving to centralise the cameo on its fine gold chain around her neck. She had changed into her most becoming dress in expectation of his return and was aware he was still in his travelling clothes.

'Well, it is a satisfying finale after her long courtship with Reverend Stuart.' Owen stood up, stretching and rubbing at his neck. 'Now, my dear Caroline,' he smiled, reading her thoughts, 'I shall wash before we dine.'

The room was suddenly empty.

For weeks, she had found it adequately filled with furnishings and the hissing fire, but now he was back and his vital presence threw everything else into shadow.

***

Reverend William Menzies watched the space between his stone gateposts with rising anticipation. Keeping well out of sight within the drawing room, nervously fiddling with the cloth covered buttons at his cuffs, he rehearsed how to greet his expected visitors.

Their reputations preceded them. Since receiving news of their intention to call at his home, the minister was aquiver with the possibilities which their arrival might bring. Catching sight of his reflection in the ornate looking-glass, he patted at his bushy grey hair, fidgeting to stop his bony shoulder blades from poking out awkwardly from under his jacket.

They were punctual. On the first bell of nine o'clock, two men in dark tail coats and shining top hats turned in off the street and crunched their way across the gravel: the knocker sounded.

'Leave the door!' Menzies called through from the hall to his housekeeper, pulling the drawing room door shut behind him. 'I shall receive these gentlemen.'

The old woman scowled at him from between the folds of her muslin cap and an elaborate starched bow, retracing her steps to the kitchen. First she was not to tidy his study nor lay a fire and now, not even to answer the door.

'This is an honour, Mr Houldsworth, and yourself, also ... my dear sir ...' Menzies shook the second gentleman's hand with an ingratiating smile to cover his discomfort at not catching his name, '... an honour!'

Whispered rumours of Houldsworth's mission to the Parish had been wafting through the local congregation since the two gentlemen booked into the Clydesdale Inn earlier in the week. Seeing strangers in the town was certainly not unusual, the Falls of Clyde and New Lanark Mills attracted thousands of people each year. Following the official opening of the Institute for the Formation of Character, there could be fifty or sixty visitors every day eager to see Mr Owen's village.

There was something different about the visit being made by Henry Houldsworth, the distinguished owner of Woodside Cotton Mills in Glasgow.

'He's a clever an' powerful man, that Houldsworth,' Charlie Dodd, an elder at the Kirk, told Menzies the previous night. 'Gillespie brought him up frae England, Manchester or Nottingham or some such place. Wanted him tae teach spinning at Woodside ... an' within twa years the Sassanach's made the mill his ane! Sharp as they come! And not backward in throwing aroond the power such wealth brings tae a canny man!'

'And is he a friend of Mr Owen? Here at his bidding?' Menzies wanted to know.

'He's a competitor, an' no mistake. It's said, he's asking questions aboot the Master of Braxfield Hoose.'

Supping on roast venison, mutton pie and four bottles of claret by a flaming fire in Menzies' comfortable drawing room, they enjoyed their evening of postulating reasons for Houldsworth's interest. They were no nearer a conclusion when Dodd stepped out into the bat filled darkness of midnight to wind an unsteady course for home.

Now, the answer might be forthcoming.

Menzies, in black clerical garb, led the party down a bleak panelled corridor to his study. Heavily draped windows prevented most of the morning's watery light to penetrate the room but as they took their seats, Houldsworth's eyes adjusted to the gloom, taking in the spartan surroundings. Rolls of papers littered the desk beside pen holders bristling with quills, ink bottles and an

135

open Bible. Two oak settles, most likely discarded pews, sat on either side of the empty, cold grate. It was immaculately clean and devoid of any comfort.

'We would beg your patience,' Houldsworth began in his deep Nottinghamshire tones, 'and understanding, Reverend Menzies. I can see you are a busy man but we would be grateful for your views on a certain subject.'

'I am your humble servant,' the clergyman clasped his hands on his lap, his gimlet eyes going from one to the other of the city gentlemen.

'May we speak in confidence?'

Menzies nodded eagerly, 'I am only answerable to God, Our Almighty Saviour.'

'We are here at the behest of several of our colleagues, some of whom are in London and hold high positions in government. Are you acquainted with Mr Robert Owen of New Lanark Mills?

'I am, Sir, indeed, I am ...'

'You are aware of the changes being made to the running of his mills in recent months? When I say mills, I do not refer to the factory floor, I speak of Mr Owen's new school and the rules he has imposed for behaviour amongst his tenants.'

'Ah, yes, his new Institute!' Menzies' bony fingers squeezed and rubbed together, suppressing an urge to clap.

'We are here for the sake of the children,' the other man said, imbuing his voice with sincerity. 'As a pillar of the community and a man of the cloth with the best interests of these vulnerable, innocent paupers, we would appreciate *your* opinion of Mr Owen's new system.'

Fired with his personal grievances against Owen, Menzies burst out with a tirade.

'For years, indeed, ever since that fine Christian evangelist David Dale, may the Lord protect him and keep him ... when that devout and wise gentleman sold his mills to the Welshman, I have been tireless in my efforts to shine a light on the dangerous and most devious actions of that gentleman! Have you been down there? Have you seen the children? Improperly dressed in little tunics ... girls mixing with boys! Touching ... holding ... The man is a Heathen! Godless! He rules over his workers in a manner which blatantly disregards the teachings of Our Lord ... they are singing rough Scotch ballads ... dancing!'

Houldsworth's square, clean shaven jaw clenched, eyelids drooping as he watched with satisfaction while the minister became more and more enraged. This was exactly what they wanted: damning evidence to remove Owen's credibility.

'You are speaking of infants, Reverend, a little dance,' he broke in smoothly, 'is that so bad?'

'It is the work of the Devil! These children should be taught the word of our Saviour, given sound moral lessons from the Scriptures instead of prancing and reeling like dervishes!'

'You fear for the children's welfare under Mr Owen's guidance?'

'He declares to know how to form a child's character,' Menzies stared at them, incensed. 'Mr Owen believes he knows better than Our Lord. It is blasphemous! His address at the opening of the Institute was the most treasonable character of both Church and State!'

'You can vouch for that?'

'Indeed!'

Houldsworth's eyes slid to his colleague: their job was done.

'Reverend Menzies, it is fortuitous we have spoken with you. As a man of good sense and with the onerous responsibility you bear for your flock, I am sure you will be relieved to have played your part in saving the souls of these unfortunates. Now, sir, may we urge you to put pen to paper and write a brief account of what you witnessed.'

'Well, if you wish,' flattered, Menzies went to his desk, fumbling for a clean sheet of paper, unscrewing the lid from the ink bottle.

'Please address it to Lord Sidmouth.'

'Lord Sidmouth?'

'Yes,' Houndsworth saw the glow of self importance on the old man's cheeks and pressed the matter. 'This will be presented as important evidence before the Select Committee at Westminster.'

'And what shall I say?' Menzies' quill hovered above the paper, the ragged plume shivering.

'What you have just told us. If you recall the specific words or rules he announced to the workers, all to the good. Keep it as accurate as you can.'

The paper remained pristine.

'Shall we withdraw,' Houldsworth suggested, rising from his seat, 'allow you peace to remember the scene?'

'The thing is,' the minister's shoulders sagged, for all that he wished to denounce Owen, he could not lie in the sight of God. 'Ye see, I did not, myself, attend the ceremony.' Seeing frowns of exasperation, he rushed on, 'As a man of God, it was beyond my capabilities to be present at such a gathering. I heard of his contemptible speech from my wife.'

'But you have seen evidence that the children of New Lanark are under the power of a man who has no Christian morals, that they are in danger of subversion?'

'Not only the children, sir, every poor soul in the mills is subjected to his will! They are being denied redemption in the afterlife ... their way to heaven barred and destined for the torments of Hell! Mr Owen is their master and they are indebted to him for their livelihoods ... I have lost count of how many letters I have penned to that gentleman but the number is large ... and yet he will not see the error of his ways. He decries the Sabbath ... pours disdain upon the Holy Bible ...'

With effort, Houldsworth restrained himself, barely listening to the irate stream of words.

'Reverend,' he contrived a smile, not meeting Menzies' eye. 'If you please, may we trouble you to make a statement of your convictions regarding Mr Owen's governance of the mills? We shall be eternally in your debt if we can have possession of the completed papers by tomorrow, before we leave town.'

Menzies was relieved at the postponement. This was his chance to bring an end to the Devil's work in his parish and he seized it with zeal. Given time to gather his thoughts he was confident he could produce sufficient ammunition to bring disgrace upon the mill owner.

Houldsworth and his companion strolled back to town through the leafy lanes, enjoying the sunshine. Their task to dig for scandal on Owen had proved fruitless.

There were no tales of an indiscreet mistress or drunken gaming parties, beaten servants, abused chamber maids or any lack in upholding the law. As a Justice of the Peace in the county, they were even unable to find a victim of merciless treatment at his hands.

In commerce, there were no grievances or incidences of sharp dealing. To the contrary, there were tales of Owen's strange habit of warning customers when the prices would fall. He would then suggest they hold back their orders to take advantage of the coming savings.

However, mainly among staunch supporters and old friends of the late David Dale, they had succeeded in amassing a file of complaints pertaining to his views against the Church.

They must stamp on his nonsense about shorter hours and his ideology of a New View of Society. A view which could not only add thousands of pounds to the running costs of mills and dent their profits, but highlight perceived abuse by many of the leading cotton barons in the United Kingdom, placing them in a very embarrassing position.

Chapter Eight

Psalms 133:1 Behold, how good and pleasant it is when brothers dwell in unity!

Surrounded by family and friends, Mary Dale married the Reverend James Haldane Stuart in the gracious drawing room of her childhood home in Charlotte Street.

The Campbell side of the family kept themselves to themselves, passing small talk with Owen with an air of haughty resignation. By the time they retired for the night, Anne Caroline was worn out, all too aware of the frictions simmering below the surface.

The newly married couple left Glasgow straight away, heading to London where Reverend Stuart was taking up parish duties. It was a wrench for Mary's unmarried sisters and Anne Caroline stayed with them for a few days while Owen attended to city business.

'We are facing a catastrophe of the greatest magnitude!' Kirkman Finlay declared gravely to his table of guests in the Tontine Rooms. 'While it is not yet through August, we shiver at frost on the morning grass and moan of the early onset of autumn temperatures. Yet, this is nothing, *nothing* compared to what is happening in the south.'

His words were met with a growl of agreement and shaking heads from the affluent merchants and bankers.

'We are staring at famine and ensuing insurrection,' Finlay continued. 'Crops did not grow, meadows grazed by bullocks and milking cows are reduced to quagmires, the carriage horses are struck with mud fever ... and now the days are drawing short and there is little possibility of a useful harvest. The reports in the Glasgow Herald do not exaggerate ...'

'A rare change,' mumbled one of the company, raising sardonic smiles.

'Mr Owen?' James Cleland enquired, 'you have recently travelled through England, what say you?'

'I can attest to the devastating weather and the shocking conditions inflicted on farmers by the lack of sunlight. There has been no summer this year, nor even what could be called a spring.

This strange, unprecedented period of blanketing cloud and rain extends throughout Europe too. We cannot seek to buy their grain or potatoes for they simply do not have it.'

'And if they did,' Robert Dalglish commented, 'does this country have the money to buy it?'

Cleland took a pinch of snuff, as Superintendent of Public Works in the city, he knew the problem all too well.

'May thanks be given to God,' he prayed, wiping his nose with a monogrammed handkerchief, 'for sparing Scotland the worst of this deplorable weather. Although we have sufficient corn for our own, we have none to spare to fill English bellies.'

'Months, more ... a year past now, of this confounded miasma!' another merchant cried. 'My agent in Manchester keeps me abreast of the matter and states even his ninety year old grandfather has never seen the likes afore. The sickening stench of potatoes rotting in the country soil is thick in the air, holding the power to make ye retch on the city streets.'

'Dark too,' Cleland said, quietly, 'I read the days are hardly opened before they're closing. Apples are rotting in the buds, bee hives piled high with dusty remnants of starving drones, exhausted and starved, unable to find flowers.'

'Is this the start of the end of the world? Are we to slowly starve to death? Is our time nigh?'

'To hear the ministers at their pulpits ye would believe it! This is God's wrath! Atonement for the destruction wrought on His people over the last two decades of Man's bloody battles.'

'Gentlemen! Our soldiers have survived the hell of war and returned home to watch their children die for want of bread. These are terrible times.'

Sitting back from the table, his hands slowly turning a half filled tankard of ale, Owen listened to the remarks.

The country was in a mess. There was a stagnant economy, no food, no employment and parishes from Cornwall to Caithness were struggling to comply with their duties for Poor Relief. Ugly scenes erupted where meagre rations of bread and oatmeal were distributed, necessitating the harassed local JPs to order a military presence to keep the peace. As everyone around the table was woefully aware, the real danger was from the people themselves and the growing tidal wave of discontent. The distractions of war had merely postponed the inevitable and now the men were home, filling their aimless days by sharing their tales of distress; feeding the flames of revolution.

'These trying times require strong, practical action,' Owen said, firmly. 'We cannot force the sun to shine, nor the wheat to grow but we can take steps to create work for the hands which lie idle today. At present, we are allowing the minds of fit, resourceful men to be filled with resentment. We need to ensure they spend their days in useful labour and generate money and food to care for their families.'

'And where do we find this food?' Doyle, a banker, demanded.

'These unusually cold, damp conditions are affecting the northern countries,' replied Owen. 'Our friends with sugar plantations in the south of the Americas are happily unaffected and, I'm sure, the holds of Mr Finlay's ships are filled with produce from the Indian and far eastern markets. We will not starve, but we may require to adjust.' He gave a cheerful smile, 'At least the cotton prices are tumbling ...'

Finlay banged the table with his fist, 'Bravo, Mr Owen,' there was only a hint of irony in his voice, 'we can always rely on your optimism to bring a ray of hope!' His jovial expression was suddenly lost, his lips setting in a line. 'Overall, we are in a dark place, my friends. Let it be God's Will that He protects our land and saves it from violent rebellion, I shall pray for our redemption.'

The angst twisting Kirkman Finlay's handsome features was shared by them all but, Owen thought, prayers were of little value if not followed up by a commitment to take action. He felt sympathy for his friend, knowing Finlay's difficult battles with the black cloud of depression.

'Come now, we must do what we can,' Owen surveyed the maudlin group, noting the bleary eyes and flaming cheeks of those whose despondency was partly the result of too much brandy. 'We must all do what we can to assist those for whom we are responsible. We are fortunate, we have factories and income, let us spread our good fortune, grow our businesses and in so doing, open our doors to more workers.'

Cleland raised his glass to him with a nod of concurrence.

'We can strive to create jobs, Mr Owen, but only God can dispel this weather,' Cleland muttered. 'And by Jings, I pray He bestows a bountiful harvest upon us next year.'

While walking back to Charlotte Street, Owen was hailed by Jim Johnston, a clerk from the Chambers.

'Owen, my good fellow!' Tall and lanky in a blue satin jacket, his spindly legs encased in matching knee breeches and white stockings, Johnston considered himself a fashion setter. 'How long have you been in the city?

'A day or so only. How goes it with you?'

The young man fell into step beside him, emanating a cloud of cologne, 'Oh, not so bad, thank you, sir, and I am pleased to see you looking so well yourself ... I wished to speak with you,' his eyes were roaming over Owen's face with concern. 'Indeed, you may already be aware of the subject ... you seem to have upset some of your fellow cotton barons.'

Startled, Owen stopped in his tracks. 'How have I upset them? Of whom do you speak?'

'Oh, few names have been divulged to one as lowly as myself and as I do not frequent the Green Card Club, I am not considered part of their 'set'. However, I do know Mr Henry Houldsworth went to your neck of the woods to dig up dirt. The spade, sir, remained clean, much to his chagrin, although I understand a minister made a damning statement against you and your ... er, considerations on the Church.'

Owen was bemused. 'I know Mr Houldsworth, he took over from Gillespie at Woodside Mill. He was at New Lanark, you say?'

'That is what I hear.'

'Why did he not make his visit known to me? I could have shown him around, answered any questions he might have about my new system?'

Johnston leaned closer, an oiled curl falling across his forehead. ''Tis hard to plunge a knife in a man's back while looking him in the eye.'

After a brief pause, Owen continued to walk, 'Well, it is disappointing to know Houldsworth and others have sunk so low. Clearly, they are provoked by the measures I am progressing through Parliament, or why else would they wish to hound me?'

143

Clocks began to toll the hour and Johnston laid a hand on Owen's arm.

'I must away! Take care, Mr Owen. I agree wholeheartedly with your efforts to force through a law for better working conditions, but I fear you may have poked a hornet's nest. These are powerful men, hell bent on keeping the old ways. Your reforms would hit their pockets, their most tender organ, and they mean to find a way to avoid that pain.'

'Thank you, Mr Johnston, I appreciate you telling me of this underhand behaviour but, really, I have nothing to fear. Let them examine my every word and action, as they should, but they will find nothing except sound reason and an honourable man.'

Johnston tipped his hat, 'I wish you a good day and good luck,' he backed away across the street, dodging between pedestrians and narrowly missing a loaded handcart, 'perhaps I shall make a visit to your mills myself!'

'You will be very welcome!' Owen called back with laughter in his voice, 'and be sure to make your presence known to me!'

'Ye can be sure!' Johnston grinned, turning to hurry away, a shining blue blur in the crowd.

***

Joe and Sam stood in the front room of Mr Baxter's house, arms folded, watching intently for any smoke escaping from the fireplace.

'Ye've nuthin' tae worry aboot on that score,' Sam said reassuringly, 'there's a guid draw up yon chimney, even on a gusty day like t'day.'

'Then whit's his game?' Joe went over to the window and gazed out over Clydesdale's hills. A strong south westerly sent deep purple clouds billowing across a pale turquoise sky, as turbulent and unsettled as the feeling cramping his stomach. He narrowed his eyes, thinking, puzzling, while watching shafts of brilliant sunshine reflect off a pure white seagull winging its way purposefully against the wind.

'Weel, mibbee he's jist an awkward beggar.' Sam threw some more twigs on the dwindling flames. 'He paid ye afore.'

Joe sighed heavily. Several weeks had passed since Mr Baxter was supposed to have handed over the final, large, payment for his completed house. Then the complaints started. One of the casement windows was sticking, the plastering looked a little uneven on the hallway ceiling, a couple of the landing floorboards creaked, the barn partitions were not as robust as he expected. They were all inconsequential little points which could easily be put right but were given as the reason for withholding money.

The last point concerned the possibility that the main fireplace, which had a large open hearth, might release smoke.

'There's mair tae it than a few wee niggles. Ah fear he disnae ha'e the money.'

Sam joined him by the window. 'Then he cannae ha'e his hoose.'

'But Ah need his money.'

'Badly?'

'Enough.'

'D'ye owe some yin or is it fer yer ane hame?'

Joe scratched at his head. 'If Ah pay ma debts, which Ah must by the end o' the month, it means ma ane hoose wulnae be feenished afore the winter.' He turned back to face the bare, echoing room. 'And this place will jist be sittin' here ... empty.'

'Naw, din nae fret, Baxter will pay.' Sam slapped his brother on the back. 'C'mon, let's gae fur a drink.'

'Gaun aheid, Ah've tae see Tam but Ah'll nae be lang.'

Pushing his hat firmly onto his head, Sam left the house and, leaning into the bracing wind, strode off towards the middle of Lanark.

There was an icy touch to the air, at odds with the dense foliage on branches tossing and swaying, sending green leaves whirling into the street. As he walked, Sam pondered on how different his life had become in the last few months. He seemed to fit into Joe's home and family with uncanny ease. Day to day living ran smoothly from waking to turning in: talking over simple domestic matters with Fiona, watching the children at play or carrying out duties in the cottage or for the animals; caring for Connor.

He was even becoming more confident in dealing with the difficult and at times heart breaking scenes with Sionaidh. On first experiencing her rages of frustration or, worse, when she fell to the floor in writhing, uncontrollable spasms, he was at a loss to help.

He held renewed respect for his brother and Fiona, and also for young Ailsa who coped so well.

Sam strove to make himself useful, gathering and chopping wood, mucking out the stables, weeding, planting and tending Cal's patch: each day rolled into the next. Taking up Mr Owen's offer of schooling for any child in the local area for a few shillings a month, Connor went down to the classroom with his aunt and cousins every morning. Each week brought a change in the introverted child. Smiles were replacing frowns, food no longer refused but eaten with relish and he joined Tom in the evening household tasks without need of persuasion.

However, in his quiet times, on his own, Sam fought constant internal struggles. Pangs of conscience and plans for the future wrestled with keeping the past buried, both of Roisin and the atrocities of war.

When he retired from the Cameronians, he foolishly believed he would be a free man to live out his allotted time on Earth as his own master. It was not long, a week, maybe two, before he realised how deeply the decades of military life were ingrained in his psyche. Nightmares of panic, screams of dying men and foul, choking clouds of gun smoke were so vivid that he would wake gulping for breath, the stench of sulphur in his nostrils.

More than anything, he missed having orders and routines.

Fiona's carefree ways and the noisy comings and goings of the children were sometimes unbearable. Rules and regulations had been his life and suddenly they were gone.

Now, he was his own master, as he had longed to be, yet the days flowed in an aimless stream with no more arduous a task than ordering up a jug of ale to share with Joe in the Tavern.

A child's piercing shriek pulled his attention to a group of huddled figures further up the road. All of the children were in the white New Lanark uniform and one of them lay on the ground, screaming.

Sam approached them. 'Are ye in need o' help?'

'He's alis fallin' ...' a young woman was kneeling, examining the little boy's leg, 'but noo look whit he's done?'

The spindly white leg was crooked, a lump protruding from the middle of his shin like an extra joint.

'It's broke,' Sam said, abruptly. 'Come, let me carry him tae yer hoose, ye'll need tae call a surgeon.'

'Aye, yer no' wrang.' She stood up, wiping grit and mud from her skirts, the tight muslin cap and clogs marking her out as a mill worker. 'Ah wid be mighty gratefu' fer yer offer.'

Trying to be as gentle as possible, he scooped the boy up, causing his cries to lapse into shuddering groans.

'We dinnae live far awa'.' The woman spoke matter of factly, hurrying along at his side, pulling her shawl tight against the buffeting wind. Occasionally, she would stroke the child's hair back from his brow, telling him how brave he was and the pain would soon be better.

On coming to a line of thatched town houses, the other children ran ahead, flinging open one of the doors and shouting for their father.

'Whit's happened noo?' A scrawny grey haired man appeared in his stockinged feet. 'In the name o' Heaven!' he took the child from Sam, 'can tha' bairn no' look where he's goin' fer yin day?'

'He'll need a doctor,' Sam said. 'If ye tell me where he lives Ah'll gladly fetch him.'

'We'll manage.' The man swung away, carrying his son indoors.

'He disnae mean tae be rude,' the woman said apologetically, offering a tentative smile. The direct look in her eyes caused Sam to give mumbling reassurance that he was not insulted.

'Ye see,' she continued, 'Wee Grant is tha' clumsy we seem tae call fer Dr Davidson jist aboot every week, but this time he's done hissel' real damage.'

An older boy hurtled out the door and charged up the street, yanking his cap off when the wind caught it, arms pumping at his sides.

'That's Paulie awa' fer the Doc noo,' she made no move to go inside, 'Ah'm grateful fer yer kindness, thank ye.'

'It wis nuthin. Ah pray yer bairn recovers an' learns tae tak mair care o' where he pits his feet.'

'Och, he's no *ma* bairn!' her laugh reminded him of Sarah's, spontaneous, girlish. 'Wid Ah be sae hairtless tae be gabbin' oot here if ma ane flesh an blood wis ballin' his wee eyes oot! Naw, he's ma brither's lad an' no doubt his Ma is tendin' tae him better than Ah'm able.'

147

Sam's smile was for more than covering his embarrassment, 'Weel, Ah'll pray fer yer nephew then!'

A sudden blast of air caused her to stagger, catching at loose strands of hair flying out from under her cap. She attempted to tuck them away with little success, asking, 'D'ye come frae New Lanark?'

'Naw, nearby, at Bankheid ...'

'Weel, Ah'll keep an eye oot fer ye ...' did Sam imagine the slight pause? 'an' tell ye how he's faring.'

'Aye, dae that!' He doffed his hat, 'Samuel Scott at yer service!'

'Ye'll be Joe Scott's brither, then?' she cocked her head on one side and this time there was no denying her friendly, encouraging tone. 'Ah thocht ye had a look o' him. Ah werk alangside yer sister, Mrs MacAllister.'

A woman's voice called from within the house, 'Ruth! Come awa' in an' close the door aginst the cauld!'

Sam raised a hand in farewell, sharing her good natured grimace at the reprimand. 'Ah'll no' keep ye, there's a storm brewing, an' no mistake.'

Head down, eyes half closed against the grit being whipped up by the gusting wind, Sam marched on to the tavern. Two questions circled in his mind: was this young woman, Ruth, married, and how soon could he speak with Rosie and find out the answer?

'Och, ye dinnae need tae ask Rosie,' Joe told him when he recounted his adventure. 'If she taks bairns tae Mr Owen's school, Fiona will ken this lassie.'

Sam swilled back the last of his ale and slammed the tankard on the table.

'Drink up, laddie! We'd best git hame!'

They found Fiona dozing by the fire, curled up on the high-backed settle, a cushion behind her head, a colourful crocheted blanket laid over her legs.

'My, you're early back ...' she greeted them, drowsily, pushing the cover away and sending something dropping to the floor: a ball of pale wool, stabbed by knitting needles holding the first few rows of a winter sock.

'Stay where ye are,' Joe insisted, taking Sam's coat to hang up with his cloak in the back scullery.

Sam shook raindrops off their hats. 'It's blowing a hoolie oot there ... an' ye look sae cosy.'

'Ah am that, an' the bairns are asleep,' she relaxed back. 'We're all tired oot wi' the dancin' an' ramblin' we've bin daen t'day. We had tae leave the walk in the woods fur the wind wis shakin' the trees somethin' terrible.'

Sam waited until they were all sitting companionably and a natural pause came in the conversation, then he related his meeting with Ruth.

'And whit d'ye say the wee lad's name wis?'

'Grant. An' they say he's alis hurtin' hisself.'

Fiona sat up straight, 'Ah ken who ye mean!'

She recalled a stocky little woman helping Ailsa with the buttons on Sionaidh's coat one snowy day last winter. It was a kind gesture, most people shied away from her eldest daughter and Fiona grasped at an indistinct impression. She was at least past her thirty years with a pleasant, plain face, not unduly lined or pock-marked, her dark brows and ready smile being the only memorable features.

'Ah mind her noo,' she said again, wondering what it was about this ordinary mill worker which caught Sam's attention. 'Aye, the bairn's alis in the wars. He's a Patterson, there's four in the school, an' the wuman ye met is his aunt.'

Sam snorted dramatically. 'Can ye tell me sumat I dinnae ken already?'

'She lives wi' her brither up in toun, but they all used tae live in New Lanark an' moved awa' when his Da', that's Grandpa Patterson, died. Ruth came tae be with them a year past ... she works in Mill Three wi' Rosie.' Fiona's eyes went pointedly to Sam. 'She's a widow. Her man wis killed in the war an' that's why she's wi' the Pattersons.'

Sam could have cheered! Instead, he nodded, smiling to himself at the warm relief brought by her words.

'She seems a pleasant lass,' he said, 'Ah've a mind tae see her again.'

Joe was kicking off his boots and stretching his legs to feel the warmth of the flames. His enjoyment of the evening was only marred by the lurking problem of Baxter's tardy payment.

'If that's all I have to worry about,' he told himself, sternly, 'then I'm a lucky man.'

The next few weeks brought a glorious colour palette of gold, crimson and bright orange leaves; scarlet rosehips and glistening bunches of deep purple brambles and elderberries gleamed from the hedgerows. Frost silvered mornings thawed into morning dew showing the tell tale tracks of deer, foxes and badgers going about their lives under cover of the growing hours of darkness.

Joe's anxiety grew. Had he overstretched himself? Was his first major building project going to be abandoned, unpaid for, left to rot as an eyesore? He cursed his naivety. He should have waited for a smaller plot of ground, one he could afford without involving a third party or relying on their money.

Every time he rode past the gate way, he was struck with an insidious, sinking feeling. Instead of pride, he felt shame, failure. All that effort, all the hopes and promises to Fiona, the sheer money and sweat; was it all to go to waste?

Ewing noticed the change in his protégée and drew him aside one evening after a Lodge meeting.

'Yer no' yersel', Joe. Is there something amiss, an' mair tae the point, can Ah be of assistance?'

It was a relief to share his worries and Joe related the difficult situation while they walked home.

'Tak Mr Baxter tae the Courts! He contracted ye tae build a hoose,' Ewing stabbed the air with his free hand, the other gripping his walking stick, ' an' that ye've done. He's no' paid ye, an' that's the end o' it!'

'The Court?'

'Ah ken a man who'll tak yer case.'

Joe whistled through his teeth. 'It'll cost me dear, Ah wager.'

'Not as much as lettin' yersel' be taken a loan of, that's fer sure.'

'Ah kept hoping ...'

'Nah, nah, it disnae work like that: hoping. Ah send oot ma bill an' if it's no' paid in time, bang! A letter demandin' payment ...'

'Tam's sent oot several ...'

'Then ye need a lawyer. Come up tae ma hoose t'morra and we'll sort this oot.'

Joe slept badly that night. Several times he awoke from nightmares of faceless, frock-coated lawyers with hooded eyes, berating him for his ignorance. Hazy courtrooms, judges with curling horsehair wigs and wagging fingers ... the facts being obscured, twisted and turned to make Baxter the victim and he, Joe, the accused.

Fiona knew he was worried and did her best to soothe him, pretending to accept his brusque explanation that it was 'jist business'. He couldn't bear to tell her the truth: he did not have the means to complete their home nor, given its half built state, any likelihood of selling it to recoup their investment.

The leaden sky mirrored his mood as he swung up into the saddle and sent Bluey towards Ewing's yard. He recalled Gerry telling him how both David Dale and now Robert Owen insisted on payment for goods within the terms agreed and did not hesitate to take legal action if the terms were breached.

'Business is business,' Gerry said.

If it was deemed good practice by those two honourable gentlemen, then perhaps it was not such a bad thing to be doing.

While Joe struggled with his problems through the autumn days, Sam and his sister, Sarah, took little heed of the season's changes, merely noticing the black evenings as a nuisance.

When evening walks were no longer possible, the Institute came into its own, for all the villagers, but especially for those courting.

After months of prevaricating, Sarah accepted an invitation from Mr Dudley to attend one of the village dances. To her surprise and pleasure, she found him to be entertaining company.

Rosie was pleased to find that she was the one person who bound the other couples together, knowing both Ruth and Andrew Dudley.

'My goodness!' she clapped her hands, the curls she tied up in rags all day under her cap were now released and bouncing at her ears. 'If we find Cathy an' her young man, we can mak up a full set fur the reels jist frae oor ane family!'

Standing close to Sam, Ruth raised up on her toes and whispered in mock annoyance,'Part o' yer family? Yer sister has a cheek tae presume!'

For a moment, Sam missed the jest in her voice and shot a worried look to the animated face at his side.

'Ye wee rascal!' he beamed, taking her hand and placing it firmly on his arm. 'Fur that, ye'll owe me a dance!'

Transformed out of their dowdy work clothes, the mill workers prided themselves on wearing bright colours, plaids and patterns, the girls weaving ribbons through their hair and imitating the fashionable ladies they glimpsed touring the factory. The men, even little Bobby Muir who cleaned the privies and usually looked like a scarecrow, took care to wash and shave. Whether urged by their wives or the thought of new sweethearts, they all wanted to look their best if they were going to the Institute.

The village shop only carried one fragrance of gentlemen's cologne and, as Sarah murmured to Andrew Dudley, in the warmth of these gatherings the scent could be overpowering.

At a quarter to ten, the musicians wiped the sweat from their foreheads and bowed to applause, signalling the crowd to disperse. In chattering groups, everyone poured out the door and up through the mill gates into the tenements. Twinkling in the dark, candlelight showed where a line of figures plodded up the hill to Bankhead. For those unable to tackle the climb, two pony traps were soon filled, crushed into the bench seats, no longer caring if their hair was in order or their skirts smooth. Despite being young in years, room was made for Mrs Gray, her bow-legs being famous for allowing her to dance but not walk.

By the time the Church bells in Lanark were peeling ten o'clock, the streets of the mill village were bare except for the two constables, lamps in hand, quietly making their first night's patrol.

***

For several months, Robert Owen remained in Scotland, riding up and down the Clyde valley to inspect his warehouses at the docks and attend to business in Glasgow. In between these trips, he devoted as much time as possible to the school.

Keeping the mills running smoothly was essential. They were the core of the village, producing the necessary income for wages, maintenance and ongoing improvements. Yet, for the community and to show a practical example of his new system, Owen considered the education and formation of character of the young generation to be of equal importance.

The dreadful weather was continuing to wreak havoc with reports of the late European harvest being even worse than predicted. In England and Ireland there were virtually no marketable or even edible crops and the north east of Scotland was battered by hurricanes and fierce snowstorms.

The corn stooks were still out in the fields when the snow came and when it was dug away they were frozen into solid lumps, useless; even for cattle fodder.

The harshest months of the year were still to come and the wearying days of rain were turning to sleet. An alarming number of desperate men were calling for help to feed their families. They turned to breaking into factories and destroying the machinery which replaced their jobs and banding together to demand changes in the government: rebellion was in the air.

Into this volatile arena stepped William Cobbett, a man who had already spent time in Newgate prison for sedition and who placed the blame for the ills of the people firmly on the shoulders of the current government. While he was touring Scotland, his supporters tried to organise a place for him to speak to as many working people in Glasgow as possible. Horrified at the thought of such a reformist addressing a crowd, the magistrates refused permission to hold the gathering in any part of the city.

The expected numbers were large and with all the usual meeting places denied to them, their plans appeared doomed. So, it was an enormous relief when James Turner, a former magistrate, offered them the use of fields at Thrushgrove, his private estate.

Turner was a wealthy tobacconist who made his own fortune from small beginnings and held a certain sympathy for his fellow working man. Fortuitously, Thrushgrove lay just outside the jurisdiction of the City of Glasgow.

Word of Cobbett's speech spread far and wide. On the misty, freezing morning of October 29th, the roads flowed with men and women, some carrying brooms to signify the sweeping away of the old ways; demanding change. From every trade and all directions, they tramped towards Royston, converging at the gateway to Thrushgrove before flooding through to fill the undulating parkland.

An emergency meeting of the Town Council called the 42nd Regiment to arms. They were ordered to stand by in the barrack square at the Gallowgate in preparation for quelling the anticipated riot.

At midday, smart in his top hat and frock coat, his white cravat tied snugly under his chin, Cobbett stepped up on the makeshift platform to give his address. While he waited for the applause to die down, he looked out at forty thousand earnest, frightened yet hopeful faces.

It was the largest gathering for political reform yet to be seen in the British Isles, let alone Scotland, and the red coated 42nd regiment expected the call to action at any moment. Around the soldiers, the city streets were eerily quiet, only the bits jangling on the horses' bridles and shuffling footsteps of old folk or children disturbed the tension.

For four hours, the crowd stood on Thrushgrove's trampled grass and listened, cheered and shouted their questions through the damp air. It was an emotional, serious speech but everyone heeded the organisers' words and remained calm.

Standing behind Cobbett in the comparative shelter of a leafless oak tree, James Turner watched the practised orator with admiration. He knew full well that by allowing the meeting to take place on his land he was putting himself in a very dangerous position. Perhaps he would be arrested or fined? At that moment, he cared little for the repercussions.

Clenching his teeth to suppress any show of emotion, he shared the feelings expressed by the crowd's jubilant whistles and whoops when Cobbett declared there should be a vote for *all* men.

He felt his conscience absolved of blame for going against the wishes of the magistrates; the rights of ordinary working men were paramount.

The events at Thrushgrove were the main topic of conversation when Owen dined with friends the next day. On this occasion, Anne Caroline was with him in Glasgow and included in the invitation to dine at the MacIntosh's. Four other couples joined them at the table and after a meal which showed little of the starvation crawling the streets, the ladies withdrew, leaving the men to their own devices.

'There are bets on Turner being charged with treason, ye know.' Charles MacIntosh told the group of men relaxing around his table. 'Hauled off to the Bridewell within the week, I would say.'

'Finlay's saying it'll take them a month at City Hall to stop trembling sufficiently to grasp a quill for the warrant.'

'Turner expected as much,' Charles Tennant muttered, accepting a glass of port. 'Stuck his neck out, showed his colours and will have little thanks for it.'

'He must have believed it to be the correct action,' Owen said, 'and there was no trouble. Those who attended would have been far more unruly had they not been given the chance to hear what Mr Cobbett had to say.'

'The black hearted Tory's were apoplectic with rage. Free speech is poison to them.'

'Cobbett!' Tennant laid his head back against the carved high-backed chair, eyes scanning the ceiling's elaborate grape and ivy leaf cornice. 'What to make of the man? I confess sympathies with his quest to root out corruption in Parliament, along with the support of others like Francis Burdett ... good luck to them!'

The retired professor, a distant cousin of Macintosh, slapped the table top. 'But some of their exclamations are pure bunkum! Universal male suffrage! I ask you? What would a factory worker in Glasgow know about politics? or why there is need for taxes ... eh?'

Owen gave the man a stern look, 'Perhaps he, this fictional factory worker, *should* know? After all, it is men like him who provide the workforce to make the fortunes to be taxed ... and thus the money to oil the machine of government. It is a simple concept to grasp and only their lack of education prevents the lower classes knowing all they need to know.'

'Quite! But, they are not educated, most cannot read.'

'And that says more about our government and society than it does about them. Given the opportunity, a man can be anything he desires.'

'Get ideas above their station, more like!' the professor grunted.

'And why shouldn't they aspire to a better life?' Owen asked.

'Street hawkers sharing the right to vote with landed gentry or admirals? Come now, Mr Owen?'

'And why not? All children should be educated and grow up to be allowed the chance to vote over issues which affect their own lives. They are human beings, just like you and me, not mere commodities to be used up and thrown on the scrap heap.'

'Pah!' the older man downed the dregs in his glass, his light hearted expression slipping into one of animosity.

Charles Tennant observed the spat. His views aligned with Owen so he saved his breath, knowing his articulate Welsh friend would state the case.

Owen's eyes twinkled mischievously, 'Take, if you will, the gentleman we have just been speaking of, Mr William Turner.' He drew the other men's attention. 'We know him as a tobacco merchant with a fine mansion and acreage, we also know of his years as a magistrate of the city. A respected and successful man, yes? Yet, gentlemen, he was born the son of a simple shoemaker, taking up an apprenticeship in the tobacco business and later moving into his High Street shop, just across from the University. One should not presume a man is ignorant just because he has not been given the tools to learn.'

After a grudging silence, the professor asked, 'Surely you do not agree with all of Mr Cobbitt's views?'

'Certainly not.' Owen knew what he meant. 'In particular, the abhorrent opinion he holds that the trade and enslavement of black Africans is necessary.'

'What did Cobbitt call them?' MacIntosh showed his dislike with a glower. ' "Lazy, laughing, fat negroes." The arrogance of the fellow!'

'My Quaker partners were outraged,' Owen recalled.

'Quite rightly so. Pray to God that bigoted man never achieves his ambition of becoming a Member of Parliament.'

'Over Wilberforce's dead body!'

'He is a strange contradiction, that Cobbitt.' Tennant mused. 'Such apparent passion for the rights of some of his fellow men and yet, utter contempt for others. The only difference being the colour of their skin.'

Charles MacIntosh set about filling and lighting his pipe, a footman standing at his side with a tray of smokers' paraphernalia and a selection of tobacco.

'There is hunger for reform,' he was saying. 'It is on everyone's lips ... from market squares to Town Halls. At least the need for change is being recognised. Let's pray we are not too late ... as happened in France.'

'Lord Sidmouth will try to suppress it,' Tennant continued his examination of the cornicing, his mind pondering the dilemma.

'Which is the worst action to take,' Owen said. 'The reforms I proposed eighteen months ago are before the Select Committee and taking an inordinate amount of time to be considered.'

'Peel dragging his heels, eh?' asked Macintosh. 'Well, hardly a surprise, given he's the largest calico printer in England, it will directly hit his own purse.'

'Perhaps,' Owen conceded, knowing this was probably one of the factors in the long delay. 'He is pleading ill health but he appears to be a man of integrity. He took up the cause, as he did before, and he managed to bring *that* into Law in 1802.'

'Weak as a kitten with no teeth,' Tennant murmured.

It was warm in the dining room and growing dim with the closing day, the rosy hue from the fire encouraging drowsiness.

'The amendments should be presented to the House and passed!' Owen continued, wide awake and clear headed, having taken only one glass of claret to his friends' half dozen. 'It is obvious to any reasonable person that it is the blatant inequality between the desperately poor and preposterously rich which causes the unrest. Steps must be taken immediately to address this ...'

'In an ideal world, of course,' MacIntosh agreed, 'but the Tories dance to the tune of their rich backers and they are not of a mind to lose one penny. It has been this way for generations; money and politics are intimate bed fellows. Oh, that the Whigs were in charge!'

'Which is exactly why this vicious circle must be broken!' Owen spoke assertively. 'And it can be, quite easily and without rebellion. It is all laid out in my writings on the subject in A New View of Society. I have given copies to Lord Liverpool and, indeed, most of our politicians on both sides of the House. If we are to stop the ferment of bitter resentment which is foaming and frothing in our midst, the changes I propose *must* be acted upon!'

'Ah, but Owen!' Tennant exclaimed, lifting his head to make eye contact with his friend. 'Your New System will take years, generations, to make a difference.'

'I grant you that, which is why it must be implemented without delay, every day that passes is a day wasted. Profound, lasting change will not happen overnight, there is no quick fix. In the mean time, let the understandably angry and bereft paupers know they are not forgotten.'

157

'If these reforms *made* money for the factory owners,' MacIntosh put in between draws to kindle his pipe, 'they would be Law already.'

'That is the irony of it!' Owen laughed. 'In the end, they will make more money after the changes. I see it at New Lanark, it is not just a fanciful thought. The production from a contented workforce on humane shifts, out-performs the current form of depressing slavery. My profits bear this out. And if one adds the inconvenience and expense of repairing damage from Luddite demonstrations, lost time in accidents and manpower while training a constantly changing workforce, my reforms and my New System do, indeed, make money.'

'Keep the pressure on them at Westminster, my friend,' Tennant smiled. 'Charles and I will create as many jobs as possible at St Rollox ...'

'And your project with steam locomotives!' MacIntosh cried.

'Ah, yes, there will be employment coming from that if all goes to plan. I am working with James Watt to build a rail line into the city.'

'You built St Rollox beside the canal for ease of transporting goods,' Owen was interested. 'Does it not suffice?'

'The canal system works, yes, but by laying a flat metal track, large locomotives can be moved to wherever one wishes by means of a steam engine. A direct line to the ships on the Clyde would be ideal. I am working on it.'

When the footmen began to light candles and shutter the windows, the party broke up.

'Oh, that was delightful,' Anne Caroline sighed, reaching to hold Owen's hand when they drove back to Charlotte Street. 'It was lovely to spend time with Mary and Margaret again.'

'You should come up to the city more often, my dear. The children are old enough to leave in Miss Wilson and Peggy's good hands. Your sisters would enjoy your company, I'm sure.'

'In the Spring, yes, that would be pleasant, but I fear I am finding the bed chamber painfully cold and damp. I do not wish to point out the dampness held inside the mattress. Perhaps I should? I fear Breen is not as able nowadays, I would not wish for anyone to be offended.'

Owen squeezed her hand, a tender note in his voice. 'You are the kindest person, Caroline. Worrying about the feelings of the servants! Oh, how I wish there were more people in the world with such empathy.'

She smiled, suddenly shy. 'I can see her efforts in instructing fires to be kept fed and the liberal use of the warming pans so it would seem churlish to complain. In my childhood, my mother was most insistent in having those stuffed feather mattresses beaten and aired in sunshine twice, even three times a year.'

'All the large carpets too,' Owen chuckled, 'the house was in uproar on my first visit to you, do you remember?'

'Oh yes, how could I forget? Sometimes, those days seem a hundred years ago, then, like now, as if only yesterday.'

'The older one becomes, the faster the years pass.' A strained tone crept into his voice.

In the privacy of the carriage, Anne Caroline lifted his hand and kissed it, praying for his plans to be acted upon. Loving him as she did, it was becoming unbearable to watch his hard work and hopefulness smothered by endless frustration.

Chapter Nine

"It is vain to talk of the interest of the community, without understanding what is the interest of the individual"
Jeremy Bentham

Much to the relief of Mr Turner of Thrushgrove and to the surprise of all those who laid bets on his imminent arrest, he was not charged with treason or sedition. However, his action of deliberately supporting radical reformists had been noted.

After a dismal autumn, winter was even worse, dripping from one overcast day to the next with little variation. At least there were some food stocks to call upon in Scotland but the docks were busy with ships bringing imported goods to feed the nation.

There were other tall ships moored in the west coast ports: the packet ships. Their gangways teemed with eager folk desperate to leave the misery behind and head to a new world, a new life.

Emigration was in Sam's thoughts too.

As well as taking Ruth to the occasional dance at the Institute, he would often meet her when she left the mills at the end of the day, collecting Connor at the same time.

Taking a lantern with him, he would escort her with her nephews and nieces, up to the market town and enjoy a companionable chat on the way. It had taken months for little Grant's leg to heal and when he first managed back to school, with the aid of crutches, Sam would let him ride home on his shoulders.

On the evening of the last day of the year, Sam strode along beside her in the bobbing pool of light. He was free of his little burden, Grant now being able to walk with the other children. Ruth was full of plans for Hogmanay and he was forced to wait for the right moment to change the subject.

'Ruth,' he plunged in, 'we've bin seeing a guid deal o' each ither fur some months now an' Ah want tae tell ye summat. Perhaps Ah should ha'e telt ye afore.' His voice trailed off.

'An' whit wis that?' she asked, guardedly.

'Ye ken Ah've bin all ma life in the military, tha' Ah've sailed tae America an' Arabia?'

'Aye, wi' yer regiment.'

160

'These past months stayin' wi' ma brither ha'e bin the longest Ah've bin in yin place. A hame, no' jist in barracks. In the Cameronians every day wis filled, frae the bugle in the mornin' tae nicht ... but here, Ah've nuthin tae dae but run wee errands tae pass ma time.'

'Yer leavin'.' She said it as a fact, her head down, concentrating on the dark, stony path.

'Ah've a mind tae sail tae New South Wales,' he blurted out, unable to gauge her reaction. 'There are nae joabs fur me here an' Ah'm nae a young man ony mair. Ah want tae see mair o' the world. Ah have the money tae tak up a scheme oot there tae buy some land, work it ... live frae ma ane endeavours.'

'New South Wales, is it?' she whispered, then cleared her throat. 'Sae, when are ye aff?'

Sam took a step forward and stopped in front of her, holding the lantern high.

'Come wi' me, Ruth? Connor and Ah wid baithe be honoured if ye wid join us.'

'Come wi' ye? Tae the ither side o' the world?'

'Aye.'

The seconds stretched out in silence: Sam was holding his breath.

'Whit d'ye say?' he prompted, gazing at her imploringly but seeing no hint of reaction. 'At least think on it?'

'Ye think Ah'll jist leave ma family an' run aff wi' ye ... like a common hussy?'

'No! We wid be merrit afore we left ...'

'Sae, yer askin' me tae marry ye?'

He swallowed; this was not going as smoothly as intended. He cursed his stupidity. Why hadn't he proposed before mentioning sailing south to New Holland?

'Will ye marry me, Ruth ?'

A smile broke the set line of her lips, shining in her eyes. 'Of course, Ah will! An' if ye wanted tae live in Timbuktu Ah wid gae wi' ye, an all!'

When he set out on his quest to find a wife, a mother for Connor, he had little idea of what sort of person he was trying to find. Ruth first appealed to him because of her sensible manner and a feeling of immediate familiarity, as if they already knew each other. From

161

the very beginning, they were comfortable sharing jokes and everyday problems. She did not have Roisin's coquettish beauty, nor her voluptuous figure, but her even features and fresh appearance held its own charm. While the other women in the village bored him quickly, he enjoyed being with Ruth; seeing the spark of a strong willed personality in her eyes, noticing endearing mannerisms. He also knew that on the days they did not meet, there was something missing.

Mindful of the children beside them, he did not kiss his bride to be. Instead, restraining himself with difficulty, he took her hand in his for the remainder of their walk.

Few words passed between them, their tightly entwined fingers saying it all.

***

Robert Owen was just drawing business to a close at the first meeting of the New Year with senior managers, when one of his oldest employees, Billy Raynes, was admitted to the room.

Sleet was smattering against the window, sliding into ridges of grey slush against the bottom half of the glass panes, reducing the already dim daylight seeping into the room. Four oil lamps and a collection of thick stubby candles fought a battle against the gloom, sparkling off the workman's wet jacket.

There was an air of anticipation and Owen glanced questioningly at the men seated around him, wondering if he had forgotten the reason for their visitor's attendance.

Shuffling his feet and staring down at his hands in embarrassment, Raynes declared he had been chosen to formally present the sincere thanks of the entire workforce to Mr Owen. They were grateful to him for reducing the working hours and giving them such good working conditions. Slowly deciphering his thick Scot's accent and mumbled words, Owen was touched by the thoughtful act.

'We wanted tae mark the first anniversary ... we've made a collection, Maister Owen, we wish tae gie ye a guid piece o' silver plate in appreciation o' all ye've done fur us.'

'That will not be necessary.' Owen shook his head, adding with a wide smile and kindly tone, 'My dear man, I am truly gratified by the thanks and your thoughtfulness but I cannot possibly accept a gift as well. Please, whatever has been subscribed, put it to a charitable cause.'

After a moment of awkwardness, Raynes conceded, doffing his cap and making his escape, relieved to have completed his task.

Owen barely felt the icy blasts when he rode back up the hill to Braxfield. Different emotions brought fleeting memories and concepts filtering in and out of his mind. The gesture of his employees was astonishing, pleasing, yet, in a strange bittersweet way, it also made him sad. He was only doing what all fair businessmen should do, nothing more. That he was considered exceptional was a cause of anguish.

He wished the antagonistic members of the Parliamentary Committee had witnessed the scene, perhaps then they could understand the importance of treating your employees well and with respect.

***

'Russians!' Cook pressed the middle of a sponge cake, nodding to herself when it sprang back. 'Grand Dukes ... in the name o' the wee man ... could we no' ha'e bin given mair time tae prepare?'

Miss Wilson was passing by the kitchen door, 'There's just the one Grand Duke,' she called, light heartedly. The house was in enough chaos without exaggerating the problem.

'Aye, but then there's a' his suite wi' him an' the Mistress telt me his Majesty's physician will be stayin' too. That's up tae a dozen ither folk tae be fed!'

'And beds to be made, although the grooms will be in the loft over the stables ...' the housekeeper was in a hurry, her mind set on preparations, 'but as they are all men, at least we do not need to change our maids' arrangements.'

Just the day before, a week into the new year, Anne Caroline received a hastily written note from Owen who was up in Glasgow. He told her to prepare for guests. Nicholas, Grand Duke of Russia, and his entourage were touring Scotland and had accepted his invitation to visit New Lanark and stay at Braxfield House.

163

Sending up a prayer for the Lord's assistance with her husband's spontaneity, Anne Caroline reached for the bell pull and informed Sheddon and Miss Wilson of the coming event.

'We have two days,' she said, quietly, 'I am sure you will be able to manage. Perhaps, we should all meet again in one hour, when we can discuss the finer points of their accommodation and meals.'

From that moment, Braxfield's corridors streamed with servants scurrying about their duties. Footmen ran up to town with lists of requirements to be delivered to the house, scullery maids washed and peeled mounds of vegetables. In the high ceilinged reception rooms, lamps were shone, every surface of wood polished, every piece of brass door furniture burnished.

Owen returned the evening before the Grand Duke's arrival and declared the house looked 'excellent' but perhaps, for royalty, the ornate brass chandeliers in the hallway should be lowered and fitted with candles.

Sheddon, quivering with unusual anxiety, oversaw the operation of ladders and footmen with a military precision of which the Duke of Wellington would have been proud. It was no easy task to arrange four dozen wax candles in perfect symmetry and also set them so soundly in their holders that they remained in place when hoisted back to the ceiling.

Miss Wilson and Anne Caroline chose the finest linens for his Majesty's bed. They decided, after shrewdly assessing the comforts and furniture of each room, that the largest of the guest apartments would be the most appropriate. Surely, royalty would appreciate the subtle oriental painted wallpaper, one of the more tasteful decorations installed by Lord Braxfield shortly before his death.

Adorned with gold braid and tassels, the turquoise silk drapes of the four poster bed were a little faded. Anne Caroline inspected the palest areas, recalling her aunt's remark that 'blue, like the sky on a winter morning in Scotland, rarely lived long before reverting to grey.'

As soon as the footmen returned the rugs from being thrashed outside and finished laying the fires, maids tripped up and down the back stairs preparing not only the Grand Duke's room but five others. The bare stone walls echoed alternately with curses and giggles among the pattering of boots and huffing and puffing as they tried not to bump into each other. Each was intent on their own work, carrying freshly ironed sheets scented with lavender water, newly plumped pillows and baskets of polishing cloths and brushes to remove any speck of dust before Miss Wilson's inspection.

On the day of their arrival, the exquisite china water jugs which Anne Caroline brought from Charlotte Street, were filled and placed beside their matching bowls.

On Owen's instructions, the village school band was dispatched to meet the Russians a mile or so downstream, at Clydesholm Bridge, and escort them up to Braxfield. When word came that the party were only minutes away, the candles on the grand chandelier were lit and the footmen scuttled back downstairs with the ladders.

Sheddon glided between the reception rooms, eyes searching for anything out of place, while upstairs, Miss Wilson rustled around her domain, closing the doors on each door as she passed it fit for guests.

'What a tae dae!' Cook grumbled, 'a week's wurk expected tae be done in a day! Ah ask ye?'

'Whit d'ye ken the Russians will be like?' Senga asked, 'Ah hope they're handsome an' romantic!'

'Whitiver they are,' Cook snapped, 'Ye'll no' be seein' them, lass. Miss Wilson an' Mr Sheddon will be keepin' an eye on ye all ... an' the back stairs!'

Robert Dale and his brother William were as excited as the servants and were thrilled to join their parents at the front entrance to welcome the royal party.

Nicholas, the Grand Duke of Russia, jumped nimbly from the carriage. He was an impressive figure in a dark blue uniform, lavishly embellished with gold braid. Tall and fair skinned with blonde curls swept severely back from his high forehead, his twenty years had not yet filled his slender frame but he carried himself with the confidence of a palace upbringing.

Behind him, the angular figure of Sir Alexander Crichton lowered himself to the ground, step by step. As physician to Tsar Alexander, Nicholas' elder brother, he was charged with accompanying the young Duke on his tour of the United Kingdom.

However, as a Scotsman who spoke fluent Russian, he also acted as translator.

Through Crichton, Owen introduced his family and welcomed the Russian Grand Duke to his home.

Robert Dale relaxed a little. The morning had been spent with their French tutor, Monsieur Lavasseur, feverishly rehearsing phrases and learning how to address a high ranking member of the Russian royal family. As his father knew only English, but the Duke was known to speak French, it had been suggested that Robert should help conduct conversations between the two: a daunting task.

Monsieur Lavasseur was adamant that the brother of a Tsar should be called Your Imperial Highness. With his expressive Gallic eyes and extravagant hand gestures, he impressed on the boy that it was 'de riguer'! However, it soon became clear from exchanges between the eight Russian officers accompanying him, and Sir Alexander Crichton, that Nicholas was simply referred to as 'you' or 'Monseigneur'.

After so much exhaustive preparation, Anne Caroline was relieved to withdraw to her little sitting room and leave the men in the drawing room with her husband. Her head was throbbing painfully and she felt nauseas so she pulled the bell cord for Miss Wilson.

'Is everything in order?' she asked when the housekeeper appeared. 'Are our Russian visitors settled?'

'Yes Madam, although,' Miss Wilson's eyebrows arched, 'I should inform you, a camp bed has been carried up to the Grand Duke's bedroom. A very ... *military* looking contraption of leather straps and metal legs. As far as I can ascertain, it is His Highness's preferred arrangement for sleeping.'

'A camp bed? Oh, may the Lord forgive my uncharitable thoughts! We have a goose-down mattress on that bed and the finest of woven cotton sheets! I hope he makes use of the pillows, at least, for the drawn thread work on the slips were my mother's own handiwork.'

'It would appear he has brought his own pillow, Madam,' Miss Wilson's nose wrinkled in disgust, 'stuffed with hay.'

'Hay!' Anne Caroline pressed a fingertip to her temple. 'We might as well have put him to sleep in the stables!' She squeezed her eyes shut, trying to blot out the window's light together with an overwhelming rush of discomfort and annoyance. 'Forgive me, my head is causing me great pain. Have Ramsay bring lemon tea to my room, I shall lie down for a while before the meal.'

In the haven of her bedroom with the curtains closed against the dying afternoon light, she lay propped up on the bolster sipping sweetened lemon balm and feverfew tea.

'Ye will feel the benefit very soon, Madam,' Ramsay soothed.

'The men were so loud and ... *large* in their uniforms.' Anne Caroline whispered, finding even the effort of speaking provoked pain. 'Although, I admit, the Duke is every bit as handsome as the newspapers declare.'

'The maids are all of a flutter and eager to catch a glimpse of any of the Russian gentlemen.' She saw the corners of her mistress's lips twitch. 'Ye can rest assured Miss Wilson will make sure there is no unseemly behaviour.'

By the time Owen came up to their room to change, he found his wife sitting by her dressing table, her maid pinning up her hair.

'I hope our young royal is finding Braxfield comfortable?' she asked, smiling to give her voice a lightness she hoped would disguise the still nagging headache.

'Our Russian friends are effusive in their thanks for our hospitality, my dear. It is a shame there are no ladies in the party, but I am sure you will be well entertained at the dinner table. Sir Alexander is an amiable man and a brilliant linguist.' He paused at the door to his dressing room, where Murdoch waited with his evening wear. 'He was born in Edinburgh, you know, but has been devoted to the Tsar and the Dowager Empress these last dozen years. He is a most interesting and well travelled man.'

Anne Caroline watched the reflection of his animated face in the mirror: she could feel his excitement. Nothing must detract from this special evening. Certainly not any concerns he might have for her physical discomfort if she mentioned she was unwell.

It was a triumph for his cause to have men of such status taking an interest in New Lanark. Thousands of people may have met the Grand Duke on his tours, but that number dwindled to just a few dozen individuals who could claim to have hosted the royal party in their own home.

The formal dinner passed remarkably easily and Anne Caroline enjoyed watching Robert Dale and William contributing to the topics of conversation. Sir Alexander deftly translated questions and answers, his deep set eyes glinting in the candlelight whilst leaning towards the children with avuncular interest. He was the oldest of the group by many years, cutting his food into tiny morsels for lack of teeth, but sampling most of the dishes on the table.

Nicholas, by contrast, picked at the plainest food and scarcely touched the wine. He leaned back in his chair, tense yet respectful, and spoke a great deal, but mainly in his mother tongue of Russian or falling into French from time to time.

'The Grand Duke is very charming,' Anne Caroline commented when they retired to bed later that evening.

Owen blew out the candle on the night stand, leaving the room bathed in dim red firelight.

'He is enjoying his stay with us, if we are to believe Sir Alexander.' He reached for the silk coverlet draped across the foot of the mattress, pulling it up over the blankets and carefully folding over the top of the sheet to cover the icy material. 'It is cold tonight but I daresay it becomes much colder in Russia. And you are feeling better now, my dear?'

She was surprised, 'Yes, although I had hoped it was not obvious?'

'Perhaps not to others, but I know you well.' He kissed her on the lips, taking hold of her hand and nestling into the warmth. 'You are the perfect hostess.'

His eyes were closed, the fan of his lashes dark against his cheek. She looked fondly on his face, just inches from her own. In the whirl of activity which now seemed to dictate their lives, these precious, quiet moments were to be savoured. His breathing became slow, lips parting fractionally as she felt the grip of his fingers loosen with the onset of sleep.

'I am very proud of you, my darling,' she whispered, 'and my father would have been so proud of you.'

She turned on her back, gazing up at the fire's idling shadows moving on the ceiling.

'Holy Father, I beseech thee,' she prayed, silently, 'keep this fine man safe and in good health. Forgive him for not accepting Your word as the Truth, for in his every action, does he not carry out his duties in the world kindly and in a Christian manner? You, my Lord, are all knowing. You see how he lives his life in unswerving dedication to improve the lot of his fellow man. Oh, I pray most fervently for him to follow the scriptures and accept You into his heart. You are the Light and the Hope and the Glory, I am your servant, Lord. Amen.'

***

'Ye'll ne'er guess whit Ah've seen?' Gavin, the boot boy, declared to the servants very early the next morning.

'We have no time for games, Gavin,' Sheddon reprimanded, stalking past him towards his office.

'Yin o' the Duke's Russians slept oot in the landin' ... all nicht! He wis lying across the doorway! Ah saw him last thing at nicht when Ah picked up the boots an' he wis still there when Ah took them back ... the noo!'

Alice was tying her apron strings, an eye on the clock.

'Did he see ye?' she asked, 'or wis he asleep?'

'Wis it the yin wi' the dark hair an' moustache?' Senga wiped the back of her hand across her brow, pretending to swoon. 'He's braw! sae tall an' handsome ...'

'Aye, he saw me!' Gavin cried, 'pit his haun oan his pistol an' watched me wi' sich threatenin' eyes Ah fair ran doon the stairs. It wis the yin wi' a muckle neb ... the auld yin.'

Cook tut-tutted, dipping her fingers in a bowl of water and sprinkling drips across the range, pleased to see them hissing and frizzling to nothing: the oven would be up to heat.

'Auld yin,' she mumbled, 'there's not yin o' those gents o'er thirty years; auld yin! Ah'll gie ye auld.'

Sheddon was intrigued by Gavin's tale and found an opportunity before the men took breakfast to ask Dr Crichton if anything was amiss with the officers' bedroom arrangements.

'Oh, do not be alarmed, I assure you, they are perfectly comfortable.' The physician dropped his voice, 'it is their custom to protect the Grand Duke, one of them always guards his bedroom door when he sleeps.'

Before taking his guests down to the cotton mills, Owen invited Nicholas and Sir Alexander into his study. He had the ear of a very influential man and was determined to make use of it to spread his vision of a New Society and his new Plan.

His report, his Plan, as he was calling it, was to aid the plight of the unemployed and the manufacturing poor, as requested the previous summer in London. He had mentioned it briefly in his opening speech at the Institute a year before and the details were nearing completion. Its inspiration was clear and obvious: New Lanark.

He proposed the government should set aside areas of land and provide materials for the poor to create their own homes. Thus producing villages, complete with schools, agricultural land and some form of manufacturing concern to generate goods for the open market. After the initial capital costs they would be sustainable, both financially and in feeding and educating themselves. The Plan sat perfectly with his New System and he was exceedingly pleased with it.

Patiently, Sir Alexander translated Owen's views and Nicholas's comments and questions. It was a deep, intellectual discussion, reaching far beyond the idea of self sufficient villages and ensuring the giant modern factories were forced to provide healthier conditions for their workforce. Nicholas was a sharp witted man and grasped Owen's principles with youthful enthusiasm.

He appeared to understand the need for taking care of the rising generation and providing conditions to form their characters through kindness and a solid education. Yes, he agreed, the infants of today were the future! There must be an end to the never ending cycle of poverty and crime caused by intolerance and lack of respect as well as unemployment due to their inability to read or write.

How much better it would be to create an able, healthy population who would naturally transfer their rational behaviour to forthcoming generations.

Nicholas particularly wanted to know the role of the Church in these plans. He listened intently as Crichton relayed Owen's firmly held opinions that spiritual beliefs were a matter for the individual and respect should be shown for all religions.

For over two hours the study door remained closed and on hearing it open, the Russian officers jumped up from their games of cards and backgammon in the drawing room and hurried to the hall.

'Come, gentlemen!' Owen swirled his cape around his shoulders, plucking his hat from Sheddon's hands. 'I wish to show you that I do not speak in vain of changing the wicked ways of the world. You will see with your own eyes how profitable manufacturing *and* providing a good life for the lower classes can be combined for their mutual benefit. If it can be done here, it can be done anywhere.'

Robert Dale was included in the party trooping down Braxfield's drive beneath the bare, arching branches of mid-winter beech trees. Having enjoyed his company the previous evening, Nicholas chose to walk beside the boy.

Speaking in French with descriptive, miming gestures to fill any gaps in understanding, Robert answered the Duke's queries on which subjects he enjoyed studying with his various tutors. As they passed the gate house, pausing to admire early snowdrops, and joined the steep cobbled road down to the village, the view was suddenly filled by the great stone structures of the mills.

The conversation turned to the business of spinning cotton.

'How much cotton do you produce a day?' Nicholas asked in French.

By chance, just the week before, Robert calculated they spun three hundred and sixty thousand miles of thread per week, so he quickly deduced how much was spun in a day.

Without pausing, he immediately replied, 'Autant de fil de cotton qu'il faut pour entourer deux fois et demi le monde.'

Walking behind him with Owen, Sir Alexander chuckled at the surprising answer.

'How well your son illustrates the enormous production of your factory! Two and a half times around the world ... each day! Well I never ...'

Taking them through the mills, the Russians exclaimed at the light work rooms and how clean the streets and storerooms were kept but it was the Institute which drew the most admiration.

As soon as they entered, a dozen or so small barefoot children scampered up to Owen, catching at his hand and excitedly showing their drawings.

Surprised looks passed between Nicholas and his party when Owen gave his attention to the paupers and answered their childish questions with as much thought as he gave the Grand Duke. This happened often, as they paused to observe each area of the work tables in the two large upper rooms, the pupils and the mill owner engaging in conversation as easily as if they were the same social status. For the Russians, this was as novel as the classrooms themselves or the simple but effective heating system of hot, steam filled pipes running up the height of the building.

The winter day was darkening into dusk when they emerged from watching a dancing display but Nicholas noticed the Village Shop and was keen to see what goods were sold.

Oil lamps and candles in wall sconces were casting a cheerful light around the well stocked store, a steel stove warming the air. The foreigners were greeted by comforting aromas of jute sacks, leather goods, trays of baking and the pine saw-dust sprinkled liberally on the floor. Mr Grant and Mr Dudley immediately stepped forward, doffing their top hats and smoothing their long white aprons, their faces wreathed in welcoming smiles.

'The supply of meat, grain and vegetables comes directly by special arrangement with local farmers,' Robert Owen guided his visitors around the displays, 'the rest of the country, as you may have observed on your travels, is suffering sorely from lack of adequate food, but, here there is plenty ... and of a high quality.'

'By Gad!' Sir Alexander clasped his hands behind his back, poking his head forward to peer at an array of pots, pans, brushes and blocks of wrapped soap. 'There is everything here! Toasting forks, pastries ... meat, by jove!'

He strolled through to the cooler back room where a housewife was watching the butcher weigh out a pound of shoulder steak.

'The company buys the goods at trade price,' Owen continued, pleased with the men's reaction, 'and can provide the villagers with all they need for their families to eat well and live in comfort. In this way, the prices can be considerably lower than in the market town up the hill and, gentlemen, all profits go towards the running of the school.'

Sarah was spellbound on seeing the officers swarm up the stairs and browse the haberdashery.

The arrival of the Russians at Braxfield House was common knowledge, the village gossips believing the striking young nobleman at the centre of the party was His Imperial Majesty, the Tsar.

With booming voices, a lively debate took place in rapid Russian. Sir Alexander eventually made it up the steps to the second floor and wandered between the men as they picked up buttons, lengths of ribbon, braid and fine quality cotton, carrying them to the lamps for closer inspection.

Nicholas was newly betrothed to Princess Charlotte of Prussia and it soon became clear that a parcel of New Lanark goods was to be sent to her as a gift.

It was nearly dark by the time they left the village and on turning the last corner of the driveway the house came into view showing its lower windows lit up from the grand chandeliers.

Robert Dale smiled to himself. That morning, he overheard a footman cursing his father's instructions to light so many candles at exactly four o'clock. On entering the hallway he stole a glance towards the grandfather clock's familiar enamel face: a quarter past the hour of four.

Anne Caroline was in the drawing room with the younger children; Jane self consciously playing the piano with David turning the pages of her music.

With a rush of excited Russian words, Nicholas bowed to his hostess with a flourish.

'He says this is a delightful scene!' Sir Alexander explained, taking a seat by the fire, 'and indeed it is.'

Sheddon took up a stance beside the open double doors to the hallway, ushering Alice and Senga into the room with trays bearing silver jugs of hot chocolate, the Owens' finest porcelain cups and dainty bowls of almonds and sultanas.

To Anne Caroline, all her children were beautiful but it was clear to even a casual acquaintance that David was an especially attractive child. The boy's glossy pale gold hair, ivory skin and dark fringed eyes caught Nicholas' attention. Singling him out, he showed off his few words of English, entertained him with card tricks and even bounced him on his knees.

Sir Alexander looked on, amused, 'The Duke says he would like to adopt your son! He would give him every advantage in the Russian Court.'

Anne Caroline's polite laugh died in her throat when she realised this was not being suggested in jest.

Setting a smile on her lips, she followed the discussion, translated by Sir Alexander, between her husband and the earnestly forceful Russian. The notion was inspired by a report which Nicholas read while in London a few weeks before. It declared the current state of Britain to be overcrowded, starving and devoid of opportunity.

'It is a generous offer,' Owen said quietly, a sympathetic expression lifting his brows. 'It is true the United Kingdom is a small country compared to the wild expanses of Russia, and also true to say much of our population is unemployed and in need of housing and food. However, this will pass. We are suffering the effects of being at war for too long and, like most of Europe, we have been experiencing poor harvests in the last year or so. My own family, thank you, Sir, are well provided for and David, like my other children, will grow to take up whatever profession he desires.'

Although Nicholas pursued his wish to take David away with him, he eventually relented, extending his invitation for a life in Russia to all and any of the residents of Scotland who would wish to travel.

Anne Caroline relaxed. Sometimes, her husband's spontaneous decisions gave her cause for alarm. The next morning, however, Owen did succeed in shocking both his family and the servants.

It was sparked by a chance remark at dinner the evening before when one of Nicholas' officers passed him a fork and pointed to the double headed eagle etched on the handle.

'The Owen inscription is the same as the Grand Duke's,' Sir Alexander told the table, 'A fine coincidence!'

To Sheddon's astonishment, his master called for the velvet lined boxes of the dessert service, comprising sixteen settings of silver knives and forks, to be wrapped as a gift for the Russian.

Robert Dale and his mother exchanged horrified glances when the boxes were presented in the hallway amid the formal farewells.

While standing at the front door waving to the departing carriages, Anne Caroline leaned close to her husband.

'I have no quarrel with giving possessions away to those who are in need or would appreciate them,' she kept her voice low, as much for the sake of the bewildered butler overhearing as for anyone else. 'But, *really*, my dear, silverware to the Grand Duke? It will mean no more to him than a handkerchief would to you.'

***

Sam and Ruth's betrothal was celebrated by both the Scott family and the Pattersons. Rosie liked her future sister in law from their first days of working together in the mill, her only concern being Ruth's comparative youth.

'Ah dinnae want tae pry,' she confided in Sarah one Sunday, walking up to Church. 'But the lassie is some years younger than me an' Sam's alis seemed much aulder, oor big brither. Ye ken whit Ah mean?'

'She's happy, Rosie! They baith are. Whit dis a few ...'

'A dozen or mair!'

'... years b'tween them matter if they love yin anither?'

'Weel, she's a lot tae tak oan. Sailin' all that way, thousands o' miles, Sam telt me. They'll be oan the ship fer months! May the Lord help her, Ah hope she kens whit she's daen.'

Rosie enjoyed her Sundays. Nowadays, they usually attended the village services, but on fine days or if there was a special occasion, they made the steep walk up to town. It was a chance to dress in her prettiest clothes, ready to meet with Gerry's sisters and their families.

His beaver hat accentuating his tall, gangling frame, Gerry walked ahead of Rosie and Sarah, with Andrew Dudley at his side. Both were men of few words and content to leave the sharing of the week's news to the females in the party.

On overhearing Sam's name, Dudley asked, 'When's your brother in law tae leave these shores?'

Gerry shrugged. 'Efter he's married, Ah wid hazard. The banns ha'e been read, but he's no' set a date.'

Sarah and Rosie glanced at each other questioningly.

175

'Ah asked Sam, a few days back,' Rosie said, 'an' he widnae be drawn, like he wis waiting fer sumat.'

'Ye noticed tae? Ah thocht that. He's haudin' sumat back.'

Rosie nodded, the brim of her bonnet bouncing. 'An' Joe's awfy doon in the mooth, an' all.'

'D'ye think Sam's havin' second thoughts?'

'Aboot Ruth?'

'Nah! Aboot emigratin'? He an' Joe ha'e bin gettin' alang grand sae mibbee they baith wish Sam wid settle doon here, in Lanark.'

'An' there's anither thing?' Rosie wondered, 'When's Joe gaun tae finish tha' big hoose o' his?'

Joe was wondering the same thing.

On being introduced to Francis Reynolds, Ewing's lawyer, Joe instructed him to embark on the necessary steps to recover the money due for the completion of Baxter's house. Since then, several letters had been exchanged with Baxter's solicitor but there was still no sign of the payment.

Then they were informed Mr Baxter was in America and there was some difficulty in communicating with him. Reynolds dug deeper. It slowly became clear that Mr Baxter was considering staying permanently on the other side of the Atlantic Ocean where he was expanding his cotton plantations.

Joe was pacing back and forth in Tam's small front parlour which now held all the paperwork for Scott & Sons.

'Sae much fur no' needing tae gae tae the Courts!' Joe's face was dark with fury. 'Noo the man's running frae his debts!'

'He's a rich man.' Tam tried to appease his friend. 'He has the money ...'

'Aye, he has *my* money an' all!' Joe spun round on his heel, 'Why did he want tae build a hoose in Lanark if he wis planning tae live o'er seas?'

Tam pushed back his chair and crossed his legs. Thin sunlight fell across his face, accentuating lines around his eyes and the growing sheen of silver in his close cropped curls.

'Ah dinnae ken, Joe,' he said solemnly. 'But, ye could be daen wi' tha' money. Donnie's men will be feenished up at Jerviswood in twa weeks an' Davey's jist aboot done oot at Cartland. There's gie few new orders oan the books.'

176

'Ah thocht the end o' the war wid see an upturn in building,' Joe continued to walk from window to fireplace and back again, his mind churning with worries. 'There wis a sudden rush o' wurk, bu' noo ... the country's plungin' back in tae a deeper depression.'

'Aye, it's the same auld story, the rich get richer an' the poor get poorer. See all that trouble at the back o' the year, rioting an' the like at Spa Fields? Folk takin' up arms,' he shook his head, 'an' last week there wis wurd o' whit they're callin' the Blanketeers, weavers doon in Manchester tryin' tae walk tae London tae demand changes sae we can all vote an' mak the country fairer for workin' people. Och, the rich ha'e ne'er had it sae guid but, whit aboot the men in the middle, you an' me, the ordinary folk jist tryin' tae get by?'

Joe stopped beside the misted window.

Through the clearer tracks of running condensation, he noticed a mother and her young daughter showing knives and a scythe to Old Calib, the blade sharpener. The figures huddling beside the tool laden handcart were making a close inspection of the blunt cutting edges. With smiles, a deal was struck and the woman reached into the drawstring bag swinging at her side and pulled out the pennies to pay.

'Damn Baxter!' Joe exploded. 'If a man gi'es a service, ye pay him! That's a fine hoose Ah've built, Ah'm makin' nae apology fur demanding whit Ah'm owed. Ah'll tak the blasted man tae Court an' win!'

'Gaun yersel'!'

Joe picked his hat off the window seat, the only clear space in the room. 'Ah'm aff tae see Reynolds,' he opened the door, letting in the loud rasping of Calib's grinder. 'We dinnae see ye up at the hoose these days, Tam. Come up an' eat wi' us t'morra? Fiona wis eskin' efter ye, sayin' how guid ye are tae ha'e the lads stayin' here.'

'Ah like the company an' they gi'e me a few bob each week sae it's a fine arrangement.'

'Ye'll come?'

'Dinnae tak this the wrang way, Joe, but Ah'd rather no'.'

'It's Sam being there, isn't it? Ye think he'll want tae talk aboot the war? Weel, ha'e nae fear o' that fur he's as closed on the subject as you.'

177

Tam's eyes remained downcast, his fingers picking at a fleck of dried mud on his trousers.

'Guid luck wi' the lawyer.'

Reynolds was closeted in his stuffy little office overlooking the Bloomgate and his clerk offered Joe a chair, mumbling between coughs and sniffs that he would be 'seen directly'. The church bells tolled the quarter hour and then the half hour before Reynolds came out, ushering a red-faced man and a stick thin woman, presumably the wife, out of the main door.

'My apologies, Mr Scott.' Reynolds took a deep breath. These days there was a rich supply of depressing cases to handle: bankruptcy, sudden deaths, evictions, and now a builder who was being taken for a ride by a wealthy merchant. He shook Joe's hand. 'Come! I will see you now.'

They went over the necessary documents required to prosecute Baxter, one being a certificate from a person of authority stating the house was, in fact, completed and fit for habitation.

'Or,' Reynolds stated, 'the first thing Baxter will say is that he has not paid you because the job is not done.'

Joe was on good terms with the architect who helped with the original plans, a fellow brother at the Lodge, so he assured his lawyer that this would not be a problem.

It was a relief to leave the stagnant air of the office. Its dust, ink stained paper and a cloying aroma of stale tobacco smoke and cologne were strong in his nostrils, causing him to sneeze, his eyes to water. Feeling more refreshed with every step, he headed straight home. He must roll up his sleeves and throw his energy into finding work.

He was in the back scullery, pulling a heavy jute jerkin over his head when he heard the front door open.

It was Sam.

'How's Cal's patch, the day?' Joe asked.

'Fair tae middling. The seeds are in an' it's in the Lord's hands noo. We can pray it's better than last year.' Sam glanced around the obviously empty room. 'Are we alone, Joe?'

'Aye.'

'Ah've bin seein' ye worryin' aboot yon hoose, an' while ma hauns are kept busy wi' chores, ma mind is searchin' fur a remedy.'

'It's taken care of, or should be in a week or so. Ah'm jist hame frae seeing the law man. We're takin' Baxter tae Court.'

Sam rubbed at the stubble on his chin. 'It's a shame it's come tae that.'

'Did ye ha'e anither solution? Tell me?'

'Ah wis gaun tae loan ye the money tae feenish yer hoose.'

Joe stared at him, incredulous. 'Whit? It's hunners o' pounds, man!'

'Aye. Ah ha'e the money an' Ah ken ye'll piy me back.'

'Naw! Ah'm fair made up wi' ye offering, but ... Ah could nae tak it.'

'Fur months, Ah've bin livin' under yer roof fur free.'

'Ye dae a lot fur us ... onyway, yer ma brither, fur Christ's sake!'

'An' Fiona and yourself? D'ye no' think ye dae a lot fur me?' Sam was defiant. 'If it wid help, tak the money.'

Joe sat down on a bench by the table and Sam took the chair opposite.

'Joe, life's too short tae pit up wi' holdin' aff yer dreams fur the want o' some pounds, pounds *Ah* can gie ye. Ah want tae see ye in that hoose afore Ruth an' Ah sail tae New South Wales.'

'Ye'll ha'e need o' every penny fur stairtin' a new life... an' Ruth an' Connor tae think on.'

'The offer's there. We'll see whit the Court says an' if Baxter piys oot ... Ah mean it, Joe, ye deserve tae be in yon hoose, if no' fur yersel' then fur Fiona and the weans.'

Joe acknowledged it as a generous offer, knowing he would never accept it but not wishing to argue.

'No' a wurd tae Fiona, mind.' Joe told him, sternly, standing up to end the conversation. 'Ah've telt Tam the same. She's content at the school room an' has enough tae vex her wi' Sionaidh's troubles.'

There was a dusting of snow on the hills of Clydesdale on the day Joe left the cottage to attend the Tolbooth. He left Bluey in the stable and walked the short distance, feeling the benefit of his woollen winter vest beneath his thickest shirt, a padded waistcoat and calf length cape.

The old council building at the bottom of the hill, near St Nicholas Church, was home to the Sheriff Court. The county jail was attached to the back of it allowing justice to be served out rapidly.

Reynolds was putting several matters before the Sheriff that day and was standing outside the Tolbooth, impatiently rising up and down on his toes, peering into the passing crowd to intercept his clients. Seeing Joe, he clumsily shook his hand, his arms being filled with a cluster of beribboned paper rolls, and sent him inside with instructions to climb the stairs to the second floor and take a seat at the back of the room.

In his wig and gown, the Sheriff commanded the anxious assembly with a steely tone and beady eyes: in this crowded, smelly room he was God.

After nearly an hour, Joe's case was put forward. Remarks were passed between Reynolds and the Sheriff, another lawyer stepping forward to join in and then, a gruff declaration from the bench and it was on to the next matter.

'Is that it?' Joe murmured to himself, regretting his thick clothes in the oppressive heat of densely packed, nervous bodies.

Reynolds caught his eye and gestured to the door.

'Whit happened?' Joe asked, descending the narrow staircase, thankful for a sudden draught of icy fresh air.

'Baxter will receive a Court order to pay within ten days.'

'And if he doesn't?'

'He'll be arrested. However, his representative made the Sheriff aware of Baxter's standing as a man of considerable wealth. In these cases, even the whiff of the Debtors prison usually suffices.'

'Why has he no' jist paid me? That's whit Ah cannae unnerstaun, Mr Reynolds.'

'It may be an oversight ... or he has his eyes set on a future in the Americas and thinks he can walk away?'

'But the hoose? Whit's tae happen tae it?'

Reynolds spied his next client limping towards them across the bustling street.

'We will have to wait and see, Mr Scott.' He revealed uneven yellow teeth as a token smile. 'Pray excuse me, I shall inform you immediately of any news and I trust you will do likewise should you receive word directly. Good day, Mr Scott!'

***

In the weeks following the Russians' visit, Anne Caroline saw little of her husband. However, unless he was in Glasgow, he made a point of joining the family for the main meal of the day and catching up with domestic matters. Anne, a composed thirteen year old, and Jane, just a year younger, were now included at the table with their elder brothers. Conversation flowed freely from Anne's excitement at discovering the works of a new poet, to Robert and William's descriptions of a neighbour's horse.

Despite his mind being taken up with business or political matters, Owen paid close attention to all the childish banter: good humoured, encouraging.

Then, as soon as Anne Caroline gave the prayer of thanks at the end of the meal, he would retreat to his study.

One of the reasons for his immersion in work was the production of his Plan. This Plan, he declared in a covering letter to the Archbishop's Committee, would alleviate the distress caused by displacement of human labour by machinery. In one stroke, it would provide employment and housing and the perfect environment to progress his New System.

Late one evening, Owen laid down his quill and sat back, clasped his hands behind his head and allowed himself a luxurious yawn. It was done.

He took a moment to enjoy the accomplishment, snuffing out the bright candles on his desk to enjoy the softer glow from coals in the hearth.

For too long, the people of Britain expected their problems and survival to be resolved by either Parliament or God. It was time to give them the tools, education and land to place their destiny in their own hands.

The Plan was received by the Archbishop's office but it was suggested that it might be useful to present it direct to Westminster. A flurry of correspondence revealed Henry Brougham to be a member of a Select Committee taking evidence on improving the plight of the unemployed poor. Sturges Bourne was the chairman of the Committee but as Owen could not recollect ever having met the man, he asked Brougham to introduce them, so he could personally present his Plan to the committee.

'You are leaving for London? So soon?' Anne Caroline exclaimed. 'I hear the roads are barely opened from snow in the Border country. Can you not postpone your journey?'

'There is no time to be lost. I have dispatched the Plan to be printed and drawn up a sketch of how the Villages of Unity and Mutual Cooperation will look when they are built. An artist is being engaged to produce the finished drawing. If I can persuade these gentlemen, then there is every possibility we can raise the funds required to put it into practice.'

They were sitting together in the drawing room, Jane and Anne taking turns to play the piano at the other end of the room.

'Am I to know your Plan?' Anne Caroline asked, laying aside her Bible.

'Forgive me, my dear! It has been in my head for so long I forget it has not been spoken!' he grinned at her, leaning forward, his face bright with satisfaction. 'It is not entirely *my* Plan, there have been several, like Mr Bellers and Mr Spence, who put this system forward before. I do not take the credit for the idea but I believe I have added to it and shall do all I can to make it a reality.'

'And it is?' she was smiling, a tender light in her eyes. 'Dear Robert, you seem to forget I cannot read your mind!'

'Basically, I am proposing tracts of land to be set aside for the building of small, self-sustaining communities: villages. These would be physically built and then lived in by the currently unemployed; the dangerously rebellious men who are suffering such distress at present. It would raise their morale and fill their minds and hearts with hope! They would be more than willing to work hard in the knowledge they were providing their *own* homes, schools and workshops. There would be a great deal for the womenfolk to do, providing food and caring for the children as well as tending the crops, milking, cheese-making and so forth.

'Each village would comprise sufficient land to support their population. In this way, with the aid of some cattle and other livestock, perhaps a small mill or factory producing marketable goods, the community would be completely self reliant.'

'It sounds very idyllic, but where would these 'villages' be built?'

'Anywhere and everywhere! This system works! I have read a great deal about the Moravian settlements, the Shakers and most recently of Harmonie, a Rappite community in Indiana in America.'

'It is also like New Lanark.'

'Exactly! I can speak from experience and show the benefits of a close knit, productive village where the residents work in cooperation to bring about a pleasurable life for *all* the inhabitants. Have we been affected by the distress of famine? No! Of riots and violence? No! Crime and drunkenness? No! Why? Because the New Lanark residents have recourse to committees of their own peers, their housing is inspected by their own neighbours, friends ... maybe even family members. It is essential to have at the root of it all my system for embracing principles of kindness and tolerance, especially religious tolerance. Only by raising the new generation in a rational society can we truly bring peace and happiness.'

Energised by the possibilities of his Plan, Owen leapt to his feet.

'The benefits are multiple!' he enthused. 'Why should any man, woman or child be rendered homeless and be left to beg on the street when they could be part of their own supportive community?'

'Surely that would be very expensive, dear. I know little of these things but these villages must require money and, as you say, these people are destitute.'

'I have made account of this. Either Parishes would offer their public land for use or subscriptions would be sought to purchase suitable land. The government, of course, could supply much of the funding for in the long run providing these villages would take away virtually all need for Poor Relief.'

If Anne Caroline was less than happy about Owen leaving, Murdoch was delighted. With a spring in his step, he strode around the servant halls and bounded up and down the back stairs preparing the trunks for London.

He would see Emily again. Walker's little house maid was rarely far from his thoughts and he was warmed by the knowledge she returned his feelings. On this trip, he would ask her to marry him!

Their stay in London was unusually short. Less than three weeks later, Owen and Murdoch returned. The manservant was bubbling with pleasure. There were certain practicalities to be overcome but Emily had, very affectionately, consented to be his wife.

183

On the other hand, Owen was quietly annoyed; maddened at wasting a great deal of time away from the mills.

Having made the arduous journey south to show his Plan to the Committee, he was informed his presence was not required and the scheme would be put forward to the committee solely by Brougham.

Frustrated, Owen spent his days waiting anxiously for their considered opinion, only to be told they would not be recommending it to be taken any further.

'Have no fear,' William Allen encouraged in his quick witted manner. 'Publicising your Plan through Government was only one option, sometimes it is best to go direct to the people! After all, it is for their benefit, let them know your work on their behalf ... show them they are not forgotten. I shall see to it that your Plan, in whole, is published in my own paper, the *Philanthropist.*'

The *Times* and *Morning Post* picked up the story and followed suit, also allowing generous column space for Owen's further letters vindicating his proposals.

The editors' leaders for the articles and public replies were encouragingly supportive, going a small way to soothing Owen's initial feeling of rejection.

Chapter Ten

"Religion is what keeps the poor from murdering the rich" Napoleon

April brought sunshine, sending rainbows arching through heavy showers, clouds building up and then dissipating into fragments, their shadows racing across Clydesdale. The swallows returned early to repair their nests and the same pair of ospreys which Cal had taken such pleasure in watching, were reunited again after their long solo migrations from the south.

The terrible, murky weather of the previous year seemed to be easing away from England. Across Europe there were reports of pastures finally showing growth, buds forming on fruit trees and the longed for seasonal rise in temperature.

For many, the recovery was too late.

In France, Germany, Switzerland and many other stricken northern countries, cities were swamped by thousands of refugees from the barren countryside. Makeshift camps huddled near soup kitchens, families in abject poverty were densely packed into squalid conditions, cheek by jowl with vagrants and discharged soldiers.

Smallpox and measles raged amongst them and for those lucky to escape those fevers, the equally virulent influenza and typhus picked off even the most robust.

Mr McGibbon, so long the doctor at New Lanark, took up an opportunity to travel abroad in an effort to address the suffering in Europe. His place was taken by a middle aged, very experienced medical man, William Gibson. Owen was pleased with this new appointment. McGibbon was a hard act to follow and yet within a week or so, the villagers were treating Gibson with open admiration.

One of the reasons for this fast acceptance of a stranger into their midst was the man's own personable character. The other was his immediate desire to inoculate the population against smallpox. Owen was wary of forcing such an innovation on the community, he did not wish to intrude further into their family lives than he did already. This was a decision for them to take individually, but he decided to give them the facts and make Jenner's procedure available at the expense of the company. Then, it was up to them to choose.

Anne Caroline found any mention of the dangerous illness ignited distressing memories. It was a subject she could hardly bear to discuss, physically wincing at the sound of the name.

The topic of affecting a program of vaccinations arose when Mr Gibson dined at Braxfield House. It was only a few days after discussing with Owen the considerable threat an outbreak of smallpox could make to New Lanark.

'I must confess,' Anne Caroline laid down her spoon, signalling for the soup course to be cleared, 'I know little of what is entailed nor of Mr Jenner.'

Gibson was keen to explain. 'There is nothing to be feared of the procedure. It has been carried out thousands of times and was brought to Britain from Istanbul where it is taken up extensively. There has always been a long held belief that milk maids who had contracted cowpox did not fall victim to small pox, or at least, not so severely. Anyway, this was seized upon by Frewster, of course, although, I'm afraid to say that few paid any attention to him, poor fellow. Edward Jenner, on the other hand, put the thing to test and introduced the practice of inserting a small amount of pus taken from the cow pox blisters ...'

Anne Caroline darted a sickened look to her husband who broke in to the doctor's words, 'Perhaps, my wife does not require the physical details?'

'Oh, my dear lady, excuse me! Of course ... and at the table! Where are my manners?' He smiled, repentantly. 'Suffice to say, that is why Mr Jenner calls the process vaccination.' He nodded encouragingly towards his hosts. 'From the Latin, vacca, in honour of the cow!'

Sheddon and a footman were laying dishes of steamed salmon, duck in a honey sauce and crispy roast lamb cutlets down the centre of the table and Anne Caroline was distinctly relieved there was no flesh from cattle.

'The results are mixed,' her husband explained, 'but there have been clear successes. Those who have been vaccinated appear to stand a better chance of recovery.'

'You say mixed results?'

186

'Unfortunately, a few vaccinated patients have died from the fever,' Gibson spoke kindly, remembering too late of Owen warning him of his hostess's tragic childhood, 'but I am reliably informed that those patients were weakened already, suffering from chronic conditions before contracting the disease.'

'Surely,' Owen cried, 'it is better than having no defence at all?'

'Jenner's motivation was and still is, to relieve the suffering and reduce the mortality caused by the pox.'

'Have you met Mr Jenner?' Anne Caroline asked.

'No, madam, I have not had that privilege. He lives in the south of England, in Gloucestershire. Although, I believe he studied medicine up here, at St Andrews University. Sadly, our paths have not crossed but I have read every word he's written!'

'Do I understand correctly that he is still a practicing doctor in his own home town?' Owen took a sip of claret, a present from a visiting London dignitry.

'Yes, he prefers to live at Berkeley with his family but has been offered other situations, I am sure. He is highly regarded nowadays. It must be said that before he proved his point, his ideas were spuriously discarded, ridiculed by the Church.'

Owen raised his eyebrows, 'As is normal practice when one tries to present something new.'

Anne Caroline was quiet for a long time, then enquired softly, 'Does Mr Jenner trust this *vaccination* to be carried out on his own flesh and blood?'

'Yes, he does.' The creases of a smile disappeared from Gibson's cheeks. 'He inoculated all his children and his wife against smallpox, with success. Tragically, his wife died just a year or so ago, from tuberculosis and ... his eldest son, from the same disease.'

'May God grant them eternal peace,' Anne Caroline murmured with empathy. 'Poor man ...'

Another long pause followed. Gibson took a spoonful from each dish laid out on the table, cursing himself for turning the tone of the evening to one of death.

Owen chose salmon and a few potatoes, flattening the fish with his fork to ensure there were no bones before placing it tentatively in his mouth: he could not abide the thought of a bone sticking in his throat.

Watching surreptitiously, he could see minute changes in his wife's expression, a deepening frown around her eyes, blinking with concentration. Once or twice, her tongue moistening her lips as if about to speak, then, thinking better of it, she would attend to her plate. He was about to break the silence when she reached for her glass of wine. Toying with the slim crystal stem, she met his gaze for a second before pointedly addressing the doctor.

'It is a matter close to my heart, Mr Gibson, I ask you to pardon my rudeness and apparent self absorption. It is not that, I assure you. My dearest wish is to protect my children, as it must be for every parent and dread of small pox has no rival.' She composed herself, as if shaking away a nightmare. 'If God has seen fit to provide the means to fight this evil, I must pray in gratitude for His guidance. Let ourselves and our children stand up to the cause of suffering and untimely death and take the inoculation ... and offer it to the villagers.'

Owen was relieved by her words. Only the previous day he was given the same argument of God's intervention but on that occasion it was for the opposite view: not to vaccinate.

***

The Scotts joined hundreds of families to take up Robert Owen's provision of vaccination against smallpox.

The demand was so great that it was arranged for villagers to present themselves at allocated times. Sarah and her daughters were the first of the family to go and reported it to be a terrible ordeal but thankfully swift. Rosie nearly passed out, having to lean heavily on Gerry's arm for support to reach the sanctuary of her bed where she lay down for several hours before returning to the mill floor.

Joe and the older children also presented themselves at Mr Gibson's surgery, deciding to lead by example and take the blade without flinching. While Fiona and the little ones received the treatment free of charge, Joe was eager to spend the pound to protect his whole brood.

The process was more painful than Joe expected. His eyes stinging with tears, he watched, recoiling at every slice of the scalpel, while his wife and children bravely bore their arms to be incised and smeared with pus.

Only Sionaidh refused to obey her parents, cowering behind Joe and screaming; arms flailing, hitting herself and everyone closeby.

'Leave her be,' Fiona pleaded. 'We'd ha'e tae haud her doon an' Ah'm feart she'll tak a fit ony minute!'

They hurried out of the doctor's rooms in New Buildings and past the disorganised queue of villagers waiting outside, finding themselves the object of bulging, curious eyes.

'It's no' tha' bad ...' Donnie shrugged, ushering Sionaidh along with a protective arm around her shoulders. 'The lass jist did nae like the thocht o' it.'

A burly porter from the store rooms jeered at the distraught girl, 'All tha' carry oan an' she did nae e'en git the pox pit in 'er?'

'Did it hurt, Donnie?' a man shouted.

'Naw! A wee scratch!'

A housewife caught hold of his arm to peer at the wound. 'Whit's a quick stab if we dinnae catch the pox?'

Donnie shook her off: it hurt like hell.

'Aye!' he used the word to mask a cry, 'ye'll nae feel it!'

Fiona nursed her own throbbing arm, her attention on Sionaidh. Urging Donnie not to linger, she noticed her daughter's twitching grimaces with growing panic.

It was too late.

With a shriek, Sionaidh buckled under her brother's arm and dropped to the ground. There was nothing they could do but shield her from prying stares. While the others encircled her, Fiona bent down, wrenching off her own shawl and pushing it under her daughter's head to stop it battering against the cobbles.

The convulsions began to subside.

'It's passin',' Ailsa whispered, her face pinched.

Sionaidh's fierce, teeth-clenching contortions and grunts slowly relaxed into gasps.

'Has there been an accident?'

A distinctive voice cut through the turmoil: Robert Owen.

It was Fiona's greatest fear to have her employer witness Sionaidh's fits. What if he cast them out? Declared their daughter

189

evil and possessed by the Devil? Would he insist on her being sent to a lunatic asylum, as they did in the cities ... condemn her ... condemn them all for harbouring someone so afflicted? She thought her heart would stop beating but it roared in her ears, pounding so loud she could scarcely hear Joe's words.

'Not an accident, Sir. Ma dochter took ill.'

Owen stepped closer, Tom and Robbie moving aside respectfully to allow the mill owner to pass. For several moments he observed the girl's quivering body, her legs still shaking, saliver trailing from her mouth.

'Convulsions?' he asked, matter of factly.

Fiona lowered her head, closing her eyes and praying for this not to be happening.

'Aye, Mr Owen, sir. Sometimes ma lass is troubled with them,' Joe used the same tone, as if it was of no particular importance.

'Have Mr Gibson take a look at her.' Owen began to move away but not before adding. 'The care of a kind family is the best remedy and I am sure she will receive that from you and Mrs Scott,' his glance embraced the anxious family. 'Indeed, from all of you.'

Fiona heard his words as if from a distance, like the times in her childhood when her brother would call out in a cave and hear the echo rebounding.

'Come, Ah'll carry the wean.' Joe put his hand on Fiona's shoulder, seeing tears on her cheeks.

'He wis nae angry,' she cried; the relief Owen's words brought could not be measured.

Ever since the first terrible day of Sionaidh's fits, Fiona lived with the dread of her daughter's plight being discovered. Each day she worried, anxious and wary in case strangers found out and refused to let Sionaidh come to the school or enter the village.

Oh yes, she heard Mr Owen's proclamations on the day the Institute was opened, telling the villagers to look after one another, make each other happy, nurse the sick. But she did not dare believe him.

For too long her life had been controlled by powerful memories of her cousin's illness. The lingering effects of the threat of having Sionaidh ripped from the family lay like shards of jagged ice in the pit of her stomach.

Now, there was no need to worry. Their family secret was out and known by the one man who could have caused the most danger. He knew the worst and stood by his own words of protecting and caring for the sick.

'It's all richt, ma darlin',' Joe leaned close to his sobbing wife, understanding the enormous change this would bring. 'It's all richt. She's safe. Ye heard the Maister, nae body's gaun tae tak her awa'.'

Toiling up the steps to their home with his daughter in his arms, Joe was soon aware he no longer held the strength of his youth. It was happening more often these days, his aching muscles and lack of stamina bringing a harsh reminder of the passing of time.

'Here, Donnie, tak yer sister. Yer auld Da's trauchled.'

'She's gettin' tae be a big lass,' Donnie swung her unceremoniously over his shoulder, like a bag of corn, 'tall tae.'

'Mind her!' Fiona and Ailsa ran beside him. 'Ye ken hoo sore her heid gets after fittin'.'

'Ye carry her, then!' Donnie cried but it was said with good nature. 'An' ye can stoap cryin' noo, Ma! She'll be grand in a wee while. Ah hope ma airm is, an' all, it's burnin' sumat fierce.'

'Mine's sae sair, Ah could cut it aff!' Alex piped up, tramping along behind them, scowling from under his mop of fair hair.

'Och, yer a babbie,' Tom teased. 'Ah thocht it wis the maist wonderful thing! Did ye see all the bottles an' instruments aroond Mr Gibson's room? Ah want tae be a doctor when Ah grow up. Ah wis lookin' aroond while ye were all flinchin' an' hollering ...'

'Ah wisnae hollerin'!' Alex snapped back, pushing his brother with his good arm.

'Robbie gave a yelp!' Ailsa giggled, 'funniest sound Ah ever did hear! An' e'en Davey,' she idolised her big brother, 'ye came oot wi' some bad wurds! Och, twas funny!'

'Funny, wis it?' Davey pulled a handful of white blossom from the hawthorn and threw it over her. 'Ah'll gie ye funny!'

Fiona slipped her hand in Joe's. Why were they all in such good spirits when Sionaidh was ill? Yet, she felt it herself. She breathed the scented air and looked upon the straggling figures winding their way up the hill in front of her. Were they all as relieved as she was to know Mr Owen did not subscribe to witch hunts and superstition?

191

Only her husband remained serious. She knew the reason and squeezed his hand, smiling affectionately into his enquiring eyes before continuing in companionable silence.

Fiona knew there was a problem with Mr Baxter paying for his house but she feigned ignorance.

In truth, she did not care if they ever moved into the new building. Compared to the homes of the gentry it was a modest affair, but in her mind it was a mansion and to be mistress of such a house was unreal, completely beyond her comprehension. She loved her little cottage with the sparrows nesting in the thatch, swallows and swifts under the eaves, the low ceilings with beams hanging with herbs and pots and pans. Wild roses and honeysuckle clambered around its deeply set, many-paned latch windows and she knew every inch of the views and the twisting branches of the old oak trees at the bottom of the pasture.

If they never moved up the hill, it would suit Fiona, but she understood it meant a lot to Joe. He was always striving to give her more. She didn't need more, she was content.

And now, when Sionaidh recovered her senses from this attack, Fiona knew she would be free to experience a deeper happiness than she had for many years.

There were only five more days to go before Baxter was supposed to hand over the money to Joe. There had been no news and Joe's mind was constantly chewing away at the dire consequences of not seeing a penny. It was not just the need to complete his home, he was now using savings to pay his men. Only one more job was on the books and Tam was out every day meeting with local councillors to catch wind of any work they might be planning. It was looking bleak.

The previous evening at St David's Lodge, he sought the advice of several Brothers and they suggested he should to go to the bank and discuss terms for a loan. The thought of being in debt to a bank did not sit comfortably with Joe but neither did the spectre of telling the hard working men on his teams that they had no jobs.

Of the two evils, the bank seemed the least unpalatable so he changed into his smartest jacket and saddled Bluey.

He was barely mounted, gathering his reins with a resigned sigh, when he heard the sound of hooves clip-clopping off the road and approaching on the softer, sandy track beside the cottage.

192

The brown, roman-nosed horse was unfamiliar, as was the young man, flushed and dusty from the road.

'I am looking for Mr Scott.' he shouted, on seeing Joe.

'Ye've found him.'

'I beg a short appointment, sir.' he tipped his hat, 'Nigel Porter, I am instructed by Mr Baxter.'

'Follow me,' Joe pointed up the road. It would be fitting to conduct this meeting, whatever it might bring, at Baxter's new house.

Porter took little interest in the building, wishing instead to come straight to business.

'The matter is this, Mr Scott. This dwelling is no longer of interest to Mr Baxter. He had wished it built as a gift for another and had expected to visit the area often and make use of it himself. However, the good Lord has different plans for his future. Some months ago, Mr Grenville Baxter, my employer's father, passed away, God rest his soul, leaving his entire estate and business matters to his son, his only son, I might add.'

Joe listened intently, hands on hips, head jutting forward towards the smaller man. He was waiting for the vital information of whether he would be paid, or not.

'The thing is ...' Porter straightened his back, his gaze slipping to the side before boldly meeting Joe's, 'the late Grenville Baxter's estate is not in the order his son expected, in fact, he finds his entire inheritance is one of debt. For this reason, he is in the embarrassing position of being unable, at present, to find the necessary means to pay you.'

Joe's sharp intake of breath forced Porter to rush on, 'Mr Scott, hear me out! He does, however, have a proposal which I travelled here today to put to you.'

'An' that is?'

'He sends his utmost heartfelt apologies for the inconvenience this has caused and begs your forbearance to allow him time to sell this property. Immediately upon the sale, he will settle all outstanding amounts due to you ... with interest.'

'Ah need this money noo! Whit your suggestin' could tak months.' Joe spun on his heel and went to the window where he leaned heavily on the sill. 'Onyway, Ah heard he wis in America. How's he gaun tae sell the hoose when he's awa'?'

Before Porter could reply, Joe swung back to face him.

'Ah dinnae see hoo his faither's debts can change the fact the man had money hisself. Ah'm nae buyin' yer story Mr Porter! There's sumat smells awfy bad aboot the whole affair. Jist a few months back, his only concern wis a smokin' chimney! Noo, he's across the seas an' no' able tae see his way tae pay a builder's chit! Has his ane money suddenly gaun up in smoke?'

'Sir, I assure you, I am telling you the truth.' Porter paused, gauging the character of the furious, forthright man standing just feet away. 'Had you been a little faster in chasing your debts you might have succeeded for, it pains me to say, as soon as the empty coffers of Grenville Baxter's estate became common knowledge, there were a great many calls on Mr Baxter.'

'But whit aboot yon sugar plantations? Ye cannae tell me tha' a man in the sugar trade is short o' money?'

'Indeed, his father had interests in the plantations but any income is directed to Mrs Baxter, the widow. No, old Mr Baxter left the responsibilities to his son, but not the profits. The unfortunate thing is ... Mr Baxter had been under the impression he would inherit a fortune and was, well, rather liberal in his expenditure in the months preceding his father's death.'

'Liberal in his expenditure?' Joe struggled with the terminology. 'Ye mean, he spent his faither's money afore the paur man wis e'en deid?'

'I would ask for your discretion, sir.'

'Discretion be damned!' Joe shouted, striding through the empty hallway. 'If ye dinnae want yer Mr Baxter tae be hauled in tae the Debtors' Prison, git oan yer horse an' follow me.'

Joe took him to Reynolds' office where, happily, they were seen straight away. With the pain of his newly vaccinated arm thumping and burning beneath the stricture of his jacket, Joe sat back and watched the other two men attempt to thrash out a deal.

From time to time, Porter would put forward an alternative solution, only to be forced to concede more in favour of Joe.

Reynolds knew his business and was a hard negotiator. Realising early in the meeting that no money was forthcoming, he ground Porter down to the best deal he could find for his client.

'So,' Reynolds summed up, after a series of intense questions. 'I believe we have reached a point when I can recommend a way to bring this to an end.'

Joe was exhausted at trying to follow the rapid conversation and turned a questioning look to his lawyer.

'If there is no money, there is no money.' Reynolds said bluntly. 'It seems the late Grenville Baxter did not hold much paternal love for his only son, leaving a large amount of money in Trust for his widow and daughters and a pit of debt and screaming creditors for his son. I shall make it my business to verify all you have told me, Mr Porter. If it is borne out to be the truth then all is well, but I warn you, this case is already before the Sheriff and he will not look kindly on any subterfuge.'

Porter's eyes were wide with innocence. 'All I have said is the truth, so help me God.'

'Mr Scott,' Reynolds fiddled with a white swan's feather quill, inadvertently smearing ink on his fingers. 'I strongly suggest you make the best of a bad deal. Mr Baxter will sign over to you the deeds of the land and the house, as it stands. It will then be for you to sell and all the proceeds will be yours, entirely yours, with no amount due to Mr Baxter.'

'All the proceeds?' Joe stared at them, aghast. The house and land were worth five times or more what Baxter owed him. 'Ah dinnae ken if that's richt ... Ah cannae see how Ah can tak sae much mair than Ah'm rightfully owed?'

Reynolds was surprised, having expected his client to grab the deal.

'Have no qualms, on that score. It is not the generous offer it first appears, but it will suffice, I believe. Remember, Mr Scott, you may have trouble selling the property and ... this arrangement has not made the slightest difference to your current demand for liquid cash for your business. Mr Baxter has not kept his part of the bargain and would be forever in your debt for your understanding, sparing him the prospect of enjoying His Majesty's prison.'

His head reeling, Joe left the men with the paperwork in the Bloomgate office, agreeing to meet them again the next morning.

***

195

Joe was not alone in struggling with the subject of debt, it was also weighing heavily on Robert Owen's mind.

The cotton mills were doing well, his quarterly reports showing a healthy and growing profit. Under the terms of the new partnership, it was agreed to plough this growth back into New Lanark for the first few years. This was allowing the Institute to be completed, new machinery installed and necessary maintenance work undertaken. All these improvements were proceeding and with money generated by brisk business in the Village Shop, the school room was beginning to pay its way.

It was his own, personal debts which hung over Owen, their shadowy presence thrown sharply into focus by a letter from Colin Campbell.

Campbell was writing on behalf of his father, John Campbell of Jura, to whom Owen was indebted and due to complete full repayment the following year. News had reached their ears of an investigation into serious irregularities at the Royal Bank of Scotland by John More, David Dale's successor. These involved the David Dale Trust and the Campbells were concerned this would endanger Owen's ability to honour his debt.

Never one to put off what needed doing, Owen laid a fresh sheet of paper before him and dipped his quill. The letter was brief, reassuring Colin Campbell there would be no delay in making the repayment of the loan from his father and he looked forward to concluding the matter, as agreed, in twelve months time.

As he dripped the sealing wax across the folded paper, he was already planning a visit to the Royal Bank offices.

Another letter was hastily dashed off to Alexander MacGregor, his lawyer, requesting him to look into the legal and financial ramifications of More's actions and how they applied to him. A third letter, more affectionately couched, was penned to his sisters in law, begging their hospitality.

Anne Caroline was drawing on her gloves, preparing to go to the village with her husband when she heard of his plan to travel to Glasgow.

'Julia wrote just two days ago to invite us to Rosebank. You are so busy, my dear, I rarely have a chance to speak of domestic matters!' She leaned towards the hall mirror, adjusting the angle of her hat and flicking a loose hair from her forehead. 'Perhaps you can stay a night or two?'

'Of course! That would be most enjoyable. Can you write to your sisters amending the arrangements?'

Watching his reflection, Anne Caroline asked, 'You will not require to spend *all* your time in the city, will you?'

'Rest assured, dear Caroline,' his eyes made contact with hers in the looking glass, 'I wish to be with you and the children and our dear sisters as much as I can and I will endeavour to keep one day entirely free for that indulgence.'

One day. One day. Anne Caroline heard his words repeating in her head as they climbed into the waiting gig and rattled off down the driveway.

The space in front of New Buildings was clustered with a mixture of carriages and tethered horses, their owners having disembarked to tour the mills. A dozen or so young village lads moved between them, offering to hold reins, pick out hooves, fetch buckets of water or generally find whatever the visiting grooms required. The numbers coming down the hill to see the mills were now so great they could not all be accommodated down by the forge and dyeworks; Cal would have noticed the change.

Anne Caroline took Owen's hand to step down from the gig, musing, 'There was a time when all one could hear were the Highlanders singing and bird song. Gracious! It is like a market town square!'

'It is certainly growing busier every year.' He offered his arm and escorted her through the gateway in the wall to the front door of their village house. 'Although, I must say, I recall many a visitor taking the tour during your father's time. On the warm summer day I first saw the mills, I declare there was a queue to enter Mill Four. All the ladies expressed an interest in seeing the school rooms ... as they do today.' He kissed her hand. 'I must leave you, the professors from Edinburgh University will have arrived and I wish to show them the Institute personally.'

He hurried away to the manager's office but Anne Caroline paused before going inside. The trees her father planted were now tall, surrounding the slope of green grass leading to the lower levels, their leafy branches jostling in a stiff breeze. It was quieter here, the commotion of people and coaches being hidden behind

197

the high wall. A couple strolled beside the mill lade, the lace on the lady's parasol flapping, her pink and white striped skirts pressing against her legs as they stopped from time to time to gaze up at the towering mills.

In this time of illness, discontent and appalling lack of employment across Britain and Europe, her husband's community stood out as exceptional. As one lady called it, "happy valley". Yes, Anne Caroline agreed, it was a very happy little valley and it was all the work of her own dear father and beloved husband.

Sometimes, Owen seemed to forget how much her father achieved, describing the village he took over as having been filled with the dregs of humanity and alcohol fuelled crime. Those comments rankled. It was not that bad, she had been there and seen for herself the reality of a thriving, content factory village. At other times, like just now, he openly acknowledged the admiration shown to his predecessor's work and her heart glowed.

New Lanark was not one man's triumph, these healthy children and the hard working, amiable workforce were the product of both her father and Owen. She felt blessed by God for giving her the good fortune to know and love them both and, she admitted, simultaneously praying for forgiveness for her selfishness, for knowing they each loved her.

A rustle sounded behind her and she turned to find the housekeeper waiting patiently at the open door.

'Ye all richt, ma'am?' the woman asked, her puckered brow showing concern.

'Perfectly!' Embarrassed to find her eyes blurred with tears, Anne Caroline pulled a handkerchief from her cuff. 'The wind is still cold despite the sunshine, it caught me unawares.'

After giving instructions for preparing beds and refreshments for her husband's guests, acquaintances from London who were keen to see the mills, Anne Caroline left the village house.

Over the last few years, her role in the community had progressively become a natural routine. She was genuinely interested in the people and did not find it at all burdensome or difficult to remember names or who was newly bereaved or, conversely, delivered of an infant. A few words of comfort, a prayer, a shared passage from the Bible, or a gift of a plant from

Braxfield's glass houses brought cheer and a little relief to those experiencing difficult times.

Whether it was cooing over a new baby being proudly presented in its best, freshly laundered shawl, or holding the hand of a distraught widow, Anne Caroline was accepted and welcomed into all the village homes. For the older residents, her calm, respectful presence as much as her delightful chuckle, reminded them of her father. A fact they always mentioned, eager to share any recollections of the great man with his daughter.

'An' he slapped me oan the back!' old Angus, a retired mill wright recounted through toothless gums, 'sayin' he'd ne'er seen sich a fine piece o' weldin' as Ah made fur him tha' day! Mr Dale wis a braw man! Peace be his in everlasting Life. There's few tae draw breath who can equal the likes!'

Anne Caroline would smile and nod, having heard the story a dozen times, but her eyes glinted with amusement as if it was the first telling.

Once her house calls were undertaken, she visited the Village Shop. If they were travelling up to Glasgow she would purchase a few gifts for her sisters and friends. It was crowded on the ground floor and she was struggling to ease her way towards the staircase at the back when Mr Dudley spotted her and came to her aid.

'Mrs Owen, ma'am! Allow me,' he gently but firmly persuaded the mass of sweating, heavily cologned bodies to part.

'Mrs Owen?' an American lady squealed, her darkly outlined eyes and rouged lips both wide with curiosity. 'Madam, would you be *the* Mrs Owen? Mrs *Robert* Owen?'

Anne Caroline nodded, uncomfortable to suddenly find herself the centre of attention.

'Oh, it is a mighty privilege to meet you, Mrs Owen,' the lady dipped into a curtsey, her hat feathers bobbing. 'This is the most charming place I ever did see!'

Several others were turning to study the mill owner's wife, the women's eyes scrutinizing her cream wool pallise, embroidered and trimmed with braid to match the flounces on her skirt. From beneath their lashes, the men admired her slim figure, deep set eyes, the thick brown hair coiled up to reveal a smooth neck and firm jawline.

Before being caught in an avalanche of questions, Anne Caroline murmured pleasantries and excused herself, allowing Mr Dudley to usher her upstairs to the relative peace of the haberdashery.

Sitting with Cathy that evening, Sarah told her of the clamour in the shop.

'Ye should ha'e seen it! nae sooner wis Mrs Owen up the last step than Ah could hear this rumble an' it seemed e'ery yin wis followin' her! Andrew bundled her in tae the wee fittin' room aff the store an' pushed me in wi' her, tellin' me tae keep the door shut till he telt me it wis clear tae come oot!'

'In the name o' heaven, whit did they want wi' her?'

'Jist tae stare, Ah think. She wis sae ... surprised at all the carry oan an' kept apologisin' fur stoapin' me frae ma work.'

'She's a rare woman, an' that's a fact.' Cathy yawned. 'We're gie lucky tae ha'e a maister an' mistress the likes o' the Owens. Ah'm wurkin' wi' a lass frae England, came up when her whole family were thrown oot a mill near Manchester. She telt me she wis beaten by the overseers! Beaten! Wi' a whip wi' five straps. She showed me her airm an' across her shoulder where the marks are still showin' ... an' that wis months past.'

'Aye, we're lucky, richt enough. An' we dinnae want fur food, neither. Ye mind Mina, spotty Mina? the freckled lassie beside me at the shop, used tae be wi' ye in the picking room? Weel, she telt me two o' her cousins died last year fae lack o' food. They were in London, a pin factory. A cryin' shame.'

Cathy chose her moment carefully, 'Mam, did ye hear Daniel Massey is hame?'

A mask fell over Sarah's expressive face, brows frowning.

Cathy continued. 'He says there wis a lot o' sailors chose tae stiy in America when the war feenished.'

Sarah sucked in air, folding her arms and remaining silent.

'We have nae heard tha' ony thing bad's happened tae Stephen,' Cathy's tone was reasonable, placating, 'sae he's probably jist stayed o'er there.'

'That's whit he wanted.' Sarah snapped. 'He wanted tae be in America.'

'Ah spoke tae Daniel, he says it's no' bad o'er there. Like here but hotter when it's hot and caulder when it's ...'

200

'We knew that frae Sam!' Sarah stood up and swung the kettle clumsily over the fire sending droplets spilling onto the coals, hissing. 'He can stiy there! Running awa' like tha' ... worrying me tae death wi' every report o' drowning an' battles at sea ...' Sarah checked herself from shouting, feeling her head would burst. 'He's in God's hauns! Ah wiped my ane hauns o' him years ago fur want o' ma sanity. Ye'll ha'e a bairn o' yer ane yin day, Cathy, an' ye'll see fur yersel' how hard it is tae dae the richt thing. Ah ken he blamed me fur no' bein' wi' his faither ... oh aye, Ah ken, but Ah did whit Ah felt wis richt in the eyes o' the Lord.' A rush of self pity flushed her cheeks, smarted in her eyes. 'An' by Christ Ah've suffered fur ma sins.'

Cathy reached for the tea pot, 'Ah'll mak some tea, eh? Mibbee Ah should nae ha'e mentioned aboot Daniel, but ye were bound tae hear the sailors are all hame noo ...'

'Naw, lass' Sarah smoothed her hand down her daughter's long hair, catching a curl at the end and twirling it round her finger. She was remorseful for her outburst. 'Ye did richt tae say.' She dropped the golden strands. 'Ah'm jist a bitter auld bisom, tak nae notice.'

They sipped their tea companionably in the dying firelight, then Cathy climbed over Lily's sleeping form in the hurly bed and settled onto her mattress, drawing her curtain closed.

For a long time, Sarah sat alone at the table, her chin propped on her hand, fragments of the day and earlier memories drifting through her mind. Giving a smothered laugh, she recalled a comment made by Andrew Dudley after helping Mrs Owen; 'how sensible you are.'

I used to be sensible, she thought, and perhaps now I am again but, oh dear Lord, how little he knew of the real Sarah.

Poor man, he was falling in love with her. She could see it in his eyes and did not discourage it. Worst of all, his sweet, good-natured ways were working their way into her own heart. There were no stolen kisses, unguarded glances, indiscreet caresses or even romantic innuendoes between them, theirs was a wholesome, staid, relationship: comfortable.

Could she settle for being comfortable with a man after the passion she felt for Sean? Passion led to heart break and God only knew the devastation that caused. If she was sensible she would let

201

their friendship develop until the inevitable question would be asked. Marriage to Andrew would mean security; a wonderful relief in her old age.

Except, of course, they could never be married because she would be committing a terrible sin against God. Her husband, to whom she was bound by the words of the Gospel in the sight of the Lord, was alive and living in America.

'Jesus,' she muttered, pushing herself up from the table and starting to unbutton her dress, 'Ah've made a richt mess o' things. Git yersel' tae yer scratcher, lass, an' stoap all this maundering.'

The first clear calls of the dawn chorus were echoing in the valley before she fell asleep, her dreams haunted by ghosts of the past.

Chapter Eleven

"How nearly equal all men are in their bodily force, and even in their mental powers and faculties, till cultivated by education."
David Hume (1741)

'I wager you wish you had never heard of Stanley Mills, Mr Owen?' Alexander Macgregor clasped his hands on the desk and looked candidly at his client.

'There was nothing wrong with Stanley Mills,' Owen said firmly. 'We just need to find a buyer for them. They should and *could* have been a sound investment. The local people were willing and desperate for work, the river Tay provided more than enough power and the machinery itself was perfectly sufficient. Why, even transport of the materials was easier than at New Lanark and many other factories which are still showing a profit. No, it was the man who managed the place. James Craig would have bankrupted the wealthiest man, a sheer incompetent! Lazy with reports, lazy with maintenance ... his only desire being to play the landed gentry and dabble in agriculture! And now we find John More is just as egocentric.'

Macgregor nodded. 'He always presented himself as a man of means ...'

'Useless and self seeking!' Owen jumped up and roamed around the office amongst piles of dusty bundled rolls of paper mounded on wooden chests. 'I heard long ago that More believed he should live in the grand style. Having taken on David Dale's position at the bank he imagined the luxuries would follow. A coach and four, liveried footmen! If Dale enjoyed these then he thought he was due them. Conveniently forgetting, Mr Dale's fortune was built on hard labour and his own cultivated intelligence. Neither of which Mr More owns even the slightest notion....'

Macgregor listened patiently while Owen gave vent to his frustration. There was the possibility of a large sum being owed to the bank by the late David Dale's Trust, most of it from the debts at Stanley Mills, but contributed to by More's bad management. The figure was running as high as thirty thousand pounds.

Macgregor smoothed the unruly moustache sprouting from his top lip, a habit his wife despised but he found strangely soothing, and eventually broke into Owen's words.

'As we both know, money does not stretch and cannot be in two men's pockets at the same time. I fear there may be reprisals on decent merchants and investors, alas, also on the income from the Trust to your sisters in law. I shall keep you abreast of matters.'

While he was concerned that Anne Caroline's sisters might suffer, Owen knew he would look after them and make up any short fall. He left Macgregor's and went straight to the Tontine Rooms, secure in the knowledge that, whatever the outcome of the More affair, the dividends from his shares in New Lanark would cover the first tranche of repayments to Campbell of Jura. He just hoped this problem with John More wouldn't spiral into further years of finding money to pay off other people's incompetence.

***

Joe spread his arms wide encompassing the stark two storey stone building, half finished barn and the footings of the second house where the walls were not yet a man's height above the muddy ground.

'Weel ...' he said solemnly, 'this is whit Ah'm landed wi'.'

Beside him, Sam surveyed the scene; damp and uninviting against the white, weeping sky.

Joe cleared his throat, he felt rough and his arm still hurt from the doctor's scalpel. 'An' nae money.'

They moved to take shelter in the barn, the rain pattering on the sodden raw timber roof and splashing noisily into puddles.

'Ah've bin a fool,' Joe started, rubbing at the back of his neck in discomfort. 'Ah over stretched masel'. Thought it wis all gaun weel an' got above masel'.'

'Not at all!' Sam took off his cocked hat and shook away the worst of the water. 'Ye did nuthin' wrang, it wis tha' bastard, Baxter.'

'Ah'm too trustin', that's whit Reynolds telt me. By the way, he's makin' enquiries because he disnae believe we've heard the truth.'

'The hoose and land are yours, aye?'

'Oh aye,' Joe broke off into a coughing fit, the exertion squeezing a band of pain across his temples. 'Signed an' sealed by order of the Court. Whit in the name o' Christ am Ah tae dae? Nae money tae feenish it, tidy it up tae sell or dae onything tae ma ane hoose ... the lads will be oot o' work afore Ah ken ...'

'Ah'll loan ye the money ...'

'Naw! It's no' tha' Ah'm no' gratefu' but until Ah ken how tae pay ye back, Ah cannae be in debt tae ye.' Joe slung his good arm around his brother's shoulders. 'Ye ha'e a lass waitin' tae marry ye an' a new life tae lead. Ah'll find a way oot o' this, Sam. Ye should git Ruth tae the kirk porch an' yersel' awa' tae the sun. Think o' Connor, o' Ruth ...'

Sam looked at his brother's haggard face: he wasn't well.

'Awa', Joe! Ah've left ye once afore when Ah should nae, Ah'll no' agin! Noo, ye should be hame afore Fiona's chasin' me fur keepin' ye in the rain wi' a cauld.'

Too miserable in mind and body to resist, Joe returned to the cottage and went straight to bed. His whole body was aching, shivers chattering his teeth and then a rush of heat would force him to kick the blankets aside, sweat trickling between his shoulder blades.

Mr Gibson was called and pronounced a severe chill, possibly influenza, although it might also be a reaction to the vaccination. He bled him and prescribed a bottle of noxious liquid and a twist of paper containing snuff tobacco to be lit by his bed when the coughing overtook him.

Fiona was alarmed, running up and down the steps to their room fetching cold water to relieve his fever or extra blankets from the kist to soothe the shivering.

'Och Sam,' she cried, snatching up a lit candle to ignite the tobacco. 'It's a mark o' how bad he is tha' the doc managed tae draw blood. Ma Joe cannae staun that practice.'

All the younger children were sitting round the table, spooning down a makeshift meal of leftovers, bread and weak ale. They spoke between themselves in muted tones, never having known their father take so ill.

Suddenly, the latch on the front door lifted and Donnie and the older boys came in, followed by Tam. His concern for Joe and a desire to offer help to Fiona overcame any thoughts of encountering Sam at the cottage.

'That's kind of ye tae come, Tam. We wid be obliged if ye can jist keep the business gaun?' Fiona's grateful smile showed she knew little of the depths of Joe's problems. 'Ah'll mak sure he's back at the helm, richt an' hearty, in nae time.'

For a while the little room was crowded, the younger boys vying for the older ones' attention until their antics and laughter became too much for their mother.

'Wheesht will ye!' she snapped, coming down the stairs from checking on Joe. 'It's gettin' late, the bairns should be asleep an' yer gettin' them a' wurked up.'

Davey followed her through to the scullery, bringing another candle to add to the weak light of her whale oil lamp. 'Dinnae fret, Ma, we're jist keepin' their spirits up.'

'Aye,' Fiona leaned against the chest of drawers where the metal washing tub lay, overflowing with bowls and cutlery. 'Ah'm weary, son.'

The guttering flame accentuated the shadows under her eyes and he was struck by how vulnerable she looked. For the first time, he realised she was growing older, not yet aged or incapable, but losing the invincible strength he always took for granted.

'Aw, there noo,' he pulled her into a comforting hug. 'Da' will be up an' aboot afore ye ken.'

She held him close, breathing his warm unique scent, enjoying the feeling of his strong arms yet loving him as tenderly as when he was an infant. It was not lost on her that he was the one giving support: how quickly they grow.

For the next few days, Fiona threw herself into nursing Joe, distressed by the sight of his ribs showing clearly when she bathed him. How had she not noticed he was growing so thin? In years past, she would have seen any changes immediately.

It was true that in the winter months they slept well clothed and it would be May or June before he cast aside his simmit at night, but she was nagged by remorse. Images of his half finished plates of food, meals missed when he snatched an apple from the barrel; always in a hurry.

He was working too hard, she decided, and needed to be taken care of properly. There was also the concern that Tom and Ailsa were coughing, were they taking the same illness? Was the whole family going down with it?

Thankfully, her fears were unfounded and only Ailsa was laid low for a few days in her bed before rallying and heading off with the others to work.

When Joe began to show signs of improvement and promised to eat the soup and cold chicken she laid ready, Fiona was persuaded to return to the classroom. Following his routine of house calls, Mr Gibson came with his bag of instruments to find his patient shaved and dressed, sitting on the front door step polishing his boots. Joe thanked him for his services but told him in no uncertain terms that further blood-letting would not be required.

'Ma neb is runnin' like the Clyde an' there's a ringin' in ma ears frae a' the gunk in there! If that's a' Ah ha'e tae baither me, Ah'll tak ma chances it'll clear. Jist a cauld.'

'Ye took more than a cold, Mr Scott, it's Influenza you've been battling. It's spreading through the town, twenty homes down with it in New Lanark and two older residents taking it bad. Keep fumigating your cottage an' keep an eye on your family!'

Gibson smiled, a gold tooth glinting, then turned on his heel and marched away, satchel swinging at his side. Without turning round, he raised his free hand in a wave, 'Good day tae ye, Mr Scott! Nothing personal, sir, but I hope I am not summoned here again for many a day!'

Joe called farewell and leaned back against the door frame.

He was as weak as one of the bleating kittens in the barn beside Rusty and Bluey but the fever was past and his head no longer ached. While lying in bed it occurred to him that he often heard the phrase, 'worried sick'. Gibson's diagnosis of influenza might be valid but he knew he had been ailing for months from anguish and uncertainty over Baxter and the lack of work for his men. Fiona's recent wheedling and coaxing to make him eat did not successfully cover the dismay he saw on her face at how little flesh covered his bones.

Now, he was ready to find a solution to his troubles. With his family out at work or in the school room, it was Sam who kept him company and, later in the afternoon, Tam joined them.

All three men had ideas. They huddled around the table, unfurled the scroll showing the original plan for the two houses, weighted it down at each corner and scrutinised it.

After hours of discussion, Joe stood up to refill the ale jug. 'Ah cannae see ony way but tae ask fur a loan frae the bank.'

'Aye,' Sam scratched at his short sandy hair. 'Whichever way ye play it, ye need money the noo.'

'Or ye could use yer savings?' Tam suggested.

'The way it's gaun, they'll be gone afore the end o' next month.' Joe poured some more foaming amber liquid in to their tumblers. 'Naw, Ah'll ask fur enough tae see it completed an' then pray mair wurk comes oor way.'

'Completed? ye mean yer new plan? or stickin' tae selling Baxter's hoose?'

Joe sat down, blowing his nose violently and then stabbing his finger at the architect's drawing.

'The new plan. Ah like it, it maks sense. Ah widnae ha'e thocht o' it withoot ye baith.' He looked up at them in turn, showing his gratitude. 'Ah'll borrow enough tae change the footings of the hoose Fiona an' Ah were tae live in. We'll mak it smaller, divide it intae four separate dwellings, back tae back an' thatched. That'll be the building the bank will tak a mortgage oan an' then Ah'll rent them oot. There's plenty call fur lodging in toon if offered at a fair price. That work will keep the teams paid an' busy fur a while, until the summer months, onyway. If things dinnae improve, at least Ah'll no' feel as bad tae lay them aff when there's crops tae be harvested.'

'An' Baxter's hoose?' Sam asked.

'We'll stoap callin' it Baxter's hoose! It's feenished, ready tae be lived in wi' a few bits o' furniture an' the like but it disnae ha'e grazing sae ... Ah've already talked tae the landlord aboot the pasture *here* an' Ah can keep it oan, use it fur the horses an' cuttin' hay ... but, Fiona and Ah'll leave this cottage an' move intae the big hoose wi' the family ... it'll be *oor* hame.'

'Aha! Aboot time too!' Sam grinned broadly at his brother. 'Or are ye jist wantin' rid o' me by movin?'

Knowing the words were said in jest, Joe lifted his tankard, proclaiming:

208

'A toast! Tae the bank gi'ing the money an' tae hell wi' Baxter an' his like! Here's tae gettin' oan wi' oor lives!'

Tam clinked his drink against theirs, wishing them all the best and wondering if he, too, should start making plans to live a fuller life.

The sadness of his unrequited yet still deeply held love for Melanie Ewing followed him like a shadow. Not a day went by that he did not dwell on what might have been: the happiness they could have shared. To others, the romance between the little one-armed clerk and the stonemason's chubby daughter was all but forgotten. Sometimes, he wished he could forget. Perhaps it was time to impose a stricter control on where his mind wandered when he was alone: he would make a determined effort to start afresh.

The day after this decision, the news came that Miss Ewing, Melanie's aunt, had died from the influenza. Not only that, his gossiping neighbour added, old Mr Ewing was down with it.

'And his daughter, Melanie?'

'Aye, they say she's taken bad.'

Once again, Tam's thoughts were in turmoil.

***

Rosebank's cream walls and crow-step gables were bathed in the glow of late afternoon sunshine when the Owens' carriage crunched its way into the front driveway.

The moment the steps were let down and the coach door opened, the children jumped out, skipping excitedly around their mother and pulling at Peggy's hand, pleading to run straight to the lawns to play.

'Welcome!' Margaret stood in the honeysuckle covered doorway, trying to keep her yapping, struggling dog from joining the children. 'We have been so looking forward to your visit!'

Anne Caroline hugged her sister. 'As have we, although I fear we may disturb your peaceful haven!'

'The sound of children laughing is never a disturbance,' Margaret assured her.

Murdoch and Ramsay followed the carriage round to the stable yard and oversaw the unpacking of the trunks.

'Ye were quiet on the journey?' Ramsay commented to the valet. 'Is there something wrong?'

Glancing round to see who could overhear, he murmured. 'Ah heard Senga may be leaving. She wis talking tae Miss Wilson in her office an' Ah'm sure she wis saying she's wantin' awa' tae be merrit.'

The lady's maid's eyebrows shot up: had she heard correctly? In the enclosed yard, the shouts of men reverberated with horses' hooves on the cobbles and the creaking carriage springs and harnesses.

'Married?' she queried. 'Tae Jack Keeble, the Sandpaperer?'

'Who else?' he smiled, sarcastically. 'E'er since he wis doon tae tak the water stains oot o' Mrs Owen's dressing table an' stayed fur a chat at the back door, ye ken how cow-eyed she's bin aboot him. They went tae the dancin' at the Institute a few times too.'

'Well, well, the French Polisher, I dare say it's a guid profession. But, och, were you sweet on her yourself?'

'Me? Awa'! She's a braw lassie but, naw,' he hefted a trunk onto the porter's barrow and reached up to catch the next one being thrown down from the carriage roof. 'Keep a secret?'

'O' course.'

'There's a lassie doon in London, at the Walkers' place in Bedford Square. Ah've bin seeing a lot of her when Ah'm there. She's the head housemaid, smart an' funny wi' it. We spoke the last time Ah wis doon there wi' the master an' we, well, we thocht if a position ever came up at Braxfield, she could come up an' we could be ... merrit.'

'It must be the spring air! Jeezo! Twa weddings frae Braxfield!'

'Dinnae say a word afore Ah've spoken wi' Mr Sheddon and Miss Wilson.'

'Miss Wilson doesn't tak kindly tae followers ... ye'd best mak sure Senga is leaving us or she'll be gie pit oot.'

Murdoch winked at her. 'As soon as we return tae Braxfield. Ah cannae wait!'

When the luggage was unpacked and while the family were taking a walk in the grounds, all the servants gathered round the kitchen table for their main meal of the day

Renwick took his place at the head of the table, propping his cane against the arm of the chair and surveying the bowed heads waiting for him to say Grace.

Irrespective of his worn out body and the palsy creeping up his arms, his mind was alert and filled with vital knowledge, born of long experience. The once thick dark hair was sparse and white, his back bent beneath the immaculately brushed jacket.

When he finished the prayer, he eased himself into his seat and cut across the rising chatter with a firm voice.

'I trust we will all ensure the Owen family enjoy a successful visit here,' his rheumy eyes hovered on the newest members of staff, 'we must not become slack in our duties. Rosebank tends to provoke a more relaxed atmosphere, probably due to the fresh air. Mrs Breen and I will be watching to ensure standards do not lapse.'

Breen raised her glass of watery elderflower cordial, catching his eye. He was still the head of the servants' hall and the look of trepidation on the younger members did him credit.

Renwick returned her gesture with a smile but while replacing his glass, his trembling fingers caused the claret to splash onto his hand. Breen looked away, pretending to be busy shaking out her serviette and smoothing it over her lap.

Ramsay saw what happened with a wave of sympathy and blushed uncomfortably. She held the Dales' butler in high regard, Mrs Breen also, and knew they had worked together for decades. It was clear they were close friends yet each emanated an aloof formality, or at least while junior servants were present.

No words were spoken at the head of the table so Ramsay applied herself to eating the minced beef and carrots on her plate, watching Renwick out the corner of her eye.

Surreptitiously, he wiped crimson droplets from his hand, folding the starched serviette so no mark could be seen.

'Miss Ramsay,' Murdoch raised his voice to attract her attention. 'Them geese on the bridge, quackin' an' snapping ... fifty or mair in yon flock, wid ye say?'

She was grateful for the excuse to join the conversation.

'I would say a hundred! A white river aroond the carriage and frightenin' the horses something fierce! The groom wis forced tae

211

jump doon tae tak hauld of their heids. I was praying we would not overturn into the river!'

'Ma Da used tae drive the geese tae Hamilton market,' piped up a fresh faced lad, one of the Rosebank footmen. 'He wid pour tar on the yard by the gate an' chase the birdies through it! Sed it stuck tae their feet sae they cud waddle fur miles wi'oot rubbin' themsels raw.'

Cook snorted, 'Mercy me! Mibbee Ah shud pit tar oan ma feet tae ease ma bunions!'

Amidst the laughter, Renwick leaned towards Breen asking the cause of the hilarity.

'Cook was saying she should use tar on her feet to ease her bunions,' she said loudly in his ear, chuckling with the others.

The butler pushed his mince around, 'Peas and onions, eh? I only appear to have carrots.'

Spontaneously, Breen and Ramsay exchanged a glance. It was a blessing Renwick could not hear the suppressed explosion of giggles.

The next morning, after sleeping soundly, Owen woke to the sound of flint on steel. A maid was kneeling by the hearth, her slight figure silhouetted against the jumping yellow flames. He waited until she left the room before rising to dress in the dim, unfamiliar bedroom with only the hissing of newly kindled coal and his wife's rhythmic breathing to break the silence.

On stepping out onto the landing, he was almost blinded by white sunlight flooding in through the high staircase window.

Since childhood he had taken pleasure in the first hours of the day when it was quiet and the air fresh. He would race through the streets of Newtown and out along the country lanes to reach his school in a rambling old mansion. It was a point of pride to arrive before the other boys, his skin tingling from exertion, feeling wonderfully alive.

Letting himself out of Rosebank's front door, he was greeted by a cacophony of birdsong. The warm scented air tempted him to wander round to the south terrace and then out across the lawn, his boots sparkling with dew. Wood pigeons cooed, swallows rose and dived high above him and soon he came to the well worn path through the meadow and down towards the river. Pink clouds of spindly cuckoo flowers and spiky golden gorse gave way to beech woods where the soft rays of slanting sunlight fell on swathes of bluebell leaves, already showing signs of early blooms.

He hoped the same sunshine was spreading over New Lanark and that Buchanan would be taking the school children up the hill on rambles to experience the glory of a Scottish Spring. Everyone should have the time and opportunity to enjoy such a day; to hear the musical notes of nature and breathe clear air. These were the simple pleasures of life, the true, free pleasures which nurtured the spirit, poured balm on the soul and refreshed the mind.

David Dale would have called it God given, he mused, and perhaps it was, who could say for sure? Whatever Divine entity created living things, they were all around them, provided in abundance.

Owen stopped beside an ancient oak tree, its trunk twice, perhaps three times his girth with deeply incised bark, rugged to the touch. The spot provided a view onto the riverbank, close enough to hear the rippling, rushing water and catch a trace of tangy damp vegetation. A blackbird hopped on the edge of the pasture overturning half rotted dry leaves, gathering grubs and worms in its beak. Its squirming load complete, it flew off to feed the brood waiting impatiently in their nest before reappearing to repeat the process. After several minutes observing the scene, Owen noticed a movement, just an arm's length away on the oak tree.

Oblivious to his presence, a sleek brown-feathered little bird crept methodically up the fissures in the bark. Owen watched, captivated by its narrow, curved beak seeking out bugs. Its perfect camouflage was only broken by glimpses of creamy white breast plumage showing as a pale crescent moving up the tree trunk or upside down beneath jutting branches.

The encounter with the treecreeper was just one of the topics of conversation when he joined his wife and her sisters later that morning. Another was his decision to make the most of the wonderful weather and spend that day with his family.

A holiday atmosphere pervaded Rosebank.

David and Richard explored the gardens, making rival dens in the shrubbery and trying to ambush one another. With Peggy in attendance, little Mary made elaborate daisy chains, adding violets and dandelions in carefully designed patterns, Then, hurrying purposefully up to the terrace where the adults sat talking, she presented them as gifts to her mother and aunts.

'What shall I make you, Papa?' she asked, anxiously, not wishing to leave him out.

'Well now,' Owen pulled his daughter onto his lap. 'I know! A bunch of as many different coloured leaves as you can find.'

'Leaves?' her high, child's voice was indignant. 'But Papa, they are all green?'

He feigned surprise. 'Are they? Why don't you go and have a look, Ann and Jane might help you.'

Mary's chubby features wrinkled, pondering the request. 'Very well, I'll have a look ... but Ann and Jane are reading in the summer house.' She gave a resigned sigh worthy of an adult, 'I suppose, I will have to go by myself.'

Anne Caroline shaded her eyes, watching her youngest child running back to Peggy where she sat on a bench positioned near the sundial. A froth of white frills under the maid's cap surrounded her amiable face, nodding and listening to Mary, gesturing to the ground beneath the copper beech and laughing.

Owen was noticing the exchange as well.

'Peggy was an excellent choice as our nursery maid,' he commented. 'She understands the need for kindness. It is as I prescribe at the Institute and the results are just as I predicted. The children are calm and good tempered between themselves and respectful of the adults. Example is everything at that vulnerable age and good, benevolent behaviour is so easily learned.'

Jean tilted her parasol lower, turning her attention to Owen, wishing to see his expression.

'Do your paupers not fight and cry like the infants I see on the city streets?' she asked. 'I thought all small children gave vent to their furies.'

'Of course, there are minor frustrations but they are never punished so they do not require to scream at unjust beatings or for lack of food or out of fear.'

'They are *never* punished?'

'There is no need, especially with the little ones who have only known kindness.'

'And the older ones?' Margaret joined the conversation, looking up from her embroidery. 'I remember in New Lanark seeing stones being thrown at one another by barefoot youths and ... name calling.' The words had been crude and offensive, spoken by boys of her own age: shocking.

'Occasionally, this still happens,' Owen used his hands in decisive gestures to illustrate his point. 'Although, always through misunderstandings, both of the cause of the disagreement and of the effect of the cruel acts. It is easily solved by sorting out the cause or respecting differing points of view. Spiteful acts have been taught through generations, it is simply learned behaviour.

'Goodwill to all men,' Margaret murmured, 'as Our Lord teaches in the Scriptures.'

'Indeed, that is so.' Owen agreed, 'it is a basic tenet in all *true* religions yet we see bullying and even killing taking place in the name of those same religions purely for want of understanding and respect.'

Jean was not convinced. 'This must be very time consuming, Robert? So much explaining?'

Owen gave an ironic laugh. 'My dear Jean, surely it is worth the time? What could be more valuable than forming a child's character so it leads a satisfying, useful life. I see no waste of time in preparing a child to lead its life without conflict and without causing pain and suffering to those around it? If its character is formed to seek understanding, there would be no conflict. Wars are much more time consuming.'

Margaret engaging her needle with the canvas once more, 'I still believe a good Christian upbringing would perform the same task as your Institute for the Formation of Character.'

'Unfortunately, it is clear it has not.' Owen responded, quietly. 'Nor have the other major religions of the world. We have the evidence laid clearly before us, look around at the world? This is the result of at least eighteen hundred years of wars and bigotry.'

Jean was studying his face. 'You believe your New View of Society, your New System, will truly make a difference?'

'Yes, I certainly do: completely. Nothing could be more clear to me. Raise a child to be rational, inquisitive and kind and you will have a fine adult. Now,' he leaned forward, his animated face glistening in the heat of the sun. 'Imagine, all children in the United Kingdom being raised this way? Move forward a further generation ... those formed in the New System will raise their children as they were raised. They will be well educated and prepared for life, taking up useful professions whether doctors or labourers, weavers or merchants, all will be kind, rational ... helpful to one another, working in co-operation for their mutual benefit. Now, dear Jean, take another step into the future to envisage the third generation?'

Jean did not answer at once and Margaret paused in her stitching, allowing herself to be swept into Owen's vision of the future.

'What would you see?' he asked earnestly, his attention darting from one to the other of his sisters in law.

'You are describing Utopia, dear brother in law. An end to repression and poverty?' Jean ventured, applying herself to give a properly considered answer. 'An end to war?' then she sighed, 'at least in this country. Although, there would still be foreigners like the French or Americans causing trouble.'

'Not if they, too, adopted the New System.'

He saw the astonishment on their faces; even Anne Caroline was taken aback.

'It can be done,' he told them, 'it is in our power to do it. And, ladies, I am pleased to say the Prime Minister wishes me to visit with him and Lady Liverpool, when next in London. Also, the American Ambassador, Quincy Jones, has written to seek a meeting to discuss my Plan.' He gave a perfunctory nod and stood up, a smile crinkling his eyes. 'In the meantime, it is deuced hot out here, shall I request Renwick to bring us some more iced lemonade?'

'Papa! Papa!' Mary bounced towards them, almost stumbling in her haste. 'See the colours!'

She thrust a bouquet of leaves into his hands.

'So many!' he leaned down, inspecting them closely.

'Some are dead,' her mouth turned down in exaggerated sadness, 'that's why they're all brown or yellow and crinkly ... but see Papa, there are red ones, yellow ones and these,' she turned a cherubic smile to him, 'my favourites, purple!'

'We shall have them placed in a vase in the drawing room,' he told her, 'and I am sure your Grandfather kept a book here which shows illustrations of all the trees and leaves in Scotland. We will look it out and discover the names.'

Jean turned to her sisters, 'As we did after our walks with Toshie. Happy times.'

'As are these times,' Anne Caroline replied. 'Mary, dear, why don't you press the leaves and we can fashion a little book?'

'A splendid idea!' Owen held out his hand to his daughter, 'Come, we will find that book together ... and,' he glanced back to his wife, 'I won't forget to ask Renwick for more lemonade.'

***

Joe dismounted at Ewing's front door, tying the reins to the ring before brushing dust off his jacket and removing his hat.

It had been a long day: long and exhausting.

Rising early, he was trotting over Clydesholm Bridge before the chappers had even woken the residents of Kirkfieldbank. The twists and turns of the valley road to Hamilton had seemed unending. It was only on the return journey, exalted by securing the much needed funds, that he noticed the fruit trees in full blossom. He waved to children scaring pigeons from the crops and took the time to follow the flight of a peregrine falcon, marvelling at its speed while stooping to catch its prey, like a stone dropping from the sky.

He pulled Ewing's door bell and yawned, worn out by the effort of riding for miles and the stress of his mission. Visiting the stonemason only added to his fatigue.

The housemaid ushered Joe up the staircase to her master's room then left, anxious and flustered. With the old mistress lying dead in the front parlour and Melanie indisposed, the daily chores with the livestock fell to her as well. There was also much to be attended to for the invalids.

The bedroom was stuffy, the air foul despite the casements being raised in both the windows.

Ewing was propped up with bolsters, his gaunt whiskered face appearing ruddy between the pale night cap and linen sheets.

'Ah'm jist hame frae Hamilton an' heard ye're no' weel. Can Ah dae ony thing fur ye?' Joe asked.

217

'That's kind, son, but only the Lord can aid me noo.' His wheezing breath quickened. 'Ah hear Mel's taken up wi' this damned affliction. They tell me little ... don't want tae bother me, after paur Lizzie ... Joe, is ma lass taken bad?'

'She's young, she'll be back tae her stove an' bakin' afore ye ken. Makin' cakes fur ye, nae doot!'

'The Quack said ye'd had this ... the influenza?'

'Aye, it's still not awa' but Ah'm through the worst.'

A burst of chirping from hedge sparrows reached them through the windows. In need of fresh air, Joe went over to look down on the yard and the tin roofed shed where he worked as an apprentice.

'It's a braw day oot there, hot,' he watched the maid tramping out to the pasture, calling to the house cow and jangling a bucket. 'If ye wid fancy takin' a seat ootside, in the shade like, Ah could help ye doon the stairs?'

'Naw, but a kind thought,' the old man's eyelids drooped.

I should leave, Joe thought, but there were things he needed to say.

'Ah've bin tae see the banker ye recommended, up in Hamilton. He's allowed me a loan frae the bank. It'll keep me gaun an' see the men richt fur a while. Ah wanted tae thank ye, sir. It wis your introductions and advice which made it happen.'

'Ye cannae dae it all yersel', Joe.' Ewing took a shuddering breath. 'Yer an awfy man fur tha'. Ye ha'e friends an' the Brothers at the Lodge. We come tae the aid of each other.'

Joe turned away from the sunny scene outside, his eyes slowly adjusting to the gloom. 'Ye ken Mel's man is in his bed an' all?' He saw Ewing swallow with difficulty, then a slight nod of confirmation. 'Sir, ye ha'e wurk on yer books, wid ye like me tae o'ersee it until he ... ye baith are weel agin?'

'Aye, that wid be grand ...' Ewing seemed to rally, eyes opening, arthritic hands grappling at the bed covers to pull himself up. 'Ah made a mistake, Joe. Ah'll admit it noo ... an' ask yer forgiveness.' He broke off, coughing, sweat beading, running into his bushy brows and beard. 'Ah should have let yer pal, Tam Murdoch, marry ma lass. Calder's nae up tae the task.' Another bout of coughing convulsed his body. 'Ah alis ha'e tae tell him whit tae dae.' He slumped back, 'Whit will happen noo?'

'Ah'll keep yer wurk richt until he's fit an' then ye'll tak over.'

218

'Ah'm past takin' over, Joe. Ah've had a guid kick o' the ba' ...
the end o' ma game's nigh. We both ken that.'

Searching for reassuring words, Joe kept his voice low, soothing,
waiting at the bedside until Ewing slipped into an uneasy sleep.

Tam was leaning on the wall a few yards from the entrance to
Ewing's yard. The moment Joe rode out onto the road, he shouted
to him, asking for news of Melanie.

'If Ah could survive this fever, Ah'm sure a strong lass like little
Mel will soon be on her feet. It's Ewing who's a worry. Ah fear it
may carry him awa'.'

'Tha' bad?' Tam tripped along beside him, trying to keep pace
with Bluey's long strides and screwing his face up against the
glaring sun every time he looked up at Joe.

'Ah telt him Ah'd keep an eye on his team up by Robbiesland.
Jist until Jim Calder is better.'

'Jim's struck wi' the influenza?'

Joe reined in, 'Aye. God help them.'

He wondered whether to mention Ewing's confession. Would it
make it any easier for Tam if he knew the old man now considered
him a better choice as a son in law? Would it change anything? No.

'Jist dinnae ask me tae gae up tae the hoose,' Tam was saying,
'it's mair than Ah could bear, but, Ah'll dae the books if ye fetch
them doon.'

'Aye, mibbee.' Joe nudged Bluey into an ambling walk. 'Come
tae the cottage later? Ah want tae tell Fiona the guid news aboot
moving up the hill an' it wid be braw if ye were there tae
celebrate.'

Tam shrugged, his arm swinging clumsily with his gait. It was
the last thing he wanted to do while Melanie was so ill, her father
possibly dying, but how else would he spend the evening? Pining?

Joe read his mind, 'Ye cannae dae onything fur her, man.'

'Ah ken that.' Abruptly, Tam stopped in his tracks, 'Ah'll be
alang later ... Ah've some messages tae fetch.'

There was no one at the cottage, even Rusty was out of her
stable, leaving the place strangely still.

After settling the mare, Joe threw himself down in the little barn
on a patch of straw, warm in the sun, allowing himself to relax for
the first time in weeks, perhaps months. Two ginger kittens, blue

eyes blinking, clambered onto his lap and soon the peaceful birdsong and warm sunshine lulled them all to sleep.

He woke to the church and mill bells tolling across the valley and was immediately struck with nerves: Fiona and the children would soon be home. How would she take the news?

Fussing around the stables, he brushed the remnants of tufty winter hair from Bluey's grey coat until it shone; birds whisking the spoils away to add to their nests.

'Yer hame!' Fiona peeped round the side of the cottage, her face lighting up. 'Ma darlin'! Ah thocht Ah heard ye here. Ye were awa' sae early this morn, afore Ah could see ye.' She flung her arms around him, 'How are ye feelin'?'

'Och, Ah'm fair enough. Ah needed tae reach a meetin' in guid time an' didnae want tae wake ye.'

'It went well?'

They walked together to the cottage door, his arm around her waist.

'As well as Ah could ha'e hoped.'

'Whit ye no' tellin' me, Joe Scott?' she gave him a sidelong look, playful but wary.

'It's a lang story, an' Ah'll tell ye ... but all ye need tae know is ...' his voice was jubilant, 'the time has come fur us tae move up the hill in tae oor ane big hoose!'

She froze. 'When?'

'Next week? Afore the end o' the month!'

Different emotions besieged her, leaving her speechless. Through all the flying thoughts and panic of leaving their home, she saw Joe's proud, expectant expression.

'My! Ye've taken ma breath clean awa'!' She kissed him, warmly. 'Whit's happened tae mak it possible sae soon? The last time Ah saw the site, the hoose wis still rubble?'

Not wanting to explain the difficulties nor the solution on his front door step, he dodged the question.

'Ailsa!' he called into the cottage, 'yer Ma an' Ah'll be awa' fur a wee while, keep an eye on Sionaidh an' if Tam calls roond, tell him tae wait fur us? There's a guid lass.' He offered his arm formally to Fiona. 'Now, Mrs Scott, join me fur a wee donder an' Ah'll tell ye whit Ah've bin up tae?'

She smothered her misgivings and took his arm.

Chapter Twelve

*"Society is produced by our wants and government by our
wickedness; the former promotes our happiness positively
by uniting our affections, the latter negatively by
restraining our vices"*

Thomas Paine (1791)

The day following Joe's visit, Ewing took a turn for the worse.

The maid thought it only right to tell Melanie of her father's
deteriorating condition, regretting her decision the moment the
words left her lips.

Leaving her husband moaning and restless in their sick bed, the
dutiful daughter staggered along the corridor, clutching at the
panelling and walls for support. She was beyond any thought of
decorum, oblivious to the state of her bulky crumpled nightgown
and dishevelled hair falling around her shoulders, tangled and free
from its habitual plaits.

Dragging a chair close to the bedside, she huddled under shawls,
flushed and burning-up yet shivering, her bare feet covered by a
blanket.

The room was noisy from the first heavy rain for weeks
pounding on the steading roofs: the storm throwing startling
lightening flashes into the bedroom. Rumbling, thumping thunder
rattled the jars on the wash stand, the tapestry bell-pull quivering
against the wall by the bed head. Miserable with fever and stunned
by grief from already losing her aunt, Melanie would not be
persuaded to leave her father's side. Even when his laboured
breaths died in the fetid air and the maid cried out, running to send
for the doctor, she remained, stroking his hand, dry-eyed with
disbelief.

With Melanie and her husband unable to make the funeral
arrangements, the matter was taken care of by Ewing's friends and
his fellow Brothers at St John's Lodge in Lanark and the Lodge he
was instrumental in having created, St David's, down in New
Lanark. It was a solemn occasion, interring two coffins: Ewing and
his sister.

Along with hundreds of men, Joe and Tam gathered in the graveyard to pay their last respects, sincerely stricken by the loss of the man who played a major role in both their lives.

'Mr Scott, may I have a word?' Reynolds fell into step beside the two friends. 'I apologise for troubling you now, a terrible loss, Mr Ewing was much respected and even loved in Lanark.'

Joe gave him a sidelong glance;'Wis there somethin' important, Mr Reynolds?'

'I discovered why Mr Baxter was so peculiar about the whole issue of the house you built, thought I should let you know.'

'And whit wis that?'

Reynolds lowered his voice, saying furtively, 'It was intended as a gift for his mistress. A place to meet, discreetly. When the lady, I use the word loosely in this context, realised he was penniless, she had a change of heart. He, of course, was at pains to ensure his wife never knew of his dalliance, especially as she has personal wealth which he relies upon entirely since his father's death.'

The explanation answered a lot of questions for Joe and he thanked Reynolds, bidding him good day and hoping he would never require a lawyer's help again.

The morning after the funeral, Joe left Donnie in charge of their own men and rode up to Ewing's yard, as he had done for days, to give out the daily orders. There were always a few new faces to be seen, hopeful figures hanging around the gateway in the chilly dawn air. Jobs were scarce, any work was better than queuing for Poor Relief. Joe pointed to two broad-shouldered lads, offering them a day's labour.

'Mr Scott!'

The shout came from the main house. Melanie's husband was marching towards him, struggling to button his jacket.

'Mr Calder ... are ye strang enough?' Joe neck-reined Bluey round to face him while abruptly gesturing to the new workmen to help load the wagons. 'Ah thocht ye were still poorly.'

'Did ye?' There was a sarcastic ring to the words. 'Or are ye trying tae tak ma business?'

Joe assessed him, noting black shadows circling bloodshot eyes, his greasy hair showing the tracks where a comb had pulled the locks away from his pallid forehead.

'Ah'm no' interested in yer business, Mr Calder. Ah telt yer late father in law Ah'd mind the men until ye were oan yer feet.'

'Weel, as ye can see, Ah'm here.' Jim Calder put his hands on his hips. 'Ah'll tak over agin the noo.'

'It's nae bother, if ye need anither day or twa tae recover an' see tae things.'

'Ah'll thank ye tae leave!'

Joe was apprehensive, the young man was trembling, perspiration shining on his unevenly shaven cheeks.

Catching sight of Melanie at an upper window, Joe asked 'How is Mrs Calder?'

'Grievin'. As well she might.' Calder started towards the group of men by the shed. 'Guid day tae ye, Mr Scott, ye can be oan yer way.'

'An' thank ye fur yer help,' Joe muttered to himself, hearing Calder bark to the new lads to 'sling their hook.'

Sending Bluey into a brisk trot, Joe clattered out of the yard and down the road, stopping beyond the first bend. Within seconds the workmen appeared.

'Ah promised ye work the day,' he told them, 'follow me.'

'Och Joe!' Tam berated him later, in the privacy of his own front parlour. 'Ye cannae jist tak mair men oan like that!'

'It's jist fur the day. Ah've made it clear. They'll no' be back the morra.'

'There's dozens needin' joabs, some walkin' up tae 'Gow an' Carluke fur a few pennies, even as far awa' as Douglas, Strathaven an' Biggar. The mines used tae tak them but even they're turnin' them awa', an' all.'

'These are hard times, richt enough. We have until ma buildings are up, then, God help us.'

***

It rained throughout the last week of the Owens' visit to Rosebank.

Each morning, Murdoch helped Owen pull on his heavy hooded cloak to ride in to the city. Every evening, soaked, it was hurriedly pulled from his shoulders and taken downstairs to dry. The pulleys above the hot pipes in the cloakroom were constantly filled: small items like little Mary's cape and Richard and David's woollen socks, hung between the Miss Dales' elaborate riding costumes.

Murdoch, Peggy and Ramsay all wished they had packed more changes of clothing for the family.

Playing hide and seek or blind man's buff and the usual indoor pursuits of painting, playing the piano, sewing and singing together began to pall. The children kept asking when they would be returning to Braxfield, they were missing their lessons and their ponies; their own favourite books and board games.

It came as a bittersweet relief when Owen decided he should go back to the mills

The night before leaving, Anne Caroline lay awake for a long time. This was where her father died. Within this house he spoke his last words, took his final breath. It held a connection to him which was impossible to explain but felt keenly, as if he was just in the next room.

Tired, but wishing to savour and store memories, she blinked into the dark. As if through smoke, she strained to make out the contours of the plaster ceiling rose, the line of the carved wardrobe which once stood in Charlotte Street, the glass wall candelabra showing pale when shifting moonlight glimmered through the edges of the curtains.

Her lips moved in silent prayer until sleep swept her away.

Murdoch lost no time in seeking out Senga when they reached Braxfield. The news was as he thought. Wishing her congratulations on her betrothal, he hurried to Sheddon's office and poured out his request.

The butler pursed his lips, mulling over the proposition.

'To offer this young woman a position in Mr Owen's household without an interview, is not an attractive prospect. You believe she would be satisfactory in Senga's position, but you are not the one to judge.'

'Mr Walker's establishment is run a' the highest standard, sir, an' she's bin there fur years. Ah'm sure she can supply an excellent reference.'

'And if she arrives on our doorstep, takes up residence as your wife and discovers the backwoods of Scotland or, indeed *you*, are not to her liking, will we be without a housemaid *and* a manservant?'

'We are as certain o' oor feelings as ony man an' woman can be afore sich a union.' Murdoch sought to allay the fears he saw on Sheddon's face. 'Sir, ma duty is wi' the Maister. Ye ken how much Ah care ... Ah've bin wi' him nigh oan eighteen years. Ye can count on ma loyalty.'

'Very well, I make no promises but I shall bring the matter to Miss Wilson's attention.'

Murdoch thanked him profusely and went about his work in the boot room and laundry. The basement corridor rang with his cheerful whistling, repeating, again and again, the catchy refrain of Burns' 'I love a Lassie'.

Cook enjoyed the first ten minutes then bellowed from the stove side, 'gie it a rest or at least gie us anither ditty. Ah'll be hearin' tha' in ma bed if ye carry oan!'

Silence. Then the tuneful notes of Bonnie Jean.

'Whit's up wi' him?' Alice moaned, taking a rest from beating a dozen egg whites to a foam.

'Ah dinnae ken, but nae doot there's a lassie at the back o' it!.'

'Ye ken? Naw,' Alice sniggered, 'he's a batchelor if e'er Ah saw yin.'

'Stranger things ha'e happened.' Cook lifted the lid of the stock pot, pulling away and shielding her face from the steam while trying to peep at the bubbling contents. 'Look at Senga, who'd ha'e thocht it?'

'True.' Alice applied herself to the beaters again, wondering if she would ever meet someone special. The next dance at the Institute, perhaps? She gave a final hearty whisk and turned the bowl upside down; the stiff white peaks never moved. Now, on to the next task.

Owen did not stay long at New Lanark, he was keen to pursue his contacts at Westminster. It seemed to him that unless he was relentlessly exerting pressure and lobbying for the Bill on factory conditions, nothing happened. Years were passing and it was still not voted upon.

For once, Murdoch did not find the journey to London arduous. This was partly because they left the Owen carriage at home and travelled by swift post-chaises and the cumbersome, but fast, Mail coaches. An exchange of letters with Emily had told his news of a conditional approval from all parties at Braxfield.

225

The valet's nerves were at breaking point by the time they alighted at Bedford Square yet it was another two hours before he met Emily again.

'The housekeeper was none too pleased,' she told him, holding eye contact, both delighting in the sight of the other. 'But I believe I've won her over. I'm required to stay until a replacement is found.'

'Och, that should nae be lang, there's sae mony folk in London, some yin must be richt fur the joab.'

She tilted her head, her teasing smile at odds with her formal black dress and modest white muslin cap, 'I thought you said I was irreplaceable?'

'Ye are tae me, ma dear. Oh, aye, ye are tae me.'

The news of Robert Owen's arrival in the city soon spread. Walker's footmen were kept busy answering the doorbell to messengers bringing invitations to dine, requests for meetings, letters imploring him to call by at his own convenience, offers to join parties and attend the theatre; soon his diary was filled with appointments.

A visit to Jeremy Bentham was high on Owen's list of priorities after receiving a letter from him complaining of a lack of communication regarding New Lanark. An afternoon of frank discussion and reassurance set the partnership on an even keel again. Then he walked through the muddy, jostling streets of the capital in the hope of finding William Allen at his Plough Court premises.

The chemist was busy, as always, but pleased to see Owen, hustling him into his study and calling for refreshments. There they spoke of the ongoing distress and famine across Europe and the growing problem of malnutrition in Britain.

Owen's plans to address the predicament and William Allen's involvement in charitable soup kitchens and his agricultural projects kept them talking late into the drizzling summer evening.

The next morning, after rising earlier than usual to attend to paperwork, and seeing it was another wet, dreary day, Owen made use of Walker's carriage. He had been invited to visit the Prime Minister, Lord Liverpool, at his city residence; Fife House in Whitehall.

Having heard tales of Lord and Lady Liverpool's close and happy marriage, Owen was not in the least surprised to find Lady Louisa at her husband's side in one of the smaller, but no less opulent, upstairs drawing rooms.

Introductions were made, Owen bowing low to the Prime Minister and then again to Lady Louisa.

Owen waited for them both to sit down before choosing his place, opposite to them. The atmosphere was formal, accentuated by the grand surroundings. Although the room was not on the grand scale of the lower reception rooms, Fife House boasted ornate, lofty ceilings and cream washed walls lined with massive, dramatic oil paintings, dark in their gilded plaster frames.

Lord Liverpool had never expected to become Prime Minister, accepting the position in a panicked flurry of activity after Percival was assassinated. He was sure another leader would be found but even with all the intervening debacle of the wars, he was still there.

He was famous for his cultured, reasonable demeanour and the genuine good heartedness of the man was plain to see.

Tall and fair, handsome in his youth and nicknamed 'Delightful' at Charterhouse, maturity brought an unattractive thickening around the Prime Minister's jowels, his chin slipping away into his starched cravat. Lady Louisa was a few years his senior but with half a century behind her, she retained the willowy figure of a girl. Poised and straight-backed in a dark blue, high necked dress of simple design, her tasteful gold and gemstone jewellery was worn without ostentation..

The shape of her deep brown eyes were not dissimilar, Owen thought, to those of his own Caroline, and her sweet tempered face stood up to scrutiny in the white daylight streaming through the windows. Only a few silver hairs shone among the dark locks swept up into a chic silk turban.

Lady Louisa took a devoted interest in her husband's career and within minutes of conversing, it was clear she was a woman of quick wit and high intellect. There were no children in their marriage to make calls on her time, giving the couple freedom to be together, travelling, entertaining and enjoying the restricted leisure time his responsibilities allowed.

As the meeting unfolded, both Lord and Lady Liverpool showed their interest in Owen's first essay, A New View of Society. They had also read his Plan for the Amelioration of the Poor and posed probing questions, illustrating a close attention to his work.

'It is a curious notion,' Lord Liverpool said slowly, thoughtfully, 'to suggest the ills of the world can be eradicated simply by forming the characters of our children to be ones of understanding and benevolence.'

Owen was quick to confirm his belief. 'It may at first seem strange to you, sir, but it is a fact and one which I can show to be true from my work in New Lanark.'

'I have received reports of your mills and your little community, describing it in the most glowing terms. However, there is a considerable difference between a village of two thousand and a country of twelve million.'

'No matter the size of the population, it is made up of individuals and families. Of that I am sure we are agreed?' Owen exuded passion. 'If each of these families conducts their lives as I have described, the next generation will be formed as useful, caring human beings. After good health, what is the most sought after goal in Life? To be happy! You will see from my essay how this can be achieved.'

'Aha! If only it were that simple!'

'With respect, your Lordship, it *is* that simple,' Owen stated. 'All it requires is for the New System to be implemented and encouraged. When the priorities of the nation are changed from acquiring money, to acquiring happiness and contentment, then cruel, oppressive behaviour would cease and harmony prevail.'

'Forgive me, sir, but in this utopian future you paint,' Lady Louisa broke in, 'there would still be a need for production of food and ...' she fluttered her fingers, 'manufacturing of goods of all sorts, would there not?'

'Oh most certainly, your Ladyship, and, I beg your indulgence, surely a contented, educated and caring population would be of far greater mutual benefit for the whole country than the way it stands today?'

The discussion turned to the provision of schooling, the radical issue of free education for the lower classes and the problems arising from the unhealthy conditions in the explosion of mills and factories.

'At present, these lowly employees are looked upon as mere commodities, to be replaced when they breakdown through illness or, in the worst cases, when they die.' Owen paused for a moment, observing the effect of his words: he *had* to make the Prime Minister understand. 'It is neither sustainable, nor moral, to treat our fellow human beings with such disrespect. That is why I have implored Sir Robert Peel to push for the new reforms.'

Lord Liverpool was nodding, 'And tell me, how does your vision, as laid out in your pamphlet, apply to the challenges and hardships we face at present with a society reliant on intensive manufacturing?'

'The one removes the other. It is exactly what I have achieved at New Lanark. Mills do not have to be evil, degrading places. They can and *should* be run to allow sufficient time for education and for people to socialise and experience the pleasant, wholesome things in life.'

He went on to explain the many benefits of a happy workforce, including high production and fewer hours lost to illness and accidents.

'My New System of teaching kindness and forbearance, tolerance and respect will allow people of different status and religious beliefs to work together, side by side. Instead of animosity and jealousy, they discover how much easier it is to co-operate with one another: mill owner with worker, master with servant. Remove the cause of the feelings of injustice and these measures, as laid out in my essay, will produce happiness.'

After more detailed debate, Lord Liverpool said, 'I am also indebted to you, Mr Owen, for your letter of a few weeks past, regarding the slow process through the House of Commons of Sir Robert Peel's Bill.' He grimaced, apologetically, 'I call it Peel's Bill, but we are all aware its origin and impetus arise from you, sir. It will have a fair hearing, no doubt about that. These things take an inordinate amount of time, but it will be read.'

'The plight of the poor is constantly on my mind,' Lady Louisa told Owen. 'My husband and I are very taken with your New System. We would both wish to visit your mills in Scotland were it a little closer.'

'You have been to Scotland?' Owen asked.

'I was there back in '96!' Lord Liverpool laughed, 'a long story and probably a boring one! Suffice to say, at the time I was Colonel of the Cinque Port Fencibles. I found myself near the town of Dumfries at the wrong time, well, the wrong time for me, anyhow. That fellow, the excise man and bard, Robert Burns, had just died and I was charged to provide Guard for his burial.' He shook his head. 'It was not a duty I relished. Many a time while in the area I was invited to make his acquaintance, it was thought a privilege but I always refused. The man was a revolutionary!'

'Ah,' Owen was pensive. 'I confess I can understand little of Mr Burns' writing, the Scottish tongue eludes me. However, I recall my late father in law, David Dale, commenting that the man's heart was in the right place. He was, with the emotional depth and clever, romantic usage of poetry, expressing the feelings of his people.'

'*His* people! He was inciting separatist feeling amongst the King's subjects. He sailed close to the wind, by Jove. A sympathiser of the reformists.' Lord Liverpool sighed. 'Your own words have been called revolutionary, ye know, Mr Owen. My Home Secretary, Lord Sidmouth, received intelligence in the form of letters quoting the statements of certain Church of Scotland ministers and other members of the Clydesdale community which purported to name you as a danger to the government.'

'Indeed?' Owen remained still, his voice quiet. 'May I enquire in what way I appear to have created this impression?'

The Prime Minister waved his hand dismissively. 'There is no need for alarm, Mr Owen. Lord Sidmouth considered the allegations against you and found them to be mere hearsay, the gossip of a housewife. These were presented as accounts, he told me, of words you may or may not have spoken on the opening of your new school in New Lanark.'

'My new Institute for the Formation of Character,' Owen corrected, realising where the slander originated: Reverend Menzies and Mr Houldsworth.

A clerk knocked discreetly at the door, reminding the Prime Minister the allocated time for their meeting was drawing to a close.

'Anyhow, Mr Owen, they held no credence.' Lord Liverpool continued. 'You have laid out your views openly, publishing them for all to see and remark upon. I note you deliberately invite criticism?'

'They will bear the closest of scrutiny,' Owen said proudly. 'I have no fear of being found lacking in my New System because they are formed from actual experience and a sound knowledge of human behaviour.'

'Your time and effort on behalf of the disadvantaged is to be applauded. It is a most absorbing theory, Mr Owen,' Lady Louisa moved forward in her seat, preparing to rise, her taffeta skirt rustling against the velvet upholstery.

'Yes, very interesting,' her husband agreed. 'I understand you are meeting the Home Secretary later this week?'

'On Thursday, your Lordship.'

They were all standing now, the footman taking up his position in readiness to open the door.

'I wish you well, sir,' Lord Liverpool shook his hand and, with another bow, Owen thanked them for inviting him to discuss his work and took his leave.

***

Cathy stood impatiently in a queue in the front room of the manager's office in New Lanark.

'There wis a letter fur me?' she asked when her turn came to approach the clerk behind the mahogany desk. 'Ah wis telt tae collect it efter work? Cathy Rafferty.'

'Miss Catherine Rafferty? Aye ...' the young man lifted papers and opened drawers. 'It were here ... oh, aye, here it is. Ye need tae piy, fourpence.'

'Whit!' she leaned across the desk and snatched it up. 'How in the name o' heaven can a letter cost fourpence?' Then she saw the sender's name and address written neatly at the top. Her pulse raced. 'Ye ken me, Philip Tait, Ah'll bring the pennies the morra, jist let me ha'e the letter noo?'

'Aye, all richt,' the lad had a soft spot for the fair-faced mill girl. 'But dinnae gae tellin' yon uncle o' yours! Mr MacAllister can be awfy fussy.'

Cathy favoured him with a flirtatious smile and hurried out the door, the letter clutched in her hand.

231

It was from her little brother, Stephen.

She stopped in the lee of a wall, shrinking back from the flood of fellow workers flowing home for the night. Pulling out the folded ends of paper and studying the handwriting she was thankful for the evenings spent in the Institute learning to read.

My Dearest Sister,

As you will know if you are reading this letter, I am alive and living in New York. It is a fine place and I am well. My service in His Majesty's Navy was dreadful beyond words, the best I can say is that it is over. It is with relief that I can write with the greatest of news, I am with Nathan Kydd! He has done well here as have many souls who left the shores of Britain to find a better life. I too have found it. You would do well to join us and all expenses would be paid by Mr Kydd.

That gentleman sends his warmest regards to you and to our mother and to little Lily. I pray you are safe and well. Please write to me, my dear sister, and forgive me for leaving.

Yours with much love and affection, your brother, Stephen Rafferty

'Cathy, whit ye daen, lass?'

Cathy jumped, nearly dropping the thin sheet of paper.

The slight figure of her Aunt Rose stood right beside her, peering up with inquisitive, darting eyes. The Scotts hardly ever received letters.

'Ah cannae tell ye ... no' the noo. Please unnerstaun, Auntie? It wid nae be fair oan ma Mam.' Cathy put an affectionate arm around Rosie's shoulders, hugging her close and joining the crowd to walk up to the Rows. 'We'll be up tae Joe's later, ye'll be there?'

'O' course we'll be there! the first nicht in their big hoose!' She sniffed, watching for any reaction. 'Weel, Ah'll pray whitever is in yon letter is guid news.'

Cathy hugged her again, keeping her expression bland and evading questions until they parted outside her tenement door.

Was it good news?

Of course, to know Stephen was alive gave a wonderful surge of happiness but the mention of her father, still calling himself Nathan Kydd, brought another, less pleasant emotion. She must tell her mother, that was clear, but when? Just before walking up to

232

town? *During* the walk? She shook her head, plodding up the dim stairway. Perhaps she would wait until tomorrow, or not tell her at all, ever? But that would be mean and, as Mr Owen said, everyone should be treated with kindness and understanding.

Lost in her quandary, Cathy thrust open the door to their room to find Sarah and Lily changing into their best clothes.

'There ye are!' Sarah turned a cheerful face to greet her daughter. 'Ah thocht we'd tak a wee gift up wi' us ...' walking around in her stays over a cotton shift, she pointed to a package wrapped with ribbons lying on the table. 'Caunels ... wax caunels. Och, they're braw! Sae smooth an' smell warm an' sweet. Andrew says they gi'e licht fur oors.'

'That's a nice thocht.' Cathy slipped the letter, unnoticed, under the blanket on her bed, throwing her shawl on top.

Pulling off her cap, she unpinned the plaits bound around her head and began teasing them apart. It was lovely to see the frown smoothed from her Mam's forehead, hear her humming in happy anticipation of the evening ahead. This was not the moment to reveal Stephen's letter

Up on the hill above the mills, Fiona was putting the finishing touches to her own hair: butterflies dancing in her stomach, thrills of excitement catching her unawares.

Joe was right, this was their first proper home. It was entirely his own achievement and she was bursting with pride. The square rooms and bare walls were now well known to her, the nooks and crannies, creaks and scent of plaster and paint being unique and cherished. It was no longer Baxter's, it was theirs, a place to make their own and share their lives. In its new found familiarity, she saw it as a different house, much smaller and friendlier than the mighty mansion her mind had created to cause her fear in the past.

The preceding weeks had been busy with preparations to move, piling belongings into boxes and bags and loading up the cart. When Fiona was down at the Institute during the day, Sam undertook the physical removal of their goods and chattels. Decades of accumulated Scott family clothes, boots, pots and pans, dozens of earthenware and glass jars filled with pickles and even more empty ones ready for the next harvest. In the evenings, with the help of Joe and the older boys, the large pieces of furniture were heaved outside and carted up the hill.

'Yon pony could pull the cart up by hersel',' Sam laughed, rubbing Rusty's smooth muzzle, 'she kens the route by hairt.'

Fiona was grateful to Sam, often wondering what they would do without him. He liked to work methodically, writing a list every evening and working his way through the tasks the next day, ticking them off as they were completed. She laughed at his almost ceremonial 'burning of the list' at night, when a new one was started.

While pressing the last hairpins into place, she heard voices outside, mingling with the evening bird calls drifting through the open window. Then there was a laugh, warm and full of mirth: Sarah and the others were arriving.

Slipping her feet into her best pumps, Fiona took a moment to compose herself, glancing round the room.

It was a mess, piled with bags and boxes all down one wall, the bed strewn with Joe's shirts, waistcoats and cravats, her shifts and skirts half covering his formal black wool jacket, piles of both their undergarments threatening to overturn and slide to the floor. The muddled garments, colourful or plain, new and pricey or old and worn-out all meant something to her, all held a little of her married life.

Joe was calling to her and on going out onto the landing, she looked down on the clamour of bodies milling around him in the hall.

Rosie saw her and blew kisses, shouting above the others, 'Lang may yer lum reek!'

With Ruth's guidance and aforethought, their only table was placed in the large front room. On returning from work, Fiona was thrilled to find it laid with cooked chicken, meat pies, pickles and bread. Added to this feast, Sarah and Rosie brought fruit cake, cheese and boiled eggs.

Rosie, not one to stand on ceremony, raked through the unpacked boxes in the scullery and sought out a large platter, carefully unfolding her parcel of greased paper to present a warm cloutie dumpling. Tam brought ale, plonking the pitcher down in the kitchen with an ironic shrug on seeing the hefty barrel Donnie carried down from the market that morning.

They ate like royalty, then, urged by the children, the hallway was used to whoop and reel to Davey's fiddle music.

It was a joyful evening. Even Sionaidh enjoyed it in her own way, wandering between the rooms, bemused but content.

Mindful of the ten o'clock curfew in the village, Joe kissed his sisters goodnight and stood out at the gateway, waving to them until they were out of sight.

'We're awa' tae!' Sam slapped his brother on the back. 'We'll walk Ruth hame an' then Connor and Ah'll bed doon at the cottage.'

'The offer stauns tae sleep here,' Fiona insisted.

'Naw, lass. This is yer first nicht, ye should jist be wi' yer bairns. Ah've imposed far too long as it is.'

'Imposed!' Fiona chuckled, her carefully styled hair was falling from the grips, swinging in tendrils around her face. Was it the ale? She felt light headed, amused by everything.

'Ah'm fur ma scratcher an' all,' Tam called from the doorway. 'Ah'll see ye the morra! It's a grand hoose, Ah wish ye a' the best.'

On going back to the parlour, Joe saw Fiona's surprise at finding Donnie, Davey and Robert lounging at the table, picking at the remnants of the feast.

'They're stayin' fur the nicht, mibbee longer,' he whispered in her ear.

Her eyes flooded with tears, lips pressing together to hold back a sob. All her children under the same roof; she could not have wished for a better house-warming present.

'Dinnae greet, ma love,' he cajoled.

She turned towards him, burying her head against his chest.

Donnie was watching and sent his father a quizzical look.

Mouthing the words over Fiona's bowed head, Joe replied, 'Happy tears.'

***

'Well, good morning to ye, Robert Owen,' Jeremy Bentham greeted his visitor from his seat behind his desk.

A sea of ledgers and papers were spread before him along with a plate of cold cuts and a bowl of stewed prunes. Slightly behind him, set safely apart, there was a tray with a goblet of small beer.

'My word,' Bentham exclaimed, 'your name is appearing all over the place ... on every ones' lips ... and in more newspapers than ye could shake a stick at!'

'Yes, my views appear to have caught the interest of the public as well as the politicians.' Owen took the chair he was offered. 'My apologies, I have interrupted your breakfast.'

'I like to put in a few hours work before taking a bite, my brain seems all the keener for being starved. Can I offer ye anything? Ye've eaten?'

'I am quite spoilt for choice at Bedford Square! It seems an extravagance given the Walkers are in Switzerland. At Braxfield, a bowl of porridge at mid-morning suffices.'

'Anyway,' Bentham returned to his topic, 'perhaps your sudden fame is not so much due to a public desire to hear your plans, as you, personally, are to the journalists? They scent a story! Someone with such a radical philosophy as your own is courting Westminster without being sent to Newgate, eh?'

'It may be radical and reformist, as the columnists are saying, but, as you are aware, it is entirely peaceful.'

'Ye have that on your side, I grant ye. Liverpool must be pleased to hear anything which might blunt the teeth of the baying masses.'

Bentham tucked his long pepper and salt hair behind his ears and settled back, giving his whole attention to his visitor.

Knowing his partner to be busy, Owen launched straight into his reason for calling so early in the day.

'I wished to tell you the recent good news. I had an extremely interesting and productive meeting with Lord Sidmouth. The upshot being, he has taken it upon himself to have my essays printed and bound in a superior manner to be sent to the leaders of Europe and the United States.'

'My, my, that *is* good news. Sidmouth, or as I always think of him, Henry Addington, was a useless Prime Minister and is proving nothing but a brutish force as Home Secretary. What else can we expect from the Tories? He fears his populace, as well he might. This island is full of desperate men, poverty stricken and starving to boot. But hanging them when they can take no more, as in York, is repugnant to any civilised human being. As ye know, I am in fierce opposition of capital punishment.'

Owen was nodding. 'Fear not! I have given him the means to quell the rising revolution and, it appears, he is enthusiastic in spreading the word. It is exactly what I wished! If governments and rulers subscribe to my New System and spread it amongst their countrymen, we will turn the tide of injustice and see the poor gainfully employed, housed and educated.'

'Have ye read the news reports?' Bentham sucked his teeth, 'their comments?'

'The gibes at my own religious beliefs?' Owen moved a hand as if swatting away a fly. 'What I may or may not believe is beside the point. It is what I *say*, what I *actually do*, my plans and desires for bettering the lot of the working classes, changing bad habits and removing bigoted attitudes ... *that* is what they should be concentrating on.'

'Nothing sells papers better than controversy. You are not a pistol waving fanatic, your arguments are reasonable and stated calmly. Unfortunately, for the ink daubed scribblers and their editors, your essays do not provide juicy fodder for their readers who have a taste for gossip and intrigue. So, they turn their minds to you, personally! Beware the sparks they will throw at ye, they may ignite and over-shadow your cause.'

'My whole philosophy is one of respecting the views of others and being kind and understanding towards one another, yet this is not enough. Southey accuses me of not founding the Plan on religion. I shall respond to him in the article I am writing for the Times. True religion is devoid of all sectarian notions and in the proposed establishment there would be full liberty for each to worship as he chose.'

'Oh, I agree! I wish you well, but they are out to pin you down like the poor fox by the hounds.'

'Well, when I leave you, I am to attend Lambeth Palace for an appointment with the Archbishop of Canterbury.'

'Are ye indeed.'

'He wishes to discuss in depth my essays and the Plan for creating villages for the unemployed. I must say, I am greatly looking forward to the opportunity.'

'That will please our fellow partners for I fear they are somewhat Evangelical in their own views. Allen in particular.'

'I will leave you to your work,' Owen stood up. 'It is a pleasant morning, dry at least, to enjoy the ten minute walk back to Bedford Square. I understand the journey south over the Thames to Lambeth Palace may be better by carriage.'

Bentham placed a hand on his desk, levering himself to his feet.

'Gracious me, yes,' he puffed, 'unless ye know the route well, ye might be lost all day!' Bentham followed Owen to the hallway. 'Come, I shall take some air, ye can leave by the garden rather than the dismal passageway from Queen Anne's Gate.'

They parted beneath a dense green canopy of elms, the squeak and clink of the wrought iron gate jarring against the harmonious sounds of distant sparrows and humming insects.

'You have a very peaceful home, for the centre of London,' Owen remarked.

'It was my father's home and I find it very congenial,' Bentham's long cheeks and high forehead were dappled with sunlight. 'Again, I wish ye luck, Mr Owen. Our fellow countrymen need all the support we can muster.'

Owen doffed his hat and set off at a sprightly pace down Bird Cage Walk.

He was pleased with the overall press coverage of his efforts, several giving favourable introductions and comments to his work. *The Morning Post's* "a real patriot and exemplary philanthropist" was very satisfactory and the *Times*' "Mr Owen is not a theorist only, but a man long and practically familiarised to the management of the poor."

Things were going the right way. His early struggles to bring attention to his philosophy were bearing fruit and bringing him powerful supporters. Before the week was out, he would be dining with two of the king's sons, the Dukes of York and Kent; valuable opportunities to garner weight behind his flagging Bill. It was still lingering in the House of Commons but, in due course, would need enthusiastic defenders to carry it through the Lords.

Owen's spirits were high as he ran up the steps of No. 49.

Walker's hallway was filled with the scent of lilies and he paused after handing over his hat to the footman, leaning close to a bountiful flower arrangement on the marble table.

'Ah, what a pleasure!' he smiled, the fragrance reminding him of Braxfield and his family. Before preparing for the interview with

238

the Archbishop, he penned a quick note to Caroline and the children. His plans were proceeding well, he wrote, but there was still much to be done and he would be detained in the capital for the coming weeks.

He sealed the letter and rang for Murdoch, then took a moment to stand and gaze out the window at the beauty of the pleasure garden and tall white terraced houses of Bedford Square.

These clean streets and spaces of trees and flowers must not be the exclusive right of those with money. In his Plan, while the buildings could not achieve the architectural splendour of those he surveyed, they would be comfortable, pleasing to the eye. He made sure there was provision for pasture land for the children to play, picnics to be taken and exercise enjoyed.

All this could be, *would be*, the future for those presently mired in poverty and despair.

At last, he was making progress.

Chapter Thirteen

"It is an honor to appear on the side of the afflicted"
Elizabeth Fry

Sam and Ruth were married within a week of Joe moving into his new home.

Before the regular Sunday service, they exchanged vows in the porch of St Nicholas Church and were solemnly declared man and wife. Afterwards, together with all the children, Ruth's brother and his family, Tam and the Scotts, they led a triumphant procession through spitting rain to gather in celebration at Joe's house.

Ruth was glowing; her plain features transformed into beauty by happiness, enhanced by the stylish gown paid for by Joe and Fiona and made and gifted to the bride by Sarah and her daughters.

Sam was bewildered. Ruth's looks, while homely and not unattractive, were not the reason he chose her to be his wife. To find her so alluringly feminine made him shy and tongue-tied after the ceremony.

'Whit's the matter, Sam?' Ruth enquired, mildly alarmed at the change in his behaviour.

'Nuthin' ...' he looked away, cheeks flaming.

'C'mon, yer no' yersel' ... ye keep starin' at me? is there a coal smut oan ma face?'

'Och naw!' He kept his eyes purposefully fixed on their clasped hands. 'Yer awfy bonnie the day, Ruth. If ye had nae a'ready won ma hairt, Ah wid be fallin' fur ye, an' that's the truth.'

'Aw, whit a braw thing tae say!' Then she nudged him, 'or are ye tellin' me Ah looked like a bag o' spanners afore?'

Fiona overheard, pretending she did not, and happily joining with their shared laughter and offering selections of biscuits and cake.

After a while, Sam braced himself and called for everyone's attention. He took up a position by the open doorway to the hall; Ruth on his left and Connor on his right.

'And now comes the hard part,' he called out, waiting for the conversation to stop, all faces turning to him. 'We must tak oor leave. We're all mercifully able tae read an' write and we must mak sure tae practice oor skills an' keep each ither close. We thank ye fur all your kindnesses and your friendship and wid beg a last favour?'

'Aye, whitever ye ask!'

'It will be hard tae tak the coach tae Liverpool, it will be hard tae suffer the sea voyage tae Sidney doon in New South Wales but ... it will be e'en harder tae step oot this door. Ah wid ask ye tae stay put, stay in this hoose an' dinnae staun at the door an' wave. We've said oor goodbyes, let us leave with a smile!'

With that, as pre-arranged with his wife and son, Sam turned and left, pulling the door shut behind them.

Joe and Donnie were the only people who knew their bags were packed and stored in the cart, Rusty already between the shafts, Donnie in the driving seat. Sam hated goodbyes and if this was the way he wished to leave, Joe would ensure it went as painlessly as possible.

Rosie dissolved into quiet tears, sinking down into a chair to be comforted, rather awkwardly, by Gerry. For Sarah, it was not unexpected. Her suspicions had been sparked by Sam's unusually long visit to her room at New Lanark a few evenings earlier.

'We'll miss them,' Fiona said to the room in general. 'We must comfort oorsels that he's no' alane an' it's no' like when he wis aff tae fight. It's whit he's dreamed o' daen fur years.'

'A toast!' Joe seized the jug of ale and moved around the room filling everyone's proffered glasses. Few noticed the tremor in his hands, the gruffness in his throat, too absorbed with their own emotions. 'To Sam, Ruth and Connor Scott!' He cried, proudly. 'Guid health, happiness an' a grand life doon under!'

The sudden absence of the war veteran and his shy little boy left a hole, even their quiet neighbour, Mrs Mclaren, shed a tear at his leaving.

Many times in the following weeks, Fiona would look for Connor amongst the children running down to school, her heart missing a beat at not seeing him. Then she would remember the reason. Laying the table or doling out food often meant the hasty removal of two places. It brought a fresh awareness of all the little chores Sam used to undertake; filling the log basket, the coal bucket, pumping water for the house and stable, tending Cal's

241

Patch and helping with the horses. As well as all the added physical work he did on the building site with Joe: unpaid, unbidden.

Fiona knew Joe was missing his brother dreadfully and tried to cheer him by recalling the happy times they shared.

'Dinnae be sad those times are o'er,' she told him, 'be glad they happened.'

It brought to mind her own brother and the games and fun they shared on the beaches many years ago. The gritty feeling of pale gold sand between her toes and the windswept cries of seagulls and the sound of breaking waves crashing and sucking on the shore: their laughter, the taste of salt on her lips and icy water lapping round her ankles. Two children playing and quarrelling but always loving each other, torn apart too soon, before they could appreciate each other, really know one another.

She wondered where he was, her big brother, wishing she could know him as an adult, talk to him, tell him she loved him and would never forget him.

***

Ever since Owen opened the Institute and brought in shorter working hours in the mills, a calm atmosphere pervaded New Lanark.

At first it was a novelty but as the months wore on new habits formed. Life was not just a daily grind of work, chores and falling asleep from exhaustion. Hobbies were explored and, weather permitting, families and courting couples took walks along the specially created woodland paths. The evening lessons provided for those who worked all day became well attended, attracting villagers of all ages. The older residents marvelled at being given the chance to learn to read.

Music and dancing was commonplace, children played shinty or with balls and hoops in the streets and the allotments rang with voices; sharing fresh produce and friendship alike.

A few days after Sam's departure, the dreary rain clouds were finally pushed away and patches of blue sky grew steadily larger. By the time the mill bell was ringing for the end of the day, the workers burst out of the doors into a scene drenched in brilliant sunshine.

A hasty dinner was eaten that evening; everyone was eager to be in the fresh air and carry out plans thwarted by the long spell of wet weather. Dozens of men tramped up the hill to their vegetable plots, pigeon or chicken coops while the women seized the opportunity of good drying weather to get the washing done.

'Weel, they'll be doon in Liverpool noo,' Sarah told Cathy as they filled three buckets with water from the pump.

'D'ye reckon? Whit a way tae stairt yer merrit life, bouncin' aroond in a Mail Coach fur hunners o' miles!'

Grasping a bucket each and sharing the burden of the third between them, they walked to their doorway with fast, encumbered steps, before setting them down with relief.

Lily was helping by putting clothes in the tub.

'Staun back, lass,' Sarah cried, emptying the first bucket, Cathy following suit. 'It'll splash!'

'There's a lot o' folk leavin' fur ither countries. Maist are gaun tae America or Canada,' Cathy rolled up the hem of her frock and tucked it into her waistband, slipping her feet out her clogs and climbing into the tub to give it a good tread. 'Och, the watter's cauld!'

Sarah laughed, 'Rather ye than me! There's sumat tae be said fur growin' auld! Lily, be a lamb an' run upstairs an pit the kettle oan?

Cathy stamped away at the clothes, one hand on her hip the other waving around for balance. This was a well practised stance, carried out since she was old enough to climb over the side of the metal tub.

She glanced around, seeing their neighbours engrossed in similar evening chores. Now would be the right time to tell her mother about Stephen's letter. The last half dozen attempts had been thwarted either by her own reluctance or interruptions.

'Mam? Can Ah tell ye sumat? While Lily's no' here an' we're alane?'

'Aye,' Sarah was pulling fluff from an old woollen shawl.

'Ah dinnae want tae upset ye ... but ...'

'Och, it's **Ross**? Isn't it? ' Sarah gave a knowing smile, 'he's asked ye tae marry him?'

'It's nuthin' tae dae wi' Ross. Ah got a letter ... frae oor Stephen.'

'Whit did ye say?' Sarah's smile froze, contradicting the dismay in her eyes.

'Oor Stephen's weel ...' Cathy kept lifting her feet up and down, no longer naturally, striving to keep up the rhythm. 'He's living in America ... wi' Nathan Kydd.'

Putting her hand to her mouth, Sarah's knees buckled and she crumpled into a heap on the ground.

'Mam!' with a whoosh of water, Cathy leapt to her side. 'Mam, are ye alricht?'

'Aye ...' Sarah gasped, covering her face with her hands.

'Ah thocht Ah should tell ye,' Cathy knelt beside her mother, rubbing her back, horrified to have caused such distress. 'Mibbee, Ah should nae?'

The commotion was attracting attention. Neighbours began calling over to Cathy: what was wrong with Mrs Rafferty? Did she need help? Mrs Young, sitting close by, pushed her knitting aside and hurried to take a look for herself.

'Is she sick?' she asked, peering at Sarah and laying a work worn hand on her forehead. 'She's nae fever.'

'Naw, weel, a bit dizzy,' Cathy lied. 'She'll be fine in a meenit.' Her mother was quiet, her breaths coming in gulps. 'Mam, p'raps we should gae up tae the room?'

In the privacy of their room, Sarah slumped down on the edge of her bed. She was trying to make sense of her jumbled thoughts, distracted by Lily's anxious demands to know what was wrong, yet unable to form a reply.

With life-long experience of her mother's turbulent emotions, Cathy decided it was best to leave her alone for a while. Surely she was happy to know her son was alive?

Pressing Stephen's letter into her mother's hand, she took Lily and the newly boiled kettle down to the street to finish the washing.

'Is she feelin' better?' Mrs Young asked when the sisters emerged from the tenement door.

'Oh aye,' Cathy said confidently. 'She'll git o'er it. She alis does.'

A few minutes later, a casement window scraped open high above them and Sarah's head appeared, calling for Cathy to come upstairs.

'Are ye gaun?' Sarah demanded angrily, as soon as her daughter entered. 'Are ye gaun tae New York tae be wi' yer brither?'

'Naw! Why wid Ah dae tha'?'

Eyes blazing, Sarah brandished the letter. 'He's askin' ye tae gae there! Tellin' ye yer faither will piy! Are ye leavin' me?'

'Naw!' Cathy cried, again. 'Mam, dinnae fash yersel', Ah'm no' gaun awa'.'

'Mibbee when ye think oan it, ye'll change yer mind?'

'Ah have thocht oan it.'

'Oh aye, a day's thocht fur sich a big decision ...'

'The letter came a while back, the day Uncle Joe flitted tae the new hoose.'

This revelation made Sarah even more upset; the tears were bubbling now. The more Cathy attempted to calm her, the more upset Sarah became, culminating in Cathy lowering her voice to a reasoned whisper, telling her mother to try and put herself in Stephen's position.

'Ye ken whit Mr Owen telt us tae dae? If we dinnae agree wi' sumat? Try an' unnerstaun' whit made the ither person dae whit they did?' She went to the door, 'Ah'm aff tae feenish the washin', think aboot it, Mam? Be happy fur Stephen? Thank God and be gratefu' he's alive.'

By the time her daughters returned to peg up the washing and string the line out the window to catch the breeze, Sarah was composed. Her red rimmed eyes and blotchy complexion telling of the stormy outburst she gave free rein to while alone.

Releasing years of pent up emotion left her exhausted but clear headed. Taking heed of Cathy's words, she realised Stephen's rejection of her was to be expected, she had, after all, refused to go with his father. It was her fault they were not a family, that her son grew up missing his father and she had to admit, her angry, at times violent, attempts to raise him must have caused resentment. She winced at the memories of slapping the little boy, shouting at him, threatening him: all to no avail. It did not bring him into line, it alienated him from her so, of course, he would rather be with his father.

It was past, things were resolving. By the grace of God, Stephen survived the perils of war and was where he wished to be and, her other painful burden of guilt, her actions were no longer denying Sean the presence of his son.

'Ah'm sorry Ah took oan sae,' Sarah told her daughters. 'Yer guid lassies. It wis a shock, t'was all. Ah should nae ha'e shouted at ye. It is grand news aboot Stephen an' Ah'll pray fur him. When ye write back, Cathy, send him his mither's love ...' she sighed, a weight lifting from her mind, 'an' tae Mr Kydd.'

The Scotts were still celebrating the welcome news that Stephen was alive when another piece of good fortune came their way.

When the market town of Lanark was granted the status of Royal Burgh by King David I, it was agreed the boundary stones of the territory must be formally checked every year. Every June for over six hundred years this duty had been carried out by a local man, given the title Lord Cornet and voted for by the Town Councillors.

The office of Lord Cornet was deemed an honour and although the duties were simply to ride or walk to all the Land Marches, or boundary stones, confirm they were in place and send a document to that effect to the reigning monarch, it was undertaken with dignified ceremony.

Mr Ewing had always been involved, both as a Lord Cornet and in later years as an official witness. Apart from seeing the group of merchants riding out the yard in their finest clothes with an air of importance, Joe just accepted it as what the locals called, the Lanimars tradition, undertaken by those of high standing in the town.

Therefore, it was to his family's unexpected delight that Joe was asked to take the position that year.

The children groomed Bluey to the patina of burnished steel, oiled her hooves and washed her snowy tail. Only the Councillors and bailies of Lanark accompanied the Lord Cornet but Fiona and Rosie made sure Joe's important role was broadcast far and wide.

***

Under a cloud strewn sky, William Allen's carriage trotted away from Bedford Square and threaded its way out of the city to the Borough of Newham.

246

Allen was taking Owen to visit his fellow Quaker friends, Joseph and Elizabeth Fry at their home in East Ham.

'Friend Joseph's wife is much involved in poor relief,' Allen said proudly. 'She is an extraordinary young woman, deeply moved by the plight of those less fortunate than herself. Her family background is one of wealth, both her father and grandfather being the bankers, Gurney and Barclay.'

'Did you say her husband, Joseph Fry, is also a banker?' Owen asked, his eyes on the passing views as the squalor of London gave way to colourful rural vistas.

'He is a tea merchant and yes, also a banker, although perhaps not the most successful in that area.' Like everything he did, Allen spoke quickly, rushing through his words as if he was too busy to waste time speaking. 'His mother was the driving force, a fine hard working Quaker lady. His uncle inherited the business acumen which, in my opinion, is lacking in the present generation of Fry men. His uncle's chocolate factory is still extremely productive, despite the war years and Tory taxes.'

Plashet House, the Fry's country residence, was surrounded by rolling parkland, graced with well spaced oaks, beech and willow trees and lush grazed meadows sloping into several ornamental, reed fringed ponds.

Owen was received with warm hospitality, being ushered into a sitting room where double doors stood open to the garden's mild air. Conversation was easy from the start and over elderflower cordial and warm muffins, Owen found his youthful hostess's views on educating the poor closely aligned to his own.

'My heart breaks for the plight of those held in prison,' Elizabeth told him earnestly. She was dressed modestly in a pale blue costume with a cream lace collar, her hair covered under a cotton cap allowing only her light brown fringe to escape. 'It is a mission of mine to remove at least some of their distress and I have recently made a little progress.'

He listened with encouraging nods and comments while she told him of the terrible conditions in Newgate Prison, where both male and female prisoners were crushed together in an atmosphere of extreme anguish.

'At last, I have succeeded in securing agreement for women to be lodged apart from men, but the lack of light, water and even the

247

most basic requirements of life are barely provided for unless the prisoners can pay,' her eyes flashed angrily, 'which, of course most of them cannot! They have only the clothes on their backs and no opportunity to clean themselves so I have been petitioning my friends for donations of any cast-offs which would be suitable and taking them into the prison myself.'

'Admirable,' Owen said, seriously.

'Attention needs to be brought to the starvation, disease and violence prevalent in these institutions. The mortality rate is appalling! I am forming the *Association for the Reformation of the Female Prisoners in Newgate* which should be far greater advanced than it is but these last two years,' she glanced away, hiding her thoughts from Owen's direct gaze, 'well ... it was a personally testing time for my own family.'

From Allen, Owen knew she was referring to the death of her small daughter, Betsy, and within months of the tragedy, the birth of another son, Samuel, their tenth child.

With a sympathetic expression, he put her at ease. 'Our mutual friend made me aware of your circumstances. You are to be commended for taking up the chalice once more.'

'Our personal misfortune is hard enough to deal with, yet we are free to find ways to ease our pain, seek comfort in our loved ones. It must be so much worse to suffer such torments while shackled in irons amidst the oppressive confines of Newgate's stone walls.'

'You are succeeding in improving their lives, Mrs Fry. It is rare to find a lady of your standing with empathy for the lower classes and to own a willingness to even contemplate their wretched lives.'

They talked of Owen's plans for making it possible for men and women to build their own villages and his New System of raising the next generation to be caring and respectful of each other.

'I have read your essays, Mr Owen, as has Joseph. I found them enthralling. I must tell you, for I prefer to speak directly, some of your remarks regarding Christianity are, how shall I say, disturbing.' She gave him an appraising look. 'However, I can see you are genuine in your philanthropy and I am pleased we have been introduced. Tell me, would you accompany me on a visit to the prison? I believe you will discover it to be as disconcerting as I do, to find our apparently civilised society treating human beings with utter contempt.'

248

Owen readily agreed and the date was set for July 25th.

The 24th of July was already marked down for a small meeting, by invitation only, at the George and Vulture tavern. His days being filled with lobbying for the languishing Factory Reform Bill, many candles were burned to stumps at night while writing and perfecting his speech for the occasion. So, it was gratifying to give his address to a full room of rich merchants and politicians.

He laid out his views and then called for the selection of a committee to investigate his Plan for the employment of the poor and ask for subscriptions to set up an experimental colony.

The response from his audience and the intense questioning which followed his speech brought criticism as well as support. Walking back to Bedford Square with friends, they discussed the success of the meeting and how best to deal with his critics.

'I have it!' he said brightly, 'I shall write a lengthy piece for the Times. It will be designed as if I am being interviewed by a third party. In this way, I can give full answers to the practicality of the scheme and allay the fears put forward at the Tavern.'

The more he wrote, the more he wished to say, waving Murdoch away and dismissing him for the night when the rest of the household could be heard retiring. Eventually, it was only the thought of being alert for his appointment with Mrs Fry the next morning which forced an end to his work.

Changing into the night shirt which Murdoch left draped on the bed, he washed his face and hands, dried them methodically and lay down. His mind was racing with thoughts on how to make this letter to the *Times* strongly worded and persuasive. It was a humid night and his long dark fringe stuck to his skin, reminding him of the need for a visit to the barber. He pushed the hair away, resting the cool back of his hand against his forehead, his eyes moving restlessly and without sight, all attention focused on the thoughts crowding his mind.

The clocks were striking the midnight hour throughout the still house before he snuffed out the candle and slept.

Newgate Prison was built to strike fear in to the hearts of anyone considering committing a crime. The architects performed their task well, creating a stone structure so fearsome and foreboding that even the innocent shuddered at its sight. Its massive frontage bore a central block and two wings, each showing only four small, high windows embedded in solid arches. Resembling an ancient fort, the impenetrable building squatted beneath a flat roof. Inside, provision was made for exercise and a concession to natural light and air by way of two courtyards, completely surrounded and overlooked by four floors of cells.

From the moment he stepped inside, Owen became aware of the nauseous odour of human waste. Mrs Fry held her perfumed handkerchief delicately against her nose, the only sign of her disgust being a slight narrowing of her eyes.

They were to be escorted by a guard, a swarthy unshaven man with vacant eyes and stains down his lurid yellow waistcoat. He carried a hoop of jangling keys which he would shake like a tambourine from time to time. Elizabeth Fry was obviously well known to him and after a brief discussion she instructed him to show them the women's cells first.

'I have begun a school for the children and to show the women the practicalities of cleanliness,' she told Owen when they emerged, slightly breathless, from the last flight of stairs. 'Even small changes make a difference to morale here.'

He had braced himself for a terrible ordeal and was taken aback to find the rooms wholesome and aired, the women smiling and the children clean. In just three months the changes brought about by Mrs Fry's thoughtful work were truly inspiring. It was obvious an effort was being made to make the bare stone spaces more comfortable and adopt routines and habits to fill the days with meaningful pursuits.

Owen observed the way the prisoners looked upon the Quaker woman who was giving her time and effort to help them in as many practical ways as she could imagine. He noted her calm, reassuring words, always supportive and encouraging, showing interest in what they had to say. Their only complaint was not having enough to do, they wished to work to pass the time, but were now trying hard to fill their days with singing, learning to read and write basic words and striving to remain as clean and healthy as conditions allowed.

After visiting the female side of the prison, Elizabeth asked to be taken to the men's corridors.

The difference was overwhelming.

It was hot, the air thick with the despicable odours of unwashed bodies and open buckets of raw sewage. Owen swallowed repeatedly, physically repulsed and deeply moved. The squalid conditions in mills offended his sensibilities to a distressing degree but this onslaught of sheer degradation was almost beyond belief.

Selecting the correct key from amongst dozens, the guard unlocked iron gate after rattling iron gate, giving access to shadowy corridors. Gruff male voices rumbled from whispers to bellows: there was no laughter.

'Most of these prisoners are waiting for transportation ships to take them to the colonies,' Elizabeth told him over the racket, 'and others will be released when their sentence is complete. That is, if these mortifying conditions do not bring an end to their lives first. I believe they all have need of skills for their future lives. At least, it might give them a chance to take up honest work and rise above the need to steal to keep from starving.'

On either side of them, behind grimy iron-barred gates, rows of narrow cells each housed a dozen or more ragged, half-clothed men, their bearded faces looming from the darkness as indistinct grey ovals with dark holes where eyes peered out, suspiciously.

As they made their way down the central corridor some of the inmates called out or stumbled forward, pushing their scrawny, bruised arms between the bars, begging for food.

Moaning and swearing mixed with angry cries and scuffles. Small groups squatted in circles on the filthy floor, playing makeshift games with torn cards or dice, barely glancing up to see the visitors. A few of the men appeared sober and rational in their despair, trying to hold on to their sanity, while others were roaring drunk on cheap gin. Spitting through rotten teeth or shouting slurred obscenities towards Mrs Fry and the jail in general, they earned a growl from the guard.

On reaching a courtyard where Elizabeth had requested boys' lessons to be held, they discovered the classes had just been dismissed. Arrangements were hurriedly made to bring the unfortunate youths back again and, from the first glance, Owen wished they had not been forced to return. Never had he seen such dejected, miserable human beings.

251

'Why are so many in leg irons?' Owen asked when they left the courtyard. 'I even saw a young boy being held in two of these vile contraptions?'

'Get out o' hand, they do,' the guard muttered. 'Irons slows 'em down.'

Elizabeth gave a helpless little shrug, 'That is the reason I was given when I asked the same question, some years ago. Who is to say? How could anyone be expected to behave well in this God forsaken dungeon? There are poor souls here who are quite deranged, they fight and bite like animals and should not be here at all. They have no memory of their crimes and should be housed away from these miseries.'

They came to a window, allowing a shaft of light to cut the gloom and a welcome draught of cleaner air. Owen paused beside it, craning to see out past the thick wall and down to the space below. Forty or fifty men were chained together, shambling in a slow circle, the metallic rattling of their shackles mingling with dragging footsteps.

Elizabeth came to stand at his side, not tall enough to see out the window but taking a moment to breathe without covering her nose.

For some time, they stood in silence, their senses overwhelmed by the awfulness of their surroundings.

Owen spoke first. 'This place, this current penal system ... it is purgatory. That boy in double leg irons? A great crime has been committed but it should be Lord Sidmouth who ought to be double-ironed in place of the boy! Our present society keeps the masses ignorant and without the tools or knowledge to provide for themselves. Then, when they are driven to crime to feed their families, they are banished to the other side of the planet, locked up in this indescribably dreadful place or punished by death. It simply cannot persist.'

'Oh, but how I wish and pray it would end,' she cried. 'Your work has the possibility to help bring change to this outrage, Mr Owen, but there are too many who turn away and forget their poor brothers and sisters.'

'Madam, I can assure you, I will not rest until everyone is treated equally, with respect and understanding. It *can* and *must* be done.'

'I agree,' she whispered.

With a wistful, wishful smile, she turned to walk towards the stairway, the guard ambling ahead holding a lantern to lead them down the windowless steps. Owen followed, almost retching when the claustrophobic stench stung his nostrils once more.

Owen was openly and warmly impressed by Mrs Fry's work. All the more so when the prison officials, whom he spoke with at length before leaving, assured him that before Mrs Fry and her associates visited the inmates, the women had been as 'lost of decency' as the men still remained.

'You see! A perfect example, if any more were needed, that human nature is plastic to good influences as well as bad ones and that if these wretched prisoners have sinned, the blame is not theirs but that of the community.'

He had been in London for a full two months and been wined, dined and invited to every meeting for good causes across the city. An afternoon of introductions to foreign officials while strolling with Charles Pictet, a brilliant Swiss diplomat, could be followed by an intimate philosophical discussion with Jeremy Bentham and his like-minded Utilitarian followers.

Society hostesses vied with each other for the presence of Robert Owen at their receptions, instructing their cooks to prepare dishes especially for his now famous 'plain' palette. The ladies were charmed by the Welshman's refined aquiline good looks and unusual accent, even the older matrons becoming quite flushed and girlish under his gaze. The men, mainly bankers and merchants, found his boundless energy and unremitting promotion of his philosophy a little wearing, agreeing he was in danger of becoming a bore 'were he not such a genuine, salt of the earth character.'

Using the medium of national newspapers like *The Times* and *The Morning Star*, Owen was finding a new way to publicise his New System and lay out his Plan for Villages of Unity and Mutual Cooperation.

The letters and speeches he wrote were published in the daily broadsheets but the printers kept the presses running to produce up to thirty thousand more copies. These were then purchased by Owen and addressed and posted to the clergy in every parish in the Kingdom. On one occasion, the weight of the additional newspapers was so great that the Mail Coaches were twenty minutes late leaving St Martin's Le Grand.

Fortunately, the New Lanark Mills were doing well, allowing Owen to spend, in just two months, over four thousand pounds of his own money in this venture to publicise his views.

Ministers on both sides of the House as well as Royalty, economists and philosophers wanted a piece of him, or so it seemed to Murdoch. The valet was struggling to keep up with his master's changes of clothing and hectic schedule. His own, personal plans were forced to change, causing sleepless nights and, at times, a strained atmosphere between himself and his future bride.

A replacement housemaid was now engaged and trained in the ways of the house so Emily was no longer required. There was also no time to arrange a wedding so she left London to stay under her sister's roof in Kent, awaiting Murdoch's instructions.

Owen's correspondence with Braxfield was joined by Murdoch's own letters imploring Sheddon and Miss Wilson to understand Emily's delay was beyond his control. It was with relief that he received word from Sheddon to say Senga was not leaving until the end of August.

With public attention and the newspapers firmly focused on Owen as the 'man of the moment', as Brougham informed him, Owen was persuaded to present his views at another meeting.

Unlike the small occasion at the George and Vulture, where it was by invitation only, this time it would be thrown open to the public.

The meeting was advertised to be held on August 14th at The City Tavern, a popular venue for such events and large enough to take the expected audience. Its purpose was stated as "for those interested in the subject will consider a Plan to relieve the Country from its present distress, to remoralise the Lower Orders, reduce the Poor's rate and gradually abolish Pauperism, with all its degrading and injurious consequences."

However, after reading his enlightening letters in the newspapers, the organisers had grossly underestimated the interest there would be in seeing, in person, the famous, wealthy philanthropist and cotton baron. An enormous audience packed the Tavern, with hundreds more being turned away at the door.

Those fortunate to hear the speaker were given a buoyant account of how the future could be if his vision was realised.

Aware of the dangers of sounding too revolutionary, Owen reinforced his statement of adhering to the Law of the country while embarking on forming the characters of the future generation and setting up villages of Unity and Mutual Cooperation. It was absolutely necessary that all institutions and laws of the kingdom must be supported and upheld.

From the start, Owen felt there was something ominous about the meeting. He went in the company of two colleagues, Mr Rowcrofte and Mr Carter, expecting a Chairman to be selected from the gathering. Unfortunately, Mr Rowcrofte's name was the only one proffered and, despite the man repeatedly declining the position due to ill health, he was pressed into the duty. It then became clear towards the end, during the questions and summing-up, that a group of young men were intent on causing a disturbance. Rowcrofte's feeble voice could barely be heard above the clamour and the meeting ended in disarray.

Owen's response was to feel sympathy for the perpetrators and that their behaviour was caused by their ignorance. However, he acknowledged to himself that his opponents were growing bolder and louder. Various sectarian papers were pressing him to declare his views on the Church and his deliberate attempts to evade giving a direct answer were starting to become an issue in themselves.

Within a few hours of leaving the City Tavern and bidding his friends good day, Owen decided it was now the time to state, unequivocally, his stance on the matter of established religion. To this end, even before Murdoch could help him change for dinner, he sat down at his desk in the bedroom of Bedford Square, charged his quill and sent a note to book another meeting at The City Tavern for the following Thursday.

At every quiet moment during the intervening week, Owen retired to his room to prepare his speech. Explaining his Plan or describing the process required for educating children, was simple, as was discussing business or the running of a profitable cotton mill. This was different. This was baring his soul for the world to see. Not only that, he would be stepping over a line which few dared to step without dangerous consequences.

On the day of the speech his fingers fumbled over everyday tasks such as winding his pocket watch or tying his cravat. He was intent on speaking the truth: the truth as he saw it. Yet, there were thousands before him who had been sentenced to death, cast out, stoned or burned at the stake for uttering against the religion of their land.

Murdoch knew nothing of his master's thoughts but noticed the slight tremble of his hand and the fractional downturn to his lips.

'Well, Murdoch, I had best be off,' Owen told him. 'I trust I will return to you, safe and sound.'

Puzzled, Murdoch bowed his head and wished him a pleasant and successful evening.

The meeting started much the same as the others with the spacious City Tavern crowded to full capacity and, again, hundreds unable to gain admittance.

After the introduction, Owen took his place at the podium and looked out at the shifting, rustling, coughing mass.

'The last meeting terminated under circumstances of some disorder,' he stated loudly. The conversations died away, attention turned towards him and arms folded in readiness for the entertainment. 'But I trust and look forward with hope that these assemblages will be in future conducted with more order and decorum.'

He then expounded his views of the harmful effects of industrial manufacturing and for bettering conditions for the poor. It was not until over half way through his allotted time that he turned to a different topic, pausing and allowing himself a moment of composure before raising his voice and projecting it out to the furthest corner of the audience.

'It may now be asked, if the new arrangements proposed really possess all the advantages that have been stated, why have they not been adopted in universal practice during all the ages which have passed?

'Why should so many countless millions of our fellow-creatures, through each successive generation, been the victims of ignorance, of superstition, of mental degradation, and of wretchedness?'

He gazed around at the expectant expressions.

'My friends, a more important question has never yet been put to the sons of men! Who *can* answer it? Who *dare* answer it, but with his life in his hand; a ready and willing victim to truth, and the

256

emancipation of the world from its long bondage of disunion, error, crime, and misery?

'Behold that victim! On this day – in this hour – even now – shall those bonds be burst asunder! never more to reunite while the world shall last. What the consequences of this daring deed shall be to myself, I am as indifferent about as whether it shall rain or be fair tomorrow. Whatever may be the consequences, I shall now perform my duty to you, and to the world; and should it be the last act of my life, I shall be well content, and know that I have lived for an important purpose.

'Then, my friends, I tell you, that hitherto you have been prevented from even knowing what happiness really is, solely in consequence of the errors –gross errors – that have been combined with the fundamental notions of every religion that has hitherto been taught to men. And, in consequence, they have made man most inconsistent, and the most miserable being in existence. By the errors of these systems he has been made a weak, imbecile animal; a furious bigot and fanatic; or a miserable hypocrite; and should these qualities be carried not only into the projected villages but *into paradise itself, a paradise would be no longer be found!*

'In all the religions which have been hitherto forced on the minds of men, deep, dangerous, and lamentable principles of disunion, division, and separation have been fast entwined with all their fundamental notions and the certain consequences have been all the dire effects which religious animosities have, through all the past periods of the world, inflicted with such unrelenting stern severity, or mad and furious zeal!

'If, therefore, my friends, you should carry with you into these proposed villages of intended unity and unlimited mutual cooperation, one single particle of *religious intolerance* or sectarian feelings of *division* and *separation*, maniacs only would go there to look for harmony and happiness; or *elsewhere*, as long as such insane errors shall be found to exist!

'I am not going to ask impossibilities from you – I know what you *can* do; and I know also what you *cannot* do. Consider again on what grounds each man in existence has a full right to the enjoyment of the most unlimited liberty of conscience. I am not of your religion, nor of any religion yet taught in the world! To me they all appear united with much, with very much! Error!'

257

There were stirrings; gasps whispered through the assembly.

'Therefore, unless the world is now prepared to dismiss all its erroneous religious notions, and to feel the justice and the necessity of publicly acknowledging the most unlimited religious freedom it will be futile to erect villages of union and mutual cooperation; for it will be vain to look on this earth for inhabitants to occupy them, *who can understand how to live in the bond of peace and unity*; or who can love their neighbour as themselves, whether he be Jew or Gentile, Mahomedan or Pagan, Infidel or Christian. Any religion that creates one particle of feeling short of this is *false*; and must prove a curse to the whole human race!'

The audience were in differing states of outrage, fury, awe and, evidenced by the cautious smiles, agreement. All were hushed and attentive, hardly daring to believe they were witnessing such an outpouring.

'Such are my thoughts and conclusions; and I know that you will hereafter ponder them well in your minds, and *truth will prevail.*'

The silence was breaking into shouts and cries of "blasphemy", ladies biting their lips, askance, fervently praying for their own salvation in the presence of such a heathen.

Owen was still speaking, he was prepared for the shock and horrified exclamations, telling them he knew he would be called an Infidel and assuring them, 'No-one here is implicated in the slightest degree in these sentiments.'

He shuffled his papers, moving to the next page where he launched in to an attack on the government.

'The interest of those who govern has ever appeared to be, and under the present system will ever appear to be, opposed to the interest of those whom they govern. Law and taxation, as these are now necessarily administered, are evils at the greatest magnitude. They are a curse to every part of society. But while man remains individualised they must continue, and both must unavoidably still increase in magnitude of evil.'

His words were creating a commotion; men barracking and stamping their feet, snide laughter, ladies pulling at their husbands' jackets, insisting on leaving and pushing and barging toward the doors with loud mutterings of dismay.

Owen was not diverted and dived back into the subject of the new villages, holding his ground to bring the speech to a calm, measured end.

To his utter astonishment, the debate which followed made no reference to religion, nor even his proposed villages of cooperation. Instead the topic of high taxation and poor government was seized upon as the cause of distress for the lower classes and a resolution was passed calling for reform.

As soon as he left the Tavern Owen handed his speech to the young errand boy sent by the Times.

'Go well, mister?' the boy asked, cheerfully doffing his cap and tucking the sheaf of papers in his jacket.

'Only time will tell,' Owen gave him a rueful smile before striding off down the street.

The next day, while walking to meet with Francis Place, Owen was suddenly accosted by the distinguished, handsome figure of Henry Brougham.

'How the Devil, Owen, could you say what you did yesterday at your public meeting?' There was humour in his eyes and a sincerely curious ring in his voice. 'If any of us in the Liberal Party had said half as much we would have been burned alive! And here you are, quietly walking as if nothing had occurred!'

Chapter Fourteen

*"You may depend upon it that they are as good hearts to
serve men in palaces as in cottages"- **Robert Owen***

Anne Caroline settled back against the upholstered settee,
enjoying her afternoon visit to her neighbour.

Comforting aromas of cinnamon toast and hot chocolate lingered
in the lofty morning room of Bonnington House. Her left cheek
and thick linen day gown were in danger of scorching from the
blazing log fire while, on her other side, away from the cavernous
open hearth, icy draughts breathed on exposed skin. Blustery wind
hummed in the chimney and sent gusts of rain spattering against
the windows, obscuring the view out over the terrace and beyond
to swaying trees and a leaden sky.

'My dear Anne Caroline, it must be very trying for you,' Lady
Mary Ross soothed her friend, 'but I am sure all those who know
your husband, know him to be a good man.'

'Oh, I do hope it is the case.' Anne Caroline dabbed at her lips
with the serviette and brushed crumbs from her lap. 'Robert always
insists a man should be judged by his actions in this world and
sincerely believes others will be of the same opinion. Oh dear,
some of the newspapers have taken against him, even those who
were sympathetic and full of admiration for his work. The girls
have made a scrapbook of clippings, but now ... poor Jane, she is at
a loss as to whether to include these recent, most damning articles.'

Lady Mary made comforting noises; what else could she say?

'It is not just down in London,' Anne Caroline sighed, 'or
confined to the Members of Parliament or the clergy, although
goodness knows what Reverend Menzies will make of him now?
No, though it may seem a small matter in the great tapestry of Life,
my husband's declaration against all the religions of the world
nearly caused us to be without our new housemaid.'

'However, did that happen?'

'I will not bore you with the details except to say, Robert's
excellent manservant, who has been with us for many years,
became betrothed to one of the Walkers' maids. I was in need of a
new maid and agreed for this woman to join our household. Well,

apparently she caught wind of the speech and having worked for years in a pious Quaker house, she became very alarmed at the prospect of employment in a household where the master entertained such blasphemous views. I knew little of this until Miss Wilson, my housekeeper, brought it to my attention.'

'Gracious!'

'The poor valet feared he would lose his sweetheart and wrote to our Miss Wilson, imploring her to confirm the very proper and Christian values of our house. It was at this point that I was informed! I must say, it is due to my housekeeper's assurances of our Christian morals that we now have a new maid and Murdoch is embarking on married life.'

'She is here already?'

'Oh yes, they brought her up with them from London and I am told she is satisfactory. A quiet, plain young woman. I must confess, since they all came home last week I have not given much attention to anything except being with Robert again.'

Raising the lid of the ornate silver warming dish and using the tongs to lift a piece of buttered toast, Lady Mary waved it towards her guest. 'Would you care for another?'

'Indeed, but no, thank you.'

'I cannot resist, very naughty, I know ...' she placed one neatly on her own plate, returning to the conversation while sprinkling sugared cinnamon on the melted butter. 'Is Robert very disappointed by the reaction to his grand new Plan?'

'Not at all!' Anne Caroline gave a hollow laugh. 'He is as optimistic as ever, saying his critics will soon see the sense in his proposals for helping the poor and even ...' Anne Caroline paused, wondering how much to confide, 'come to agree with his philosophy on religion. Anyway, he is steeped in the mills again and, of course, the school.'

Chewing delicately, a sheen of grease gleaming on her chin, Lady Mary pondered the situation.

'In all the time I have known you both, I have to say your husband has never given the impression that he is *against* the Church, which is, perhaps, why I find it difficult to understand this great furore over his declaration. You, my dear, are the most ardent of Christians, a devoted member of the congregation, like your father before you. Your children are raised as Christians and in the village there are regular, well attended services provided, even for the smaller sects. When I bring the Highland preacher down from the north for communions in the summer, Robert pays for and makes all the arrangements for the Highlanders to take the service in Gaelic ... never have I seen him stand in the way of spreading Our Lord's word.'

'It is true. Yet, he would do as much for Pagans and Jews, and what would Reverend Menzies say to that! It is just my husband's way. It is intolerance he detests.'

'And that is the nub!' Lady Mary popped the last sweet morsel into her mouth. 'I profess, on that score, I must agree with him.'

A particularly strong gust of wind droned at the window, flaring the flames into yellow tongues licking over the logs in the wrought iron grate. Anne Caroline pulled her shawl around her, not looking forward to the drive home.

'Autumn is upon us,' she said, quietly. 'Are you going to Balnagowan for Christmas this year?'

Lady Mary rubbed her hands together and stood up, 'It is uncommonly cold, come, let us take a turn around the room before my toes lose all feeling.' They linked arms and began to walk wide, slow circles. 'We have decided to stay here. The children are pestering me to hold a Christmas Ball. Well, hardly a ball, more a large house party, because my relatives will be coming over from Ireland.'

'It appears that this English custom of celebrating Christmas Day is being embraced north of the Border,' Anne Caroline said. 'I received excited letters from my sisters in Glasgow just the other day, full of news of social engagements.'

'When we stayed in London over the winter season there was a ball or sometimes two, everyday in the darkest months.'

'Do you miss those times?' Anne Caroline asked, measuring her steps to keep in time with her friend while making the tighter turn by the grand piano.

'On empty days when the rain falls like a curtain and the roar of Corra Linn's crashing water sounds in every room, yes, on those days, I become melancholy. Yet, I cannot say that I miss high society any more than I miss the other carefree days of my youth.' Lady Mary gave her friend one of her frank, no-nonsense looks. 'The Lord has given me a fine house and healthy children and I am

262

blessed with an interest and aptitude in horticulture which Bonnington's grounds allow me to indulge. I am content, I ask for nothing more. However,' she raised her eyebrows, 'it might be fun to brighten the darkest days with some music and dancing at Hogmanay, don't you think? Please come? All of you?'

They returned to the fireside, exchanging places by mutual arrangement: two scorched cheeks were more becoming than only one.

'Oh, I must tell you!' Anne Caroline was shocked at herself for forgetting, 'splendid news! My sister Mary, now living in the south of England ... she has a baby boy! David Dale Stuart.'

***

At eight o'clock on every school morning, unless the weather was too unkind, all the children trooped out of the Institute. Only the infants who were still too unsteady on their feet to benefit from the activities stayed indoors. The rest, both boys and girls, were used to this routine and knew exactly where to line up, the steps of the dances and, for the boys, how to drill and march. A dozen or so of the older children made a merry little band with fifes, whistles and drums to accompany their fellow pupils.

Fiona enjoyed supervising this morning exercise, never failing to be proud of her little charges. It made a colourful display of tartan trimmed white tunics, the children's feet, bare until the harshest months, flying through formal quadrilles and familiar Scottish reels in unison.

Due to the early hour, this activity, designed to wake the children up and fill their lungs with fresh air, did not attract the same audiences as the dancing classes held later in the day. Few visitors arrived before mid morning and those were mainly businessmen or academics who were there to view the machinery and factory, not the school room.

If Owen was at home, he often came down to watch the dancing. Standing to one side with Mr Buchanan, he would clap in time to the drum beats and discuss the progress or any problems arising within the school. If there was no pressing business, he might follow them back into the Institute to spend time observing the classes and talking with the infants.

So, Fiona was not surprised when the mill owner appeared at the Institute door early one morning. The ground floor was packed with all one hundred and ninety two village children under the age of ten years: an undulating carpet of white uniforms, well brushed hair and pink faces.

'Good morning to you, Mrs Scott,' Owen greeted her. 'I see Mr Buchanan is engaged at present. Be so good as to pass my instructions on when he is free?'

'O' course, Mr Owen, sir.' Fiona dipped a curtsey, noticing a stranger standing behind him.

'I have brought Mr Macaulay to see our children. He would like to stay with you for most of the day, please ensure he is given every opportunity to examine the pupils' progress.'

'Ah'll be sure an' tell Mr Buchanan, sir.'

Owen turned to Zecheriah Macaulay. 'You will have a most splendid time. I would introduce you formally to Mr Buchanan but I do not wish to take him from his duties. He is an admirable chap.'

The teacher was shouting out names from the register and ticking each child off as they called back 'Aye!' Throughout the process there was a quiet, high pitched murmur of young voices, all tranquil, willing and good humoured.

'A far cry from my school days,' Macaulay commented. 'We were forced to stand at our desks without uttering a word for fear of the strap.'

'There is no corporal punishment, no punishment at all. No rewards either. Yet, as you will see for yourself, the children are docile and keen to learn. They *enjoy* their school days. Why? Because they are constantly engaged in interesting pastimes; exploring, learning.' Owen excused himself and headed towards the door, calling back, 'Stay as long as you wish!'

With a signal from Buchanan, the haphazard crowd formed into rows. Then the door was flung open and one of the older boys rapped twice on his drum, the other musicians putting their instruments to their mouths and bursting into tune. Buchanan strode to the front and they all filed outside.

The retired but yet spritely Sergeant Major, clean shaven and with his long grey hair neatly tied back in a ribbon, marched at the rear. He was attired in a smart, almost military styled outfit: back straight, chin up, his arms swinging stiffly at his side. For nearly an hour the children danced and sang, with short interludes to catch their breath in the cold air. During these pauses, they watched the older boys marching in formation, backwards and forwards to the Sargeant Major's commands.

Macaulay was mesmerised. It was not so much the display of reels or the precise manoeuvres performed by the boys, it was the way the children reacted to each other and to their teachers. They were taking pleasure in what they were doing, eager to try their best and, even more surprising, helping one another.

The younger infants, those under five years of age, were grouped together and would occasionally forget where to turn in a dance. They were immediately and patiently rescued by their friends and aided into the right place. Molly Young, the young assistant, tripped around between them, gently prompting with words for the songs or taking their little hands to guide them.

Once inside again, flushed and bright eyed, they dispersed to their lessons. The older children ran upstairs to the largest of the school rooms where forms and desks were placed in Lancastrian lines with a corridor down the middle. The smaller room on the second floor, with a gallery for an orchestra and the main space left clear for dancing and singing was surrounded by walls hung with large, brightly coloured paintings of wild animals. Even on a dull autumn day, the high, many paned windows allowed sufficient light to keep the use of lamps to a minimum.

With an older student stationed in each area, they set about different subjects and Buchanan gathered twenty or thirty of the oldest, nine and ten year olds, to teach elementary reading, writing and arithmetic.

Macaulay noted the texts the teacher chose for his pupils to copy or read aloud were taken from the Bible and when another group, furthest away from Buchanan, broke into song, it was in a simple rendition of a hymn.

After several hours of quiet industry, the mill bell rang for the workers' meal time break and the pupils left their tasks and hurried home. For a few, the distance was too far and downstairs at the fireside, Fiona, Molly and three other assistants supervised the doling out of porridge, mackerel and potatoes. Then the babies were tucked up in blankets to take a nap.

When lessons resumed, Macaulay spent the afternoon moving from group to group, observing. The atmosphere was calm, genial, like the warm rooms themselves: wholesome.

'I have never seen so many contented children gathered in one place,' he declared to Owen when they walked up Braxfield Road together much later that evening. 'The pupils are very well behaved and not only well versed in geography and basic natural sciences, they are also openly delighted with their knowledge. The quality of the discussions I heard among ... mere children ... would put many an adult to shame!'

'Tell me?' Owen asked, ardently, holding a lamp high to show their way in the darkness. 'Apart from returning to Braxfield for a light meal, you have spent the whole day witnessing my system. Which part did you enjoy the most?'

'My word! What to say?' Zecheriah Macaulay laughed out loud. He was in high spirits from such an entertaining and inspirational day. 'The enormous globe! Why, I was quite ridiculously enchanted with it myself! And the game ... the game where one child has a wand and the other pupils call out a place, a river or country or some such location as to be so obscure and hard to find that they hope they will win the game and take up the challenge themselves. My goodness, there were some places I did not know as accurately! Ah, and the sewing amongst the girls. So attentive and neat while they stitched away. The seamstress was instructing them in producing useful, purposeful items. Then again, the manner of recalling the times tables of arithmetic, singing the lines ... a wonderful device.'

'And the activities?' Owen pressed him.

Engrossed in their discussion, they turned into Braxfield's driveway, boots crunching on the gravel, tall hats bowed forward. The moist night air glowed in a misty circle around the lamp, allowing a short tunnel of light to break the pitch-darkness.

'The dancing, without a doubt. Even the little ones knew their way through tricky steps and, I must say, Owen, there were upwards of eighty spectators over the afternoon filling the gallery.'

'It is only by witnessing the true benefits of my new system that it can be judged.' Owen stated, flatly. 'Those who denounce my philosophy and attack it with irrational arguments are ignorant to the truth. No amount of criticism and hot air can change the facts, it is simply a matter of time before they are accepted.'

They reached the corner of the driveway and saw the glow of Braxfield's windows.

'Well, *I* think you are on to something, Owen, and I do not say that lightly. As you know, it was Mr Brougham who urged me to visit and asked me to explore the possibility of setting up a similar school, a free school, for the children of London.'

Owen was quick in his response. 'Free to those of all religions?'

'Free to *all* pauper children, yes.'

'You have my unreserved support, Mr Macaulay and, of course, Mr Brougham and your other partners as well!' Owen bounded up the front steps, reaching for the door handle just as Sheddon opened it. 'Tomorrow, we will discuss this further!'

***

Lady Mary Ross's festivities over Christmas and Hogmanay were a treat for the whole Owen family. Robert Dale, William and Ann rekindled and cemented early friendships with the Lockart Ross children. On several crisp mornings they sought permission to ride over to Bonnington to enjoy the short hours of daylight together, the adults following later in the day.

Lord Leinster, Lady Mary's younger brother, took a liking to Owen and they would find a quiet seat together away from the hubbub of the children and party games. With a tray of tea and bowls of nuts or sugared dates and currants, they mulled over philosophical questions, their support for Catholic Emancipation and issues touched upon by Paine's 'Rights of Man'.

An ebb and flow of guests moved up and down Bonnington's driveway. Donning heavy cloaks and fur hats and muffs, couples admired the grounds and crunched their way over a carpet of beech masts under the trees' spidery branches to the Pavilion to view the spectacle of Corra Linn. The halls and reception rooms of the great mansion thronged with tipsy conversation to a background of a varied programme of music.

The young ladies had an eye for attracting attention to themselves, taking it in turns to give harp or piano recitals, their hopeful admirers standing in little groups around them, turning their music sheets and clapping on the final note of every rendition. The company grazed from plates of venison, pheasant and pigeon, spooned lush sauces and pickles over thick slices of baked ham spiked with cloves, dark with caramelised sugar.

Anne Caroline was pleased to join her husband at several of the parties. It was a novelty to dress up for a formal occasion and she found the steps of favourite dances, enjoyed in her youth, came back to her with ease as soon as they took up their positions.

Owen danced with grace, his footwork neither showy nor laboured, it was a skill he honed as a boy in Wales but rarely used as an adult. It was a shame, Anne Caroline thought, her hand in his, smiling at each other in the candlelight while gliding, bowing and curtseying with their friends.

Owen's work and views on the Church were now famous throughout the land and nowhere more so than locally. His enemies shunned him, some of his acquaintances and even those he once thought of as friends, were cold in his presence or openly hostile. Landed gentry from various county estates no longer included the Owens of Braxfield House on their invitation lists.

Conversely, his true friends grew closer and he was attracting a new group of admirers among those who recognised the benefits of his radical essays.

Over the festivities at Bonnington, two young men specifically asked to be introduced to Robert Owen. The cheerful, bantering atmosphere of yuletide celebrations and a house full of children did not allow serious discussions, but enough passed between them for Owen to invite them to his home.

From that day on, Captain Donald MacDonald and Alexander Hamilton became frequent visitors and consequently, close friends. Hours were spent by Owen's fireside, deliberating on the essay, a New View of Society. Both men were well connected and soon the number of followers began to grow, articles appeared in news sheets debating the merits of the formation of character from childhood, schooling on the lines of New Lanark's system and his proposed Villages of Unity and Mutual Cooperation.

Alexander Hamilton was a desultory young man, newly home from the war and thoroughly disillusioned with the world. His family, the Hamilton's of Dalzell, were immensely wealthy, owning thousands of acres of land beside the Clyde twenty miles downstream from New Lanark. Luxuries of race meetings, balls and theatre parties bored Alexander; everything bored Alexander. Until being persuaded to accept Lady Mary's invitation and meeting Owen, his life held no meaning.

He was shocked to the heart by the cruelty of war. Experiencing the terrible sights and sounds of extreme violence and the gore of battle had left him wounded, inside. The scars were invisible but deep and weeping.

Occasionally, Anne Caroline would meet him in the hallway and pass a few words, always parting with a feeling of compassion.

'He tries to disguise his hurt,' she wrote to her sisters, 'I am not sure which is the most disturbing to see, the lost, hopeless look in his eyes or the valiant effort he employs to disguise his pain. I pray the interest he is showing in Robert's essays will give him hope for the future and the will to live.'

Captain MacDonald, Alexander's friend, was a much more confident character. He had served in the Royal Engineers and understood what Owen was doing and felt it grossly unjust that religious bigotry and upper class small mindedness should hold back such important work. Riots and unrest were reported daily. Starving, desperate people would not be suppressed forever, something had to be done.

Captain MacDonald threw himself into promoting 'Owenism', as people were now calling it, bringing the example of New Lanark to people's attention.

Early in the new year of 1818, Macaulay brought a group of London gentlemen up for a lengthy visit. Samuel Romilly, William Leake and Lord Dacre were close associates of Henry Brougham and John Walker. All shared a desire to provide education for the poor and where better to research the subject than at Robert Owen's school for pauper infants.

Fiona recognised Macaulay the moment he walked into the classroom, returning a respectful curtsey when he nodded in her direction.

'Yon London gents, friends o' Mr Owen, were at the school again today,' she told Joe that evening, seeking him out in the workshop he'd made at one end of the barn. 'They seem awfy taken wi' the bairns' lessons.'

269

With the aid of two oil lamps and tallow candles in sconces on the wall, Joe found he could work long after darkness fell. The few local jobs they could secure were keeping the teams in work but it was a week by week dilemma.

Fiona perched on a stool, as had become her habit over the winter, her thick wool shawl drawn tight around her, hands tucked under her arm pits. Here, while he worked or sharpened tools and set things fare, they discussed their day. Private jokes were shared, plans made for finding better furniture for the children's rooms and tittle tattle from the mill village. Joe let her prattle on, enjoying her company if rarely paying attention but giving an occasional comment when he thought necessary.

'When are ye pitting these oan the gate posts?' Fiona nodded towards two lumps of stone on the floor. 'Eh, Joe? Yon sculptures Davey brought doon frae his pal?'

'Och, Ah forgot,' Joe left his workbench, pleased to have been reminded. 'We'll sort them this Sunday when the lads are here.' He rolled one over to catch the light.

Hewn out of sandstone, each slightly larger than a man's head, were two skilfully chiselled lions' heads. Their mouths were open as if roaring, manes writhing in deeply cut waves.

'He's a clever lad, Robert Forrest.' Joe ran a finger over the animal's vicious features. 'Davey wis tellin' me he's mighty pleased tae ha'e purchased these fer a few shillings last summer fur Robert's had a bit o' luck an' noo his things are twice the price.'

'Whit kinda luck? It's alis guid tae here o' some yin daen weel.'

Joe went back to his bench, tired now, his concentration broken. He started to tidy away his tools and brush up the dust.

'Ye ken he works oot o' Orchard Quarry? Weel, the hunt passed by in search o' the fox, hounds an' horses kickin' up dust an' the bugle deafening folk, so Davey telt me. Yin o' the men, all in red wi' a red excited face tae match, spied Robert chiselling an' hammerin', nae bothered wi' all the noise. This gent, Colonel Gordon they cry him, he took a liking to the feenished pieces lying aroond. Telt him tae come up an' see him at his hame! Noo he's payin' the lad tae mak things an' telling all his posh friends.'

'Och that's grand! Ah wish him all the luck. D'ye ken he'd dae the same wi' Davey? He's a michty guid carpenter, an' no mistake.'

270

Joe smiled fondly, 'Aye thinkin' o' yer ane chickens, lass!'

'Aye! An' prood o' every yin o' them.' There was a long, comfortable silence until Joe blew out the candles, turned down the wick on one lamp and picked up the other.

'Come, Ah'm done fur the nicht.'

'This wee barn works jist dandy fur ye!' Fiona took his free hand, 'an' look at the half moon. D'ye ken Sam can see it?'

'Aye, weel, mibbee no' richt noo. Ye're the teacher, ma darlin', ye tell me?'

'Ah'll ask Mr Buchanan if we can ha'e anither lesson aboot the moon an' Ah'll piy attention this time!' She laughed and he cuddled her close.

Every day might be proving a struggle for money, but there was no denying the pleasure the whole family were taking from their new home. Through the bare winter trees dividing his two properties, moonlight played on the thatched roof next door. His strategy was working; it now housed four families, their rents providing a vital addition to his meagre income.

***

Long stemmed snowdrops reached their fresh white beauty and faded to droop, tinged with brown, passing on the promise of Spring to plump green cushions of yellow primroses. A mild spell fooled hedgehogs from their slumber, woodpeckers drummed and streams bubbled with mating frogs,

Daylight was waning on a windy afternoon in March when Joe heard the news about Jim Calder.

He was at the back of his house checking Bluey's shoes for wear and hoping the mare's hooves would last another couple of weeks before trimming. He could do without a farrier's bill to add to his financial woes at the moment.

'Joe!' Tam's shouted greeting startled the horse and Joe dropped its foot hurriedly and jumped back.

'Woah! Ye nearly had me crushed, Tam!'

'Ye all richt?' Tam made a wide path behind Bluey's swishing tail.

'Aye, but ye ken how she taks when the wind's blowin' in her ears!'

'It's Jim Calder, ha'e ye heard the news?'

'Naw?'

'He's bin taken awa' tae the Tolbooth an' flung in the Debtors' Prison.'

'Whit! Who telt ye that?'

'Up at the market. It's oan every yins lips. Whit will happen tae Melanie?' Tam's rugged face was filled with despair. 'They're sending in the bailiffs tae Ewing's hoose ... closing the yaird.'

'When did this happen?' Joe walked into the barn, reappearing with tack in his arms.

'Yesterday, he wis in the court, so they say, an' the JP sent him straight tae the jail. If Ah'd known Ah'd ha'e bin there, perhaps ... tae help Melanie ... but, Ah never heard tell of whit wis happening until the noo!'

Joe listened with disbelief, all the time expertly restraining Bluey's snaking head while swapping the rope halter for the bridle. Tethering her again, he rapidly slid the saddle into place and buckled the girth despite the animal's agitated side-stepping.

Tam told him all he knew. Desperate to obtain work, Calder let it be known he would undercut all the other quotes for jobs, whilst also keeping up appearances by entertaining and befriending the factors of surrounding estates. It secured him contracts but at such a cost that soon his wife's dowry was spent so he resorted to mortgaging his late father in law's home.

'He had nae paid fur materials fae months when the writs stairted tae come in.' Tam said, dolefully. 'They say his debts are mair than the hoose is worth sae ...' his voice cracked with bitterness, 'how could he run doon that business? And, Joe,' he repeated, 'whit will happen to Melanie?'

Joe grabbed his hat from the workshop and swung himself up into the saddle, perplexed.

'Ah dinnae ken, Tam, but Ah'm awa' tae find oot! Yer sure ye've heard richt? Ah'm nae gaun up there fur a flea in ma ear?'

'Aye! Honest tae God, Joe. Ah wish it weren't ...' Tam clamped his hand across his mouth, his face contorting. 'Och, that's a lie! Ah wis shocked tae hear it but,' he looked up, directly at his friend. 'May the Devil strike me doon, but Ah'm no' sorry.'

When Fiona arrived home she found a woman sitting at her kitchen table huddled in a heavy cloak her face creased with lines where plump cheeks once dimpled.

'Mrs Calder?'

'Och, Mrs Scott ...' Melanie's chin crumpled.

Joe came through from the scullery with the coal bucket swinging in his hand. 'Fiona! The stove's jist lit ... Melanie will be stayin' wi' us fur a wee while.' His expression told her to accept this without explanation.

'Weel ... come and we'll find a place fur ye tae sleep an' ...' Fiona looked askance at the two kists and bulging carpet bags beside their guest, 'a place fur yer things.'

Assuming a welcoming smile and busying herself with Sionaidh, she hoped to successfully hide her astonishment and the dozens of questions bursting into her mind.

There was an atmosphere of calamity in the air, unsettling and draining. It caused the Scotts to speak in hushed tones, tiptoeing around the stranger in their midst. Curious, Sionaidh kept going over to stand beside Melanie and studying her closely without speaking until one of the family would pull her away.

In these dark months, Joe usually lit the big fire in the front parlour as soon as he came home and they would sit comfortably together, but not that night. Hugging the warmth of the range, they ate their meal, tidied up and went about their chores. All the while, Melanie remained as if stuck to her seat.

It was only when Ailsa and the younger children were settled upstairs and Fiona suggested they share a pot of tea, that Melanie's tale unfolded. It was hard to believe her life had changed so dramatically and so quickly, in the space of a week.

Calder would be held until his debts were repaid but there was scarce chance of that happening. The house, his major asset, was already in the hands of the bank and with unpaid interest mounting on a heavy mortgage, there would be little left even if it sold quickly.

'Ah have nae hame,' Melanie whimpered, 'nae money an' but fur ye, Joe, Ah wid be in the Poor Hoose this nicht.'

'It'll ne'er come tae that,' Joe told her abruptly. He was tired, Fiona looked exhausted and Little Mel, as he always thought of her, was now repeating herself through her sobs.

'Ah've pit some blankets in the front bedroom,' it crossed Fiona's mind to explain the state of the bare room, their own lack of money, but the thought passed. 'Ah'll shew ye up ... the lads, Donnie an' Davey are awa' t'night ... at a pal's,' she avoided mentioning Tam's name. 'Come wi' me, Mrs Calder. We all need tae rest.'

'Please, call me Melanie? Or Mel?'

'If ye like,' Fiona was past caring, in less than six hours she would be rising again and every muscle in her body ached to lie down.

At last, Melanie was persuaded to try and rest. They led her up to the bedroom, closed the shutters and laid a candle and tinderbox at her side.

'D'ye ken she'll sleep?' Fiona whispered to Joe, climbing into bed.

'Well, if she disnae, Ah wulnae ken, fur as sure as there's a moon in the sky, *Ah'll* be sleepin'.'

He blew out the candle and they wriggled and kicked the blankets into a comfortable position before falling silent.

'Sam wid ha'e seen the moon afore us ...' Fiona murmured.

'Uh?'

'Ah asked Mr Buchanan ... aboot the moon ... an' he telt me they see the moon afore we do ... every nicht.'

'Unless it's cloudy.'

'Oh aye,' she yawned, 'unless it's cloudy.'

Chapter Fifteen

*"Faith consists in believing when it is beyond the **power of** reason to believe." Voltaire*

Following Melanie's unexpected arrival under her roof, Fiona tried her best to comfort the young woman. Given that the Scott family left the house before daybreak and did not return home until after sunset, the few hours they shared were invariably spent in the kitchen; talking.

Joe escaped to his workshop or on Freemasonary business, the children made quick work of their meal and melted away into the big house or out to the barn, leaving Fiona to tend to their guest.

Melanie's conversation consisted mainly of 'if only' and 'whit's tae happen tae me?' accompanied by tears leaking and shining on her ravaged face.

As the days spread into weeks, Fiona began to dread opening the back door of her beautiful new home, knowing the doleful, awkward evening which lay ahead. So, it was a welcome surprise to come home and find Melanie busy at the stove, mouth watering aromas of fresh sponge cake and scones greeting them at the door.

'It kept ma mind aff the bad things,' Melanie said, shyly, indicating the plates and trays of baking on the table.

'Aye,' Fiona bristled, noting the stack of pots and pans, empty flour bags, empty currant jars, the small stump of sugar cone ... 'Ah see ye've bin busy.' She took a deep breath, asking tersely, 'Is Joe in the barn?'

'Aye,' the nervous smile on Melanie's lips was a pathetic improvement from the previous weeks of doom. 'Wid the bairns like some fruit scones the noo?'

'Naw!' Fiona snapped, ashamed to see the woman wince. 'They git oot their tunics richt awa',' she explained, unable to keep annoyance from clipping her words. 'An' then dae their tasks aroond the hoose afore we sit doon tae sup t'gether.'

'Oh, aye ... weel, we can ha'e them fur supper. Ah wanted tae thank ye fur takin' me in tae live wi' ye.'

Sending the children off to their chores, Fiona excused herself and marched outside to find Joe.

'She thinks we've taken her in! That she'll be livin' wi' us!'

Taken by surprise, Joe stared at his wife, chisel poised, mallet raised.

'An' noo,' Fiona's expressive eyebrows rose and fell with her words, dark pupils sparkling with pent up frustration, 'she's used up ma flour an' everythin' frae the larder in yin day!' She spoke through gritted teeth. 'She disnae unnerstaun we ha'e tae watch the pennies. That's all ma wages fur a week gone in yin day! The egg basket has twa left! Twa! There wis a dozen this morn! She's made scones fur the whole o' Lanark ... we're no' a bakery. Och, Ah'm vexed fur her, an' she's grievin' fur her aunty an' her faither an' all, but ... Ah'm truly sorry, she cannae stiy here, Joe. God knows where she can live but this is oor hame ... *ma* hame an' Ah cannae bear every nicht o' listening tae her gaun oan an' oan!'

The sound of the back door opening was followed by Ailsa shouting to Sionaidh, calling her back inside.

'Ah ken it sounds selfish,' Fiona went to the door, peering into the darkness to see her daughters, 'an' God help me mibbee it is, but Ah want Donnie an' Davy an' Robert back! Ah dinnae blame them fur nae wantin' tae be here but ... they're doon at Tam's squished intae a wee room ... Melanie's no' kin ... no' like Sam an' Connor. Ah dinnae mean we throw the lassie oot but, sae help me, Joe, Ah want ma kitchen back ... she cannae stiy here!'

Fiona whirled out, pulling the door shut behind her and Joe was left in the still workshop, speechless.

He had no idea Fiona was irritated by Melanie. His mind was so occupied by business matters that he thought all was well at home. He laid down his tools and idly blew a cloud of dust away from the gravestone he was engraving.

It was in memory of Ewing and his sister, commissioned by St John's Lodge with the Freemason's symbol beneath the names and dates. Melanie was bereft, without a family member; only Joe to turn to in her time of need. Then a thought occurred to him and his shoulders relaxed, a long sigh escaping.

Tam was surprised to find Joe at his door so late in the evening and even more surprised by the discussion which followed.

276

In the time it took for Joe to utter the words, Tam's life changed completely. With his heart hammering in his chest, he struggled into his jacket, jammed his hat on his springy hair and accompanied his friend up the hill.

'When did ye last see Mel?' Joe asked when they neared his door. Their breaths foamed in the air, every footstep crunching into spiky frost. Spring's early bid to overtake winter was being icily rebuffed.

'It's bin a fair while, Ah cannae rightly mind.'

'She's changed. The last years have nae bin kind tae her, they've taken their toll.'

'The paur lass.'

'Whit Ah'm tryin' tae tell ye is Mel's nae the same tae look at ...' Joe struggled not to be cruel. 'Ye ken she wis alis ... cheery an' ... weel, fat.'

'She's a big lass, aye, but tha's neither here nor there tae me,' Tam said earnestly.

In the darkness, Joe could hear his fond smile. 'She's nae sae plump noo, Tam, as Ah say, she's changed. She's aulder lookin', drawn, an' there's nae easy way tae say it, but it disnae suit her. Ah jist wanted tae warn ye.'

Tam tapped Joe on the arm. 'We did nae care fer each ither fur oor guid looks, ye ken, or Ah wid nae ha'e stood a chance!'

'Ah'm jist sayin'.'

On entering the kitchen and seeing Melanie, Tam was not appalled, nor disappointed. She was as she was. In the first glance, he accepted the change in her appearance, the bags beneath her eyes, the lines creasing her features. When their eyes met, all thoughts were instantly overcome by the strong personal connection.

Melanie was non-plussed, blushing scarlet and rising from the table in astonishment.

'Melanie,' Joe went straight to her, taking her by the elbow and steering her towards the hall door. 'Tam wid like a word. Ye can speak in private in the parlour.'

Fiona jumped to her feet, amazed by the unfolding scene. She snatched up a candle to ignite an oil lamp and handed it to Joe, patting his arm encouragingly.

Like a lamb, Melanie allowed herself to be guided away from the supper table, watched by the children's silent, inquisitive stares.

After shuttering the windows, Joe left the couple standing awkwardly in the lamplight surrounded by the looming shadows of the large cold room.

As he pulled the door closed he heard Tam murmur, 'Aw, lass, it's gaun tae be all richt.'

Joe took his place at the table where Fiona had laid a plate of scones, cheese and pickle and immediately began to eat.

'Weel?' she asked, expectantly. 'Whit's gaun on?'

'Tam's askin' Mel tae work fur him, tae be his housekeeper.' Joe gave a meaningful glance down the table at his children. 'She needs a joab and a place tae live an' he's bin sayin' fur a while that he needs some yin tae keep his hoose.'

'Aw, ye clever man!' Fiona blew him a kiss. 'Ah should ha'e thocht o' that! Won't there be gossip?'

Joe shrugged, 'And why wid that be? Reverend Menzies has a housekeeper ... there's mony a man in the toun wi' a woman who does fur him.'

'He's awfy lucky,' Tom said through a mouthful of sponge cake. 'Mrs Calder maks a grand cake!'

Fiona beamed, 'An' there wis Ah full o' remorse efter running tae ye earlier. Ah wis fair beratin' masel fur ma lack o' charity but noo ... mibbee it wis fur the best.'

Later, when they were alone, Joe confessed his own guilty feelings about Melanie's misfortune. For the first time in years, there were more contracts on his books than he could handle, many being to complete Calder's unfinished work.

Months of security lay ahead for Scott & Sons.

***

Emerging with the babbling crowds at the end of an evening's dancing at the Institute, Sarah and Cathy walked back to their door chaperoned by their dancing partners. It was a habit now, walking slowly, arm in arm in the fresh air. All along the Row people were calling goodnight, breaking off to enter the tenements, the whispered calls of last minute messages echoing with stifled laughter.

Ross and Cathy hung back, the darkness cloaking stolen kisses.

Sarah was growing uncomfortable with their growing intimacy. She wondered how long this courtship was going to take before Ross plucked up the courage to ask her daughter to marry him.

'Ross's a nice lad,' she said conversationally, her voice low. Lily was asleep in the hurly bed, arms flung back, pale hair fanned out around her shoulders.

'He's no' a lad, Mam, he'll be twenty five soon an' he's a skilled weaver.'

'He's jist a lad tae me, the same as you're a lassie.' Sarah stepped out of her pink satin dress and gave it a good shake before folding it neatly. It was two years old and well worn but by ringing the changes with different short lace or embroidered lawn overlays, her wardrobe appeared varied. It was a trick she learned at Holroyds and passed to many of her customers in New Lanark.

'Lassie! Ah'm twenty two years auld noo! Ah'm no' a bairn.'

'Och, a ken that.' Sarah bit her lip, the music and fun of the previous few hours was receding, leaving an emptiness. 'Dinnae dae whit Ah did, Cathy. Promise me? If ye care fur the lad ... Ross, dinnae dae onything ye should nae, until yer merrit.'

Cathy shook her head with embarrassment, muttering, 'Awa'! Grant me some credit, Mam.'

'Ah'm jist sayin' ...'

'Onyway,' Cathy moved to beside the fire, barefoot and ready for bed in her long cotton shift. 'Ross wants tae marry me. He asked me.'

'And?'

'Ah telt him Ah wid be happy tae be his wife, but in the summer time.'

'Ye ne'er said onything ... when did he ask ye?'

'A month past.' Cathy reached for the hair brush on the dresser and methodically brushed her hair, her back to Sarah. 'He's a guid man an' earns enough tae piy a rent oan a room fur us, e'en wi'oot ma piy. We've bin talkin' aboot it ... we dinnae want tae rush it. He's bin tae the Manager's office an' pit his name doon fur a room, but it wulnae be until August.' She turned to face her mother, her expression lost in the shadows. 'Ah wrote tae Stephen an' telt him ...'

'Yer brither kens aboot it an' he's thoosands o' miles awa' an' yit ...' Sarah's eyes shimmered with tears, 'ye did nae e'en think tae tell me?'

'Ah wis gaun tae, Ah said as much tae Ross this eve. An' Stephen wulnae ha'e the letter yit, sae, please Mam, calm doon ...' there was irritation in Cathy's whispered words, 'ye alis git sae upset!' she glanced at Lily who stirred under her blanket before turning on her side, asleep.

'Ah'm happy wi' Ross,' Cathy continued, her vehemence no less forceful in hushed tones, 'an' Ah want tae marry him an' live in oor ane room, here in the village where we baith wurk an' oor friends an' families are all aroond. But wheniver Ah think oan leaving ye alane ... weel, Ah worry aboot ye, tha' ye'll git all doon an' sad like when Da' left ... an' Stephen.'

'Ye worry aboot me?' Sarah's voice wavered and she reached towards her, hugging her tight. 'Och, ma darlin' chiel, ye must ne'er worry aboot me, Ah'll be jist fine. Ah'm happy fur ye, truly. Marry Ross, may the Lord bless ye an' gi'e ye every happiness. Ye must no' let ony thoughts aboot me keep ye back.'

They stoked the fire for the night and swung the swee over the bright coals for a pot of tea. Talking softly, they took down the dry washing from the pulley; folding, sorting, piling mechanically. They mused on Rosie and Fiona's reactions, and pondered over fanciful ideas of entwining fresh flowers in Cathy's hair and forming a posy of the same blooms, then fashioning silk ones of the same hues to adorn her skirts.

From Braxfield Road to the furthest end of Caithness Row, and throughout New and Nursery Buildings, the nightly ritual eased into slumber. Prayers were said, men, nodding under nightcaps, left their pipes and fireside chairs to clamber into bed beside their snoring wives. Quiet descended on the village, soothed by the Clyde's rippling, constant flow blending with a faint rustling amongst the cocoon of woodland. Only the distant, muffled cry of a baby disturbed nature's peace.

Muffled up with thick knitted jumpers beneath their uniform heavy cloaks, the night wardens sauntered through the village, lamps swinging, watching as the low lights glimmering at cracks in the shutters slowly faded away.

Groups of roe deer, ears and tails flicking, moved on the edges of the village. Badgers merged with the grey landscape, trotting along their well worn tracks to snuffle for worms on the grassy slopes beside the Institute. Thin, restless clouds occasionally parted their veil over the half moon, allowing its brilliance to throw sharp shadows and flash briefly in the lines upon lines of glass windows.

Sarah did not draw the curtain across her set-in bed, preferring to lie on her side, gazing past the legs of the table to the hearth's red embers. Her prayers were being answered. She thanked God for taking mercy on her sinful ways of the past and promised Him faithfully to never stray from the road of Godliness again.

There was no point in looking back, scolding herself for being so foolish to follow Sean away from the path of Righteousness. God had punished her severely for her sins and she must be eternally grateful to have been given the strength to break free.

This was a wholesome life, a good, worthwhile life and she would strive to hold on to it for as long as the Lord allowed.

The next morning, she rushed to tell Andrew Dudley the happy news of Cathy's engagement. He was delighted by her excited chatter, the youthful skip to her step when she ran up the stairs with her skirts swinging, the ribbons of her bonnet flying out behind. Unable to keep the smile from her lips, the serving girls and customers alike soon knew all about the impending Rafferty wedding.

When the mill bell released the factory workers for the mid day meal, Sarah almost ran out of the shop and down to find Fiona.

Along with the usual visitors to view the schoolrooms that day, Owen was giving a detailed tour to James Mill, another mutual friend encouraged by Henry Brougham to visit the school.

Mill, Scottish by birth, was a small, pale-faced man of middle age with bushy eyebrows and long side burns, making up for a lack of hair on the top of his head. Like Brougham, he was a past student of Edinburgh University and, also like Brougham, journeyed to London as a young man to earn a living as a journalist.

Owen was pleased to extend hospitality at Braxfield, sometimes entertaining half a dozen or more to breakfast and twice as many for dinner.

As a follower of Jeremy Bentham's belief that society should be ruled with the object of achieving 'the greatest happiness for the greatest number,' Utilitarianism, as it was known, James Mill was intrigued by Owen's essays.

'Did ye hear the men talkin'?' Sarah asked Fiona at the end of the day, 'Mr Owen and his pal?'

Fiona buttoned up her jacket and tucked away loose strands of hair beneath her cap. 'Wee Jeannie an' twa ithers have caulds an' snivelled an' greeted a' day, paur weans, sae Ah did nae hear much o' onything the day. Whit were they sayin'?'

'The wee yin, baldie, ye ken, weel, he wis sayin' sumat aboot taking Mr Buchanan doon tae London an' stairtin' a school doon there.'

'Ye sure? Oor Mr Buchanan?' Fiona cried, face screwed up with disbelief. 'Naw, Mrs Buchanan wid na want tha', wid she? An' ye ken who wears the troosers in tha' hoose!'

'Sounded like it tae me, but Ah could be wrang.' Sarah shrugged. 'He's michty guid wi' the bairns, is Mr Buchanan, Ah hope he disnae leave the village. Lily learns a lot fae him.'

'Aye, Alex an' all. It wis Mr Buchanan who pit oor Tom up fur the clerk's joab in the counting house, itherwise he wid be in the mills.'

The women exchanged commiserating smiles.

'Nuthin' we can dae,' Fiona said, waving to Alex to head for the door and taking hold of Sionaidh's arm. 'We'll jist ha'e tae trust in Mr Owen tae find us anither Buchanan if this yin leaves.'

Anne Caroline was as surprised as the villagers to discover the plans afoot for John Buchanan and his family to leave New Lanark.

'Mr Buchanan has never travelled further than Lanark in his entire life!' she exclaimed, 'He was born in New Lanark and is a simple soul, you declared as much yourself when you appointed him as the head teacher. Is he happy with this arrangement?'

Owen was standing at the bedroom window, waiting for his wife to finish her toilette before descending to dinner with their guests.

'He appears to be very happy,' he told her, 'and although I insisted he should be given time to review the proposal, he agreed within the day. His wife is a capable woman, if a little stern and I expect it is more her choice than her husband's. However, the deal is done! It will not be for a while, premises must be found and so forth but I must find a good replacement and have him work with Buchanan to learn his ways.'

Ramsay took the soft clothes brush from the dressing table and smoothed away a couple of loose hairs from the back of her mistress's strawberry pink satin gown. Her expression gave nothing away as she gave a final tweak to the velvet bow of Anne Caroline's pendant and handed her the long matching evening gloves. This was gossip to be shared downstairs, later.

Cook was in her element. The menu called for rich sauces, marinated pigeon breasts, stewed mutton with plums and sultanas, various white fish served in short crust pastry parcels and syllabubs decorated with crystallised ginger.

'Lord love Mr Owen fur bringin' us sich guests!' she strained a pot of spinach and passed it to a maid to press through a sieve before adding a pint of thick cream. 'The London gents appreciate a richer dish an' Ah'm fair enjoyin' makin' it!'

'A splendid table, thank ye, Mrs Owen!' Mill enthused to Anne Caroline at the dinner table amid the rich scents of gravy and vases of hothouse lilies. He reached for another ladle of mutton stew. 'Are you coming up to the city with your husband next month?'

'Alas, no,' she inclined her head, graciously, her ruby earrings reflecting the candlelight. 'Dear Robert will be taken up with business while there, leaving me alone without a thought of how to occupy my time. Anyway, travelling is so tiring and I prefer to stay with the children.'

Mill looked down the table of guests to the four oldest Owen children. The boys were in earnest conversation, Ann and Jane maintaining quiet but interested expressions.

'I was impressed by the methods adopted in the village school,' he said, carefully selecting a forkful of meat, 'and look forward to starting a similar establishment for paupers in London. I cannot say I agree with all your husband's theories but I wholeheartedly concur on the provision of education for all. It is absurd to decide on which child to confer knowledge on the grounds of the Church his parents' attend or their wealth. Preposterous.'

To veer the conversation away to a lighter subject, Anne Caroline ventured, 'Do you have children, sir?'

'Indeed, I do, and I make it my priority, above all the other work I undertake, to teach my eldest son, John, myself.'

'Gracious, Mr Mill, I was under the impression you were an author and now held a position with the East India Company. It is to be admired that you also find the time to teach your son?'

'I do not care for admiration, however kindly intended. It is my duty as the boy's father to ensure he receives the stimulus he requires. He is a brilliant scholar.'

With a motherly chuckle, Anne Caroline asked, 'How old is John?'

'He is in his twelfth year.'

'Ah, my dear Jane is nearest in age, there beside her father,' she nodded proudly towards her dark haired, vivacious little girl.

'By the age of eight, John was fluent in Greek,' Mill proceeded to tell her, his voice matter of fact and clipped. 'He has read Easop's Fables in their original forms as well as texts by the Athenian author Diogenes Laërtius and educational theorist Isocrates and, of course, pieces of Plato. After his eighth birthday we moved to Latin, where he quickly became competent, so algebra and geometry were included. He is now studying political economy through the writings of the Scotsman Adam Smith and my friend, the economist David Ricardo.'

Startled and horrified in equal measure, Anne Caroline could merely smile and offer her congratulations.

A supercilious smirk flitted over Mill's face, his mouth opening as if to speak again, then closing firmly, bringing the exchange to an end.

Owen was quiet, observing the company and listening to the flow of topics. Once or twice, he caught Anne Caroline's eye beyond the flower arrangements and Sheddon's precisely placed candles.

'Am I right in thinking you found Mr Mill an awkward guest?' he asked, kicking off his slippers at the side of the bed. 'Your end of the table seemed a little strained.'

'Yes, Mr Mill is a strange man. Are you sure he understands Mr Buchanan's methods, *your* methods, in the classroom? For I confess, he does not appear to share them.'

'Well, he is a staunch supporter of free education for every child in the country and is keen to provide such a school. Brougham tells me since the publication of his book, what was it called ... *The History of British India*? Anyway, Mill finds himself offered a lucrative position with the East India Company and he has money which he wishes to invest in the next generation, an admirable thing to do.'

'That *is* a charitable act, I agree.'

'Yet, while I have not read his book, I have been given mixed verbal reviews by mutual friends. He may express religious tolerance, which once again is an aspect of his character to be applauded, but he is extremely derogatory regarding the Hindus and Muslims of India. I have no desire to read such a book, especially as I am told he did not even have the courtesy to travel to the Indian colony for the purpose of research.'

'May the Lord forgive me,' Anne Caroline yawned, 'but I did not take to the man. However, I may be mistaken and can only wish the venture well.'

No sooner was Mr Mill away from New Lanark than another set of guests arrived and Braxfield's servants braced themselves for the accompanying long hours and heavy work.

The Institute's classroom provided many different lessons and the arrival of John Winning, an accomplished local artist and his daughter, Janet, also a talented draughtswoman, proved a successful addition. Fiona loved the classes as much as the children, taking up the offer of creating her own little pieces whenever possible. Seeing a finished sketch by Winning of the New Lanark mills, Owen was struck with an idea.

'My dear, look here!' Owen burst into her morning room, a pile of small labels held high, their strings flying around his fingers. 'These will show everyone our charming factory!'

Anne Caroline laid aside her sewing and reached for one to examine.

'Why! they are little pictures of New Lanark.'

'Exactly! There is no need for any understanding of the language or even being able to read. Our cotton will be instantly recognisable throughout the markets.'

'What a clever idea.'

'I felt it would be a distinctive and noteworthy addition! Our cotton is sold all across Europe and Allan Stewart's secured major customers for me in St Petersberg in Russia. I shall send samples up to them, I am sure they will approve. I must take some with me to show my London partners.'

Owen's next trip south was looming, bringing to an end one of the longest periods of having him at home. The thought saddened Anne Caroline, she was growing used to having him at her side.

In writing to her sisters to tell them of her husband's imminent departure, she invited them to stay. Their reply came swiftly, asking if they could accompany their brother in law to the capital because they wished to visit Mary.

Anne Caroline read the letter, penned by Margaret, with a growing feeling of desolation. She knew they were keen to see their sister and meet the new baby but the reality of not being included in this reunion caused a stab of rejection. Instantly chiding herself for such selfishness, she took the letter through to Owen.

'Of course! How delightful! We shall make a merry party down through England.' He misread the frown clouding his wife's usually contented expression. 'Have no fear, Caroline, I shall take great care of them.'

Before leaving, Owen examined the mill's accounts for the first quarter and was pleased to find that profits were up. This was the first year the company was paying out interest to the partners and he knew the figures would placate some parties and reinforce confidence in others. His own, personal, account was buoyant despite his heavy spending on promoting his views and paying back the first tranche of his debt to Campbell of Jura.

Owen felt no need or desire to accrue wealth. Nevertheless, after providing for his family, paying his servants and running his house, he required sufficient to publicise his essays and cover the expenses of travelling to spread the word.

However, knowing it would please his wife and children, as well as himself when in residence, he spent several hours with the gardener the day before his departure. He wished to improve the flower garden around the front of the house. Any questions, he said, should be addressed to Mrs Owen in his absence and all expenses referred to his secretary, Mr Clegg.

Six weeks after Owen and Murdoch set off for London, and having fallen into a comfortable routine on her own, Anne Caroline received a letter from Owen and, in the same delivery, one from Julia.

Owen wrote to tell her of an invitation from Monsieur Pictet and their mutual friend, Monsieur George Cuvier, to accompany them to Paris and then on a tour through Europe. He was in the process of writing to John Walker to accept his long standing invitation to stay at Walker's house in Lucerne, Switzerland. It would be the perfect opportunity to take up the many introductions he was being given to meet influential leaders and reformists across the Continent.

Anne Caroline strained to decipher her husband's notoriously difficult, rushed, hand-writing.

Pictet and the Walkers thought it would be fun for the Dale girls to join the party and matters were in hand to secure them a passage to France where they would all meet in Paris.

Taken aback, Anne Caroline opened Julia's letter and read confirmation of the forthcoming 'adventure' on which her sisters were excited to be embarking.

She laid the letters side by side on her bureau, smoothing them flat with the palm of her hand while holding her breath to gain control. Was it jealousy she was feeling? This heady emotion of anger and frustration, was it because *she* was not part of their plans for such an extraordinary holiday?

She walked unsteadily to the window and gazed out across the garden.

The ormolu clock on the mantelshelf ticked its way through minutes; the only sound in the still house. She watched thrushes running across the lawn, deep blue spires of delphiniums stirring in a breeze, butterflies dipping in and out of the herbaceous border. Spring was beautiful at Braxfield, summer brought picnics in the dappled shade under the chestnut tree, long evenings sitting on the terrace watching the swallows.

How long would the tour of Europe take them away from Scotland? A month, no, more, surely? Three? Four? Would autumn be sending frost to this verdant scene before she saw Robert again? Tears welled up, spilling over and trickling down her cheeks; dripping onto her dress to leave dark, wet marks. She made no move to wipe them away.

Had she been invited on this Continental expedition, would she have accepted? The question lay unanswered while she cried but through the release of emotion, the bitter hurt of being left behind began to subside. No, she would not have accepted; her place was at home with the children. It was her duty to keep the house running smoothly, to supervise their growing family while Robert travelled far and wide to spread his vision of a better world.

Suddenly aware of her self-absorption, she turned from the window, pulling a handkerchief from her cuff and composing herself. A glance to the clock told her it would soon be time for Peggy to bring the younger children down to the drawing room. Then Robert and William's tutor would be leaving and Ann and Jane's music teacher arriving.

She reached for her Bible, flicking through the pages to a soothing chapter and settling down on the window seat. There was much to be done but first she would find solace in the Lord's word.

***

When Robert Owen was away from Braxfield little changed in the day to day running of the New Lanark Mills. It was one of the interesting factors noted by his ardent supporters, Alexander Hamilton and Donald McDonald.

A recurring criticism from sceptics of Owen's New System was that it was paternalistic. This was evidently untrue and could be easily demonstrated if his detractors made the effort to visit the village.

The system of Silent Monitors maintained a steady watch on behaviour and productivity, not because of fear of dismissal or punishment, but from personal pride. No-one wanted to have their slack attendance or poor performance telegraphed to their co-workers. They were all working for the good of the community and knew their work was a necessary contribution.

The village Committees, made up of residents and selected amongst themselves, ensured the houses were kept clean and tidy. Drunken or disorderly behaviour was similarly addressed and more serious offences, such as petty theft or fighting, were dealt with without resort to calling in outside forces like solicitors or the courts. These incidents were rare because everybody worked together, cooperating with each other to keep a smooth atmosphere: from the school room to the village shop, the store rooms to the farm on the hill.

Their reward was far more than the monthly wage paid by the Company, it was a high quality of life.

Early on a bright Sunday evening in August, Cathy and Ross's wedding took place.

They chose to take their vows at the end of the service, wishing to sit side by side throughout the sermon with their friends around them and anticipation mounting.

The young couple were asked to hang back after the ceremony in the meeting rooms at the top of New Buildings, while the congregation hurried to form a crowd around the entrance. A roar of cheering and whistling erupted when the new bride and groom stepped out. Holding hands and laughing, flower petals were showered over them, golden in the slanting rays of evening sunshine.

The evenings, especially Sunday evening, were when the residents had the village to themselves. They were used to prying eyes while they worked, just as the children had grown accustomed to strangers watching them in the classrooms or dancing. On the seventh day, it was a relief to relax, attend the Church and enjoy their leisure time.

Cathy's long fair hair was loose around her shoulders, crowned with pink and white wild roses, hedge-parsley, sweet scented creamy honeysuckle, mallow, fine sprigs of yellow lady's bedstraw and long tendrils of tiny ivy leaves. She held a posy of the same flowers tied with narrow satin ribbons of pink, yellow and white, the ivy and ribbons cascading down the front to reach the hem of her pretty rose pink and white flower printed cotton skirt.

'Ha'e ye e'er seen sich a bonnie bride!' A woman cried. 'Ah saw Mrs Rafferty oot gatherin' yon flowers this morn. Ye ken, Ah want her tae mak ma dochter's dress when she marries!'

Amidst the calls of 'guid luck' and rowdy clapping and yelps of congratulations, Cathy and Ross led their friends, and anyone who wished to follow, along the Row to the Rafferty's room.

'Thank the Lord it's a braw day,' Rosie laughed, bustling along beside Gerry. 'Ah've asked the lads frae next door tae help wi' carryin' oot the tables an' Donnie an' his brithers promised me they'll tak care o' carryin' doon the food ...'

Gerry stalked along beside her, pleased the day was going well but wondering when his wife would stop organising everyone.

It was not long before the party was underway with Davey and some friends sending spirited fiddle music bouncing off the high stone tenements, echoing around the village.

Within moments of the first notes, Fiona was swaying and clapping her hands to the beat.

'Ross!' she called across the clamour, catching his attention, 'Grab yer wife an' stairt the dancin'!'

She pulled Joe into a clear space, persuading others to join them for a reel with Cathy and Ross at the top of the set.

Andrew Butler reached for Sarah's hand, 'Leave the food platters, come an' dance?'

Taking their place at the end of the line, Sarah savoured the lively scene. Although neither Tam nor Melanie wished to dance, they were self consciously dressed in their best outfits, shyly encouraging others and returning playful banter.

Sarah wished them well, knowing there were folk up in town who crossed the street to avoid the wife of a debtor living indiscreetly with her former admirer. Tam was still regularly insulted in the tavern with drunken accusations of stealing a man's wife when the beggar was in jail. More difficult to shrug off were the disgruntled comments of his neighbours, calling him a Godless sinner and worse.

Let them have their views, Tam deserved a bit of luck and as Joe said, he was 'like a dog with twa tails' since taking in Melanie.

Sarah's eyes passed over the dancers, Molly, Ailsa, Robert, little Lily partnering her tall cousin, Donnie, and onto the jostling people beyond. It was noisy, babbling with chatter, whoops, clapping, clogs and steel capped boots scuffing the cobbles, squealing girls and music.

When it came to their turn to join the dance she threw back her head and entered the fray, beaming and looking fondly on Andrew's cheerful face.

Arriving in their final position at the end of the set again, she patted her chest and fought for breath, loving every minute but aware her age was showing. It was then that she became aware of being watched by a man standing behind Andrew, partly shielded from view by an older couple. The figure's stillness caught her attention and the feeling of his eyes boring into her.

The fiddles came to a crescendo and then stopped, leaving the party in a moment of deafening silence. Couples began bowing and curtseying in mock formality, applauding haphazardly and surging towards the tables laden with ale casks and food.

Forcing herself to give all her attention to Andrew, Sarah asked him to fetch her some ale. She waited until he turned away before glancing in the direction of the stranger, wondering if it was her imagination. The street was full of people joining the celebrations, young and old, children dodging between the bodies.

He was still there. The instant their eyes met, he dropped contact, taking a step backwards and jerking down the brim of his top hat.

Sarah glimpsed his profile and smothered a gasp. The straight nose, thick dark brows, strong chin and swinging, jaunty stride when he moved away were those of a man she thought she would never see again.

Incredulous and doubting her own eyes, she found herself following his retreating figure, calling out to him to wait. They were moving against the flow of party goers and nearly at the end of the Row when he heard her, his footsteps slowing, then stopping, his hand on his cane, back still turned.

'Sir?' she asked, softly, suddenly unsure of herself, moving to his side and looking tentatively up at his face.

No words were spoken, none were adequate to translate the anguish of the love, despair, and longing they felt for one another.

She could see deep lines around his mouth, dark shadows under his eyes and his cheek bones were more angular but age had not dimmed his striking good looks nor reduced the mischievous sparkle in his eyes.

'Sean?'

'Sarah ... I didn't wish to disturb ye,' Sean's Irish brogue shivered through her, 'but, the truth be told, I did want to see you. And Cathy ... and little Lily. I mean you no harm, I just wanted to ... see ma girl on her wedding day.'

The tooled leather boots, beaver hat and expensively tailored jacket and breeches told of wealth. His hand resting on the silver topped cane was clean and manicured, displaying jewelled rings, glinting deep gold like the watch chain strung across his embroidered waistcoat

'Is Stephen wi' ye?' She heard her voice, clear and even, yet part of her brain was telling her this was not happening, it was a dream.

'No, he is holding the business together until I return.' Sean's eyes were flicking over Sarah's face, refreshing the memories of his wife, gathering new ones.

'When d'ye leave?'

'Soon.' The music was striking up again and his voice became low, earnest. 'You will be missed, no-one can know I am here.'

'Yer still hidin?'

'Nathan Kydd doesn't hide, it is only here that my previous life might be resurrected. Can we talk afore I leave?'

Without hesitation, she nodded, noticing how tense he was, trembling.

'Tomorrow?' he asked, urgently, 'seven o'clock? Come to the Clydesdale Inn.'

'T'morra ...'

He raised his cane and started walking away, 'Go back, before there are questions ... I'll pray for tomorrow.'

'Who wis tha'?,' Rosie asked, when her sister returned to the throng. 'A city gent? On a Sunday nicht?'

Sarah pulled her wits together and returned a rueful smile, finding the lie came easily to her tongue. 'Aye, he wis wondering whit all the noise wis aboot! Whit are they like?'

'Nosey beggars,' Rosie laughed. 'There's those who want tae join the ceilidh or tae *watch* the ceilidh and those,' she pointed to several shuttered windows dotted about the tenements, 'who call a glass o' ale an' dancin' the Devil's work an' say we'll gae tae Hell.'

Sarah experienced the rest of the evening as two people.

The proud mother of the bride behaved as expected, smiling and laughing when appropriate, hugging Cathy goodbye with genuine pleasure, exchanging animated chatter with her neighbours and family. All the time, the encounter with Sean was rarely from her mind; flashes of relief in his green eyes, the jolt of recognition, the dark curve of his lashes when he looked down, the shape of his lips ....

He was here. She would see him again tomorrow yet it was not joyful anticipation which kept her awake until dawn nor any thoughts for her daughter on her first night as a married woman. It was dread. If he wanted her to go with him, was she strong enough to resist?

The next afternoon, the clock in St Nicholas' tower was striking seven when Sarah walked briskly past the Church doors and down the Bloomgate.

A group of tourists were disembarking from a carriage at the door of the Inn and she slipped up the steps behind two older ladies, their husbands standing back courteously to allow her to pass. Inside, the mahogany panelled hallway was filled with people moving purposefully between potted plants and high backed chairs arranged in groups around the spacious flag stoned floor.

Sarah hovered inside the door, willing herself to remain calm. She shouldn't have come, she told herself, biting her lip and half turning to leave.

'Mrs Rafferty?' a drawling man's voice asked, its owner was standing at her side, bowing politely.

'Aye.'

She had never seen the man before for she would have remembered his distinctively high forehead and olive skin, his grey streaked hair hanging smoothly to his shoulders from a centre parting.

'Adam Dewson, your obedient servant, madam,' he announced. 'I am instructed by Mr Kydd to escort you to his side.'

She followed the dapper figure through open double doors to a smaller seating area where a coal fire warmed the stale air. Several guests were relaxing, the men quiet with their pipes and newspapers, the ladies gossiping. A side window allowed a shaft of light to pierce the scene, showing a figure rising from his seat in the furthest corner.

Sean came towards her with the aid of his cane, bowing for the benefit of their audience. Making a show of asking loudly after her health, he ushered her towards their seats commenting on the luck of enjoying two dry days of weather coming together in Scotland.

'Thank you for coming,' he said quietly, releasing the brass buttons on his tailcoat and leaning forward in his seat. 'I wondered if you would.'

'O' course, how could ye doubt it?'

He gave a hollow laugh and coughed, pulling out a garishly patterned silk handkerchief to cover his mouth.

'Oh, I doubted it!' he shook his head, 'I ruined your life.'

'Ye ne'er forced me tae be wi' ye, Sean ...' she looked around guiltily, realising she should not use that name, but unable to bring herself to call him by any other.

'Ye were so young, innocent,' he held her gaze, fondly, the tone of his voice was wistful, kind. 'Yesterday, when I saw you dancin' and smiling your sunny smile, it cut through me like a knife. You looked ... happy, like the first time I saw you all those years ago. I caused you nothing but misery, took you away from your family and the chance of a good life with decent people.' She saw torment etched on his face, his movements were edgy, awkward. 'I never meant to do that,' anguish distorted his words, 'you must believe me ... I *hate* myself for what I did to you.'

'It's true, ye gave me grief,' she whispered, 'an' Ah cannae deny Ah've suffered but e'en wi' all that's happened, Ah dinnae hate ye.' She made to touch his hand, hurriedly pulling back at the thought of being seen. 'We have three fine children an' Ah praise the Lord fur them.'

'Oh Sarah, ma darling Sarah, how I've missed you but just as I miss you and the little ones I also know it would have been wrong, a mistake ... if you had sailed with me to America.'

She was hurt. 'Why? D'ye ken how many times Ah've cried masel' senseless fur no' gaun wi' ye?'

'It was a hard, cruel crossing. There was fever on board an' things were little better when we docked. There's a bad, wicked side to me, Sarah, ye've seen it an' I'm ashamed of it, but it is the way it is. My love for you and the children is strong yet the Cause for my brothers in Ireland is in my blood, running in my veins. I cannot abandon my homeland, not even for you.'

294

'But ye have,' she said sharply, 'look at yer fancy clothes an' jewels .... an' makin' yer hame in America? How are ye helping yer friends in the Cause?'

'There are many ways of making a fortune in the New World. It was easy with my skills at the card table.' He saw her disgust. 'Men with wealth need entertaining, when money itself is plentiful their greed must be fed in other ways and I supply whatever they need. It is amusing to fleece the politicians and the new breed of pompous bigots! I keep enough to fool them, make them believe I am a business man, but t'ousands of dollars are put to good use to free us from the English.'

'Ha'e ye no conscience?'

'Oh, I have a conscience ...' he spoke too loudly, hastily lowering his voice, fidgeting in his chair, 'which is why I do what I do and why we are sitting here today.' He checked to see if they were being overheard and she noticed how breathless he was. He sat back and cleared his throat, restless in his chair. Then, satisfied he could speak candidly, he continued, with an earnest expression in his eyes imploring her to understand. 'We parted in dreadful circumstances, ma dearest Sarah. Ye will forever be in my heart, special and dear to me to the day I die. I beg your forgiveness and wish ye all the luck an' happiness in the world.'

Leaving a long space while she considered his words, she murmured, 'Sae, ye dinnae want me?'

He flinched, sucking in air between clenched teeth.

'I *want* ye, oh, that is never to be doubted. There is not a woman alive who can take your place, I've never found another you. But the paths we choose to follow are so far apart that in being together we can only achieve misery.' He gave a roguish smile, two gold teeth catching the light. 'We both have years of experience to remind us of that fact! Ye survived, thank God, an' not for any help from me. Ye are strong. I cannot, for my own sanity, put ye through that again.'

Sitting straight backed, tense, in her chair, Sarah felt a rush of understanding. Much as she wanted to disagree, she knew he was right. They were ill-suited, complete opposites in character, with nothing in common besides the weak, youthful moments of passion which created their daughter over twenty years before. In that moment of clarity, all the yearning for what could have been, what might have been, disappeared.

'I've never known ye so quiet.' he said gently.

'Ah ha'e nuthin' tae say,' she took a shuddering breath, studying the stranger in front of her, a stranger she once knew intimately. 'Ah've loved ye sae long, an' sae dearly ... an' God bless ye, Ah believe Ah alis will, but yer richt, if we had nae bin sae taken wi' lust we would ne'er ha'e bin t'gether.'

Admitting their mistakes with open honesty brought about a strangely calm atmosphere. They spoke of Cathy's wedding, of Lily and of Stephen's hot headed ways. Of the clubs he ran in New York, the opportunities for work and wealth in the other States.

'I will send you money,' he sat back and folded his arms.

'Ye will no'!' she blurted out, 'efter tellin' me it comes fae gamblin' an' *hoors*,' she mouthed the last word. 'Ye can keep it. Ye were richt, Ah wis happy at the Dale's hoose when we met an' noo, aye, Ah'm content ... happy.'

'An' the man you were dancing with? Does he make ye happy?'

She was about to answer but asked instead, 'Does oor Cathy ken ye're here?'

'No. It is best tae say nothing of our meeting.'

'Fur her sake, or yours?'

He shrugged, rubbing his brow, 'perhaps both. Although it pains me, my dear, I believe we should part now.' He started to cough, patting at his mouth with the handkerchief, his eyes becoming bloodshot and watering from the effort of catching his breath.

Dewson appeared within moments, proffering a tray with a tumbler of opaque liquid. Sean grasped it and drank, spluttering a little before resting back in his chair.

'Are ye ill?' Sarah asked anxiously, seeing a sheen of sweat dampening the hair falling across his temples.

'A chill ... caught on the voyage. Dewson is keen to see I live to take him home again.' He waved a hand in the man's direction. 'Ma ill gotten gains have provided me with a manservant, would you believe?'

They parted quickly and, outwardly, formally, conscious of the surrounding eyes and ears.

'I am grateful we had this time together,' Sean murmured, holding her hand tightly between his. 'Bless ye, ma dearest.'

She tried to smile, their eyes exchanging heartfelt goodbyes, seeking contact until the last moment.

'Fur better or worse, ye are ma husband,' she whispered, 'ye'll alis be in ma hairt. May the Lord ha'e mercy oan ye, ma darlin'.'

Chapter Sixteen

"Courts of law, and all the paraphernalia and folly of law
cannot be found in a rational state of society."
Robert Owen

Charles Pictet's friend, Monsieur Cuvier, arrived in London to accompany Owen to Paris. They travelled to the south coast where a French frigate waited, specially dispatched to collect the party. There was barely a swell on the sea on leaving England, but to Owen's dismay, for he had never sailed before, a severe westerly blew up half way across the Channel. Their vessel was tossed around like flotsam in the hazardous conditions, not arriving in Calais until after sunset.

Owen's first sight of France came through a porthole from his seat in the cabin below deck. He cried out as he spotted the quayside lamps, apparently bobbing in the distance, and there was shared relief and exuberance at surviving the ordeal.

An atmosphere of adventure embraced the three gentlemen, taking their friendship to a deeper level and reaffirming that they had more in common than their ages; all being in their late forties.

After settling their masters into their rooms at a coaching inn, Murdoch and the two French manservants were directed to a hayloft above the horses' rustling stalls. The yard was bustling with coachmen and stable lads, rowdy with buckets clanging, oaths and jokes exchanged in foreign tongues. Tuneful melodies from a mouth organ added to the spontaneous exclamations from a group of squatting figures huddled over a card game. Drained from the fearful journey and desperately missing Emily, Murdoch lay down on the hay, covered himself with his cloak and fell asleep almost instantly.

The next morning, the weather being less unruly, the party boarded a magnificent carriage sent for their comfort and set off along the road to Paris.

Any problems Owen might have encountered in the practical matters of understanding the language were smoothed away by his French companions. Having been chosen by the Swiss Republic as 'envoy-extraordinary' to the Congress of Vienna in 1814, and again the following year to the Congress in Paris, Pictet was a shrewd and capable man. He was also entertaining company, as was Professor Cuvier.

Jean Cuvier, or as he impressed on Owen at their first meeting, 'call me Georges, no-one calls me Jean,' had been placed in charge of education by Emperor Napoleon. With bristling, greying, chestnut hair, a large nose and a small, thin lipped mouth, the French zoologist looked perpetually surprised and curious, a fitting trait for such a brilliant scientist.

Happily, the return of the Bourbon monarchy did not end his career but instead brought about his prestigious appointment as Chancellor of the University. Although a Lutheran, he placidly tolerated Owen's religious stance and refrained from giving vent to any impulse to convert the Welshman to his own views.

The high, rattling, carriage rolled along the country lanes drawn by four well-muscled bay horses. Bred for stamina with shaggy feathers flowing around their sturdy legs, they ate up the miles. Sitting up top, the valets and the coachman passed few words, the two young footmen, lads of not yet fourteen years, bounced about on the back seat, waving cheerfully to everyone they passed.

In more comfort within the cab, the three gentlemen ate simple fare and drank light ale or claret, rocking gently and, all the while, discussing their views. School systems, Owen's pet favourite and the main reason for Cuvier's interest, the government's harsh policies to quell the social unrest and, a topic returned to again and again, Nature.

Every turn of the road revealed another scene to be noticed and commented upon. Groups of sweet chestnut and hazelnut trees baked in the sun amongst gently rolling land. Lush meadows melted into watery marshes, vivid with every hue of green foliage, speckled with wildflowers and bright scarlet poppies.

Wide, slow moving rivers, edged with poplars and flowering shrubs, meandered through the shallow valleys where stone hamlets clustered around windmills and medieval churches. The peace of the hot day was only disturbed by the clatter of the coach and the cries of startled pigeons or waterfowl as the travellers passed by, leaving a cloud of dust in their wake.

Stopping at a village to water the horses and allow them time to rest, Owen and his friends chose to stretch their legs and wandered down a track to the riverbank. Around them, bird song filled acres of apple orchards, domed wicker bee hives buzzed with activity and elusive grass hoppers chirruped. Dragonflies darted or hovered along the water's edge, shimmering red, green and blue above the reeds.

'This was an excellent idea,' Owen told Pictet, plucking a poppy bloom and pushing it into a buttonhole. 'I am rejuvenated already and the journey has just begun.'

'You are the youngest of us three,' the Frenchman laughed, 'is it your youth you are seeking?'

'Not at all! It is just that for more than three years I have been pushing for reforms in Government and they are stagnating. The Bill is lying as if in that river, barely moving on its course.' He pushed his fingers through his hair and looked down the river, his blue eyes dark and wistful, 'In the meantime, thousands of poor people, mainly women and small children, are suffering.'

'Do you believe your suggestions will become law?' Cuvier asked, his strong accent and carefully chosen words adding weight to the question.

'Oh yes, they will.' Owen's tone was firm. 'I have no doubt. You see, it is just plain *wrong* for factories to treat their workers as they do at present.' he explained. 'It cannot continue, it is untenable. The only question is, how long will it take before common sense and decent humanity prevails over greed? The ingrained behaviour of those with power, abusing their power, is a hard habit to break.'

'Well, mon ami,' Pictet slapped him playfully on the shoulder, 'wait until we arrive in Paris, I have friends I wish you to meet and I am sure they will raise your spirits!'

'My spirits are rarely lowered, my friends! Now, with this joyous scene to behold ... and your genial company, I am already recovering from any frustration with Westminster.'

France was just emerging from decades of warfare and revolution, as well as having suffered the worst weather in living memory for the previous four years. The horror of small pox, measles and other deadly diseases lurked in the shadows. Whole villages were decimated, adding hundreds, every month, to the rising death toll since the catastrophic famine of 1816.

300

Despite this turmoil, Owen found Paris to be as comfortable as any city, London included, and also as filthy, foul smelling and socially divided.

Cuvier was eager to introduce him to the salons and coffee houses frequented by the leading philosophers, scientists and politicians of French society.

During the day they met under gaudy awnings in cafes beside the Seinne and joined picnics on the grass among shady trees in the parks. In the evenings, they went to clubs and private houses, walking through dimly lit, narrow streets filled with music and foreign chatter; warm with the aromas of fresh bread or frying garlic.

Owen ate lightly. Unsure of the strange dishes placed before him, he chose easily digestible soups which, as usual, he left to cool before tasting. Bread and cheese with various cuts of cold, cured meat became his staple diet, a preference kindly mocked by his new gourmet friends but quickly forgiven with effusive Gallic charm.

The Prime Minister granted Owen a meeting within two days of receiving the letter of introduction written by the French Ambassador in London. Owen's arrival in Paris had not gone unnoticed, encouraged, no doubt, by knowledge of the Duke of Kent's patronage and the dozens of copies of Owen's essays sent out by Sidmouth a year before.

The little information Owen had discovered about, Richelieu, the Prime Minister of France, did not fill him with optimism. This was a man from a wealthy, royalist family who had lived through the Revolution and seen his estates stripped from him, close friends murdered. As an ally of Marie Antoinette, he was famous for having risked his life to warn her of the approaching hordes, giving her just minutes to escape the palace. With the monarchy removed by the rabble, he eventually turned to the Russians to fight against Napoleon, taking a high rank in the Russian Imperial Army.

Now, back in Paris and with Louis XVIII on the throne, Owen was given to understand Richelieu had been persuaded, against his first inclinations, to lead the government. In this position and as a staunch monarchist, he could not turn down a recommendation to speak with a man known to be close to the Dukes of Kent and

Sussex, the sons of Britain's King George III, and brothers of the current Prince Regent.

Their appointment was conducted behind closed doors, accompanied only by an interpreter.

Owen took his seat opposite Richelieu, a man a few years his senior. His short curling grey hair and clear cut features projected a strong character, augmented by years of military training and the immaculate grooming of an aristocrat. They were in an echoing, ornately plastered and gilded room, the windows drawn up to allow bird song and the splash of fountains to fill the humid air.

Pausing between sentences for the translator to pass on the information, Owen explained in detail his system for raising the new generation in a kind and caring manner, instilling only good habits and providing a sound education. He gave examples from New Lanark, showing the Duke how he could create a happy, respectful and satisfied population who would work together in strong communities without religious intolerance.

'I give you the tools to heal your country ... these are tried and tested ...' he concluded, 'revolution does not have to be by force ... slowly, through one or two generations, you can bring about previously only dreamed of happiness. This is the time, this is the moment! Grasp it and it will be done.'

Richelieu posed several intelligent questions, all answered concisely by Owen.

'It is no secret that I was against the Revolution,' Richelieu then told Owen through the translator, 'however, it is clear we cannot go back to the old ways. Your views are interesting, more than interesting. I believe them to be sound, Monsieur Owen, but I do *not* believe we are ready for such radical change. Perhaps, in time, we could achieve the society you propose, but now? I do not think so. It is not the time.'

The response was more hopeful than Owen had expected and they parted formally and on pleasant terms, with Owen inviting the Duke to visit New Lanark.

Among Cuvier's illustrious circle, none shone brighter or held more respect than the venerable mathematician Simon Pierre Laplace. To Owen's immense delight, the snowy haired Laplace often joined impromptu philosophical debates held over claret and walnuts when the cloth was drawn.

302

For the first week or so Owen listened and observed the animated conversations as an outsider, speaking only if specifically drawn into a topic by a bilingual member of the party. As his presence became familiar, he began to be included more, greeted with genuine warmth and invited to private dinners in their homes. Several were excellent English speakers but those who were not fluent would mime their way through anecdotes for his benefit, often causing raucous hilarity with ridiculous gestures and contorted expressions.

One evening, while dining al fresco in the little garden behind Cuvier's town house, Owen found himself seated beside Laplace. Moths and mosquitoes danced in the drifting pipe smoke, attracted by the candlelight, repulsed by the tobacco.

Laplace turned his attention to Owen, fixing him with a direct stare and asking a question. Not understanding the language, Owen gave a self-effacing smile and looked to Cuvier, sitting opposite, for help.

'Ah, Marquis Laplace wishes to know more of your philosophy!' Cuvier reached for the decanter and charged their glasses. 'Speak, Mr Owen! I shall be your translator!'

There were half a dozen other men at the table and they fell silent, lounging back in their chairs, their eyes on the quiet 'Englishman' while he laid out his vision. Most of them already knew Owen's work, several had even read his essays, but all wished to hear Laplace's views.

Laplace was renowned for picking up on the minutae of a subject, creating problems where few existed and complicating matters whenever he set his mind to a task. He listened intently, probing for weaknesses in Owen's argument for the formation of character and demanding to know why there was resistance to this New System.

While Cuvier translated, Owen was fascinated by the subtle changes of expression flitting over Laplace's face. The drawn down brows, then a half smile, lop-sided and gentle, then a frown and gruff remark; his eyes darting from Cuvier to Owen, to the moths, the candles, but remaining focused within his mind. This was a man who used complex mathematical equations, physics and statistics to calculate the stability of the solar system, the speed of sound and explore the existence of black holes.

What would such a mind make of his philosophy?

The candles burned low, dripping wax and almost guttering to a close before being replaced by an unobtrusive servant. Bats flew through the dark garden, frogs croaked, but the men around the table were oblivious to their surroundings, leaning closer, engrossed in the debate.

Distant bells rang out across the city, clear in the dewy air. It was growing cool and Owen sat back, finishing his monologue by reiterating his belief that the changes he proposed would not happen overnight. They would be thorough, steady.

On being told this final statement, Laplace smiled and launched into a torrent of French, causing sighs and murmurs of agreement from his audience.

'He refers you,' Cuvier's voice was tired but tinged with satisfaction, 'to his principles, derived from physics, to favour evolutionary over revolutionary change.'

Owen nodded emphatically, eyes shining.

Cuvier continued, 'In response to you he says, "Let us apply to the political and moral sciences the method founded upon observation and calculation, which has served us so well in the natural sciences?"

There were mutterings of accord and rye smiles amongst his friends.

' "Let us not offer fruitless and often injurious resistance to the inevitable benefits derived from the progress of enlightenment; but let us change our institutions and the usages that we have for a long time adopted only with extreme caution. In the face of this ignorance, the theory of probability instructs us to avoid all change, especially to avoid sudden changes which in the moral, as well as the physical world, never occur without a considerable loss of vital force.'

Cuvier, their host, surveyed the candlelit faces surrounding his table.

'Gentlemen,' he rose from his seat, 'an inspiring evening, I thank you all. Let us adjourn indoors before the chill on our skin reaches our bones.'

Hearing of Owen's presence in Paris, Duc de la Rochefoucault, a cotton master, invited him to tour his cotton spinning factory. The reputation of New Lanark's high quality yarn was famous in

Europe and Rochefoucault, confident in his own product, wished to show Owen his business. It was an interesting day because, casting his professional eye over the French cotton, Owen saw it was of almost the same fineness as at New Lanark. However, although of slightly inferior quality it was four pence per pound more expensive.

Amongst the scores of influential and interesting men and women to which Owen was introduced while in Paris was a Prussian geographer and explorer, Alexander Von Humboldt.

Humboldt was a superb raconteur, charming and quick witted. Not only was his intelligence revered, like that of Laplace, but his strong Germanic build, square jaw and thick, attractively tousled dark hair blessed him with conspicuous good looks. Having spent many years travelling in harsh, primitive conditions, he was revelling in the intelligent company he found in Paris. The ladies at the *soirees* adored him, flirtatiously demanding to know personal details of his times in exotic countries. He was often to be found surrounded by an enrapt audience, telling exuberant tales of his expeditions throughout South America. How he plotted the course of the Orinoco River, trekked to Quito, the exhausting effects of altitude whilst climbing the mountain Pinchincha or being shocked and severely injured while capturing electric eels.

'Humboldt is a fine man,' Cuvier told Owen one afternoon while making their way to meet a few friends; one being the man in question. A little exercise was the order of the day, probably a stroll around the park, and then a light meal at a local tavern.

'I admit to finding all your friends to be stimulating company. They are receptive to new ideas. It is very refreshing. I fear many British gentlemen, the clergy and upper classes especially ... they are steeped in tradition. "If it has been this way, it shall always be this way!" They are frightened, as blinkered as a nervous horse, made blind to any new suggestions which might disturb their habits.'

They wandered on, talking, hands clasped behind their backs, dust from the well worn path clouding their polished boots. Willow trees dipped their weeping branches into the lazy river, mirror like, until the waters rippled in the wake of small boats. It was popular for young men to hire a boat and woo their sweethearts with their rowing skills. Soft giggles and cries of praise drifted between the riverbanks and Owen paused to enjoy the scene.

In the stern of the boats, young women in flowing pastel outfits relaxed against cushions, their faces hidden by the fluttering satin fringes of their parasols.

'Here in France,' Cuvier continued, walking on along the path having seen the colourful displays on the Seine a hundred times before, 'we were taken to the brink and beyond. Our uprising and the decades of bloody war have opened our eyes, even the eyes of those who dared not see! What has all the death and pain produced? If we look at the map of Europe, the borders have returned to virtually as it was before Napoleon.'

A family approached on the narrow path and they stood aside, receiving a polite smile and 'merci' from the oldest child, a boy of six or seven. Cuvier's eyes instantly flooded with tears: three of his four children had died young and the sight of the boy brought its usual stab of desolation.

'And the monarchy?' Owen was saying, unaware of his friend's distress.

Cuvier composed himself; 'No one has won ... Once again, a Bourbon king sits upon the throne of France. Yet, beyond the material things, oh, I assure you, the changes are deep. The revolution has truly enlightened our minds and stirred our consciences and that is far more powerful.'

'It is tragic,' Owen said, shaking his head, 'that Man must resort to war? Bigotry and greed have become entrenched, consented to as part of everyday life as if it is normal. My system would bring about a society where this sort of behaviour and suppression could not survive and ... all without a drop of blood being spilt.'

Cuvier gave him a shrewd look, 'We study science, facts, to discover the world around us but you, Mr Owen, you have turned the mirror, you study people. Observing, noting reactions. I am sure you will enjoy speaking with Humboldt.'

'He lectures at the Institute, I understand?'

'He is the, how d'you say? Leading light? of the Institut de France! No mere Professor! He is still compiling his notes from his grand adventure in the Americas, a task he expected would take perhaps a year or ... three,' Cuvier laughed, again searching for the right words in English. 'I think twenty years will not be enough! He has read your essays, you know, and is curious.'

When Humboldt joined them in the park, he brought with him a young scholar, Mariano, a black haired, dark eyed Peruvian, and regaled the company with the boy's brilliance.

It was not until later, when the group of friends took over several tables outside a tavern on a little side street that Owen and Humboldt spoke together. They drank coffee, ate stuffed olives and discussed Owen's projects, the others occasionally chipping in with comments.

Finding a rapport with the Prussian, Owen asked him why he became an explorer.

'I am a naturalist, Mr Owen! If I am to learn the mysteries of the natural world I must visit the forests, mountains and coastlines, see them, touch them and study them scientifically.'

'It is a fascinating subject, my friend,' Owen said, with feeling. 'I believe there is much benefit to be had from spending time in the countryside, close to Nature.'

'Indeed! My work proves the *unity of nature*, all parts of the natural world relate to one another, everything is interwoven, dependent. That is why certain plants can only grow in a particular soil, or above a specific height from the level of the sea ... it is all tied together, working together to make the whole planet ... the whole universe.'

Cuvier cleared his throat, 'Our Lord God created the universe, Humboldt.'

'That is still a question.' Humboldt replied, swinging round to face Cuvier, eyes smiling. 'Perhaps he did? I cannot say but, as a physicist, I require evidence. Yet, it is a fine 'hypothesis', to quote our esteemed mutual friend, Laplace. However, physics, as the name implies, can only explain the physical aspect of the natural world. The greater power, if it exists, is one above our knowledge, a divinity perhaps?'

One subject moved into the next, with Owen finding common ground to debate on every topic.

Following the hostility and rejection he suffered from declaring his own religious position, it was refreshing to discover, as they talked, that he was with a fellow Deist and one who also detested the hypocrisy of certain religious attitudes.

Owen's most audacious appointment in Paris, arranged by Prince Edward the Duke of Kent, was with His Serene Highness the Duke of Orleans.

Before leaving London, Owen was warned of the recent personal tragedy befalling the Duke of Orleans: his baby daughter, Francoise, had died. It seemed impolite to intrude on this personal grief but then, in August, the city buzzed with the heartening news of the birth of a healthy son to the grieving family, poignantly christened Francois.

Despite all the pomp and ceremony of the royal apartments the Duke of Orleans turned out to be unexpectedly sympathetic towards Owen's work. He had read the beautifully bound copy of A New View of Society, sent to him by the British Home Secretary, and wished to discuss it at length.

Owen was impressed by the man's strength of character. It must have been hard to be born into the Royal Court with a father who held admirable but dangerously pro-revolutionary views and then be thrown into a civil war. While his father was sent to the guillotine, the young Duke escaped into exile, his sympathies still with the working people of France. Although he was a far more popular figure than the King, unfortunately for Owen, he held none of the power.

'How long are you staying in Paris, Monsieur Owen?' the Duke asked at the end of their meeting.

'I have been here a full six weeks but will be leaving for Geneva in a few days.'

'Ah Switzerland! It was my haven of safety when I was forced to leave Paris with my sister. You must travel outside the city, the country is magnifique!'

'I shall be staying with my friend and business partner, Mr John Walker, at Lucerne ...'

'You will enjoy it! My journey was less peaceful. France was in uproar and my father and brothers imprisoned so I, at not yet twenty years, was deemed an embarrassment to Switzerland. I took to the road with only the companionship of my dear valet, Baudouin, a true and trusted man.' The lines around the Duke's mouth drew down, his gaze drifting, seeing memories. 'We were young fugitives, like so many at that time of terror. Barns and hedgerows were our beds for too long a time until we came to

Reichenau, on Lake Constance?' he looked at Owen as if he should know the place. 'No matter, a beautiful little town. I taught there, at the boys' school of Monsieur Jost. It was there, coming back from skating with some pupils on a snowy day ... I heard of my father's fate by the blade of the guillotine.'

'A terrible tragedy, your Serene Highness,' Owen offered, feeling the man's emotion. 'Is that when you left for the United States of America? Where you met our mutual friend the Duke of Kent?'

'No no ... I spent many years travelling in Europe, using different names!' He gave a hearty laugh as if it was a game, the pain in his eyes showing the desperate truth. 'As far to the north as Finland, so very different from my homeland: interesting times. It was later that I sailed to the Americas to join my brothers ... they were in exile in Philadelphia. Have you been?'

'No, I must confess this, France, is as far as I have travelled.'

'Then you should go! It is a wonderful, young country. Travel opens one's mind ...' he gave another guffaw, this time with mirth, 'although, I think perhaps your mind is already open, mon ami!'

***

The Dale sisters, accompanied by Giggs, arrived at Cuvier's house in Paris during a heavy rain shower. Owen was out at the time so it was Anne Marie Cuvier who welcomed them. Relieved to discover these fashionable Scottish ladies both spoke excellent French, she explained the reason for their brother in law's absence.

Tired from the journey, they were encouraged by Madam Cuvier to rest until dinner. They were entranced by the pretty bedrooms with ornate dark wood furniture, their walls painted with birds of paradise and flowers. Lace curtains under colourful silk swags draped the small pane windows. On drawing the layers back, Margaret felt a thrill at seeing the views across a private courtyard, trees, and beyond to spires and the exotically different roofline of Paris.

Much too excited to lie down for long, they were waiting in the drawing room when Owen returned.

'Scientists and scholars ... The Duc d'Orleans!' Jean cried, offering her cheek for a brotherly kiss. 'Robert, my dear, Madame Cuvier informs us you have spoken with Royalty!'

'Jean,' Margaret rebuked, joining the family reunion and enjoying a warm embrace, 'you know that Robert is on close terms with our own Royal family these days, it is no surprise he is invited into such society in France.'

'What is he like?' Jean asked, ignoring her sister.

They sat by the fireside and Madam Cuvier excused herself politely, smiling sweetly but overwhelmed by her parlour being filled with babbling English chatter.

For Owen, it was very pleasant to be with family again and he looked fondly on their familiar faces with the added relief of conversing smoothly in English.

Murdoch was in the outhouse attending to laundry when he glimpsed the portly cloaked and bonneted figure of the Charlotte Street maid. Dropping the collar he was starching and choking back a cry, he rubbed at the condensation on the window and peered out. He was not mistaken. Forgetting all formalities, he ran across the puddle strewn courtyard calling her name.

'Och Giggs! Ah've ne'er bin sae happy tae see a well kent face in all ma life!' He rushed towards the lady's maid and hugged her.

'Well! there's a welcome, an' no mistake!' she laughed.

They were standing in the back hall with pattering, splashing rain pouring from a broken gutter outside the open back door. A young footman struggled to pass them, weighed down with the Miss Dales' trunks , his hair already soaked and plastered to his head.

Murdoch guided Giggs through to the large room where the servants ate their meals.

'Ye ha'e nae idea whit a difference ye bein' here will mak tae me!' His words echoed off the bare walls. 'The last six weeks ha'e bin sic a trial fur Ah cannae unnerstaun a word they say ... Ah'm fair vexed wi' it all.'

'Ye paur soul,' she chuckled, 'weel, Ah can imagine. Three days in yon rattlin', heavin' carriage has bin bad enough fur me but noo we can ha'e a richt guid blether.' She beamed up at him. 'Ah ha'e sumat fur ye, it'll pit a smile oan yer face.'

'Whit?'

'Twa things ... but ye'll ha'e tae wait until Ah've seen tae ma ladies an' then Ah'll gie ye them.'

Whistling happily, Murdoch returned to his chores. When he found pursing his lips became impossible with an irrepressible smile on his lips, he burst into song.

Evening was settling on the household before Giggs could find a moment to deliver her surprise.

'Here ye are,' she declared, 'this is frae Mr Renwick an' the rest o' them in Glesgie,' she handed him a bottle of Hosh malt whisky. 'And this,' she produced a letter, 'is frae Miss Wilson doon at Lanark. She sent it tae me at Mrs Stuart's, askin' me tae pass it tae ye.'

Alarmed, Murdoch unfolded the paper and held it close to the nearest candle.

It was not from Miss Wilson, only addressed in her hand, the letter was from Emily, his wife. It was short, affectionate, telling him she was well and, by the grace of God, he was to become a father before the end of the year.

***

'Oh look, the horse chestnut trees are turning!' Anne Caroline pointed to the woodland at the end of the lawn, enjoying showing Braxfield's garden to Lady Mary. 'I always remember the grand old chestnut tree at Charlotte Street, a favourite of my father's. He would comment on its progress through the year as others might discuss a friend.'

'Such glorious trees, giving us a spring display of flowers and the earliest copper leaves.'

'The boys will be happy,' Anne Caroline smiled to herself. 'Games of conkers are not far away and the yearly fun of picking hazelnuts from the trees down by the river.'

'I fear the summer is drawing to a close for another year.' Lady Mary leaned down to smell a full blown moss rose. 'Oh! No French perfume can compete!' She took another sniff before releasing the deep pink flower, a petal falling to the ground. 'Is Robert still in France?'

'I believe they are all in Switzerland now. The last letter I received was from Margaret, telling me of their safe arrival in

Paris, but it was written a few weeks ago.' She led the way through a newly planted timber archway where tendrils of sparse purple tinged honeysuckle leaves struggled up the supports, their first year's growth coming to an end. 'I know they planned to journey on, straight away, to stay with Mr Walker and his family in Lucerne.

'All those miles in a carriage,' Lady Mary sensed a lowering in her friend's mood, 'I do not envy them! And ghastly foreign food! Gracious, the dishes they serve in London are bad enough,' she grimaced, 'eels and offal, but I'm told the French are worse and eat frogs and snails ... doesn't bear thinking of, my dear!'

Anne Caroline appreciated her efforts to bring humour to the subject and responded with a laugh, changing the subject to take her on a tour of the orchids in the hot houses.

In fact, day to day life was surprisingly good, even without her beloved husband in residence.

Robert Dale and William were now almost full grown young men and she was astonished at how remarkably similar their deep timbred voices were to their father's in tone and accent. Having their company, and that of Ann and Jane, at the dinner table made for companionable evenings. During the day, there was plenty to be overseen at Braxfield and her visits to the mill workers' homes filled most afternoons.

Every Sunday, she attended Church, twice. In bad weather they rode in the carriage, otherwise, she walked down to the village to hear the sermons given by the minister of her father's Old Scotch Independents Church. All the children went with her; little Richard and Mary bringing up the rear of their processions with Peggy.

At sixteen years old, the tall, dark haired Robert Dale was catching the eye of the village girls. He had inherited his father's lean figure, high cheek bones and deep set eyes which were attractively combined with his mother's rounder features. The villagers knew him from the classes he taught in the Institute and they liked his friendly manner as he went about his business.

However, it was his little ten year old brother, David, who the older women cooed and clucked over. They restrained themselves, with difficulty, from ruffling his yellow hair or affectionately pinching his cheek as they would their own grandchildren.

'He's a bonnie bairn,' Sarah commented one Sunday morning, watching David and his family walking sedately up the road towards Braxfield House. 'He'll be a hairt breaker soon.'

Rosie nodded, but she rarely noticed children.

'Will Cathy be up at Joe's?' she asked Sarah, climbing the steps to go to Joe's house.

'No' the day, Ross's Ma's no' weel, sae they're roond at her's. Ah gather Tam an' Mel will be there, though.' Sarah shot her sister a sidelong look. 'D'ye ken Tam's all richt? The last time Ah saw him he wis fair doon in the mooth.'

'He telt Fiona he's worried aboot Jim Calder getting oot o' the jail an' takin' Melanie awa' frae him.'

'Naw! Tha' scoondrel should leave them in peace! There's folk want tae hound him oot fur driving Ewing's fine business intae the grun.'

Rosie paused for breath on the steep hill, laying her hand on her side to ease a stitch.

'Dear Lord, this hill will be the death o' me! Ma auld bones wulnae manage it soon!'

They turned to gaze down at New Lanark's roofs and the hundreds of smoking chimney pots.

Sarah began walking again, 'Ah hear a lad frae Nursery Buildings has taken o'er Cal's patch.'

'Aye. Ye ken, Ah miss Cal like the De'il, Sarah. D'ye no'?'

'Every day. Ah went up tae his grave the ither nicht an' laid some flo'ers. Ah suppose ye niver get o'er losing some yin ye love. Ye jist, weel, ye jist ha'e tae keep livin' an' mak the maist o' it until the Lord sees fit tae tak' ye up an' then ye can be t'gether agin.'

'Until then, we can keep him in oor thochts,' Rosie said seriously. 'That's whit Ah dae. Ah feel if Ah think on him, mind his funny ways an' all o' tha', then he's still wi' us. Ah dinnae want him tae be forgotten.'

'Cal will ne'er be forgotten.' Sarah's voice was soft.

It was weeks since her encounter with Sean and in many ways she felt calmer and more settled than at any time since they first met. Yet, she was troubled by memories, selective, happy memories, of the young Irishman she once knew.

'If ye love someyin,' Rosie was saying, 'a little o' them stays wi' ye long efter they're gone. Like Sam an' wee Connor. It hurts no' tae see them. How does yon Robert Burns pit it, 'tis better tae ha'e loved an lost than ne'er tae ha'e loved at all.'

'An' Stephen,' Sarah murmured, adding, unspoken, 'and Sean.'

When they turned into the driveway, laughter could be heard and on following the sound, they discovered Joe kneeling in the corner of his workshop.

'Come, quietly ...' he sat back on his heels. 'At least some yins makin' use o' this, Ah've a mind tae leave it.'

The intricately woven grass, straw and tiny twigs of a blackbird's nest was lodged between a slab of stone and the barn wall. The lining of dried mud was empty of eggs, any chicks having long since fledged, and was now partially covered over by windblown wisps of hay. Under the hay, four or five tiny dark brown mice peered out.

Rosie screamed and hurried away to the back door, calling to the Lord for protection.

'Aw, whit bonnie wee things,' Sarah whispered. 'Their eyes and ears are much too big fur their wee bodies. Did ye e'er see sich a sicht!'

Tam and Melanie arrived in high spirits, bringing news of the satisfactory outcome of months of worry. After much soul searching and discussions, the couple decided they must do something to free Jim Calder from Debtors' Prison. Neither could truly appreciate and enjoy their life together knowing the man was mouldering in a cell in Hamilton.

'Sae, Ah paid his ootstandin' debt,' Tam said bluntly. 'In exchange fur his freedom, he's leavin' us in peace an' will ne'er come back tae Lanark.'

'He wid nae ha'e dared come back!' Rosie cried amid the others giving congratulations,'but Ah'm fair made up fur ye baithe.'

Joe enjoyed the Sunday gatherings of the whole family. If Fiona commented that he was quiet during the meals, it was for no other reason than sheer satisfaction. From his seat at the head of the table, he watched their faces and listened to their chatter feeling no need to speak. It was enough to know they were all well and he, Joe, was providing for them.

314

Ironically, this was sometimes made possible by the misfortunes of others. It was not only Calder who fell victim to the hard times, all around Clydesdale, indeed all across the land, bankruptcy was bringing the bailiffs to clear once thriving homes.

The long, oak plank table and ten chairs, a dresser and three strong kists, (two having elaborately engraved brass work, much to Fiona's delight) came from an auctioned estate at Cleghorn. Four wide brass bedsteads, a fancifully carved dressing table and matching wash stand, from near Carmichael, and other household items from weekly sales at the market.

After conducting their own businesses, Joe and his Brothers at St David's Lodge, were spending any free time they could find to raise money for charitable guilds and churches to distribute rations to the growing number of poor in the area.

Fiona felt the time was right to broach another idea to her husband, but chose the moment carefully. She noted Joe's good humour when he came in the door one evening and his decision not to go out again, given the rain. Then, she waited until the haggis and mashed turnips and potatoes were eaten, the table cleared and the children dispersed to their evening pastimes.

'Ah've set a fire through by,' she told him, removing her long apron and smoothing her hair. ''Tis a while since we sat in the parlour, quiet like, by oor ane hearth.'

The flames soon took hold with little encouragement from the bellows and she eased off his boots, propping a footstool under his heels.

'Yin day, Ah'll sew a tapestry cover,' she patted the threadbare cushion. 'Ah wonder how many feet ha'e rested there? Noo then, that'll keep the draught aff yer toes.'

She sat down beside him on the leather upholstered settee, kicking off her pumps and drawing her legs up under her skirts to lie cuddled up against him.

It took a while for her to reach the subject and when she did, Joe smothered a smile by kissing the top of her head.

'Tom's daen awfy weel,' her words were casual, 'he's a bright lad an' findin' the office work easy.'

'Aye, he has mair brains than the rest o' the family pit t'gether.'

'Ye ken he's alis doon at the Institute, reading? He spends his wages oan book. O' course, that's efter gi'ing me some fur his board. He's a guid lad.'

Joe was happy to take the bait. 'Ye think he's still hankerin' efter being a doctor?'

'Aye. He wid need tae gae tae the Grammar school fae that, get learnin' in the Latin and Greek.' She wriggled her arm from under her and took Joe's hand, still gazing into the fire. 'Ah ken it's expensive but ye said we had a wee bit o' money noo an' that wid be well spent ... sending oor son tae the Grammar.'

'The last years ha'e bin tough but, aye, we ha'e the money fur it. If the carry oan wi' Calder an' tha' numskull Baxter ha'e taught me onything, it's tae be mighty carefu' of o'er spending.'

'But ye reckon we could send Tom tae be a scholar?'

'Aye, Ah wid think sae. Ah'll ask, shall Ah?'

She lifted her head to look into his eyes, offering her lips.

'Sae that wis whit the fire wis fur,' he mumbled between kisses, laughing, 'yer an awfy wuman!'

Settling back against him, she yawned and stretched. 'Och, not at all, Ah jist fancied sittin' by the warmth wi' ma man.'

'Aye richt,' he chuckled, squeezing her hand.

'Ah'm worn oot t'nicht.'

'Ye work too hard, ma darlin',' as he said the words, he realised how true they were and was struck by conscience. 'Whit am Ah thinkin'! If we ha'e the money tae send Tom tae the Grammar, then we can afford fur ye tae feenish work.'

'Feenish work?' she was shocked. 'Ah love ma work! An' would nae we need ma wages e'en mair?'

'Perhaps ... then, could ye tak a cut in oors? Dae less days? Rosie wis saying sumat aboot a neighbour o' hers daen tha'?'

'No' in the school, at least, Ah dinnae ken ...' The thought appealed to Fiona. 'It wid be easier fur me if Ah had mair time tae look efter Sionaidh, although she's settling in tae the laundry work no' bad these past months.'

They talked for hours, with only occasional interruptions when Fiona put Sionaidh and the younger ones to bed and the older boys came home.

When the basket of firewood was empty, they decided to turn in for the night.

316

'Ye gae oan up,' Joe said sleepily, 'Ah'll dae ma roonds.'

It was his rigid routine. Every stone, every slate and piece of timber on his property had been hard won. It represented his life's achievement and he allowed himself cautious pride but it also brought responsibility. Ewing had instilled in him the importance of insuring his home, his tools, his horses. Even in the days of scratching for work and making other savings, Joe always made his insurance payments.

Each evening, he checked the horses, secured the workshop and damped down the fires in the grates. Upstairs, he looked in to each of his children's rooms, confirming no candles were left burning. He knew of many accidents, having personally smelt the acrid soot of the destruction when called in to rebuild or demolish the remnants.

Since the first night they spent in their home, he carried out this ritual every evening. Once or twice, bone tired, he had gone straight to bed, but after tossing and turning he eventually fumbled his way downstairs, lit a lantern and did the rounds.

Fiona was already asleep when he reached the bedroom and set down the lamp, quietly extinguishing the flame.

Tawny owls were hooting from surrounding trees, their exchange moving into the distance. He listened, following their progress while he undressed, his eyes growing accustomed to the darkness, distinguishing the lighter cracks of the outline of the shutters.

Was this large house really his? Did the healthy profit lines in Tam's account books actually belong to him? Was a son of his going to be a scholar? It seemed unreal, yet wonderfully, comfortingly true.

Chapter Seventeen

"The true triumph of reason is that it enables us to get along with those who do not possess it." Voltaire

The night before leaving for Geneva, a banquet was held for Owen at a restaurant in the centre of Paris. If he had been in any doubt of his popularity it was dispelled by the crowd of elite professionals, politicians and philosophers flocking to the event.

For Jean and her sisters, this was their first experience of French high society. They were fascinated by the unusual manners, chic, sometimes outrageous and daringly provocative fashion, and the peculiar food. Their brother in law, they were told, was the 'lion of the salons' and even Laplace favoured them with his presence, bringing with him members of his intellectual circle at Arcuel.

When they boarded Pictet's carriage the next morning, Owen was sorry to be leaving the inspiring company of his new Parisian friends.

The primary reason for his tour of the Continent was to visit schools in Switzerland. Henry Brougham had travelled these same roads a few years earlier and urged Owen to experience the establishments first hand. This was not purely to research different methods of teaching, it was also to seek out a possible boarding school for his sons.

Tutors were all very well but Robert and William needed to broaden their horizons. The schools available to gentlemen's sons in Britain were rife with bullying and ancient, unsavoury practices which both Owen and Anne Caroline found abhorrent. These institutions, some boasting hundreds of years of existence, methodically instilled religious and class intolerance. They prided themselves on turning out bigoted, self-satisfied young men who felt they were above other men, indoctrinated to believe they were different, special.

Any place of learning which condoned whipping and the use of oppressive ways to intimidate their students, was instantly struck off Owen's list. His friends, Pictet, Walker and Brougham all gave glowing reports of the schools he was about to examine.

A week of whirlwind activity was spent in Geneva meeting Pictet's colleagues and the leading reformists and merchants residing in the city. The Dale sisters adored seeing the sights and readily took up the kind invitations extended by the wives of Owen's contacts. Never the less, the constant receptions, theatre outings, recitals and concerts were so far removed from the gentile life they led in Glasgow that it left the young women worn out. They quickly adopted the habit of rising after midday, resting or taking a quiet stroll in the afternoon and then preparing for the evening.

So, when Owen declared he wished to travel to Lucerne and stay with John Walker, they joined him on the journey.

Walker's rambling three story stone house charmed them from first sight. Sprawling among vineyards on the slopes above the lake, against a back drop of towering snow capped mountains, it appeared to grow out of the hillside. Long balconies and terraces faced south, shaded by colourful rambling roses and tangled white jasmine, vibrant geraniums and lavender spilling from large terracotta pots.

'Breathtaking!' Jean Dale sighed, standing on the main terrace and gazing out over the dazzling mirror-calm water to a hazy horizon of craggy, white topped peaks. 'I would never tire of this view, nor the hollow ringing notes of the cowbells in the distance. The air is so clear!'

The quieter pace of the Quaker household suited the Dale girls.

Sarah, John's wife, made them feel welcome from the start. Her life revolved around her ten children and an assortment of pets, which she enjoyed at a leisurely pace between prayers and meals of simple food. Emphasising how much they appreciated the hospitality in Geneva, Margaret spoke for her sisters when she admitted having found it rather 'fast'. It therefore came as no surprise when they elected to stay by the lake when Owen returned to the capital to tour schools with Pictet.

Giggs was sorry to see Murdoch driving away with his master, but was heartily relieved to be staying in this comfortable, countryside haven. She had not enjoyed her short acquaintance with the servants and facilities in Geneva and Paris: noisy, filthier than a Glasgow slum and very, very smelly, was her verdict.

319

Owen was excited by Pictet's itinerary for viewing three schools, chosen for having received high praise for their innovative ways of educating the poor.

The first was a Catholic school, run by an earnest old priest by the name of Father Oberlin. The man himself was genuine in his intense desire to offer basic schooling to children from the poorest families in his community. However, on being shown several hours of classes, Owen was disappointed to find the master relied on religious teaching, strongly projecting Catholic principles to the young audience and using the old techniques of making the pupils learn passages off by heart.

In Yverdun, Pictet took pleasure in introducing Pestalozzi. They took refreshments and discussed, through Pictet's able translation, the new theories of this pioneering teacher. Owen listened with rapt attention, recognising that the school was certainly in advance of others. As with Father Oberlin, Owen told Pictet as their carriage trotted home, it was the honest simplicity of the gentleman, Pestalozzi, which was so engaging, rather than his school.

To work efficiently and produce the desired results, an education system must be self regulating, able to be delivered by anyone. He doubted very much whether the value of the systems would remain if you removed their two inspiring fathers from their own establishments.

The third place to be examined was Hofwyl.

Here, Owen met Monsieur de Fellenberg who ran two schools, one for the poor and another for pupils from wealthy or upper class families. There was too much to take in during a single day and the visit ended up lasting three days.

Owen was thrilled by what he found.

As soon as he reached his room in Pictet's Geneva home, Owen wrote to Anne Caroline. He had discovered Hofwyl, the finest boarding school for Robert and William.

'I found that M. de Fellenberg possessed rare administrative talent and a good knowledge of human nature. His school for the poor was admirably conducted and the schools of the upper class are two or three steps in advance of any I had yet seen.'

He sent instructions for a German tutor to be found and for the boys to be given a good grounding in the language.

When Dunn, the one armed postman, delivered Owen's letter to Braxfield, drifts of autumn leaves lined the driveway. More news was to come, this time from Jean's pen, stating the sisters would be returning to Scotland before the weather closed in for the winter. Owen, however, wished to extend his tour but as they now considered themselves seasoned travellers, they were not alarmed at the prospect of making the journey home without their brother in law.

Owen, Anne Caroline read, would be travelling to Frankfurt with John Walker, who was fluent in German, with the intention of presenting his essay to the Congress.

Since the decisive victory over Napoleon at Waterloo, certain countries had agreed to send representatives to a regular meeting to discuss European problems. Delegates for the Congress of Aix la Chapelle were converging on Frankfurt, giving the perfect opportunity to meet with these influential leaders.

When Rosemary Pemberley came for a visit to Braxfield House, Anne Caroline confided her dismay at the length of time her husband was in Europe.

'My dear, you should be proud,' Rosemary placated. 'Your husband is now a statesman. The newspapers have been filled with his name, government committees take notice of his work and the Duke of Kent is amongst his closest friends.'

'Oh, I am proud of him, Rosemary, and I pray for his success. It seems so many people now require his presence, so many projects and issues ... and the Bill in Parliament is still not passed into Law. That will, no doubt, call him away to London as soon as he comes home.'

'At least he is not a soldier going into deadly battle,' Rosemary sniffed. 'Some of my dearest friends in Glasgow lost their husbands and sons to the war, never seeing them for years on end and then, with a letter or a knock on the door, they are told they will never see them again.'

'You are right, I am being foolish. Lord forgive me for my selfish desires. Yet, in many ways, my dear Robert *is* fighting. He is fighting for the rights and health of the poor and little thanks or support is he getting for his efforts. It is perhaps just as well that he is abroad and not reading the horrid remarks about him in the newspapers.'

321

Rosemary's plump face quivered with indignation.

'Well, clearly, those who say these nasty things have not been to New Lanark!'

'I shall be patient, dear Rosemary. There is much to be thankful for in my life, I am blessed in so many ways. When one hears of terrible misfortunes, like this deadly small pox epidemic in London at present, I feel truly humbled to be spared that suffering. I should ask for nothing more.'

'Indeed, you should not,' Rosemary's tone was slightly teasing. 'Anyway, for most ladies in your position, this house and your charming newly designed garden would be satisfaction enough.'

Anne Caroline smiled good-naturedly.

One day, Robert would be in the very chair where Rosemary was now sitting. Then, the memories of his months of absence would vanish and, once again, she would have her husband at home.

***

In the middle of November, Queen Charlotte died in Dutch House, in Surrey. She was fondly remembered by the older generation for making art and music fashionable, staging exhibitions and concerts in the capital.

At her invitation, leading artists and composers, like Zoffany and Mozart travelled to England to entertain the Court. Even women of the middle and lower classes prayed for her soul on hearing of her passing. They were thankful for her charitable work and patronage of the Lying-In Hospital in London and her almost radical views on girls being given a proper education.

With the King under close guard, declared completely insane, deaf and blind, the Queen's supporters took comfort that her eldest son, the disreputable Prince Regent, had at least seen fit to be at his mother's side when she passed away.

Owen sailed back from France and passed through London during this time of mourning for the Queen. He stayed only long enough to give his condolences to his friends the Dukes of Kent and Sussex before heading north to New Lanark.

Receiving advance warning of his return, Anne Caroline instructed the coachman to take the Braxfield carriage up to town to wait for the Mail Coach.

Robert Dale and his younger brothers and sisters painted and cut out letters of brightly coloured card to make welcome home banners, stringing them across the drawing room mantelpiece and up the first flight of banisters in the hall. Everyone dressed in their Sunday best and on Sheddon's command, the servants gathered in the hall, running up the back stairs to take their place just moments before his arrival.

Fussing with her hair and jewellery, Anne Caroline felt light headed and anxious. She glided from room to room giving unnecessary instructions, straightening the boys' jackets and flicking back unruly curls from her daughters' faces.

Of course, she realised later, there had been no need for concern. This was Robert, her kind, understanding friend and husband.

He cared little for the frills and superficial niceties of life, his whole attention being absorbed by the people and their spirited welcome. His affectionate greetings with the children and open appreciation for each of the servants standing in line, was immediately familiar, yet respectful. It was as if he had only been away a week.

Their first fond embrace at the front door was overtaken by the clamour of the children, all wishing to speak to their father at once. Then the celebratory meal was enjoyed in high spirits, cook providing special 'plain, cool' dishes just for the master, followed by the family sitting around the fireside hearing snippets from his travels and answering his queries of news from home.

Then they were alone.

She blushed at the memory of their shared pleasure of being reunited as husband and wife and thanked God for his safe return.

A few hundred yards away, at the back of the stable yard, a light glowed at the middle window of a line of low thatched cottages. Inside, cradled in Murdoch's arms, Emily listened to his tales of the expedition through Europe.

She was now too large and close to her time to be working in the house but, with Murdoch away, everyone rallied round to look after her as her confinement drew close. Miss Wilson had consulted with Mrs Owen about suitable accommodation for a married couple and new baby.

After several discussions, the under gardener, Stubby Drew, as he was called on account of having cut the tops off four fingers on his left hand in an argument with a scythe, was moved into a room over the stables and Emily took over his one up, one down cottage. Had it been a palace, she could not have been more proud, taking personal delight in brushing her own front door step.

The snow fell heavily that night, blanketing the hills, trees and roofs of Clydesdale and muffling any sounds in the still air. The next day, its beautiful purity was briskly scarred by teams of men shovelling and gritting, lining the roads with piles of brown stained snow, pock-marked with Lanarkshire's red road chippings. For days on end, low banks of pinkish grey clouds crawled across the sky, delivering their frozen load in tiny, spiralling flakes. Roads became clogged, turnip fields, kale patches and haystacks lay smothered, livestock huddled together, shoulder deep in drifts.

Calling on all the strong men and boys in the village, New Lanark recovered quickly. The shop, school and mills carried on as usual and by the afternoon the labourers, screwing up their eyes against the brilliance, were dispatched to help the farmer at Bankhead.

Beyond Owen's mill village, hardship tightened its grip with every snowfall.

Throughout Scotland and Northern England where the freezing weather hit the harshest, Parish ministers wrung their hands in anguish. Messengers appeared on foot, bundled up against the chill, announcing the roads were too treacherous for the wagons bringing provisions for Poor Relief.

Newspaper reports told of gangs of machine breakers attacking mills, fuelled by their pent up resentment at being made redundant and left destitute. Printed beside these articles ran leaders in bold typeface, declaring the rising death toll from small pox; over seventeen hundred victims, so far, in the current outbreak in London alone.

Thousands of homeless, starving families turned desperately to begging, ransacking barns and store rooms. Scarlet coated soldiers stood guard in market places, ready to break up fights and stop looting, often resorting to drawing their swords and firing warning shots over the scuffles. The moors and woodlands whispered with furtive figures trapping and snaring game, netting rivers and stealing into dovecotes to snatch birds and eggs. Many stumbled in straggling columns along the snow mounded drove roads in search of the very basics of survival: food and shelter.

Owen read the newspapers with a grim expression, shaking his head at the Government's outrageous refusal to pursue his Plan.

A few days after arriving home, he was visited by Captain MacDonald and Alexander Hamilton. The young men wanted to know how his essays were received in Europe.

'Oh, they agree with me, by and large, but it was at once enlightening and disturbing. Enlightening because many of the highly intelligent men I was fortunate to meet, face to face, had already read the essays and knew my views. They could find no flaws in my arguments.' Owen stood up from his place by the fire, moving around the room, restlessly. 'It was equally disturbing to see how much is yet to be done to translate words and agreement into action. There is so much *talking, deliberating* ... and no *doing*.'

MacDonald shook his head, 'But did you succeed in having your New View essay presented at the Congress?'

'Yes. I spoke with Castlereagh, who was there with the Duke of Wellington representing the British, and he put it to the Congress, together with two memorandums which I wrote while in Frankfurt especially for the occasion.' Owen stopped pacing, his back to his friends, looking out onto the blue shadows of his frozen garden.

A recollection jumped to mind of a hasty, unplanned meeting with Tsar Alexander, elder brother of the Grand Duke Nicholas who stayed at Braxfield. It was on the pavement as the Tsar and his retinue left their hotel and Owen offered him one of the bound copies of his essays. The Russian gave a cold, offhand response, declining the papers with the feeble excuse that he did not have pockets and telling Owen to see him another time. Owen made no further attempt to see the Tsar, disliking his manner.

He turned away from the window, shrugging away the unsavoury memory, saying, 'On my return through Paris, I heard reports that my papers were amongst the most important laid before Congress. Now, they just need to act.'

When Hamilton and MacDonald took their leave, Owen left his study, dressed in his hooded, long wool cape and fur lined gloves, and set off down to the mills.

325

It was already darkening into night although it was not yet four o'clock. His footsteps crunched on the frozen gravel and he looked around, forcing his attention out of the seething frustration in his mind. Ahead of him, the silhouettes of bare trees stood out starkly, black against the lighter sky, the snow covered ground shimmering like silver.

Walking down Braxfield Road into the village, he heard the familiar distant, churning water wheels and the rush of the river. Closer, high-pitched and excitable, came strains of fiddle music and the laughter of small children dancing in the playground outside the Institute.

A wavering golden glow told of the braziers positioned to provide light and warmth for the pupils to enjoy their daily exercise outside during the dark months. A group of older women appeared, bent under their cloaks, ambling towards the Rows. They carried heavy wicker baskets filled with produce from the Village Shop, resting them on the snowy ground from time to time and rubbing their arms; waiting for each other, chatting.

A young clerk came hurrying out of the Counting House and almost took a tumble on the ice, his arms flailing to regain his balance. Seeing the old women's gaze upon him, he clowned around, pretending to totter unsteadily towards them on the slippery cobbles.

Owen watched, straining to follow the exchanges.

After some more jesting around, the women's figures rocked, their hands self-consciously covering toothless grins as the clerk scooped up their baskets. Piling them on top of each other with ease, he proceeded to escort the women to their doors.

A simple act of kindness.

In less than three years since opening the Institute, the effect of his speech had already created an atmosphere in the village of sound, genuine friendship. This was how he knew it would be, the foundations had been laid in the preceding fifteen years and, to some extent, in his late father in law's time. Yet, no-one could deny that in that short space of time, despite wars and famine all around, it was his methods which produced this happy community.

He was consumed by an uncharacteristic rage. This is how mankind could be living, *should* be living.

Walking swiftly through the village he visited the Shop, warm and well stocked, the Counting House, a hive of activity with clerks bent over ledgers in pools of lamplight. Then, passing the schoolyard and smiling and raising a hand in greeting to the little ones who called out to him, he went on past the lade and into Mill One.

The roar and heat of the main work rooms hit him with their usual force, particularly after the peace of the icy streets on that still winter afternoon. The Silent Monitors were mainly yellow or white, good or excellent work, although there were always a few blue and the occasional black sides showing beside some of the workers. Invariably, it was the same culprits, usually single men or women who spent their wages in the grog shops and taverns in the market town up the hill.

Down in the basement picking rooms, he paused at the doorway, watching dozens of children preparing the raw cotton, their little bodies covered with a fine film of white. This was a dusty job and he was constantly assessing how to ventilate the rooms better. At least they were all over ten years of age and would be attending the schoolroom in a few hours.

Two small girls looked up from their handfuls of cotton and smiled at him, their keen eyes examining him from hat to boots. He returned an affectionate, fatherly smile and left them to their task.

Marching back up the hill to Braxfield, he was no longer sickened with frustration but revitalized: his views *would* be accepted, his Plan *would* be adopted and, most pressing, the Factory Reform Bill *must* be passed into Law.

The early snow melted away, allowing easier travel which was grasped upon by Anne Caroline's sisters. Feeling apathetic and out of sorts from the anticlimax of returning from the Continent, they invited themselves to Braxfield for Christmas and Hogmanay.

The house was suddenly full of people, music, games and an almost continuous round of visitors and food. The Lockhart Ross children were home from boarding school and Lady Mary was holding recitals and afternoon luncheon parties, encouraging her guests to walk to the Falls of Clyde.

Amidst this social whirl, Murdoch's baby daughter was born. All the servants rejoiced at the news, showering him with congratulations while running about their chores. At first, he was thrilled, overjoyed, then the sleepless nights of living with a fretful, colicky newborn began to take their toll. Taking pity on him, Miss Wilson suggested he sleep in his old room, purely over the time the Owens were so busy entertaining. He seized this peace and quiet, too exhausted to feel any guilt at leaving Emily alone at night and prayed she would understand.

Rosie and Sarah implored Joe to attend the Institute for the Hogmanay Ball which was being organised by the villagers. He would have preferred to avoid it but the arrival of a letter from Sam brought real cause for celebration.

My Dear Joe and all the family

We have arrived safely in Sydney after a wearisome voyage of more than 100 days. Walking on dry land again has been hard to master! I am writing this before we leave to travel the road (the only road) one hundred miles west across the Blue Mountains. I am told there is good land there so I have purchased 150 acres at a trifling sum and been granted a servant, a cow, four bushels of wheat and the right to market wheat in the King's Store at Bathurst. When we have a home, I will write again, until then my dear family I send most affectionate wishes and love from Ruth, Connor and myself, always your loving brother, Samuel Scott. I must add, we find ourselves governed here by a most able man, Lachlan Macquarrie - a Scot!

This heart warming news from the other side of the world meant Joe was easily persuaded to join the ceilidh and ended up thoroughly enjoying himself.

A large contingent of Highlanders from Caithness Row joined the celebrations, persuaded, no doubt by Kyle and Freya Macinnes. The older residents harped back to the 'guid auld days of Big Lachie and an 'ootside bonfire', but conceded the warmth of the Institute was a far more comfortable arrangement.

Just before the Bells, a shout went up in Gaelic, telling everyone to go outside. Understanding, Fiona hustled her family out through the front door along with hundreds of Highlanders.

Kyle and two other men were standing beside a brazier setting fire to stout, spirit soaked leather balls, attached to chains. A fiddler struck up a tune, another joining in and soon everyone was clapping and hollering. Whirling the chains around their heads, the men made great sweeping movements, creating a blazing display of streaming flames in the black night air.

The light show came to a crescendo as the bells rang out to signal the end of the old year and welcome in 1819.

'Happy New Year, ma darlin'' Joe kissed Fiona, hugging her tightly and thinking of Sam and his family with renewed relief. 'May it be a guid an' healthy year fur us all.'

***

In early January, John Buchanan and his family were waved away to start their new lives in London. The school in Westminster was nearly ready to open its doors to the poor of the parish and Brougham, Mill and their partners were eager to have their teacher installed.

The new head teacher for New Lanark, Finlay Wallace, was very similar in background to Buchanan. A fresh faced, well groomed young man in his mid twenties, he was a resident of the village, newly married to a girl who worked on the throstle machines in Mill Two. By the time he took over the classroom, he was already well trained by both Owen and his predecessor to carry on the good work.

With the disappointing response to his Plan to help the poor and further delays in processing his Bill to better the lives of mill workers, Owen was delighted to see at least his education methods were being embraced.

There was also a delightful interlude of several days when John Griscom, a Quaker from New York, came to visit New Lanark and stayed at Braxfield House. By sheer coincidence, Griscom had just returned from making almost exactly the same tour of Europe as Owen.

Many hours were spent by Braxfield's log fire pondering the merits of communal living, sustainable small scale farming (his father had been a farmer) and social regulation amongst the Shakers, Moravians and Rappites.

In late March, in the grey of dawn just before sunrise, Dr Gibson plodded home after a long night dealing with a difficult birth in Caithness Row. Villagers were waking to sleepy morning routines, children darting out on errands to the water pumps or emptying the slop buckets. Early workers were already on the streets, yawning and gathering in huddles at each of the locked Mill doors, ready to be let in to light the lamps and fire up the stoves.

The doctor was sorely in need of his bed but found Maude Wishaw's eldest boy waiting for him, begging him to visit his mother.

The Wishaw's room was on the fourth floor of Double Row and Dr Gibson paused half way up the dark stairwell to settle his breathing and ease his aching calves, letting the boy run nimbly ahead.

'She's no' weel, Doctor,' the patient's anxious husband informed him in an urgent whisper, holding up a thick stump of guttering candle and pointing towards the set-in bed.

Gibson pulled back the half-drawn bed curtain and assessed his patient, standing to one side to make use of the thin light filtering through the window.

The woman was in her early thirties and known for keeping poor health. This was not the first time little Ben Wishaw had come to his door seeking help.

However, this time it was not the lack of flesh on her bones which sparked the physician's attention. He picked up her limp hand and saw flat red spots spreading up her forearms and a few showing on her face. Quickly, he loosened the drawstring around the neck of her nightgown and examined her chest where the skin was damp to the touch, fevered but unmarked.

'Light!' he cried abruptly, dropping to his knees at the bedside to make a closer examination. 'Bring the flame closer! How long has she been unwell?'

'Aboot a week noo,' Mr Wishaw lit another candle and held both over his wife. 'She wis troubled wi' a sair heid, an' then telt us her pains were doon her back an' all o'er ... but, ye ken, Doctor, Maud's alis got sumat tae moan aboot.'

Gibson's practiced eye found two or three spots where blisters appeared to be forming, but perhaps it was just a sheen of sweat distorted by his own fears?

'I wish you had called me earlier,' he muttered. The patient was showing all the symptoms of one of the world's most feared diseases: smallpox.

Knowing the panic this diagnosis would bring upon the village, Gibson bled the groaning woman and made her as comfortable as possible, telling her husband to stay with her and bathe her forehead with cold water every hour.

'I shall return before midday and see how she's getting along,' he began to pack away his instruments.

'Ah cannae miss ma wurk, Doctor.' Wishaw grumbled. 'The weans will stiy an' see tae their Ma, an' Ah'll come back up in ma dinner oor.'

'It would be better if you stayed here ...' Gibson said firmly.

'No' better fae me, thank ye, Doctor.' Wishaw picked up his cap and opened the door, 'Ben, mind yer Ma,' he pointed at the boy and backed out the room, banging the door shut behind him.

At nine years old, Ben accepted his responsibility with a shrug from where he sat, cross legged, on the mat beside the hearth. Around him, his four younger brothers and whimpering baby sister stared balefully at the strange man at their mother's side: intrigued, trusting.

Gibson looked kindly on them. 'Come to the window, all of you.'

None of the children were showing symptoms of the illness and he was relieved to see all but the baby bore the scars of inoculation. On checking Maude's arms, he discovered she too had been given the cow-pox vaccination. Perhaps he was wrong?

Praying there was another reason for Mrs Wishaw's illness, Gibson made his way wearily down the stairs and out into the fresh air. Above Mill One, the bell swung into action; this was the first bell to signal the main gates were open and it was time to head to the factory floor.

Bathed in the scarlet glow of the rising sun, a growing flow of workers streamed out their tenement doors and flooded down the hill, calling to one another, gossiping and waving their children goodbye at the open Institute door.

Dr Gibson headed to the managers' office with a heavy heart. There were two and half thousand souls in New Lanark, all living and working together in close conditions. The recent reports from the cities across Britain showed the current smallpox outbreak to be especially virulent. Over the last three decades, one in fifty died from the pox, but this current strain was taking as many as one in four.

Gibson looked on the fiery ball in the sky, shading his eyes against its radiance to see blood red streaks in the wispy clouds. On any other morning, he would have marvelled at God's creation. Today, it seemed the Devil himself was looming over the horizon to spread pain and tragedy on the mortals below.

An emergency managers' meeting was called as soon as they received the physician's report of a possible case of smallpox in the village. It was decided to watch and wait; say nothing until the diagnosis was confirmed.

A messenger carried a note up to Owen at Braxfield House, informing him of the situation. Owen responded immediately, politely asking Gibson to inform him as soon as he knew how the situation was unfolding.

They did not have long to wait.

By mid-day, Maude's condition was critical, the red marks spreading down her body, those on her hands clearly showing as raised blisters. Without a chance to rest, Gibson saw three other residents with early symptoms.

As soon as Owen heard the news, he addressed a rapidly convened meeting of the senior managers.

'It appears, gentlemen, that we have the pernicious disease of small pox amongst us. We should count ourselves fortunate to have a strong, healthy population, many of whom have been vaccinated. Be vigilant, double the efforts of cleanliness and ensure infected households are kept separate from others. The victims are only contagious when showing signs of distress from aching heads, shivering or fever.'

'With the aches there may also be nausea and vomiting,' Gibson interjected, 'the early signs are similar to the Influenza.'

'Until that time,' Owen continued, 'you cannot catch the pox, but as soon as it shows itself the illness must be immediately reported and the families given support. Dr Gibson has the aid of good women of the village who will assist in his duties. Together we will get through these difficult times. Please, reassure all those affected that Sick Pay will be paid.

Gerry was appalled. 'Sir, we will have to tell everyone ...' he asked, his voice was high and agitated at the thought of Rosie's reaction, 'that it is the pox?'

'Yes, but in a calm, measured manner, Mr MacAllister. Fear spreads as fast as fire and can in itself be terrifying. Let this be treated simply as a physical disease for which many have been successfully vaccinated. And, it must be stressed, from which the majority recover.'

The bell was ringing out again across the mills when Gibson finally dropped onto his mattress to catch some sleep. This time it rang to mark the end of the day.

Having woken to a bright normal day, the workers ended their shift by being gathered together in groups and told of the smallpox outbreak.

'Ye gae in tae the jennies wi' a smile,' a woman muttered, ramming her bare feet into her clogs, 'an' come oot a few oors later wi' fear in yer hairt.'

'It's in God's hauns noo,' someone cried. 'Pray tae the Lord.'

'D'ye ken yon scratches the Doc gave us will save us?'

Rosie shivered, 'Only time will tell, God help us all.'

Within the week, twenty new cases were diagnosed, then the numbers accelerated, coming thick and fast until whole tenement blocks were marked with a red rag tied on the front door. Up in Lanark, the story was the same and soon everyone knew someone who was laid up with the pox.

There had been epidemics before which took away the old, infirm or very young and when Maude Wishaw died the sadness was tempered because she was known to be sickly. It was when one of the labourers succumbed, a strapping lad of eighteen years, that real fear gripped the village.

Fiona and Molly opened the Institute each morning to greet fewer and fewer children and the workforce in the mills dwindled to half within a fortnight. Not all the absentees were ill, children stayed at home to care for their parents, and the reverse was true. Grandparents and neighbours rallied around each other, doing what they could to ease the suffering or, in the worst cases, dealing with the aftermath of death.

The disease struck randomly, infecting perhaps one or two in a family of eight, passing mildly for some and taking a severe toll on others. Gibson could find no pattern except for reporting that in a high proportion of those vaccinated, some having been given the cow pox two or three times over previous years, the symptoms were lighter and recovery faster.

Anne Caroline was consumed with worry, insisting the younger children remain at Braxfield and when visitors called for Owen, she politely refused to meet them. Any contact with the outside world brought about a renewed panic and her immediate withdrawal to pray and seek comfort from the Bible.

After watching the disease's trail of devastation from the side lines, the Scott family were suddenly drawn into its clutches.

Sarah brought the news, breathless and shaking, hammering on Joe's door at first light. Gibson had been called to Rosie in the night and Gerry was valiantly tending to her needs.

Having nearly lost her some years before, Gerry refused to leave her bedside, his long face growing ever more mournful.

'Ah've bin doon wi' food fur Gerry,' Fiona told Joe, returning with her empty basket. 'He wulnae let me through the door fur fear o' spreading it tae us.'

'An' Rosie?'

'Nae change. Gerry says the fever's as bad as he's seen it an' the spots are fu' o' pus. He sed the yins aroond her eyes mak it tha' she can hardly see.'

Joe was sitting at the kitchen table costing out his latest job. He laid down the quill, resting the inky nib against the base of the candlestick, and took his head in his hands. He was drained by worry for Rosie and the spectre of the pox pouncing on more members of his family.

'They should shut the school,' he said, his eyes on Fiona, assessing her in the dim light: was she flushed? more tired than usual? Sickening? 'There cannae be mony left takin' the lessons?'

'There's enough. Molly's doon wi' it sae Ah ha'e tae be there. The wee bairns need some yin tae keep an eye oan them if their mithers are weel an' at the jennies or the mills will stoap ... an' then where will we all be?' She bustled around between the scullery and the range, pulling out pans and chopping carrots and potatoes before setting them to boil. Then, seizing a wooden bowl, she went out the back door calling back over her shoulder, 'Ah'll jist pull some kale'.

It was a damp evening, light in the cloudy sky but already dark on the ground. She picked her way to the vegetable patch, trying to avoid soaking her skirts on the mounds of collapsed yellow grass on either side of the trampled path.

Something was moving silently beside her, sending a waft of air to brush her cheek. Instinctively, she ducked low, covering her head with her arms, the bowl falling from her fingers.

'Och the De'il tak ye!' she cried out in a rush of terror before focusing properly on the pale, shifting, swooping shape of a barn owl.

She watched the bird's eerily soundless progress as it flew close to the contours of the land, rising over walls and dipping down into the valley until it was lost from view.

Turning into their gateway, Tom saw his mother with the kale and stopped to wait for her. She was brushing at her eyes, shaking her head as if to rid her mind of thoughts.

'Whit's the matter Ma?'

She hadn't seen him and looked up sharply, grateful for the dusk.

'Nuthin' ... nuthin', ma darlin'.' Her tone was bright, forced. 'Come away in. Can ye licht the fire in the parlour, there's kindlers in the basket ...' she prattled on, too quickly, trying to banish the lingering image of the white bird.

All evening she assessed her family with the eyes of a watchful collie dog, terrified of finding any trace of fever or a rash. She knew the stories they told of barn owls, that they were harbingers of death. She had laughed at such old wives tales, decrying them as mere gossip and ridiculing those who believed the nonsense of Old Bel and her cronies.

Now, with Rosie dangerously ill and disease in every shadow, her sinister twilight encounter was not so easily dismissed.

Fiona woke to the sound of knocking, a rhythmic shaking of wood against plaster. Joe was already stumbling out of bed, scrabbling to light a candle in the darkness.

'It's jist Sionaidh fittin' ...' Joe whispered.

Together they hurried to Sionaidh's bedside, half asleep but carrying out the routine they so often performed. The fit passed, leaving the girl listless and moaning.

'It's all richt noo ...' Fiona soothed, stroking her daughter's hair, noting the cool forehead and clear skin with relief. 'Ye can sleep ... hush sweet hairt, it's all o'er.'

Joe stood up, yawning and shivering with cold, looking around for a safe place to set down the candle before returning to bed.

'Fetch ma shawl?' Fiona asked quietly.

'Aye,' he knew she would keep a vigil until Sionaidh was peaceful and then see to changing the bed linen.

From behind him, Ailsa murmured and he glanced round, whispering 'Yer sister's all richt, gae back tae sleep.'

The blankets were trailing off the side of Ailsa's bed, her slim figure spread awkwardly on the mattress showing bare legs below the night gown, her woollen socks kicked off.

Snatching up the candle again he approached her with a feeling of dread; Ailsa was red with burning fever.

'Oh dear God ...' his words were no louder than a breath.

'Da?' Ailsa mumbled, 'ma heid's bustin' ... an' ...' she lurched forward, retching, coughing and spluttering.

Fiona was instantly at his side, clutching at her daughter to hold her forehead while she vomited.

By morning, Alex and Robert were also feeling unwell. Joe sought out the nearest Lanark doctor, Davidson, and, finding him out, left a message requesting a visit.

'If it's the pox,' Mrs Davidson told him plainly, 'ye've tae keep yersels tae yersels. Doctor will ca' as soon as God grants him the time. Ma husband has just the yin pair o' hands an' a score or mair cases roond here wi' the same problem.'

The mills were still working but some workrooms had only half the usual employees at their stations. The Overseers stood about disconsolately, their thoughts on stricken relatives, wary eyes following their colleagues in search of early symptoms.

Molly Young recovered well. Within three weeks of taking ill, she was back in the school and joining those women who, like herself, were now considered immune and helping to nurse the sick throughout the village.

Sarah and Lily moved anxiously from day to day with bated breath. They were worried sick about Cathy, checking everyday to make sure she was still well: asking after Ross. As Rosie improved, Gerry took ill. Sarah was too scared to help her

336

weakened, blotchy sister to take care of her husband. Instead, ridden with guilt but unable to conquer her dread, she took to leaving pots of soup, boiled eggs and bread or cuts of cold meat at Rosie's door.

For Fiona, the weeks of caring for her family passed in a haze of anguish and exhaustion. She ached at the sight of three of her children deformed by a thick layer of fluid filled pimples. The alarming disease covered their bodies, even erupting inside their mouths and noses, but particularly swathing their hands.

Ailsa and Robert spent a miserable ten days before rallying while Alex was less than a week at the height of his infection. Fortunately, all three were left with only a few scars and Fiona was relieved to see Ailsa's face bore just three or four noticeable pock marks around her chin. The girl was not favoured with pretty features but had always taken pride in her smooth, peachy skin and glossy hair which were the envy of her friends in the mills.

Knowing the incubation period could be up to three weeks, Fiona counted off the days with chalk marks in the back scullery. By eighteen days, with her invalids recovering and the rest of the family still healthy, she began to breathe more easily.

'Ma'!' Robert shouted from the hallway, 'that's Sionaidh fittin' agin!'

'Och, she's havin' a bad time o' it jist noo ...' Fiona ran to where Ailsa and Robert were crouched at the foot of the stairs trying to stop their sister from thrashing against the bottom step.

'Ma ... look at her hauns ...' Ailsa caught a waving, jerking hand showing livid red marks. 'She's doon wi' it ... aw, Christ in Heaven, she's taken the pox!'

It was worse for Sionaidh. Not only would the fever bring about more fits but she was the only one of them without protection.

'She's a strong lass,' Dr Davidson tried to comfort them. 'Apart from her fits, she is rarely ill, or so ye tell me, eh, Mrs Scott?'

'True, doctor, but ... look at her ... the ithers were ne'er as bad.'

The physician could find no words to deny what was clear to everyone in the room.

It took ten days for the deadly virus to consume Joe and Fiona's eldest daughter. She finally lost her hold on life during a violent seizure, lying limp in Joe's arms, her mother kneeling at her side stroking her hair. It took several seconds before they realised she was no longer breathing, neither daring to be the one to put it into words.

Distraught, Joe stumbled out the back door, walking blindly towards the doctor's house. Why was he rushing, no one could save her now? He left word for Dr Davidson to come to his house and set off down the road, head down, striding past his gate posts and on down towards the mills.

Giving a curt rap on Rosie's door he went straight inside.

'Sionaidh died.'

The words were out before he took in the scene before him.

Dr Gibson was leaning over the bed, Rosie at his side, and at that instant they drew the blanket over Gerry's still form, covering his face.

'Aw, Rosie ...' Joe cried, seeing the streaks of tears on his sister's devastated face, 'no' Gerry too?'

Chapter Eighteen

"All that is necessary for the triumph of evil is that good men do nothing." Edmund Burke

Dr Gibson recorded three hundred and twenty two cases of small pox in the village during the epidemic, two hundred and fifty one having received the vaccination. He was adamant that the village's vigorous program of inoculation proved invaluable, cutting the fatalities to far below the national average.

Only six victims died in New Lanark, a mercifully small addition to the death toll in Lanark and across Clydesdale. For those left scarred, blinded or bereaved, it was the darkest period of their lives.

Off a narrow vennel in the back streets of Lanark, the jingling bell on the undertaker's door had become an ominously familiar sound to its neighbours.

It was a dull, breezy day when Joe heard it, standing politely aside to let a man leave before entering. It was Kyle Mcinnes.

'This is a grim time,' Kyle muttered, stepping outside. 'If your task is as hard tae bear as mine, Ah'm fair grieved fur ye.'

Joe found it difficult to speak. 'Ma dochter, ma eldest lass, an' ma sister's man. You?'

'Ma ...' he faltered, continuing through clenched teeth, 'Ma lady, Freya.'

Shocked, Joe stammered, 'Och, mon ... ye must be gutted, tha's a tragedy. Ah'm sair vexed fur ye, truly.'

Kyle nodded, lips pressed into a downward line. 'A grim time.'

Fiona heard of Kyle's loss with no emotion, all feelings she possessed were entirely taken up in the agony of losing Sionaidh. She went through the motions of daily life but barely saw beyond her cloud of misery.

In her own down to earth manner, Rosie donned her new mantle as a grieving widow with a brave face, allowing only the solitary evenings by the fireside to witness her desolation. The sight in her left eye was permanently damaged, the iris showing cloudy and white, the rim red and weeping. She refused to let this hamper her duties and was back on the factory floor at the big spinning mule the day after Gerry's burial.

When there were two clear weeks with no new cases being reported, Owen set off for London. A new opportunity was on the horizon due to the death of the Member of Parliament for the united boroughs of Lanark, Selkirk, Peebles and Linlithgow. Owen would be put forward to stand for the vacant seat. Between his other engagements, he spent hours at Bedford Square writing his manifesto, eager to gain a seat in the House to further his cause.

Murdoch relished his time away. It was not that he loved Emily any less since they married, but the experience of living with a new baby was bordering on intolerable. For too long, he enjoyed the batchelor life, pleasing himself in his leisure time, sleeping soundly in a neat, tidy bed room and spending hours reading or simply dozing. No amount of hard work for his master caused him to feel the irritable weariness induced by his tiny, noisy daughter.

Spring blossom gave way to lush foliage and young birds appeared, fluffed up with down, chasing their parents for food. Carpets of bluebells shared their peppery perfume beneath unfurling ferns, humming with bees, fluttering with butterflies. Nature laid out her beauty in every colour and design yet there were few people in a frame of mind to enjoy her display.

Only the wealthy could take the time to promenade in gardens and parks. The middle classes struggled and millions of working British people lived hand to mouth, day to day, under ever greater hardship and oppression.

'It is disgraceful,' Owen said forcefully, while dining with the Duke of Kent. 'I understand Sir Robert Peel has been ill but really ... I first brought the dire conditions in the mills to his attention over *three* years ago! Yes, yes, I know there have been unexpected events ...'

'Napoleon's return rather filled the diaries.'

'Of course, but that matter is now dealt with and still we allow this abhorrent system to persist in our country. We are supposed to be civilised! Pah! Look at the recent report on Gortons and Roberts' Elton mill; filthy, no ventilation, the children half clothed and half fed, no instruction of any sort! To do nothing about this, and that mill is not alone, is to agree with these wretched practices.'

'I understand a handful of physicians were purchased to supply statements to the contrary.'

'For some mills, yes, it must be the case, for no person in their right mind would say it was *not* injurious for a child of ten years to stand for sixteen hours a day! My word, few of the men on the Committee could stand for *two hours* without reaching for their cushioned seats and a stiff brandy. And yet, the reports were delivered, accepted, which is farcical, and entered into the minutes.'

'Well, in my opinion those medical men are ruining their reputations but perhaps their pockets are filled enough with bribes to allow retirement in a single act.'

'And the unrest!' Owen threw his hands in the air. 'After witnessing the direct result of suppression and unemployment in France, there are still no solutions in place to feed or provide gainful labour to the country's homeless.' He stood up, uncomfortable with frustration. 'I have given them my Plan! There are many successful examples overseas like the Harmonists and Shakers, or as far back as Beller's plans ... They can see for themselves, should they bother to look, that the villages I propose are designed on sound principles. They do not need to take my word for it, look at George Courtauld's pamphlet on Harmonie or John Melish's ... or ... my friend, the Quaker who visited New Lanark in the spring ... Griscom! All eminently sensible gentlemen.'

'I hear Courtauld's in America again?' the Duke queried, 'I gather his son, Samuel, has turned his business around and is making it a fine affair.'

'Indeed, sir, Courtauld's silks are amongst the best.' Owen would not be diverted, returning to his topic. 'There is absolutely no need for poverty in our country, as I can demonstrate. One visit to New Lanark would suffice!'

'Owen, my dear fellow, I have heard rapturous accounts of your community. I tell you now, I shall press for another Select Committee ...'

'I am grateful, Sir, but with respect, there has been enough talking! Now is the time to *act* before we have an uprising.'

'We shall bring in a fresh Committee! Hold New Lanark up as an example.'

'They have received a multitude of statements ...'

'I shall send my physician up to Scotland. The good Dr Grey Macnab is reliable and independent minded yet highly respected. He is not averse to calling a spade a spade or vice versa ... you know what I mean, eh?'

The Duke smoothed a palm across his bald head, his brow creased with concern.

Since the Duke's return to England the two men had grown even closer, at ease with each other to share their disappointments as much as their achievements. Owen was known to be trustworthy in a society where that trait was rare. Prince Edward was able to confide his dire financial situation and seek advice without fear of reading it in the papers the following day.

His father, the king, although now completely mad and confined to a padded room in Windsor Castle, had treated him with contempt throughout his adult life and his brother was of no help. Parliament would not even grant a rise to his income since his marriage which had forced him to retreat to his wife's country to save expenses. The burden of a larger household was proving altogether impossible to maintain and he was relieved to have Owen's straight forward, analytical business mind to consult.

Had he been born the eldest son, it would now be Edward who held the reins of power and stood in the king's shoes. The obese Prince Regent, Prinny to his friends and enemies alike, did not share the liberal views which the country so urgently required and which Edward understood.

Prince Edward was also indebted to Owen for a personal loan: a serious amount of money which allowed his return to England. In return, as well as royal assurance that the debt would be repaid, he gave Owen a gift. It was a gold and deep red cornelian ring, the stone engraved with the Prince's profile but as Owen was not one to flaunt wealth, it lay at home in his desk drawer.

'Please,' Owen said impulsively, 'come to New Lanark and see for yourself that all I state is true. A happier, more productive community you will not find on this earth.'

Edward smiled, used to Owen's extravagant language.

'I should be honoured but I cannot leave my wife at this sensitive time.'

'Ah! I completely understand,' Owen cried at once, remembering the Duchess's delicate condition. 'I trust the Duchess is well?'

'Capital! the babe should be here any day now, I'm told. But what do I know of these things! Have no fear, I shall not be diverted from our project although I regret travelling will be off the agenda for a while.'

As expected, baby Princess Alexandrina Victoria arrived a few days later, on the 24th of May. The Duke, a proud father for the first time at the grand age of fifty, was charmed by her. Her birth on British soil was the main reason for his return from Germany. His brothers having no living, legitimate children, he took delight in introducing the infant as 'the next Queen of England.'

Yet, even in the midst of his personal celebrations, he did not forget Owen and was as good as his word.

Macnab was dispatched to report on New Lanark, and the Duke urged his other influential contacts like the Whig MP for Southampton, Sir William de Crespigny and General Desseaux to 'see for themselves' the practical evidence to back up Owen's words. Owen was back on the London political stage once more, spurring the tardy Sir Robert into action with the Factory Reform Bill.

On a light midsummer evening, Owen attended a meeting called by the Duke expressly to draw support for his Plan of Villages of Unity and Mutual Cooperation. It was held in the gracious surroundings of the Freemason's Hall and in the capacity of his presidency, the Duke opened the meeting.

He was famous for oratory skills and asked the audience to deliberate on Owen's Plan for alleviating the unemployment and poverty of the working classes. Passionately, he declared that no matter what Robert Owen's private religious beliefs might be, 'Owen allowed the fullest religious liberty at New Lanark.'

Afterwards, making his way back to Bedford Square, alone, Owen was acutely conscious of the scale of the destitution and overcrowding on the streets. Makeshift shelters under bridges and in narrow alleyways were crammed with humanity: unwashed, stinking and foulmouthed with desperation. Urchins and ragged, starving ex-servicemen spilled out into the main roads to beg or steal enough to survive the day.

Food was expensive but gin was cheap, its addicts keen to forget their depression and hunger in its comforting fog.

'This cannot continue,' Owen thought bitterly, catching sight of a young woman, emaciated in face and body. Spitting on a stained grey rag, she crouched down beside her infant and wiped at its filthy face.

'I *will* change this,' he murmured to himself, looking back down the jostling street to see the mother huddling down in a doorway, hugging the child on her lap. Would they sleep there for the night?

Braziers were being lit; hazy, smoking spheres in the growing dusk. He could feel the despair; the hopeless desolation of having no power, no home, no food and not even the right to gather together to complain.

The scene rippled through tears smarting in Owen's eyes and he strode on down the street.

'I am trying to help you,' he wanted to shout. 'I *will* help you, but they are still not listening ... one day they will ... I will not give up.'

***

Fiona stormed through her back door and flung her shopping basket on the table, ripping at her bonnet ribbons with shaking fingers.

She was only working four days a week at the Institute now, sharing her duties with a woman from Caithness Row. This arrangement allowed her more time to rest, sorely needed since Sionaidh's death, and that afternoon she had decided to visit Lanark market.

The town was busy, everyone seeking a bargain, haggling to take a ha'penny off this a farthing off that. Peddlars shouted their wares between exchanges of abuse with the permanent stall holders, angry at sharing customers. Beggars, many maimed from the war, held out their hats with pitiful requests.

A glut of soft fruit from the fertile Clyde valley had brought several smallholders up to sell their produce. Strawberries, raspberries, plums and damsons were offered for a penny a punnet to anyone willing to risk the wasps hanging over the stalls, buzzing in the warm, sugar-scented air. Choosing the deepest crimson berries, Fiona paid her tuppence and turned to browse a pile of blankets and that was when her day turned sour.

'It's Mrs Scott, isn't it?' a woman asked, her extravagant straw hat and bows proclaiming her higher status in the town.

'Aye,' Fiona dipped her head politely, trying to recall where she met this grey haired matron who fancied herself as well-to-do; a wife of one of Joe's colleague's? 'Guid day, Mrs Snodgrass.'

'Ma dear,' her sharp, kohl lined eyes surveyed her prey, studying her face. 'Are ye unweel?'

The condescending tone made Fiona bristle.

'We've recently suffered a bereavement. Guid day tae ye, Mrs Snodgrass.'

'Oh my dear! I had no idea ... not your husband, I hope?'

That was when she should have walked on, Fiona knew it now but instead, her manners forced a response.

'Oor dochter ... wi' the sma' pox.'

'Terrible, terrible ...' she tut-tutted, then shot a shrewd look. 'Which one? I recall ye had two lassies.'

'The eldest.' Again, Fiona made a move to turn away but a gloved hand gripped her arm.

'Och, the daft one? Weel,' the woman gave a sickly, pitying smile, 'that's no' sae bad, then, eh? It's better if they die at birth, I'm sure.'

Fiona only meant to push the woman's hand away but the force of the blow sent Mrs Snodgrass backwards, knocking against baskets of squawking chickens: feathers and screeches filled the air.

Fiona fled.

Her clogs echoing on the Wellgate's cobbles, she hurried home, muttering the rudest rejoinders she could muster, eyes blazing, her heart banging violently in her chest. Vague images of the scene hung in her mind: Mrs Snodgrass's open, gummy mouth, her bonnet askew, skirts flouncing above darned stockings and blue veined bare thighs.

How dare that bisom be so cruel; how *dare* she!

Since returning to work and meeting acquaintances in the village, a few awkwardly avoided Fiona but everyone else showed kindness, understanding.

When Joe came home, she told him the whole horrible tale and he held her while she cried.

'She wis oor sweet Sionaidh,' Fiona murmured, sniffing with tears and leaning into his embrace. 'She wisnae daft, jist different. An' Ah'll tell ye summat else fur nuthin', she wis a better person than yon snippy Mrs Snodgrass. Sionaidh ne'er hurt a soul wi' word nor deed.'

She felt Joe tense.

'She ne'er meant tae harm Cal,' she whispered, 'it wis an accident. Joe?' she reached up and caressed his cheek. 'She wis an innocent bairn.'

After a pause, he sighed. 'Aye, Ah ken it wisnae her fault.' He gave her a reassuring squeeze. 'There are plenty folk who dinnae unnerstaun people or things tha' are different. We forget ither folk are no' like the yins in Mr Owen's village. There's plenty nastiness in life, ma love, ignorant bodies who dinnae care aboot ithers, like yon Snodgrass wifey. Ah see it all the time at ma work but nowadays ye dinnae see it doon at the mills.'

'It scares me, Joe. Up in toun the day, there were that mony beggars an' Ah saw fightin'. An' up the vennels, bodies lyin' aboot, stinkin' o' drink.'

'It wis alis like tha', weel mibbee no' sae mony beggars. All the touns are the same an' in Hamilton there's places ye wouldnae venture.' He gently eased her away from him and stood up, kissing her on the top of her head, liking the fact she was not wearing a covering over her hair. 'The de'il only knows whit the cities are like.'

He held his hand out to her and pulled her to her feet, determined to raise her mood.

'Ye ha'e seven hungry mouths tae feed, sae pit yer mind on tha', ma lass!'

When they were all gathered around the kitchen table, scraping up the last of the stew and dumplings and delving into bowls of strawberries, Joe called across the babble to gain attention.

'Ah had a man call oan me the day, a Mr Minto. D'ye ken,' he looked at Donnie and Davey, 'the rumours flyin' aboot a while ago aboot men clambering aboot an' measuring fur a bridge tae be strung, high up above Kirkfieldbank, between the Cartland Crags? Across the Moose river gorge?'

346

'Aye,' Donnie kept chewing the last mouthful, 'but that's sheer cliffs, Da', a michty drop tae span.'

Joe grinned, 'The plans are made, by Mr Thomas Telford no less!'

'Naw! Yer pullin' oor legs!'

'Ah swear it's nae lie. Whit's mair, Mr Minto has engaged Scott and Sons tae dae the wurk !' Joe waited for the garbled questions and cheers to subside. 'No' all the wurk, mind! He's contracting several stonemason businesses an' ither trades as weel. It's tae stairt soon an' will pay us an' oor teams through many months.'

'Whit a difference tha' will make, eh?' Davey exclaimed, in awe of such a project. 'Ah wonder where they'll pit it?'

'Where the cliffs nearly touch, wid mak sense,' Tom said, picturing the dark, narrow chasm where only ravens and peregrines ventured.

'It will be like pittin' a bridge o'er the Falls o' Clyde, way up past Corra Linn, ye can see them frae Corehoose side.'

'Aye,' an' that's the ither place we've bin asked tae tender fur, the new building at Corehoose. Ah'll be o'er there wi' Tam t'morra. All of a sudden, we seem tae ha'e a lot o' wurk, sae, we'll mak the maist o' it!'

**

Robert Owen came back from London to fight for the parliamentary seat vacated by the late Sir Buchanan Riddle. However, in the end, the little time he managed to spend on gaining support was not enough to secure him a place in the House of Commons. It was a setback, but they would try again at the next election, probably in four years time, and allow more time to canvas the voters.

'Oh dear,' Anne Caroline murmured to herself one morning on receipt of a black edged letter. 'Oh no, that is a shame. God rest his soul. Robert? My Uncle James has died. I know you were not always on the best of terms with him after you ended his contract here but will you be able to attend the graveside?'

'I bear him no ill will. He left the mills of his own accord. Of course, I will go. I daresay his nephew, David, will be there but I will represent our side of the family.'

'Poor Marion, I will write directly. My sisters know her better than I these days, but I must visit her when we go to the city.'

In all, Anne Caroline felt the funeral passed as smoothly as she could have wished. It was pleasant to renew her acquaintance with her Aunt Marion, their last meeting being at Mary's wedding and now she could tell her about baby David's arrival. Despite the sad circumstances, they found they shared more in common than in previous years.

During the small reception which followed the burial, the Haddow family were surprisingly friendly towards Owen. From her seat beside her sisters, Anne Caroline watched with relief as her husband and Marion's son, William Dale, held a lively debate on George Melish's recent pamphlet on self sustaining communities in the United States.

Owen told her afterwards in the privacy of their Charlotte Street bedroom, 'I am not sure if it is the idea of the communities or simply leaving this country for new horizons which appeals to William. I gather several of their Haddow relatives in Douglas are considering emigrating.'

'Mmn,' Anne Caroline peeled off her long gloves, 'my father would not have approved. He was so determined to keep Scots in Scotland.'

'To be forced to leave from sheer poverty and hopelessness is more what your father was railing against, my dear. Leaving by choice, is quite another thing.'

Anne Caroline opened her mouth to speak, thought better of it and allowed the subject to change. William Kelly, her father's manager for many years, was also paying his respects to the widow. Since leaving New Lanark, Kelly's fortunes had gone from strength to strength with mills in Bute and a splendid town house in Glasgow. While he passed a few words with her, he had studiously ignored her husband. Obviously, the rift of nearly twenty years was still not healed.

The Owens were barely back at Braxfield when news came through of a terrible incident in Manchester.

'It was only a matter of time,' Captain MacDonald declared, alarmed and excited by the horror of the report.

348

Owen scanned the newspaper article covering the front page of the Glasgow Herald, beneath it lay a copy of the Times with the same story.

'They're calling it Peterloo!' Hamilton groaned. 'Editors can find a catchy headline for even such a tragedy.'

Nearly sixty thousand people had turned out, peacefully, dressed in their Sunday best to hear the orator Henry Hunt. Banners calling for Reform, Universal Suffrage, Equal Representation and Love were held aloft, the poles topped with red caps, an easily recognisable symbol of liberty.

By all eye witness accounts, the meeting was calm and well ordered but magistrates, watching from a window some distance from the crowd, took fright at the increasing numbers flocking onto the field.

The militia was called in and the Riot Act read, telling them to disperse. Few could hear the officer's voice above the throng so the mass of bodies not only remained but steadily grew larger.

The magistrates' agitation turned to panic. Standing in reserve were over one thousand trained soldiers from the Hussars, Cheshire Cavalry and Special Constables but the order to arrest Hunt was sent to the local yeomanry.

Captain Hugh Birley and Major Thomas Trafford commanded this haphazard paramilitary force of local men. Many held private grudges and had already consumed more ale than was good for them that morning.

Instructed to seize Hunt, Captain Birley sent his men forward with cutlasses, swords and clubs. Spontaneously, the crowd linked arms to block their way and try to protect the hustings. Drunk and ready for a fight, the yeomanry charged into them, lashing and cutting at whoever stood in their way.

To the magistrates, watching from afar, it looked as if the people were attacking the soldiers and the Hussars were ordered in to the fray to gain control. Mayhem ensued, leaving eighteen dead and over seven hundred seriously injured from trampling and being cut down by swords and sabres.

'The speakers and organisers are to be put on trial for Treason,' Owen read out loud, then slapped his hand on the desk and sat back. 'Good grief! Did you see the last line? The Prince Regent sent congratulations to the magistrates and Lieutenant Colonel Guy L'Estrange of the Hussars.'

'To be fair,' MacDonald interrupted, 'they say L'Estrange realised the people were only defending themselves and tried to stop the carnage, but by then it was too late.'

'There will be more of this,' Hamilton went over to the window, leaning on the wall and gazing sightlessly at the garden. 'How much longer, in these enlightened times, will the government be able to justify being voted for by only two percent of the population? The tide is turning, people want true leaders who understand their needs, not a few wealthy men voting for others in their elite circle.'

Owen smiled at the irony. 'If only others of your status shared your views, Alexander! Your family are amongst the richest in the land. It is heartening to hear your opinion.'

Perhaps spurred on by the shocking events in Manchester, a delegation from the Guardians of the Poor at Leeds arrived to examine the conditions at New Lanark. Mr Edward Baines, proprietor of the Leeds Mercury, Mr John Cawood, a wealthy manufacturer, and Mr Robert Oastler, a highly respected member of his community, took rooms at the Clydesdale Inn and made several in depth visits to the mill village.

They were unanimous in their praise, stating their report would reflect the admirable methods employed by Mr Owen and his thriving, contented workforce.

Slowly, New Lanark was returning to normal although it would be a long time before the villagers could relax their guard against the pox rearing up again. The monthly dances in the Institute restarted and the long, light evenings saw families taking advantage of the woodland walks and allotments.

The new herbaceous borders and trellises of climbing roses in Braxfield's gardens were repaying the gardener's hard work, many fold. As one species passed its full blown perfection, another took the spotlight, spreading rainbows of colour across the views from the drawing room.

On the afternoon before her two eldest sons were to leave for Switzerland, Anne Caroline instructed Sheddon to lay their main meal on the terrace. The air was mild and the sky a deep unfathomable blue from horizon to horizon, a light breeze ensuring midges would not be a nuisance.

'I shall take this memory with me and hold it close,' Robert Dale said, dreamily, tilting his head back and closing his eyes; the sunshine warming his face. 'What a chorus! the sparrows are loud today, competing with the bees! Ah, a blackbird! And ... perhaps my favourite, the curoo curoo of our wood pigeons.'

'You have not lost your love of romance, dear Robert,' his mother mused from under her parasol. 'You will remember to write to us, won't you? You have a particular way with words and we will all be eager to know how you are enjoying Howfyl.'

'No, Mama,' William teased, raising one eyebrow in a well practiced arch. 'We will forget you entirely! I shall only remember Albga,' he clicked his fingers and immediately a wriggling white puppy hurried over to lick his hand. 'Yes, Albga, I shall write to you,' William joked, but the affection was real, causing a brief shadow to dull his tone: he would miss their new pet. 'Anyway, Papa,' he said brightly, 'from your descriptions of Monsieur de Fellenberg's school, we will be kept far too busy learning about agriculture, new horsemanship skills and javelin throwing, quite apart from the modern sciences.'

'It is a fine place,' Owen sipped some lemonade, adjusting his position in the garden chair to allow Mary to sit on his lap, 'and I am confident you will both have a marvellous experience. Apparently, you will take hikes into the mountains, which I can recommend. Did I tell you I climbed Mount Rigi in the Alps?'

'You climbed a mountain?' Anne Caroline giggled at the image this conjured in her mind.

'Indeed I did!' Owen laughed. He was personally proud to have kept pace with his much younger companions, despite nearing his fiftieth year. 'Two of John Walker's boys, Francis and Edwin, were planning an outing to collect butterflies on the lower slopes and on hearing the summit gave a view over France and Germany and to more than a dozen lakes, I asked if I might join them.'

'Oh, I hope Will and I can climb mountains,' Robert opened his eyes again, blinking, 'was it difficult?'

'A scramble at times, although more a steep walk than a climb, but worth the effort. At the peak, we ate smoked fish and black bread, a wonderful picnic! Invigorating! It reminded me of the fresh air of the Highlands but on a grander scale.'

The conversation flowed from one topic to the next, with David and Richard asking as many questions as their elder brothers and sisters. Anne Caroline observed them quietly, committing their cheerful voices and the comfortable family atmosphere to memory, to be replayed and enjoyed whenever required.

***

Fiona liked the new teacher at the Institute. She had not thought that she would, but, she did.

'Och, we had a grand time the day,' she told Sarah, herding her small charges back into the building after a country ramble. 'We went up in tae the woods an' had tae write doon all the different things we heard. Jings! Ah thocht it wid be aboot five or six, but no! hunners!'

Sarah was laying out squares of various different coloured cloth, one for each of the twenty three children at her table.

'Weel,' she said, huffily, 'if they've bin ootside all yon time, Ah hope they've washed their hauns afore ma sewin'?'

'Aye,' the smile died away from Fiona's lips. 'Whit's wrang? It's no' like ye tae be snippy these days.'

Sarah was about to answer when they were interrupted by Mr Murray showing a group of visitors the sewing and handiwork table.

'Tell me later ...' Fiona murmured, noticing Sarah's strained expression. 'Ye alricht?'

'Naw ... but Ah micht as weel be here as onywhere.' She doled out little pincushions. 'Keeps ma mind busy.'

The end of the school day was becoming easier for Fiona. The first months since Sionaidh passed away, she dreaded walking out the door with only Alex by her side. It made her feel she was missing something, had forgotten something; incomplete.

That day, she pushed sad thoughts away and waited for Sarah outside the Institute door.

'Come,' Sarah said brightly, patting Alex on his curly blonde head and setting off towards the shop. 'We'll buy a biscuit for yer Auntie Rosie. Will ye be a guid lad an' tak it up tae her fur me?'

352

'Only if Ah can ha'e yin?' the little boy retorted, cheekily.

'Weel noo, laddie,' Sarah said with a frown, 'ye should wait an' see if Ah wis gaun tae gi'e ye yin fur bein' helpful.'

They came out the shop a few minutes later with Alex clutching a paper bag containing two ginger parleys.

'Ye can eat yin wi' yer Auntie Rosie,' Sarah instructed, 'an' no' afore, mind. Aff ye toddle!'

Fiona waited until he was out of earshot then asked, 'Sae whit's the matter that ye didnae want Alex tae hear?'

Sarah glanced around, 'Come up tae mine an' Ah'll tell ye.' Her voice dropped to a whisper, 'It's aboot Sean.'

Fiona never knew of Sean's visit to Scotland to see Cathy's wedding. So, as soon as they reached the privacy of Sarah's room there was a lot to be related in the short space of time before Lily returned from the mills or Alex from his errand.

'Ye see,' Sarah was reaching the end of her tale, her composure slipping. 'Ah thocht that wis the end o' it. Sean went on oan his way an' Ah wid get oan wi' ma life. Then, a letter arrived frae Stephen. It wis written tae Cathy,' she brushed a tear from the corner of her eye, 'he disnae write tae me ... but he telt her ...' her tongue wouldn't form the words, her voice suddenly high, 'Sean's deid.'

'Deid!' Fiona rose from her seat and put her arms around Sarah. 'Aw, that's a shock fur ye.'

'Stephen said his Da had no' bin weel fur years, a disease in his lungs the medics say.' Sarah turned brimming eyes to her friend, 'he wis coughin' sumat fearful when Ah saw him ... he wis dyin', Fiona. That's why he came o'er tae see us.'

She broke down into sobs and Fiona stroked her back and made soothing noises, not knowing what to say.

'Whit's upset me,' Sarah took a shuddering breath, 'is whit Stephen wrote. He said his Da telt him tae mak sure Ah knew when he passed awa' ... he wanted me tae be free.'

'Tae be free? Whit did he mean?'

'Jist that. He knew Ah wid nae marry or let go o' him until yin o' us wis deid ... an' noo he is ... an' Ah feel, oh Fiona, Ah dinnae ken whit Ah feel but it's nae a guid feelin', Ah can tell ye that.'

Fiona sympathised, but as soon as she returned home, she confided the story to Joe.

'He wis trouble from the first moment she laid eyes oan him,' she said, bluntly, 'an' he's still causin' grief frae beyond the grave. Mercy me, Joe, Ah hope this will be the end o' it, Ah truly dae.'

'Perhaps she'll mak mair o' Andrew Dudley noo.'

'Gie her time tae grieve!'

'She's had years already, none o' us are gettin' ony younger. I wid like tae see her settled wi' a guid man, taken care of, proper like. She ne'er had that frae that Irish skellum, an' ma sister deserves some happiness.'

A tremor ran through Fiona, causing her to shake her head to cover the sudden discomfort.

Happiness? Surely it was the most fragile and elusive emotion anyone could feel? There, one moment and then vanished. If she ever felt it again, she would hug it to her heart and prize it dearly.

***

Rosie worked hard at keeping busy. Her duties as the stair superintendent and daily work in Mill Three took care of a large portion of the day. Neighbours and family included her at their tables for meals in the evenings or to join them for walks on the new woodland paths. The problem came after ten o'clock when everyone retreated to their rooms.

Since Gerry died in the Spring, she would fill the hours before bed by reading the little pamphlets Fiona bought for her from Lanark market, mending or knitting. The cast iron range she inherited from Gerry's father was pressed into action baking gifts of bread, scones and oatcakes and bottling fruits and chutneys.

When the days began to draw in, the prospect of the long dark evenings took their toll. No matter how physically tired she made herself, she could not sleep. Tossing and turning, the nights stretched interminably. Often, she heard the distant strains of Lanark's clock striking the hours of three or four before achieving peace.

On a cold November morning, she woke to the chapper's loud rap on Mrs Bennett's door, across the landing from her own room. Settled in the warmth of her blankets, now all she desired was to sink back into oblivion but did not dare risk closing her eyes again for fear of being late for work. She fumbled in the darkness for the tinderbox and lit the candle beside her bed.

Another day had started.

'By, it's gie cauld,' a fellow worker greeted her at the mill door. 'The winter's here. There wis ice oan the cobbles this morn.'

Rosie shivered beneath her shawl and fell into step with the women trudging up the stairs. It was still dark outside but at least the spinning rooms were brighter and warm from the hot air flowing out of vents from the basement furnaces. Leaving her clogs at the door and laying her shawl neatly over them, she entered the familiar room.

The humid heat eased her tense shoulders and she took up her position beside the immaculate Crompton's mule. She was proud to see the white side of her Silent Monitor displayed to the room.

This was the best part of the day; gossiping with the other women before the din of the machinery drowned out their voices. It was companionable, comfortable, and a prelude to hours of intense methodical work to fill her mind.

The Overseers started the gears and all Rosie's attention was immediately directed to her portion of over thirteen hundred spindles. The massive mule, running down the entire length of the workroom, moved backwards and forwards on iron wheels, sending streams of white cotton whirring through its rollers. The noise was rhythmic, changing four times in a minute to carry out processes which used to require hundreds of pairs of hands.

Concentrating on their tasks, few people noticed a man dash through the door, nor the frantic exchanges with the floor manager.

All of a sudden, there came the crashing and grating of metal on metal. Men began charging between the machines, hauling back the gears to grind them to a halt. The women jumped or were pushed backwards, staring around at each other, shrugging and shouting, the children leaping out the way.

'Fire!' as the churning mules slowed and stopped, the Overseers' desperate cries could be heard. 'Fire! Get out ... get out!'

Frozen to the spot, Rosie tried to make sense of the scene of panic. She saw the others rushing for the door and the children's frightened faces, bodies shoving her this way and that in their haste, but her mind would not believe it was really happening.

355

This must be a nightmare? Had she fallen asleep again and was still in her bed?

A man's arm grabbed her roughly round her waist, jolting her out of her shock and into the chaos. Abruptly, she became all too aware of the danger and let herself be swept towards the door.

Then she was running down the corridor with the crowd, bare feet slapping on the boards, sucking in cold air. The clamour came to a halt when everyone jammed into a squeezing, terrified queue on the narrow staircase. Each step sent a chill shooting through her, a knot of fear aching in her chest, sucking away her breath.

On descending to the first floor, they joined the women from the lower work rooms and the crush became worse. Cries and garbled shouts were growing more agitated, provoked by a strong smell of smoke.

Was the fire below them or above? Were they cut off from their only escape?

At the top of the last descent, Rosie was pushed from behind, losing her footing and stumbling. She reached out to grab at arms, clothes, anything around her, trying to break her fall. Then she was toppling, dropping down amongst trampling feet and swinging hems, her head smacking onto the flagstones.

On the other side of the mill lade, Sarah was setting up for the day in the fitting room above the shop. She was going about her normal routine and chatting with the other staff when her eye went to the window. It was the rapid movements of men carrying lamps which drew her attention.

'Whit's happenin' o'er at the mills?' she asked, curious but unconcerned. Her mind was on the new items to be displayed before the door opened for the day: boxes of fancy buttons and silk ribbons.

'Ah dinnae ken,' two shop girls joined her to take a look, holding their candles behind them and peering out. 'It's too dark, Ah cannae see ...'

'There's a bell ringin'?' Sarah cocked her head to one side, 'Can ye hear it?'

Her eyes searched the lifting dawn, struggling to discern roof top from sky; the far, wooded horizon from clouds. In the foreground, darker shapes were spreading along the road in front of the mills.

Distorted by the twilight, it appeared as if an ominous black, pulsating wave was flowing up the hill.

'Ladies,' Andrew Dudley came hurrying up the stairs into the haberdashery, a lantern swinging in his hand. 'We must remain calm. There is no danger to anyone on this side of the lade, so please do not panic. A fire has broken out in Mill Three but I am sure it'll soon be brought under control ...'

'A fire ... Mill Three!' Sarah's knees threatened to buckle and she leaned heavily on the window ledge. 'Ma sister's in there ...'

'Dinnae fret,' the older of the girls stroked Sarah's shoulder. 'Look, Ah cannae see ony fire an' there's hunners oot in the street, she'll be wi' 'em.'

'Ah pray tae God she's safe,' Sarah muttered, all thoughts of displaying buttons erased from her mind. 'Ah must find her.' She tore herself away from the window and turned to Mr Dudley. 'Can Ah gae oot an' find her?'

'Everyone is to stay inside, that's the order from the manager's office. Ye ken we have a fire engine an' dozens o' men trained tae deal wi' a fire breaking oot. Leave them tae dae their joabs.'

He saw the dread on her face and wanted to take her in his arms but refrained, saying more softly. 'Ah cannae let you out, there's enough people oan the streets. They'll be takin' a roll call. Mr Owen's orders.'

'Mr Owen's no' here!' Sarah cried, wondering if she could push past him and then deciding not, all in the same second.

'He doesn't need to be here, it's all written doon. The managers know what tae dae, calm yersel'.'

She bit back a curse and returned to the window.

The view did nothing to settle her fears.

From where she stood, most of Mill Three was hidden behind the bulk of the Institute but now, rising into the early morning sky, she could see twisting columns of smoke. No sooner was the smoke visible than the unmistakable, flickering orange glow of flames could be seen. Within seconds, the Institute was turned into a solid black silhouette surrounded by vibrating red light.

The moment the alarm was raised, Mr Murray took charge of his pupils in the Institute. The rear windows of the Institute overlooked the stricken mill. They were just yards from the

357

disaster with only the lade and a narrow road separating the classrooms from the fire.

Calmly, he addressed the morning assembly, sending them all to the new School building. Fiona was aghast, knowing Rosie would be at her work at the top of the burning building.

The sudden emergency took her breath away, instantly sparking traumatic memories from her childhood. This was no time to allow those demons to rise, it would help no one if she went to pieces.

Joining Molly and the older children, she helped to shepherd the pupils out of the main doors, picking up the smaller infants and taking the toddlers by the hand Outside, the air was strangely still but heavy with smoke and voices. Men's deep, raw shouts rang over the higher shrieks and sobs of female workers running from the mill, half clothed and scared to death.

The straggling line of more than two hundred children made slow progress through the playground and down the frosty slopes below Caithness Row. To their innocent eyes the spectacle was a dramatic event to be savoured. It took firm persuasion to keep them moving, especially over the bridge which afforded the best view.

The second floor of the school held two big rooms and Murray stood on the first landing, directing them to file into the largest one and sit down in rows.

They were safe: what to do now?

The fire was taking hold. Great furling waves of flame shot out through the lines of tall windows, sending exploding shards of glass showering over the men below. With caps and jerkins drawn over their heads, they valiantly pumped water with the fire engine. Using the water from the lade, yards of hose and bucketful after bucketful of water, they battled the inferno.

Their efforts appeared to make scant difference. Above the roar and crackle came resounding crashes of internal timbers falling deep within the structure. The roof was giving way in wide holes, each surrendering in a shuddering, sliding mass of tiles.

With the strong walls of Mill Four and an additional gap of several yards between the school and the fire, Mr Murray surveyed his pupils. He was aware of the change in mood from excitement to fear. Methodically, he called out the morning register until he was satisfied they were all present.

'We may have to be here for a wee while so we will take our usual lessons!' He applied a wide smile to his words and clapped his hands together. 'Sargeant Major, please take the older children to the other room and conduct your exercises indoors today ...' He then carried on giving instructions with an air of forced normality.

Outside, in the sepia light of daybreak, flying red embers swirled in the black smoke before dropping into the lade, hissing and splashing. Everyone from Mill Three and the mills on either side were rigorously counted and double checked, then told to go home for the rest of the day. When the mothers started to collect their children, Fiona asked if there was news of any one being killed or badly injured.

'The yins wi' burns or cuts and bruises are here, doon the stairs,' one woman told her. 'Ah dinnae ken aboot how bad they are but nae body's deid. Thank the Lord.'

When all the pupils whose mothers worked in the stricken and evacuated mills were collected, Fiona approached Mr Murray.

'Mr Murray, sir, ma man's sister wurks in Mill Three. Ah'm awfy anxious aboot her. Can Ah mak sure she's alricht?'

He rubbed his smooth, clean shaven chin, 'I would prefer you tae stay here, in this building. It's much too dangerous tae be walking aboot ootside.'

'Maybe they'd ken doonstairs?' Molly put in, 'there are some folk doon there who came oot o' the fire? Dr Gibson's wi' them.'

'Very well, ye can ask, but ...'

Fiona was already out the door and racing down the stairs.

The lower rooms were crowded with women sitting on the floor with their backs against the walls, others standing around chatting, crying, comforting one another. Their bare arms and feet were smeared with soot, their hair and clothes thick with the pungent stench of smoke.

Dr Gibson and several village women were at the furthest end of the room, attending to dozens of patients; some laid on tables, others sitting dazed and dishevelled in their thin cotton shifts.

Fiona was half way across the room before she recognised Rosie as one of the women needing special attention. Hurrying to her side, she saw her eyes were closed and her head swathed in bandages.

'Doctor?' Fiona cried, not daring to touch Rosie. 'She's no' deid is she?'

'A bad knock to the head.' he said gruffly, glancing up. 'You're her brother's wife, aren't ye?'

'Aye,' Fiona was shaking.

'She fell down the stairs and may have a few other bruises here and there but she's very lucky. One of the men saw her fall and picked her up before more damage was done.'

' She'll be alricht?'

'There will be a scar, I've had to stitch the wound. Tricky place foreheads, the skin is stretched across the skull, ye see, gapes when it's split open.'

Fiona swallowed; then again. Nausea was swamping her, making her dizzy.

'Thank ye,' she managed to croak, gaining control. 'Why's she no' awake?'

'Oh, she will be soon. She passed out when she saw the needle. That reaction can be a blessing, ye know, then ye don't feel it when ...'

Fiona cut him off, sickness cramping her stomach.

'Ah must git back tae the bairns upstairs, thank ye, sir, thank ye!'

Wondering how best to look after Rosie, she collided with a large figure while hurrying towards the stairway.

'Joe!'

His arms went round her, pulling her fiercely against him, pressing her face against his coarse jute cape.

'Lass! yer all richt?' he released her to see for himself. 'Where's Rosie?'

Quickly, Fiona explained, then asked why he was there.

'Ah came as soon as Ah saw the smoke. Thank God oor bairns are in Mill One ... Ah spoke tae them in the office an' they telt me ye wid be here.'

'Can ye tak Rosie up tae oor hoose? We can look efter her?'

'Aye, Ah'll see tae it.'

He watched her run up the stairs until she disappeared from sight, allowing himself a moment to let the relief steady his breathing.

From the moment he saw smoke rising from New Lanark, panic had gripped him. Leaving Bluey in her stall, he ran straight down to the village, almost falling on the steep steps.

Town's people from Lanark and early carriages full of visitors were already gathering on the upper road, viewing the spectacle with gruesome fascination.

As he descended into the valley he could see through the bare winter branches that Mill One was untouched. This was where Ailsa, Lily and Robert worked and he paused for a second to catch his breath. Then, he took in the sight of Mill Three's inferno and his anxiety returned, sending all thoughts to Rosie.

From what he saw, the six story mill would be completely destroyed. It seemed like only yesterday that he and Tam were breaking rocks and mixing mortar to build the massive structure. Now, the worst had happened and their creation was dying amidst a roaring blaze.

It was several days after Mill Three was destroyed before the news reached Owen in London. He was profoundly grateful to read there were no fatalities or serious injuries but this initial relief soon gave way to the hard reality of how to cope with keeping production flowing and orders completed. A few frames had been salvaged from the west end of the factory and insurance would cover the replacement of the rest of the machinery and rebuilding the mill.

In the meantime, winter was upon them. His employees needed work and hard won, lucrative contracts must be fulfilled.

Sitting down at his desk, he penned letters to his partners to inform them of the damage. Then, as the cause of the blaze appeared to have originated from one of the small stoves on an upper level, he wrote to his senior manager asking several pertinent questions.

Evening was reaching into night when he rang for Murdoch to bring a light meal up to his room. While he worked, utterly focused on charts and figures, more candles were lit and coals replenished several times in the little tiled fireplace.

He was laying out safeguards to remove as many fire hazards as possible and restructuring the remaining mills to allow for continuous use. Although he spurned all-night working, he devised a shift system to ensure each employee only worked his or her

361

standard hours. In this way, he could keep everyone in work and meet the required production figures.

The clocks were ringing out the midnight hour when he finally snuffed the candle and fell back against his pillows.

He was tired, mentally as much as physically. The last ten months had been fraught with setbacks including the misfortune of disease striking his mills, yet they still showed a profit. Now, there was the fire's destruction.

Switching his mind away from the loss of Mill Three, he was thankful his Factory Reform Bill was due for its final reading.

Then, he received another crushing blow.

In an effort to save money, the Duke of Kent had taken up residence in Woolbrook Cottage, down in Sidmouth, and only occasionally visited the city. So, on receiving a note from the Duke asking Owen to call by that afternoon, Owen was pleased to make his way to Kensington Palace.

'Owen, my dear chap, thank you for coming ....'

When the niceties were over and the two men were alone, the real reason for his invitation was revealed.

'There is no easy way to tell ye this. The Select Committee has voted against presenting to the House of Commons your Plan for building Villages of Mutual Cooperation.'

'But *all* the reports were favourable!' Owen was incensed. 'You know yourself, Dr Macnab was glowing in his recommendations! Saying that the children are superior in point of conduct and character to all the children he had ever seen! The independent reports from the Guardians of the Poor could not have been more enthusiastic ... why have they rejected taking it any further?'

'Well, although the brilliant economist Ricardo stood in favour of your Plan, not to mention Brougham, Sir William de Crespigny and many more shrewd intellectuals, it was thought to be too costly ... '

'More costly than a Revolution? More costly than providing Poor Relief to millions in the coming years?'

Edward continued, 'but also, unfortunately, in his summing up, our Chancellor, Nicholas Vansittart, reminded the committee of your words from two years ago regarding your stance on religion. Indeed, he read a lengthy quote where you denounce all religions of the world. It appears, they took it to heart. Wilberforce stated

362

they believe there should be a Christian foundation to any community founded in this country. There are many in power who are staunch members of the Anglican Church and, as you know, recently, the Archbishop of Canterbury withdrew his allegiance to you.'

With no expression, Owen asked, 'What was the result of the vote?'

'The motion was lost, one hundred and forty one to sixteen.'

'Their ignorance is astounding! Throughout the country we have men rioting, demanding action to allow them the basic dignity of earning a living and feeding their families ... and we have ... this! Where is the humanity in this decision? Where is their so called Christian charity?' He pushed both hands through his hair and grasped his head, trying to contain his exasperation. 'What other measures are they going to put in place to quell the growing swell for revolution?'

'Liverpool is set to have his Six Acts passed within the month.'

'All suppression! Since the carnage at St Peter's Fields there have been uprisings in Huddersfield and Burnley ... there are women's groups being created to call for reform and countless other clubs and underground meetings demanding their voice be heard. Politicians do not grasp the danger of their actions.'

They sat for a while, deep in thought.

'Good gracious,' Owen started again, 'was France not evidence enough of the outcome of such a lack of understanding of human nature. The Government are running scared, with good reason! I doubt if Sidmouth has sufficient spies to reach every inn and parlour where desperate men plot his downfall.'

Edward leaned towards Owen, sharing his friend's genuine grievance and seeing his bitter disappointment.

'Perhaps, we should leave your Plan a while and then try again,' he said, placating. 'At least, Peel's putting your factory reforms before the House. Are you staying to hear the result, I am sure it will be successful.'

'I must return to Scotland because of the fire, there is much to be done. At any rate, I have read the amendments and it bears little relation to my original Bill.' With a heavy sigh, Owen stood up, preparing to leave. 'Ye know, sir, religious bigotry and greed have no conscience. They render a man entirely selfish, unable to empathise with those around him. It would be laughable if it were not so dangerous, for not only am I castigated for allowing *all* religious freedoms, but the Catholics are persecuted for holding *different* religious views.'

The Duke pushed himself out of his chair and they walked together to the door. As a strong advocate for Catholic Emancipation, he had no rejoinder, no excuse for his fellow Peers in the House of Lords nor the Members of Parliament.

'These are dark days,' Edward said, solemnly, 'but we will overcome. You still have my solid support, my good friend. I trust you have a safe journey north and I look forward to your return.'

As the carriage pulled away, Owen raised a hand in farewell to the royal figure standing in the doorway; overhead lanterns shining on his bristling side burns and bald head.

That image of his friend remained clear in Owen's mind for the rest of his life.

The four weary, hopeful, exasperating years throughout which Owen struggled to improve the lives of factory workers, finally came to a close. The Factory Reform Act passed into law but it was so watered down it was as useless as its predecessor.

Owen had proposed that no child under ten years of age should be employed in factories, the new Act said nine years old; he wanted a maximum ten hour working day, the new limit was set at twelve hours. He wanted all employees of sixteen years and younger to be provided with basic education, there was no rule laid down, nor any system for inspection or enforcement.

Bitterly dissatisfied, Owen latched on to its one redeeming feature: a precedent had now been set for Parliament to become involved in the management of factory conditions. Still, it was deeply disappointing after so much work.

A few weeks later, he heard of a more personal loss.

After catching a cold, the Duke of Kent was taken severely ill and despite the attendance of several doctors, he passed away in the Devon cottage on the 23rd of January 1820.

Just six days later, his father, King George III, died in London and the country was thrown into a frenzy of preparations to dissolve Parliament and crown George IV.

Chapter Nineteen

"Mr Owen's practical rules of life are, in fact, all without an exception to be found in the books of divine revelation." Dr Henry Grey Macnab

During the freezing winter days following King George III's death, Parliament was adjourned and the lengthy process of a general election began. Allowing time for preparations and canvassing, there would then be more than a month between the first and last borough declaring their results before reconvening on 14th April.

This vacuum offered an ideal opportunity to the fermenting revolutionaries and reformists.

Pushed to extreme measures to achieve a new system of government, the Spenceans planned to assassinate the leading figures in the Tory Cabinet and seize control of the country.

They had attempted a coup before, in 1816, and narrowly avoided death or transportation. This time their audacious plan was to take place when Lord Liverpool and his ministers were attending a dinner at 39 Grosvenor Square: Lord Harrowby's London residence.

The idea was proposed by George Edwards at a secret meeting a few weeks after the king's death. Assuring them he could provide the weapons required, Edwards showed a newspaper report to the thirteen leaders of the faction which stated the date and time of the dinner. Thistlewood, the head of the group and a known radical, was eager to embrace the plan and when the meeting dispersed, he hurried off to garner more support.

Unfortunately, what Thistlewood and his desperate colleagues did not know was that Edwards was a spy for the Home Secretary: the reported dinner party was a hoax.

One of the conspirators, a Jamaican born coloured man, William Davidson, was suspicious of Edwards. Davidson was well educated, having once studied law and had also worked for Lord Harrowby in the past. With these qualifications, he was the obvious choice to be elected to call at the house in Grosvenor Square to find out more about the important dinner. When the servants told him Lord Harrowby and Lady Susan were not in the city, his misgivings about Edwards were reinforced.

Thistlewood, however, would not be convinced of any problems and decided to go ahead. He rented a hay loft in Cato Street, close to Harrowby's, where they would meet and arm themselves before the event.

On the evening of the fabricated dinner party, Edwards alerted the Bow Street Runners to the plot and they swooped on the gang as they were preparing to leave for Grosvenor Square.

The newspapers were full of the story. It came as no surprise to Owen. There was a palpable feeling of discontent in every town and city, even in smaller market towns like Lanark.

While Joe was sitting in his kitchen chatting with Tam one evening, his son, Robert, came through the back door.

Tall, dark haired and lean like Davey, but without the flamboyant character of his elder brother, he was now in his twenty first year and an accomplished weaver.

'Yer late this eve, son?' Joe welcomed him with a smile.

'Aye,' Robert was the quietest of all the Scotts, preferring to listen and watch than enter the fray. 'Ah wis asked alang tae a pal's hoose ...' his voice trailed away.

'How's wurk?' Tam asked genially, pulling out the chair beside him and gesturing for him to join them at the table.

'Nae sae bad.' Robert sat down and took the tankard of small beer his father slid towards him.

'Tam an' Ah were pondering oan buyin' anither horse tae pull the cart,' Joe told him. 'Rusty's gettin' gie stiff of a mornin' an' yer Ma wulnae let me tak her tae the knacker's yaird sae she'll be turned oot in the pasture.'

Robbie nodded, his mind obviously elsewhere, then blurted out, 'Ha'e ye heard o' the United Scotsmen? Ah've jist bin hearin' whit they plan tae dae, an' Ah'm fair vexed aboot it.'

Joe leaned forward, resting his elbows on the table. 'Whit did ye hear?'

'Ye ken weavers an' many ithers are hardly earnin' enough tae live? Mind all the trouble years back? Weel, it's nae better noo, worse, mair like. There's gaun tae be an uprising ... all roond Scotland. They want every yin tae leave their joabs an' demand proper wages an' a break frae English rule.'

'When's this tae happen?' Tam was alarmed.

'They have nae sed yit. They'll tell every yin in factories an' mills an' leather works ... *every yin*, an' we'll all walk oot.'

'That'll cause a muckle load o' trouble,' Joe muttered.

He had heard rumblings through his contacts at the Lodge but there were so many voices demanding change it was hard to tell who would act and who would follow. He just hoped this did not include his own men who he relied on turning up to work on Cartland Bridge and several other contracts.

'The thing is,' Robbie said, 'Ah sympathise wi' all the demands o' these United Scotsmen ... but, weel, doon at New Lanark we already ha'e whit we need. Perhaps the piy is a wee bit less than Ah could mak in the city but look at everything else? Yer treated wi' respect, an' the orders are fur fine quality, a pleasure tae weave, no' jist ony rubbish. Nae body's worn doon, the oors are fair, ma wages are ne'er withheld an' we ha'e Sick Pay an' a doctor oan call ... why wid Ah want tae walk oot ma joab an' cause trouble?'

Joe looked him squarely in the eye, 'Then dinnae dae it.'

'But whit if every yin else does?'

'Ye ken the folk at the mills, they're no' daft. They're no' gaun tae lose their joabs by daen sumat stupit. After all that Mr Owen's done for that place an' all the villagers? Every yin work t'gether doon there, tae stoap production wid hurt themsels an their families as much as the maister. Naw, Ah cannae see any yin causing him grief.'

Under cover of darkness, late on Saturday 1st April, scurrying figures dodged through the streets and parks of Glasgow. Carefully timed to evade the patrolling Constables, they put up placards calling for an immediate national strike.

The word went across the country like a strong westerly wind.

On the Sunday, printed copies of a proclamation were liberally distributed throughout central Scotland, signed *Committee of Organisation for forming a Provisional Government*. It asked everyone to stop work from that day onwards and stated their aims were to have a more responsive government and electoral reform, ending, *" we are but a brave and generous people determined to be free."*

367

On Monday morning, thousands of employees did not report for work. Hundreds of scuffles broke out where speakers called for an end to English repression and the return of a Scottish Government for the Scottish people.

Ramshackle bands of determined men marched to Carron Iron Works to find weapons, others walked from Strathaven, expecting to join up with larger forces of Radicals. The magistrates were ready for them and called out the militia. Ordinary men and women armed with pitch forks and sharpened sticks were no match for the slashing sabres of the Hussars.

For a week, skirmishes and violent unrest swept through the industrialised counties of Scotland with over sixty thousand workers taking part in the strike.

It did not take long for the ringleaders to be arrested and the country began to simmer down: production returned to normal.

Then, the trials began and the truth started to emerge.

'It was all engineered by government spies! Again!' Captain Donald MacDonald was furious.

A new fervent follower of Owen's philosophy, Abram Combe, was with the group, mulling over the happenings of the previous weeks.

'These poor wretches,' Abram said with feeling, 'with a genuine passion to better their country ... they've have been played like puppets.'

'And been hanged for it,' Alexander Hamilton shuddered. 'It was Sidmouth's spy who handed Baird the weapons and encouraged the training for an uprising. Now, the Tories have created the perfect climate of fear to show their quaking voters what terrible danger they were in ...'

'And "how well the Tory Government's policies dealt with it".' MacDonald finished for him, groaning. 'Another Tory landslide is on the cards.'

'Sidmouth will justify it by saying he was only flushing out the revolutionaries.' MacDonald tapped his unfilled pipe against his palm and roamed around Owen's study at Braxfield. 'Meanwhile, women and children have been killed in the riots and thousands of hours of labour lost to the economy. A dreadful time! Hardie and Baird swinging at Stirling and that man from Strathaven, who surely did not deserve the gallows, strung up in Glasgow.'

'I hear they even arrested Turner and threw him in the Tolbooth for a day or so! He's out, of course, but it was a warning to him after allowing reformists the use of his estate at Thrushgrove.'

Owen had remained silent but added, 'Don't forget the twenty unfortunates on their way to the Penal Colonies. What an irrational society we live in at present, gentlemen.'

Hamilton slouched back in his chair, glancing at Owen warily, wondering how he would answer his question.

'How did your mills fare?'

'There was no disturbance,' he replied simply. 'Why would there be?'

MacDonald cleared his throat, not wishing to press the subject but needing to hear the truth. 'I heard you lost some workers?'

'In the last month, yes, a few have gone to Catrine and one family to a mill in Glasgow. They had given their notice before this uprising.'

'Sir,' Combe asked, 'may we know why they left your mills?'

'Of course! The father of the family heading to the city is a devout Catholic and wished his children to receive a Catholic education, which I assume means he wanted more emphasis on religious teaching in the school. The ones going to Catrine did not like so much dancing, although I suspect it was the slightly higher rate of pay they were after.' Owen folded his arms. 'My friend Kirkman Finlay runs a good establishment over there, but they will soon discover the lack of benefits they took for granted here.

'Good factory conditions are only a small part of my village. It is a *community*, the people here care for each other, co-operate with each other to make it a pleasant, respectful place to live. It is also virtually self-sufficient and their children receive not only a superb education but will grow up to be happy, rational adults.'

Hamilton flung his arms wide in an uncharacteristic show of enthusiasm.

'Well, *we* know that, my dear sir!' he cried, 'But how the devil can we make the rest of this damned island see they have the solution to the problem staring them in the face!'

The prediction that Lord Liverpool and his Tories would return to government came true. Owen was not successful in his bid for the Linlithgow Boroughs but took it in his usual philosophical way.

369

However, as a direct result of the cloud of fear and radical ill-feeling looming over the land, a silver lining appeared.

Given the evident well-being of New Lanark while the rest of the country was drowning in despair, they asked him to make a Report to the County of Lanark. They particularly wanted him to outline measures to address the ever increasing problem of unemployment which was draining the local Parishes' Poor Relief Fund.

Owen accepted the brief, relishing the opportunity to present his Plan for spreading the benefits of free education and mutual co-operation to a different public body.

***

Joe opened the bedroom shutters and gave a sigh of relief.

Blue sky stretched to the horizon above the sparkling spring countryside. This view always filled him with a satisfying feeling of pleasure but today he was especially pleased.

'Up oot yer bed, lazy bones!' he teased Fiona, 'it's a grand day!'

She responded by covering her head with the cotton sheet, a joy in itself, being a new acquisition after a life time of rough blankets.

Today, Lanark would be alive with merriment to honour the arrival of a statue commissioned by the town of the historic figure of William Wallace. The Scotts felt personal pride in the event, not just because Joe was involved with organising the celebrations but the sculptor, Robert Forrest, was a friend of their sons.

Joe washed and shaved with extra care, mentally running through the programme for the day. On the chair beside the wash stand, Fiona had laid out his clothes; white shirt with double back cuffs, cream breeches, blue taffeta waistcoat, starched white cravat and, over the back of the chair, his best black tail coat.

'Mind ye dinnae git Bluey's hair oan yer jacket!' Fiona cried, standing at the back door, barefoot and wrapped in her shawl to kiss him goodbye. 'Ah'll meet ye at the Toon Hall.'

Fiona waved Robbie and the younger children away to New Lanark. Then, after a rush to clean grass stains off his knee breeches, hugged the now long-legged, earnest Tom and sent him on his way to the Grammar.

Left alone in the sun filled house, she took her time braiding and styling her hair and dressing for the occasion. She enjoyed her days off work, sometimes taking on a task; a new counterpane for Ailsa's bed or scrubbing and polishing the copper pans she found at the market. Other days, she chose to sit on the window seat in the front parlour and just gaze out at the ever changing scene beyond the glass.

Like drifting clouds, her moods could change within seconds, taking her from singing a cheerful tune to sobbing uncontrollably. It only took a chance reminder of Sionaidh to cut her to the quick: the scent of honey, the sight of a piece of clothing she once wore or one of her daughter's favourite blue ribbons in the sewing box.

For some reason, which she could not fathom, she found her loss easier to bear on sunny days. Tying a posy of pretty yellow silk roses to her hat, she tried it on for effect and smiled at her own reflection.

It was quiet in the house, sunlight warming the floorboards beside her dressing table, highlighting specks of dust swirling in the air. A bumble bee was buzzing and knocking against the landing window, the sound accentuating the silence.

She adjusted her hat's brim to a jaunty angle and secured it with pins, tucking stray curls away from her forehead and drawing others down around her neck. Going to the full length mirror, another recent bargain, she turned this way and that. She liked the way the matching green and pale yellow bodice and short, petal shaped overdress, complimented the long cream underskirt. A lady visiting the school had worn a similar outfit and Fiona was very taken with it. With Sarah's help, she sought out the same design among the village shop's patterns and, after insisting on paying her, asked Sarah to make it up.

'How strange,' Fiona mused, assessing the chic figure in the looking glass, 'Ah could pass fur yin o' Mrs Owen's lady friends.'

She felt a burning desire for her parents and brother to see this apparition. What would they say of her owning this solid, spacious house with its own staircase and attic rooms? Oh, how she wished they could meet her dearest Joe and the children. What would they think to see their daughter grown up, growing old, dressed in fine clothes with scent on her wrists and silk flowers on her hat?

It was a silly thought. Both her parents were dead and her brother was thousands of miles away, if not also deceased. With a shock, she realised he would be past his half century if he was alive, a sobering thought.

Tam and Melanie came to her door and they all walked up to town together, looking forward to the excitement of a parade.

'Och look!' Fiona pointed to a mass children in white tunics, four abreast, marching ahead of them along the Wellgate. 'Ma weans frae the school! Aren't they bonnie?'

'They're no' yer ane bairns,' Tam laughed, 'whit are ye like, Fiona!'

'They feel like ma ane, Ah ken them tha' weel.' She watched them with a sense of satisfaction, noting the approving glances of the town's people. 'E'en auld Mistress Hardy cannae stoap a smile frae crackin' her face.'

Melanie giggled, nudging Tam. 'An' there's the Reverend Menzies. Ah wager he wulnae pass the time o' day wi' me,' she turned a toothy smile to the minister, enjoying his discomfort when he recognised her as the woman he described as a harlot.

'Dinnae court mischief, lass,' Tam warned.

The undercurrents in the community ran deep. To the visitors, the colourful crowded streets and fluttering bunting were a wonderful sight to behold. They were oblivious to the snubs and subtle rejections, clever one up man-ships, petty victories of securing the best vantage point or wearing the most expensive garments.

The Owens, accompanied by Ann, Jane and their younger sons, walked up from Braxfield House by way of a path beside Castlebank. Little Mary was not well, struck with an upset stomach and confined to bed, much to Dora's disappointment because she had to forego the outing and stay with the child.

Not being used to walking, except to attend church in the village, Anne Caroline was finding the steep hill tiring, requiring several pauses along the route. Holding a parasol in one hand and her husband's arm with the other, she managed to lead their own procession up the High Street and through the bustling market place. Heads turned as they passed, some fawning to curry favour, others awkwardly antagonistic. They were followed by half a dozen of their servants, led by the impeccably turned out Mr Sheddon and Miss Wilson, demure and prim, if rather warm, in her Sunday coat and hat.

No sooner was Lady Mary Ross waving to the Owens and insisting they stand beside the Bonnington party, than the resounding beat of pipes and drums thrummed in the air, heralding the procession.

Two enormous gleaming brown and white Clydesdale horses drew the cart bearing the statue, their manes and tails plaited and beribboned, brasses sparkling. They were led by a man at each side, holding their great, nodding heads for fear of losing control amid the din of skirling pipes and whooping, whistling applause. Behind the cart, Donnie and Davey lifted their friend, the man of the day, Robert Forrest, onto their shoulders.

The young sculptor waved and cheered along with the crowd, his cheeks scarlet and his wavy brown hair, so carefully combed that morning, flying from his head in disarray. A few paces back, his assistant, John Greenshields, was similarly carried down the hill, thrilled with the reception.

Loud cheers rose from the visiting contingents from Carluke, Forrest's home town and also from Lesmahagow, where Greenshields was raised.

It was a proud day for Clydesdale, celebrating the works of local artisans for their creation of a fine tribute to Scotland's hero, William Wallace.

Joe stood close to the church door beside several of his brothers from the Lodge. His hands clasped and unclasped behind his back, a serious expression squaring his jaw. While his eyes surveyed the crowds, all his attention was on the complicated mechanics of hoisting and levering the statue into place. Despite checking and double checking the ropes and running through the procedure with his sons and Forrest the night before, he was eager to have the job completed.

At last, the speeches were over and the carved figure hauled into place. It was at least three times the size and bulk of a man, its rugged features copied from an ancient drawing which purported to be an accurate depiction of the famous freedom fighter.

Once secured and hailed again with applause, the pipe band escorted the horses and the empty cart back up the hill.

'Good day, Mr Scott,' Anne Caroline greeted Joe outside the Town Hall. 'I trust the statue will not topple on any unsuspecting passers by?'

'Mrs Owen,' Joe removed his hat, bowing his head. 'It'll no' budge, ye ha'e ma wurd oan that, Madam.'

Owen turned towards him, nodding an acknowledgement to Fiona.

'Mrs Scott, Mr Scott. What a fine display. I understand you were part of the organising committee, sir, an excellent outcome.'

Again, Joe gave a brief, polite bow. 'Thank ye, sir. We are gie pleased it went sae weel.'

'You are involved in building our new bridge across the Moose river, I hear.'

'Ma teams are part of many, but aye, it's coming alang weel. Mr Minto and Mr Telford mak the task easier wi' their detailed plans.'

Owen's eyes were intense with his characteristic enthusiasm. 'When will it be finished?'

'Anither year, at least. It will mak a grand difference tae trade fur the toon.'

'Indeed it will. For my mills alone, it will allow the wagons to avoid the winding valley road and approach Lanark by way of Carluke and across the moors. I can imagine it removing an hour or more from the journey.'

A young voice piped up, 'I'm sure the horses will appreciate the new bridge as much as any one.'

The adults looked round to find young Jane Owen..

She blushed, her eyes as lively as her father's, as dark as her mother's.

'Well,' she continued, 'the poor creatures have to drag those wagons up and down that awful hill at present. If there is a bridge, I am sure it will be much easier.'

While walking home that afternoon, Fiona recalled the Owen's daughter.

'She's the spittin' image o' her Ma as Ah remember her oan the day we were wed by Mr Dale, de ye no' ken?'

'Aye, bonnie wee lassie. She's mair like her Grand Da' than the ithers.'

'An' that's a guid thing. He wis a true gentleman and a fine Master. Not that Mr Owen's no' a kind man, fair and decent tae us, but he's sich a busy man.'

Joe squeezed her hand. 'It wid ha'e bin guid if he had won the seat for parliament last month.'

'Whit went wrang? Every yin ye talked tae afore the day of voting sed Mr Owen wis sure tae win. An' then, he didnae? How come?'

'It wis complicated, ma darlin'.'

'Dinnae gi'e me tha' 'it's complicated' nonsense, ma lad!' she raised their clasped hands and kissed his fingers. 'Tell me, whit happened!'

'There's a rumour, although Ah've heard it's true, that his opponents played dirty, took oot the men who were declared to support Owen and ... weel, they entertained them wi' drink an' all sorts. They could hardly staun' up when the day came, that's whit wis sed by those who saw them.'

'They got 'em drunk?'

'Aye, an' Mr Owen could see whit happened but by that time the ballot wis past.' Joe pushed back his hat and rubbed at the sweat on his forehead. 'Life's no' fair, lass, no' fair at all. If it had bin me, Ah reckon Ah'd ha'e punched them! But when the result was read oot in the Toon Hall, all hell broke loose, wi' people callin' it a fix an' corruption! It wis Mr Owen who pulled the meeting tae order. John McDiarmid from the bank telt me. He wis there, an' he sed Owen stood on a chair and pleaded for calm.'

'Awa'!' Fiona fell quiet, thoughtful.

'Ah telt ye it wis complicated,' Joe teased.

'Ah wis jist thinkin' ...'

'Steady, lass, ye'll need a lie doon if ye dae too much o' that!'

She aimed a smack at his arm, laughing. 'Mr Dudley wis tellin' me how Mr Owen tried tae mak it law fur all the factories tae be run like New Lanark. But it didnae come tae much an' there's still some paur bairns wurkin' in dreadfu' places. He must be gettin' awfy fed up wi' people no' takin' notice, but he's alis friendly an' sae keen tae show folk his mills.'

They came to their driveway and stopped beside the gateposts, admiring the carved lions with renewed appreciation.

'My, we can be prood o' these!' Joe patted a lion on its craggy, curling mane. 'Ah reckon Robert Forrest will be famous soon. His work's sellin' frae a yard at Crossford an' there's talk o' pieces being bought by toffs fur their gardens.'

'Are we toffs noo?' Fiona asked, coquettishly, playing with the lace trimming on her neckline. 'Look at us, Joe Scott, wi' oor hoose an' you lookin' sae handsome in yer polished boots an' felted hat. Ah feel like a lady in this frock, it's as light as a feather. Sarah did a bonnie joab.'

'Ye alis look like a lady, ma darlin', ye dinnae need fancy trappings. It's in ye, the way ye walk an' treat ither folk.' He was being serious, quietly admiring her and seeing her as the townsfolk would see her at his side. 'It's taken thirty years but this is whit Ah've wanted fur ye frae the day Ah first saw ye.'

'Aye, an' Ah kept tellin' ye, Ah didnae need onything but ye beside me.' She stepped closer, 'This is a fine hame an' Ah'm fair made up wi' it, but, wi' oot ye, Joe, it wid be nuthin'.'

'Ah feel the same,' he whispered, allowing a moment of companionable silence before a smile crept into his voice, 'fur wi' oot ye, who wid mak ma tea ... Ah'm starvin'!'

***

The mill bell began to ring and Sarah took off her spectacles, folded them carefully and laid them in their little box.

Stretching and yawning, she started to pack away her things for the day. The other girls were in a hurry to go and she was soon alone with the dust sheeted cabinets and neatly stacked rolls of material.

Glancing out at the sunny view of the Institute, she noticed Davey walking slowly along the street. He kept pausing and looking around and at one point gazed up at Nursery Buildings and along the line of windows towards the shop.

She waved but he didn't notice and turned to wander down through the open iron gates and off into the crowds of workers streaming from the mouths of the mills.

He was dressed very smartly, she mused, unusually so: his long hair cut and tamed to fall neatly to his collar and, for the first time in years, she saw no plaits or thin leather straps woven into it. Perhaps the rumours were true and Marie MacInnes, Kyle's pretty daughter, was succeeding in her quest to win his heart.

Or was Davey filling in time before a meeting? She knew Joe was hoping to tender for rebuilding Mill Three but had been told no work would be done for a while. A shame, she thought, for although the rubble was cleared away it left a gaping charred hole and rusting pipes and girders around the waterwheel which stank of soot, both in the rain and on a hot day.

'Sarah?'

'Och Andrew, Ah didnae hear ye come up the stairs.'

'Are ye all richt?' His pale face loomed over her with such an expression of concern that she was taken aback.

'Aye, jist tired, weel ma eyes are tired.'

'It's a lovely eve an' I wondered if ye wid join me fur a stroll up tae Lanark and we could see the new statue of Wallace?'

They arranged to meet in an hour and she went home to change, finding Lily waiting at the top of the stairway.

'Mam, Ah heard there's a joab up at Braxfield Hoose fur a maid! Can Ah ask aboot it? Ye ken Ah dinnae want tae spend ma whole life in the mills like you an' Auntie Rose. It wid be perfect!'

Taken by surprise and feeling insulted by being described as spending her whole life at the mills, Sarah did not respond.

'Mam? It's an under housemaid they're efter, an' Maisie Brooks says they're awfy nice tae work fur up there, kind, like at the schoolroom. Her cousin is a scullery maid in the hoose an' she's only twelve, Ah'm fourteen noo ... Please Mam?'

Sarah swung the swee over the grey coals and hooked the kettle into place.

'Whit does it piy?' she asked.

'Ah can find oot? Can Ah gae tae the office an ask? Can Ah?'

'Och, away ye gae! But dinnae tarry, Ah'm aff fur a walk wi' Mr Dudley soon an' we've still tae eat.'

Her last words were said to an empty room and she sat down, scowling at the floor.

I haven't spent my whole life in the mills, have I? The thought niggled. Of course not, there was picking fruit in the Clyde Valley, then Glasgow and success at Holroyd's and now I'm senior seamstress in the shop and an assistant teacher. These achievements soothed her and she went to the cupboard to fetch the eggs for supper.

It was as she put them in the pan and reached for the kettle that she realised the fire was cold.

Muttering oaths at her own stupidity, she turned her money bag out on the table. Finding a penny and three Spanish coins impressed with New Lanark's stamp, she scooped them up and ran back down the stairs. Mr Grant would still be in the shop and she was sure she had seen some mutton pies being taken through to the larder for the night.

The sign on the door said closed but she could see figures moving at the back and knocked for their attention. Begging for their forgiveness and understanding, a pie was retrieved and she hurried back outside.

At the same moment, Lily was coming out of the office. She saw her mother and then looked back over her shoulder, talking animatedly to someone inside.

'Ma Mam's here noo ... ye can ask her yersel'?'

Lily's voice was clear on the air and Sarah rolled her eyes: she did not have time to discuss a new job. Then she saw the man behind her daughter and laughed.

'Och it's ye, Davey,' she called, hastening her footsteps towards them. 'Ah'm in a rush this eve ...'

As he emerged from the shadow of the doorway, the sun brought him into sharp focus. The similarity was remarkable, even the line of his brows above almond shaped dark eyes and the cleft in his chin were those of her nephew, but this young man was a stranger.

'Oh, Ah beg yer pardon, sir ...' she cried, flustered.

'I don't wish to be a nuisance, ma'am,' he spoke with an attractive North American accent, bowing deferentially from the hip. 'I understand this is a strange request,' he gave a chuckle, 'but I hear from your daughter that you have lived here for a long time?'

'Aye, since it wis built, tae be honest,' recalling her daughter's hurtful remarks earlier in the evening, she added, 'Ah mean, Ah wis awa' fur mony years but Ah'm back again noo.'

'I am in search of someone and have traced them to these mills. They were owned at that time by a Mr David Dale? Would you remember anyone from so long ago?'

Sarah's heart began to race, 'Who are ye seeking?'

'My aunt. She was just a child then, Fiona MacDonald.'

'Fiona ...' a choking sob robbed her of speech. With tears pricking her eyes, the pie fell from her fingers and she flung herself against the man, hugging him with such ferocity he staggered backwards.

'Aye,' she cried, 'Ah ken Fiona ...' the words stumbled through her tears. 'She's ma greatest friend an' merrit tae ma brither.'

'Are ye sure she is the one?' embarrassed, he gently disengaged himself from the emotional, clinging woman. 'Ma'am, I have seen many registers and lists in my quest and the name Fiona MacDonald is not uncommon ...'

'Och son, look at ye? Ye are the image o' her, an' no mistake. That's why Ah thocht ye were Davey, her son. The twa o' ye are like twins!'

'She is here ... alive?'

'Aye, she's alive.' Sarah stood back, releasing him. 'Ah'll tak ye tae her. Oh, she will be sae happy ... *sae happy*.'

Lily was bouncing up and down, 'My name's Lily and she's my aunt too! What's yer name, sir?'

'Gideon MacDonald,' the smile he gave her was full of warmth. 'I pray to God we are truly speaking of the same lady. When can I meet her?'

After a contented day of pulling weeds from the vegetable patch, Fiona was in the kitchen when she heard the sound of hooves and voices beyond the open back door.

'Who's that?' she asked, busily mashing potatoes. 'Will yin o' ye tak a keek? Ah should ha'e shut the door but we need the draught.' She looked down at her soiled blouse and drawstring skirt, her bare feet still dusty with earth. 'Och, Ah'm no' dressed fur visitors.'

Joe and the older boys were not yet home but the rest of the family were sprawled around the table, hot and tired from a long working day.

Only Ailsa slid from her chair, 'It's Auntie Sarah ... an' a man oan a horse?'

Fiona gave a final battering to the potatoes and banged the masher sharply on the edge of the pan.

'Whit's she bringin' a man here for at this time,' she tightened the chequered kerchief she used as a hair band and pushed her loose hair away, shaking it to fall down her back, 'she kens when we tak oor dinner.'

'Coo ee!' Sarah called from the back step, already coming into sight, 'Fiona? Are ye there?'

'We're aboot tae eat ...'

379

'Ne'er mind that,' Sarah was grinning from ear to ear, 'there's some yin ye ha'e tae meet ...'

Fiona stared at the man walking towards her, unable to breathe, blinking in disbelief.

It was her brother. It couldn't be her brother, this man was young.

Her hand flew to her mouth, stifling a yelp. Was she seeing a ghost? Had she suddenly died and this was her brother taking her to Heaven?

Her eyes probed his face for clues and she started to tremble.

Then he was speaking; 'Please, I did not mean to frighten you.' He was shocked, instantly recognising his own likeness to the woman in front of him.

Any trace of doubt vanished: this was his aunt.

Bracing himself, he said slowly, 'I'm Gideon MacDonald, your brother's son. I promised my father I would try and find you and now ...' his voice broke, 'I believe, I have.'

***

Joe rode through his gates to find a strange horse tethered outside the barn. The large brown beast turned an enquiring head, ears pricking, before resuming its doze. Its saddle flaps bore the stamps of a Glasgow livery so it would be well used to strange surroundings. These hard working horses were usually docile, unlike the Scotts' new pony. Donnie had it between the shafts of their cart that day and it was proving to be a handful. Knowing he would soon be home, Joe wanted the yard clear.

Leading Bluey straight into her stall, he pulled off her tack, threw a bucketful of oats and bran into her manger and went in search of the visitor.

He was a few steps into the empty kitchen when he heard Fiona laughing. How long had it been since he heard his wife laugh like that? It was genuinely relaxed, full of amusement, heartfelt. Pleased but curious, he went to investigate.

'Joe!' Fiona jumped from her chair in the parlour and ran to him, glowing with excitement. 'Oh Joe, the grandest thing has happened!'

Gideon stood up on seeing Joe and approached him with great respect, hand outstretched. This was the man who married his aunt and through sheer hard work took them out of poverty and into this beautiful house. He liked him the moment their eyes met and knew instinctively that the feeling was mutual.

'Ma guidness!' Joe exclaimed, when the initial explanations were made. 'This is a braw day!'

'Sarah has taken Alex awa' wi' her tae see the statue an' the ithers ha'e gone too.' She was clasping her hands against her breast and swaying, unable to keep still, her hair swinging around her shoulders. 'They thocht we needed peace tae talk an' we've no' stoapped since they left.'

Joe's attention was still focused on Gideon, 'How did you find Fiona?'

'It's a long story, but as I told ... my aunt ...' he shook his head, closing his eyes for a second, 'it is strange to be able to say that.'

Joe indicated towards the seats and they all sat down again.

Gideon composed himself. 'Where to begin? My great uncle,' he started, falteringly, 'became friendly with an officer on the ship which brought them from Scotland. Mercifully, that officer spoke the Gaelic, for it was the only language my family knew. My great uncle beseeched him to find out what had happened to my grandmother when he returned to Glasgow.

'You must understand, my great uncle was very distressed at having been forced to abandon members of his family. He had no choice because my grandmother was fevered and the Captain denied her passage. My father told me the ship's officer was as good as his word and made enquiries of the authorities in the city. When he next docked at Wilmington, he sent word that, as they feared, my grandmother's name was listed as having died that year, buried by the city in a pauper's grave.'

Joe glanced at Fiona. She had heard the tale earlier and remained silent, tears welling in her eyes.

'There was no information about my aunt. My great uncle died shortly after that, along with other members of our family in the terrible yellow fever epidemic. It was then that my father moved inland to Lancaster County. Life was hard for him but he never gave up hope of finding out what happened to his sister.'

'Is your father still alive?' Joe asked, gently.

'Yes, although he suffers with his joints and is scarcely able to walk this last year.'

'And your mother?'

'My dear mother died some seventeen years ago, my little sister also.' Gideon tilted his head back, unsuccessfully hoping to disguise his pain. 'Then there was just the two of us for a time until he married again; a pleasant woman who cares for him and helps to run the farm.'

Joe was very surprised. 'You are a farmer?'

The young man in front of him appeared more like a member of the gentry; sophisticated in manner, well-dressed and with smooth, manicured hands.

'My father is a farmer and I worked with him when I was young. I went to Sunday School with the other local children but it seems the minister decided I had a brain which should be encouraged. Whether that is right or wrong, who am I to say? Anyway, my father wanted me to 'make good', as he would tell me, not struggle and end up like him. So, when I was twelve, he sent me to school. First in Philadelphia,' he grimaced, 'a cruel, spartan establishment which I hated but its very horror inspired me to learn quickly in order to escape. Then, I was fortunate to be sponsored to attend the College of New Jersey at Princeton.'

He paused, expecting the name to excite a response but neither Fiona nor Joe knew the importance of the place.

'Anyway,' Gideon cleared his throat, 'you asked me how I found my aunt? I was sure that because my grandmother's death was recorded in the city records, and the last time my father saw his sister she was refusing to be parted from her mother, then the authorities in Glasgow would have taken her in.

'It seemed plausible? A starting place for my search? On arriving in Glasgow a few days ago, I lost no time in visiting all the hospitals and Poor Houses and enquiring to see their registers for the year and month of my grandmother's death. That was the one fact I knew to be true. Sure enough, there it was: child, orphan, Fiona MacDonald.'

Joe moved in his chair, crossing his legs and rubbing a hand over his mouth. Fiona lowered her gaze, knowing that if she caught his eye they would both break down.

Gideon carried on, but, acutely aware of their discomfort, he lightened the tone of his voice.

'Beside the entry was the date in October 1788 when she was apprenticed to David Dale at his New Lanark Mills.' He sat back, 'Of all the places in Scotland, New Lanark Mills are well known in the United States because of the philanthropist, Robert Owen, so I hired a horse and rode to the famous mills.'

'They ken Mr Owen in America?' Fiona was amazed.

'Oh yes, his essays are published in the main newspapers and magazines. I have read his New View of Society myself.'

Joe nodded, 'Well, that explains why we ha'e sae many American visitors in the village! Tell me, did the mill office say Fiona wis a Scott noo, merrit tae me, an' where tae find her?'

'No, sir, they asked me to return tomorrow when they will have retrieved the records of that era. We have young Lily and your own sister to thank for my presence in your house today!'

Beyond the windows, the setting sun was dipping below the horizon, colouring the sky with a crimson glow and turning feathery clouds to gold.

Suddenly realising how late it was, Joe stood up, asking, 'Where are ye lodging?'

'I was planning to find a room for the night in the town and possibly for the next. I was keen to spend as much time as possible on my mission, however, I must be back in Glasgow by Friday night.'

'Ye will stay here, Ah insist.'

Fiona was delighted, 'Oh aye, of course ye must! Joe, Gideon's travelling wi' men frae Philadelphia,' she pronounced the name carefully. 'They're oan their way hame after touring all roond Europe.'

'I am a journalist,' Gideon shrugged, standing up to address Joe directly, 'or I wish to be a journalist. At present I am acting as a clerk for two writers, a general assistant, you could say.' He straightened his jacket. 'Thank you for the invitation, I will gladly accept. Now, my horse. Please tell me the best arrangement and I will see to it.'

While the men were in the barn, Sarah and Mr Dudley arrived with the children and almost immediately, Donnie and Davey drove the new pony and cart into the yard.

This led to more introductions and joyful disbelief until Fiona chased Alex and Ailsa indoors and upstairs to bed. They were over excited, infected by the atmosphere of something out of the ordinary happening but not truly understanding the importance of the American guest.

Seeing them settled, Fiona stoked the range and placed the kettle to boil before standing at the door to watch the figures in the dusk. Behind her in the shadowy kitchen lay unwashed pots, pans, dishes and crumbs but, for tonight, she was blind to the clutter.

She feasted her eyes on her family.

Bats flittered over their heads and midges danced in clouds around the storm lantern over the barn door. It was cooler now, the air sweet with grass scented dew and wild honeysuckle.

After a chorus of 'cheerios', Sarah and Lily walked briskly away, escorted by Mr Dudley holding aloft a borrowed lantern.

'My brother's son, under my roof,' Fiona murmured to herself, 'whoever would have thought such a moment would come? Sometimes good things do happen, wishes can come true.'

***

Fiona woke very early the next morning, tip toeing her way through her morning routine in the sleeping house.

When Joe roused from sleep he saw her quietly styling her hair at the dressing table already dressed in her best outfit, the one she wore to see the statue installed.

'Ye no' wurkin' the day?' he asked sleepily.

'Did Ah wake ye? Ah could nae sleep an' got tae thinkin'.'

'See you, an' all this thinkin' ...' he chuckled, lying back on the pillows, memories of Gideon's arrival coming to mind.

'Ah should be wurkin' but if Ah ask Susan nicely, she'll tak ma place fur the day, Ah'm sure she will when she hears aboot ma nephew.' She pushed some more long hair grips into the tight braids wrapped around her head. 'Ah want tae be wi' Gideon while he's here.'

'The lads and Ah will come back a bit earlier t'nicht, an' all. Shall Ah ask Tam up?'

'Aye, an' Ah'll chap Rosie's door an' ask her too. She wis daen night shift yesterday but that wis the last yin fur a few days. Ah want her tae meet Gideon or she'd be awfy hurt.'

Fiona's arrangements went smoothly and at ten o'clock she was free to meet Gideon outside the Managers' office.

'The ledgers were very helpful,' he greeted her, 'Mr Dale ran a tight ship, as does Mr Owen.'

'Whit did they say aboot me, in the books?'

'They showed your change of name and an address in the Row. The next entry, which I admit was pointed out to me by the young clerk, may have been more difficult to find, but he knew you. In fact, he told me you were one of his teachers for years.'

'Oh aye, Ah've worked in the school e'er since marryin' Joe.'

'I cannot see you as a disciplinarian!' he narrowed his eyes, assessing his aunt. 'My recollections of teachers, both male and female, have not been good, traumatic, at times.'

'Och, we're no' like that here! Come an' Ah'll shew ye! Tell me, *a bheil Gàidhlig agaibh?*'

'*Tha, beagan,* but only a very little! My mother did not like it when my father taught me phrases, even he speaks American now, like a native.'

It was strange for Fiona to take the role of visitor in her own school. Her pupils gawped in awe at her stylish dress and upswept hair, telling her how bonnie she looked and begging her to bring the hat to class the next day so they might learn how to make the silk flowers.

With enormous pride, Fiona ushered Gideon slowly through the Institute's rooms. Together with a party of a dozen or so other visitors, they hovered beside work tables, watched dancing classes, and viewed an exhibition of well researched and identified exhibits of plants, rocks, drawings of insects and animals: all collected from the woods around New Lanark.

'My goodness,' Gideon enthused, watching a history lesson and seeing the children pointing out how one discovery in the world was made at the same time as certain rulers were in power or a natural disaster occurred.

'I like the way they keep the lectures short and encourage questions and debate afterwards to apply what they learn to their own lives ... inspiring. ' He was engrossed in the pictures on the walls. 'There are few books?'

'Mr Owen disnae want the bairns annoyed wi' books until they're aulder, the top classes. He believes there's plenty tae learn an' explore in the world aroond them afore that. Onyway, it comes oan gradually. The pupils learn their letters because they want tae write wee labels or find oot aboot a burd or tree, sae the learnin' comes naturally.'

'Ingenious!'

After showing him the new school building, they bought shortbread and wandered down to the lowest terrace to admire the river and the refreshing sight of Dundaff Linn.

Fiona poured out her story of the early years and her gratitude to Mr Dale. How she learnt the Scots tongue and met Joe, and his role in building the massive mills. Gideon was astounded and expressed an interest in seeing inside the buidings.

For the first time since leaving the factory floor, more than a quarter of a century earlier, Fiona entered the thundering noise of the spinning rooms. Breathing through her mouth to cope with the sweltering heat, a torrent of past images leapt to mind. She found it little changed, the air cleaner perhaps, but still with the distinctive aromas of lamp oil, grease from the machinery, lime and whitewash and raw cotton.

The tour drew to an end on a woodland path where they sat down on a bench overlooking the village rooftops.

'You know, aunt,' Gideon said quietly, 'when my father asked me to find you, he also asked me to bring you back with me, to Pennsylvania. He was tortured by thoughts of you being alone in the world. I will ask you, but only because I promised to do so, do you wish to come back with me to America?'

'Ye ken ma answer already, Gideon, but ye must thank yer faither fur makin' the offer. Ma place is wi' Joe, an' as ye can see, Ah live in the best place in the world.'

'Aha!' he laughed, 'with respect my dear aunt, you have not travelled, how can you say that?'

'Wi' confidence,' she replied with mock indignation. 'Ah dinnae need tae travel the world, the world travels here. Every day, Ah hear the cries o' the visitors. Ah've heard it called Utopia,' she patted him on the arm, catching his eye. 'Ah didnae ken whit the word meant an' looked it up. 'An ideal place where all is perfect, socially and morally', that's whit it said. An' that's whit it is.'

The evening of celebration was enjoyed by everyone, especially Rosie who took a shine to the good looking American and cornered him in the front parlour after their meal. Gideon admitted to Davey later that he found Aunt Rose, as everyone called her, intimidating.

'Aye, she has that way.' Davey looked fondly across the room at his diminutive aunt helping to clear the table. He felt protective towards the slight figure, straight and neat beneath her lacy cap and the wispy fringe covering the puckered scar across her brow. 'She's a tough auld burd but as kind as the day's lang. Ah grant ye, she can also be a nosey wee bisom at times!'

The newly found cousins talked late into the night, discovering differences and similarities in each others' lives and cultures: vowing to keep in touch.

On leaving for the Institute the next morning, Fiona said her goodbyes quickly. She knew her brother never learned to write nor read, except the very basics, and implored her nephew to write on his behalf.

'Here's a letter fur him, please mak sure some yin reads it tae him? And here,' as well as the letter she pressed a small cardboard box into his palm. 'There's a stane in there, a precious stane.'

Gideon put it in his pocket and took hold of both her hands.

'I saw your collection of stones,' he said softly, 'as soon as I arrived. You see, my father has the same. He keeps them in a pewter dish on the mantelshelf.' His words were husky, indistinct. 'He told me their story.'

Fiona's vision was misting, her chin crumpling. 'I wish ye a safe journey an' guid health.' She hugged him, squeezing him tight and knowing the affection was returned. 'Tell yer faither Ah love him, Ah alis will ... and tell him no' tae worry aboot me ony mair ... Ah have a guid life.'

Chapter Twenty

*"I have a long and arduous task before me to convince governments
and governed of the gross ignorance under which they are contending
against each other, in direct opposition to the real interests of both."*
Robert Owen

Much to her delight, Lily Rafferty was engaged as a junior housemaid at Braxfield House.

Miss Wilson placed her under Emily's guidance, allocating her a bed in the attic of the servants' wing. She would be sharing the low-beamed space with five scullery and laundry maids but was pleased to see they each had the luxury of their own mattress, set in sturdy wooden frames. She soon discovered they were not the only occupants, having a rustling bat roost at the east gable and noisy house sparrows and swifts beneath the southern eaves. Hanging from the highest timbers were the papery grey globes of old wasp nests and the other girls told her Miss Wilson needed to know straight away if they returned and the gardener's boy would see to them.

'Our new maid, Lily, is full of interesting little bits of information,' Miss Wilson reported to Anne Caroline, setting a fluted vase of pink and white roses on the mantelpiece.

'Did you say she is from the village?'

'Born and bred in New Lanark and a wee chatter box. My goodness, she's a clever lass. She's only been here a week and she's quite won over everyone downstairs.' The housekeeper smiled at a recollection. 'Her mother is the needlewoman, Mrs Rafferty.'

Anne Caroline looked up from the list she was compiling, amused.

'Of all the children in the village, who would have thought it? Mrs Rafferty was our housemaid in the village house when my father was alive.'

She loved having her husband at home so much nowadays but Anne Caroline was exhausted from the relentless bustle of organising Braxfield. Owen threw open his doors to everyone who showed an interest in his work which meant they were continuously hosting large numbers to the main meal of the day. The drawingroom was becoming more like a hotel reception area than a family home and with new servants engaged to aid Cook and Miss Wilson, it was a large household to supervise.

Sarah was cautiously pleased with Lily's new position. While she was relieved her daughter was no longer in the factory, she soon discovered the novelty of living alone was not to her liking.

'Rosie, how d'ye manage it?' Sarah asked her sister, meeting her in the street beside the water pump one blustery evening. 'Ah cannae thole it. Oors o' bein' alane, but ye seem content? How? It's no' e'en eight o'clock an' the light's gaun.'

'There's alis sumat tae dae in the hoose,' Rosie chewed on her gums, her few remaining teeth were causing problems. 'Or Ah gang next door an' play dominoes wi' the Carruthers or walk doon tae the Institute an' ha'e a chat wi' whoever's by the fire. If there's a body who's grievin' or poorly, Ah call in fur a wee blether. That sort o' thing.'

Sarah sighed, hauling her heavy bucket to one side, replacing it with Rosie's and helping to pull the pump.

'Ah'm no' sayin' it wis easy,' Rosie added, 'after Gerry wis taken, God rest his soul. Ah felt it bad. Ah could nae sleep nor eat proper an' sat aboot wi' ma dark thochts and self pity. It taks time tae adjust. Ye'll git used tae it.'

Their buckets filled for the night, they parted and Sarah trudged back up the stairs. Was this it? Her little room was neat and tidy, her second best dress hanging from the pulley, pressed and ready for the next day. It was oppressively quiet except for the distant murmur of voices from other rooms and occasional moans of wind in the casement windows.

By the morning, her mind was made up.

While eating their midday meal with the school children, she whispered her decision to Fiona.

'Ah'm gaun tae marry Mr Dudley.'

'Aw Sarah! that's wonderfu' news! When did he ask ye?'

'Och, he has nae asked me yit, but it seems the best thing tae dae.'

'Whit? He has nae asked ye? The twa o' ye ha'e bin courtin' fur years an' years ...'

'An' Ah've bin waitin' fur the richt time.' Sarah retorted, primly. 'That's Lily awa', an' Ah'm gaun daft alane in that room. Noo's the time. All he needs is a wee bit of encouragement.'

Fiona spooned down the last of the broth. 'Weel, if that's whit ye want, Ah wish ye success. Ah ken Joe wid be gie pleased.'

'Ye reckon?'

'Oh aye, he likes Mr Dudley.'

'Joe wid like ony body ither than Sean, isn't that the truth?' Sarah gave a rueful smile. 'That's settled then.'

When the forthcoming marriage was announced, Joe was, indeed, pleased.

'An' that's no' all,' Fiona told him, perched on the stool in his workshop having their evening chat, 'they're tae live in the Row, at Sarah's.'

'No' at Dudley's?

'He wis sharin' wi' anither man, big Charlie Forth, ye mind him? Cheery lad, bushy beard an' a wart oan his neb the size o' a conker.'

'Oh aye,' Joe murmured, not recalling him at all.

'He's a mill wright in Mill Four.' Fiona rubbed idly at a mark on her skirt, 'Ah'm glad they're stayin' at oor place. That's how Ah alis think on it, 'oor place'. That's where the bairns were born, weel, all but Alex. It's a special room that.' A wistful look came into her eyes, gazing at Joe. 'We spent oor first nicht t'gether there.'

He felt her watching him.

'Ye wee romantic, ye!' He teased. 'An' here's anither thing, there's ne'er bin ony body in there but ma family. It wis newly built when we came o'er fae Douglas. We were the first tenants.'

Fiona sat quietly, recalling moments from the past and suddenly Calum and Sionaidh were alive in her mind.

Wincing from the empty ache of missing them, loving them, she pushed her mind to a different subject but the memories swam back into view. Sionaidh as a baby, propped in the wash basket chewing a clothes peg, chubby and newly washed, lying on the old rag rug playing with her own toes. Cal sitting at the table, flicking his tangled fringe from his eyes, metal tankard in his hand.

Not wishing to spoil Joe's contented mood, she said nothing, but felt a change within her, a settling: coming to terms.

Telford's spectacular design for the three span bridge over the Moose river at Cartland Crags was nearing completion. The hours spent agonising over their estimate were paying off. Tam and Joe were quietly satisfied to discover Mr Minto was recommending them to his contacts for future work.

Yet, Joe's loan from the bank was a constant nagging concern. The interest rates were high and the spectre of Jim Calder's rapid descent into the Debtors' Prison made Joe determined to pay the money back as soon as possible. Having a steady income and more contracts lining up on the horizon, he decided to make large, regular repayments until it was settled.

An appointment in Hamilton was already arranged when Tom brought home a letter from the Master at the Grammar School.

Fiona and Joe read the contents carefully while Tom sat awkwardly on the other side of the kitchen table, picking at his nails.

'He says yer a bricht lad,' Joe told him. 'Ye'll soon be completing yer time at the Grammar an' ha'e passed all the tests and examinations wi' high marks.'

Fiona kept tight-lipped but her expression was full of motherly pride.

Joe was glancing at the letter while he spoke, 'He maks the suggestion that ye gae tae Glesgie University an' tak up medicine.' He laid the paper down and fixed his son with an intense, enquiring stare. 'Ah ken ye telt yer Ma and me ye had a notion tae be a doctor when ye were a bairn. This university learnin' ... it wid be hard, ye wid be awa' frae Lanark, livin' in the city. Is this whit ye truly want, son?'

'Aye, more than anythin', but, Ah ken it'll tak money, an' ye've already paid fur the Grammar. If ye can see yer way tae piy fur this, Da', Ah swear tae God Ah'll repiy ye.'

Fiona could no longer restrain herself, 'A son o' mine at the university! A doctor! Och, in the name o' the wee man, Ah'm the proodest mither in the land!'

To repay the bank or send his son to Glasgow University? The dilemma was short lived.

'O' course ye can gae!' Beaming, Joe reached across and clapped his hand on Tom's arm, squeezing it tight. 'Ye've done weel, lad, very weel. We are gie prood o' ye!'

***

The subject of repaying debts was also on Owen's mind.

Finally, a settlement had been reached with the dismissed manager of Stanley Mills, James Craig. Although he owed the David Dale Trust considerably more, a payment of fifteen hundred pounds was agreed to bring the matter to an end. Craig was incapable of paying more but remained at Stanley House while the mills lay silent, mothballed, mouldering.

On a more positive note, Owen had paid the full amount owing to Sir John Campbell of Jura and settled the unsavoury case with his old partner, Humphrys. The calamitous mismanagement of the David Dale Trust and the repercussion's of More's bankruptcy were also under control.

His fortune was now his own with no restrictions to save cash to cover those debts. It was a gloriously free feeling, especially as the mills continued to generate profits, making him a very wealthy man.

Owen's Report to Lanark was received well, with encouraging interest from the County Sheriff and a committee of six influential local gentlemen.

This time, Owen had laid out the Plan in close detail, showing how they would provide employment, education and give the residents self sufficiency in both food and income. He also addressed another issue which was currently high in the public interest: the value of currency.

The Bank of England's change in currency, from gold to using paper bank notes in 1797, was supposed to only last for six months beyond the end of the war. The war was long since over and the question of a 'standard value' was the topic of the moment

Owen argued, 'that the natural standard of value is, in principle, human labour or the combined manual or mental powers of men called into action.'

It was a fact, he pointed out, one which could be demonstrated, that the labour of a man was more than sufficient to maintain himself. It was also a fact that with the mechanisms and tools now available, that same man could produce ten-fold, even one hundred-fold: yet, people were starving.

Why?

392

If poverty was not created by any lack of production of wealth, it must be created by the means of circulating that wealth: the currency. The old, in many ways fairer method of barter was now discarded in favour of money. So, it stood to reason, it was the means of valuing money that was creating poverty.

These radical views were included in his report as he described the currency to be adopted within the new villages: labour notes.

For several years now, he had been following the progress of self sufficient communities and was heartened by confirmation of his own views. Harmonie, a successful settlement in the United States run by Reverend George Rapp, was an interesting example. Owen wrote to him, sending his essays and describing his Plan, requesting an exchange of useful information.

This correspondence with Father Rapp gave Owen further evidence that he was on the right track. Also, new methods in agriculture sprang to Owen's attention when an acquaintance in England invited him to inspect his land.

'You have every area of your Villages planned out!' Donald MacDonald congratulated him. 'From the schooling to the housing and natural pleasure gardens and now, even the way they till the soil.'

'Using the spade rather than the plough has been shown to give a higher yield. It is used to great effect in market gardening, indeed, it is considered the norm. So why would anyone not use it to feed their own families?'

MacDonald turned his hand from side to side, looking doubtful, 'It is very labour intensive.'

'And what is the major problem we are facing today?' Owen raised his eyebrows, 'Mass unemployment. Our other problem? Starvation. Both of these evils would be removed.'

'It certainly makes sense,' Donald agreed, 'but when did sense ever get in the way of the government controlling the people?'

While her husband pressed for the uptake of his Plan, Anne Caroline made the most of the time he was at home. Their elder daughters were taking a keen interest in the village, especially in the classrooms.Their local tutors were becoming redundant and Anne Caroline asked for recommendations from friends to find a boarding school to further the girls' education.

Owen was a firm believer in girls receiving a sound education. He was closely acquainted with many clever, capable women, particularly amongst the Quakers, like Elizabeth Fry. It was borne out again and again that an educated woman was just as competent and capable as a man under the same circumstances. He was very much in favour of his daughters, like his sons, expanding their knowledge and gaining experience of life.

A girls' school in leafy Russell Square in London was thought to be suitable, under the tutelage of Miss Whitwell. They would not be too far from their Aunt Mary, now the mother of two little boys. Also, the Walkers, home from Switzerland, extended an open invitation to the girls to visit Arnos Grove whenever they wished which gave comfort to Anne Caroline when she bid farewell to Ann and Jane.

However, in a surprising turn of events, within a few months of them arriving, Miss Whitwell was so taken with all she heard and read of Owen's school that she decided to travel north and teach at New Lanark. Arrangements were hurriedly changed and the girls moved to Miss Vates' care at Cannonbury House.

It took the household at Braxfield a while to adjust to the absence of the older Owen girls and Miss Wilson shared her mistress's unsettled feelings. It was hard enough without the boisterous energy of Robert Dale and William bounding round the house.

Now, the high ceilings and panelled corridors also lacked the giggles, singing and girlish chattering voices of Ann and Jane.

Apart from Mary's laboured efforts when her teacher came to call, the piano lay covered in a lacy cloth, providing a surface for flower arrangements. The harp, a favourite of Ann's, gleamed invitingly but silently beneath its daily polish.

David and Richard were calmer in nature than their older brothers which came as a relief to Miss Wilson after Robert Dale's youthful escapades. Although they rode their ponies and played with the dogs and cats in the stableyard, climbed trees and gathered nuts in the woods in autumn, they went about these hobbies in a quiet companionable manner, little Albga trotting devotedly at their heels.

It was Mary who caused her mother concern. The little girl's pretty baby plumpness was deserting her but it was not her features, attractive or otherwise, which were a worry, it was Mary's frequent bouts of ill health.

Rosemary Pemberley comforted her friend by saying Mary reminded her of herself at that age, not yet into her eleventh year. She declared how sickly she was as an infant but it passed. The wonders of lightly applied kohl around the eyes and rouge to the cheeks and lips would transform Mary in later years.

The arrival in the village of the youthful Miss Whitwell caused quite a stir. She brought with her boundless energy and many talents. One being the creation of rolls of painted canvas depicting the Stream of Time. It laid out events, wars, monarchs and discoveries in chronological order. A firm line was drawn to mark the end of each century making it a superb and welcome tool for History lessons.

Unfortunately, her startlingly modern views on 'free love' were not so appreciated.

A year of boarding school was sufficient for Ann and Jane. They enjoyed the opportunity of meeting new people and gaining an insight into life beyond New Lanark. Dances, poetry readings, theatre outings (much discouraged by their mother in her letters) and days out in the country at Arnos Grove, all added experience to their previously very sheltered lives. They especially savoured sharing time with their Aunt Mary and playing with their little cousin David and baby James, but both were pleased to come home.

They returned with a more confident air about them, their manners and bearing having matured from childlike to accomplished young ladies. Ann, her hair pinned up under a wide brimmed, peacock feathered hat and turquoise riding habit, arrived home looking older than her seventeen years. It was only when she rushed to hug Miss Wilson and Peggy that her youth was revealed.

Soon, there was more rejoicing.

After nearly three years at Monsieur de Fellenberg's school, Robert Dale and William came home to Braxfield.

Spotting the yellow bounder from a window, Anne Caroline ran from the front door and embraced them the moment they climbed down onto the gravel.

'Let me look at you!' she cried, noting how lean and broad shouldered they appeared. Their unique features, so indelibly imprinted in her memory, were more defined; sharp, no longer boyish. 'Why you are men! Thank the Lord you have safely returned.'

They brought with them Charles Walker, one of John Walker's sons, who would be staying with them at Braxfield and learning the business of cotton manufacturing.

Receiving word of their arrival, Owen rode straight back from the mills, greeting them all with hearty hugs and calling for everyone to gather in the drawing room.

'I am sure we all wish to know your adventures,' Owen raised his voice over his chattering family, waiting for quiet to fall before continuing. His eyes were on Robert and William. 'Tonight is just the beginning of sharing recollections, there is no rush. From us all, Sheddon, Miss Wilson and the servants as well ... welcome home!'

The whole family cheered, reaching out to their oddly unfamiliar brothers to clap them on the back, give playful thumps on their arms, the girls giving them more kisses on their cheeks. Then the clamour of questions rose again.

The brothers took up a stance by the fireplace, telling tales of alpine walks, the beauty of the land and forests, swimming in ice cold lakes, singing hymns at the top of peaks.

'You don't speak as you used to speak,' Mary said pertly. 'You sound ... different, foreign.'

'That is no surprise,' Robert Dale exclaimed, no longer able to ignore Albga's appeals for attention and kneeling down to ruffle the dog's glossy coat and pull his ears. 'My, how Albga's grown! Will and I have lived, breathed, dreamt and thought in German for so long, it is hard to know we are Scottish.'

William was laughing, taking over from his brother, 'Robert even fooled a pipe merchant in Hamburg. The man boasted he could tell where anyone came from by their accent and placed my brother as German, more accurately, from Hanover! We admitted our homeland but granted him credit because many of our tutors were Hanoverian.'

Charles was settled into one of the larger bedrooms at the front of the house while preparations for a large family meal were underway downstairs in the kitchen. The steamy room was filled with servants. Miss Ramsay and Peggy were seated at the coolest end of the table, near the door, lending Miss Wilson a hand to make paper swan table decorations.

Her face a shining beetroot from the well stoked range, Cook was putting the finishing touches to sauces and checking the progress of two roasted legs of lamb: her maids scurrying to her orders. Through this crowd, a scrawny little scullery maid tripped to and fro on her bare feet, swamped by her over large cap and ankle length tunic. She had slyly perfected a way to carry away pots and pans to be washed whilst sneaking tidbits from the dishes already laid out on the table.

Into this bustle, Sheddon put his head round the door from the corridor.

'I must warn you, the family are retiring to change for dinner and the young masters are on their way downstairs ...' he dropped his voice to an urgent whisper, 'they are here!'

Robert and William strode into the kitchen. The servants jumped to attention, papers flying, aprons and caps pulled straight.

'Mercy!' Cook cried, allowing herself to be embraced, 'Ah wid nae ha'e recognised ye fae the scamps ye used tae be!'

Miss Wilson and Peggy were also caught up in affectionate hugs, crying out in embarrassment when they were lifted off the floor. It was a joy to have 'their lads' back and they scrutinised the men's faces as keenly as if they were their own sons.

Watching from the sidelines, Lily was overwhelmed by the sudden appearance of such fashionable, handsome young men. The Owen children had been present throughout her whole life, but were always known as distant, revered figures, usually with their mother at church or as tutors in the classroom.

Seeing them at close quarters she was taken aback by how tall and full of life they were with their white teeth, tanned skin and the easy, demonstrative way they showed their warmth to the servants.

Throughout the meal, snippets of the Owen brothers' travels were brought downstairs by the footmen serving the table.

Lily listened, awestruck. Not wishing to move from the kitchen in case she missed the stories, she declined having a rest before her later duties.

Instead, she made herself useful by trimming wicks and chipping away dripped wax from the servants' candles; one of the least favourite jobs given to the lower maids. Then, finding the special pan, she melted down these scrapings with the shortest stubs and poured them into moulds to set.

'On the way home, their boat wis caught in a storm,' a footman relayed, whisking trays of dirty crockery through to the scullery. 'They were crossin' the English Channel. Three times they were turned back an' neely ran agroond on sandbanks.'

On the next visit to the kitchen; 'Their teacher bought them a crereche? Ah dinnae ken that's the wurd but it must ha'e bin a gig o' coach o'some sorts. They used post horses tae pull it an' travel hame, hunners o' miles through Europe. Yin time, they pit the coach oan a boat an' floated doon the Rhine! They say the cliffs were as tall as Corra Linn, the gorge as narrow. Och, the masters had some trip!'

After clearing the table cloth and laying out fruit and nuts, they brought the next instalment.

'They stayed at a castle, wi'a Baron Munchausen?' the footman made a face. 'Dined in the garden yin day, they say, under a tree. An' when they dined in the hoose it wis at a grand table in a lofty hall, the ceiling as high as a church. The Baron an' his family sat at the top an' the servants *at the same table* ... at the ither end. Bye, frae whit he says aboot the Baron's dochter, it sounds like Maister Robert left his hairt wi' the lass!'

Lily lingered over her task until Sheddon appeared and the gossip was brought to an end.

What adventures! How exciting it was to work in Mr Owen's home. She couldn't wait to tell her mother on her next visit home.

***

The committee considering Owen's Report to the County of Lanark was presented with very good news.

Alexander Hamilton of Dalzell offered to lease the county up to seven hundred acres of land to build a Village of Mutual Co-Operation as laid out by Owen. This offer was received with gratitude, on the understanding that the decision would not be made until after further examination.

By the following summer the Plan was brought before the House of Commons once more and debated vigorously but, once again, the motion to pursue Owen's vision was lost.

This time, there were two main objections.

The first was gloomily familiar: Wilberforce, supported by Canning and Lushington, opposed the motion on the grounds of Owen's religious stance. They considered any new community to be created in the British Isles should be founded on solid Christian principles. Lord Londonderry, however, objected to it due to the paternal character of Owen's proposed government.

'Some people just do not *understand*.' Owen said solemnly, becoming used to the bigoted ways of the members of the establishment. 'They cannot grasp how a community can work together and enjoy the mutual benefits of their own labours. Paternal! Can they not see the whole essence of the Plan is to develop self regulating, co-operating villages without jails, lawyers or an over arching church!'

MacDonald grunted, his young face black as thunder. 'The irony, of course, is utterly lost on them! They call your ways Paternal, while you seek for people to work together to create good lives for themselves, under their own control. And these politicians would prefer to rely on the strict adherence to an all seeing, all knowing, yet invisible, Father: God.'

'However, there is a more sinister aspect, I fear, one which was made abundantly clear to me in Frankfurt several years ago.'

Captain MacDonald was interested, 'And that is?'

'A sumptuous dinner was thrown by Monsieur Bethman, a well known Frankfurt banker and he invited the secretary of the Congress, Monsieur Gentz. He arranged for us to be introduced. Now, Monsieur Gentz was in full confidence of the leaders of Europe. I told him that the means now existed for society, if founded upon the principle of union, could saturate society with wealth sufficient to supply the wants of all through life. Do you know what he said?'

MacDonald shook his head.

'The learnéd secretary replied, apparently speaking for the governments, "We know that very well, but we do not want the mass to become wealthy and independent of us. How could we govern them if they were?" Oh dear, Donald, I have a long and arduous task before me to convince governments and governed of the gross ignorance under which they are contending against each other, in direct opposition to the real interests of both.

'One day,' he clenched his teeth for a moment, deep in thought, 'they will see. That day will come when our children, our rising population, are raised free from prejudice and closed indoctrination.'

Although less frequent, Owens trips to London continued, as did the increasing flow of carriages bearing journalists, educators, intrigued professors, economists and concerned members of the public. As Owen lost allies in government, he gained them many fold in other walks of life.

An aspect which Owen found very satisfying was to see the personal interest his children were showing in New Lanark.

Robert Dale, William and Charles Walker were eager to learn the business side of the mills. They were taught not only the administration of gaining orders, finding and paying quality suppliers, managing the warehouses in Glasgow and running the workforce but the mechanics of the factory floor itself.

Owen knew the value of having firsthand experience of his trade and encouraged them to rise early and work alongside the employees. Many times, they would strip down to their shirt sleeves and crawl beneath a broken machine. When they reappeared after completing the job, their filthy, sweaty faces were radiant with achievement, earning them due respect from their colleagues.

They oiled wheels and gears, repaired and re-installed snapped leather straps and made replacements for sheared bolts. Kyle Macinnes was loud in his praise for the 'lads' when they visited his forge to be shown the basics of metal work.

For their part, Ann and Jane were no less involved, but in a different way. They joined their mother in her visits to elderly or bereaved residents, as well as calling in to congratulate new mothers or sit with the sick. Ann spent a great deal of time in the classrooms and took a special interest in pupils who showed real promise. After asking her father's permission, she offered private tutorials to these protégés at Braxfield, diligently conducting her lessons as if a trained teacher.

In the late summer of 1822, Owen was invited to tour Ireland. It was arranged by the Duke of Leinster, Lady Mary Ross's brother, because many of the Irish nobility and politicians wished to hear Owen's vision of a New Society and his Plan to eradicate poverty.

When Murdoch broke the news of another long spell away from Scotland, Emily was furious. They had two children now and she was not at all happy about being abandoned for months. So, when Murdoch packed his master's trunks, his wife's complaints were ringing in his ears.

Nevertheless, early on a dark autumn morning he climbed aboard the carriage and set off with Owen to meet the Mail Coach in Lanark where Captain MacDonald joined them on the trip. Armed with copies of Owen's essays and a large drawing of his planned villages, the little party set off to join their boat at Liverpool.

As usual, Owen left his agent, Clegg, and his managers in charge but now that his sons were there, he felt a weight of responsibility lift from his mind.

Ireland was in a terrible state, worse than the mainland. It sorely needed a solution to the crisis other than the one chosen by the tens of thousands leaving their homes and sailing to the New World.

It was several weeks later, while Owen was in the south of Ireland, that a situation arose concerning one of the children at the Institute.

Ann was very fond of one of the pupils, a pretty little girl called Margaret, who came to her at Braxfield for extra lessons.
On discovering the child's mother was removing her from school and sending her into the mills, Ann became very concerned.

'She has such potential to rise in society!' Ann told her family one afternoon at their main meal, 'is there nothing we can do?'

Anne Caroline knew of the girl and shared her daughter's disappointment.

'If she is ten years old, Ann,' she said reasonably, 'this is the age a child can enter the mills. I daresay her family require the money.'

'That is as maybe, but she is much too clever to be a mill worker ...' Ann's features were downcast. 'Her manners and her sweet, witty intelligence, they will be lost in the rough labour on the factory floor. She is special, Mama, I am sure you have seen it for yourself.'

There was a general murmur of agreement round the table. Despite being a dozen years her senior, Robert Dale had noticed Margaret from the first time she came to church with her family. The mother was a striking woman, slender and graceful with the complexion and refined features more expected from aristocratic breeding. Her daughter showed even more promise and if there was ever to be a beauty at New Lanark, surely Margaret would grow up to take that accolade.

As Ann rightly pointed out, the little girl's spirited intelligence singled her out from the crowd as much as her lovely face and shimmering hair.

Ann would not give up so easily; 'Even in Papa's factory, the harsh routine of mill work will crush her. It will take away all her ambition and her parents will deny her any further education to better herself.'

'Well, that cannot be helped, my dear,' her mother told her again. 'If they wish her to earn for the family then that is all there is to the matter.'

Ann pondered on the problem and the conversation moved to other topics between the others, until she burst out, 'We could adopt Margaret!'

'I cannot imagine your father would wish another child,' Anne Caroline chortled at the notion. 'While it is common knowledge that he dearly loves and shows great affection to all the village children in his care, he has seven of his own.'

'We could ask him when he comes home,' William said, sensibly.

'That would be too late. Father will be in Ireland for months to come and Margaret will reach ten years in a few weeks.'

'You could write to him?' Robert suggested, 'he can only say no?'

Ann returned a shining smile, 'Oh yes, I shall write to him! I shall pray to the Lord for Margaret to become a member of our family.'

Anne Caroline was neither pleased nor displeased. A lingering sensation of nausea had been plaguing her, on and off, for weeks, leaving her tired and uncomfortable. The meal was nearly over and she looked forward to retiring early so she brought the conversation to a close by wishing her daughter well in her mission.

Anne penned a sixteen page letter to her father and entrusted it to Dunn the postman. Eventually, she received a reply and ran from room to room telling her mother and all her brothers and sisters in turn.

If Margaret's parents were agreeable, Owen would adopt the girl into his home to be raised as part of his family.

***

In New South Wales, west of the Blue Mountains, the rolling plains of Bathurst baked in the sun; a haze smearing the line of the horizon into cloudless blue sky.

Shielded from the heat under her tattered straw bonnet, Ruth Scott threw a wheat sheaf up on to the wagon. This was her third attempt and seeing it settle firmly into place she enjoyed the satisfaction of completing a full load. Their mule dozed in the shafts, occasionally shaking its head to dislodge a cloud of flies.

It was very quiet, barely a breath of wind, just the bleats of sheep in a distant pasture, the buzzing of flies and the rustling of her feet when she walked on the dusty ground.

Flicking wisps and seeds from the loose sleeves of her smock, she retrieved a covered basket from a patch of shade beneath a group of trees. Gurgling noises told her the baby was waking but he was a peaceful child.

She laid the basket carefully on the driving seat and clambered up beside it, wincing as something jabbed her hand. Finding a sharp husk embedded in her scratched, calloused palm she drew it out with her teeth and spat it out before taking hold of the hot wooden handle of the brake.

'Ah'll tak this load in tae the barn!' she called, her voice thin in the void above the yellow stubble.

Sam looked up from sharpening his scythe, shouting back to her to take care and wiping sweat from his face with the back of his hand.

Waving in reply, she flicked the reins several times, calling abruptly to the mule before it lumbered forward.

Sam's light hair was now long, bleached white and falling around his shoulders; he carried on swinging the blade methodically through the remaining patch of golden stalks. He kept glancing towards the rocking pile of wheat until she was safely up the incline, between a stand of leafy trees and disappearing from view behind their timber steading.

This was a good day, not too hot nor wet, if they kept up the hard work the harvest would be collected by night fall. Connor was checking the sheep with the help of their four workers but they would be back within an hour or so. The farm labourers were emancipists who he took on two years ago and were proving to be reliable; keen to return to normal life. The sheep, along with fruit trees and crops of soft fruit, were a new addition to their farm and one which they were assured would reap benefits. He hoped so.

Life was tough and bleak at times, but he never doubted it was the best decision he had ever made. Now that the basic house was built, a structure he knew his brother Joe would probably condemn on sight, Sam felt more secure. The first years almost broke his marriage, but they were through that and since Joseph was born the companionship was returning to their relationship. He knew from other settlers that women complained when there was no water, no stove and the same monotonous food rations for months on end. Perhaps Ruth was not so bad. She worked beside him, sometimes tight lipped and sullen, sometimes angry and tearful but never blaming.

Connor, on the other hand, was in his element. The once slightly built, shy child had grown into a well muscled, confident young man, taller than his father, as dark in colouring as Sam was fair and as strong as an ox. He was also proudly determined to make a success of their new lives.

Sam only had to look at his son's face to know he had done the right thing. Why had he put it off for so long? He asked Ruth this question one evening whilst sitting outside on the wooden porch watching the sun set.

'It wisnae the richt time.' She said simply, nursing Joseph. 'There's a time fur everything, an' this is oor time tae mak the maist o' life. Fur all the grief an' trials this adventure has gi'en me, Ah'm thankful te ye, Sam, an' yer sons will be thankful. This land

404

has opportunity for their futures. Ah wid despair bringin' a bairn in tae the world in the old country, but here, their life's their own.'

***

The Irish embraced Owen's New View of Society and after six months of hospitality, private meetings and dinners in his honour, the tour culminated in a meeting at the Rotunda in Dublin.

Like the preceding meetings in London at the City Tavern, thousands of people flocked to attend. Amongst the audience were the earl of Meath, Lord Cloncurry and a number of clergy.

Owen spoke boldly of bringing their suffering to an end. By creating Villages of Co-operation, his Plan would vanquish the starvation and poverty presently killing their country.

They did not need to wait for Poor Relief from a government hundreds of miles away across the sea, they would build their own self sufficient communities with their own hands. Feed and educate their children under their own control and by applying his methods for the Formation of Character, happiness would abound.

His long speech, nearly three hours, was accompanied by outbreaks of spontaneous applause, and although the Lord Mayor, chairing the proceedings, was moved to call for order occasionally, it was in good spirit. In the discussions at the end, it was members of the Protestant Party who put forward objections, declaring his Plan was immoral in its tendency, contrary to revealed religion and generally subversive to the established order.

However, their voices were in the tiny minority and such was the uptake of people wishing to hear Owen's views, more meetings were held. His speeches were reported in the broadsheets, the *Evening Mail* and the *Patriot* and MacDonald noticed the attendance of journalists from the *Dublin Report,* a substantial pamphlet, taking copious notes when Owen spoke.

At the fourth meeting, a more private affair, the Hibernian Philanthropic Society was formed. With strong support from Sir Frederick Flood, Sir William Brabazon, Sir Capel Moyneux, General Browne and many other members of the higher social circle, Owen's plans were showered with subscriptions. This money would be used to buy the necessary land and materials to start the remedy to Ireland's ills.

By the end of the meeting, bank notes covered the secretary's ledgers and scores of influential names were added to the list of subscribers.

'It went exceedingly well,' Owen said pensively, looking out the carriage window to a soft spring evening. He was driving back to Lord Cloncurry's city house with Captain MacDonald. 'We will see what the government has to say? Surely, with such obvious and fervent support, they cannot block this remedy any longer?'

It was David Ricardo, the economist, who received the memorial from the Hibernian Philanthropic Society. He was chairing a Select Committee to consider the employment of the poor in Ireland and read how Owen's Plan was receiving tremendous support from that area of the United Kingdom.

Ricardo mused on the subject for a while, conferring with colleagues. Perhaps they should consider Owen's Plan again in close detail.

Owen came back to Braxfield to find New Lanark buzzing with visitors and Abram Combe in the throes of starting up a cooperative business in Edinburgh. The excitement of this excellent news was compounded by Clegg's announcement that, at last, a buyer had been found for Stanley Mills. The purchaser was James Buchanan, a cousin of Kirkman Finlay, in partnership with gentlemen from Glasgow.

So, Owen was in a buoyant mood when he broke the seal on a letter from David Ricardo.

It stated how they appreciated Mr Owen's suggestions to create 'establishments of good education and early moral habits,' but the Committee was not of a mind to recommend them further. They felt the society he was proposing, one of equality and mutual co-operation, was too far removed from the established way of things and could only be seen by the eyes of a visionary.

Owen was politely requested not to present his Plan before the House of Commons again.

***

406

For a few days after this final rebuttal from the government, Owen was quieter than usual. He attended to paperwork, inspected the accounts with the managers and could be seen walking slowly, purposefully, around New Lanark.

Over the winter, Robert Dale had taken a deep interest in the school and was compiling a book on the revolutionary new techniques his father was applying in the classroom. Owen visited the classroom, discussing his methods with his son, always with a ready smile for the children and no hint of ill humour, but his family knew he was hurt.

As was his way, Owen soon left his disappointment with the government behind. The tragic news of the untimely death of Alfred Walker, one of John and Sarah's younger sons, brought his priorities clearly into focus.

The capricious nature of Life was too precious to waste. He was past his half century and there was so much he needed to do that he would not be diverted from his Vision.

He took heart from the extremely supportive comments he was receiving daily from visitors and in letters from abroad and delved into making further improvements to the methods of teaching. One of his changes was deciding it would be more beneficial to the children's general knowledge to study geography instead of reading the Bible. Within days, this perceived blasphemy was relayed through the local grapevine to Reverend Menzies.

Seizing on this 'outrage', the local ministers called an emergency meeting and soon the Glasgow Chronicle was declaring that Owen had 'banned the Bible' in New Lanark.

William Allen and his Quaker partners were alarmed and a deputation was sent to speak with Owen and discover the truth.

'This is nothing but a malicious exaggeration,' Owen told Allen calmly, standing at the side of the Institute's largest classroom. 'See here, the Bible has not been banned. It is still read throughout all the classes. However, if these children are to learn useful knowledge during the short time they have in the school, a firm grounding in geography, history and the natural sciences will be more applicable in later life.'

Allen appraised the tunic clad students, noting the bare legs and feet, the familiar way boys and girls mingled around the work tables.

'I have mentioned it to you before, Mr Owen, there is not enough emphasis put on their religious instruction. Furthermore,' his mobile features and inquisitive eyes were searching across the room, 'these pupils are almost indecently clothed! It cannot be right for members of the opposite sex to be so ... naked while in physical contact! The dancing ... there is too much dancing! No ... No, Robert Owen, there must be changes made if I am to continue to be associated with this establishment!'

Owen argued his point of view throughout Allen's stay at Braxfield but to little avail.

'You are a brilliant businessman,' Allen said solemnly on their last morning together, 'of that there is no doubt. In spite of the disastrous market conditions over the last ten years you have consistently turned a profit. Even in '21 and '22, gracious, those were terrible years, yet you have given us a clear 15% on our investments. I congratulate you. But, and with this I am *adamant*, there must be greater attention paid to the word of the Lord and, I insist, the children must have different uniform.'

Shortly after Allen's visit, two separate publications by local gentlemen came to the fore. Stirred by Owen's Report to the County of Lanark and encouraged by certain members of the local clergy, these works were antagonistic towards his claims for bettering New Lanark. Their authors, the Reverend Aiton and William McGavin, told of workers leaving for Blantyre and Catrine mills where conditions were just as good, they said, and wages were higher.

They celebrated the previous benevolent owner, David Dale, whose evangelical religious beliefs had provided the village with comfort and schools long before Owen arrived.

Coming thick and fast, so many rejections and criticisms would have caused most men to give up their crusade: not Robert Owen.

'Robert, my dear,' Anne Caroline, appealed to him, while walking in the garden one morning. 'You have a fine and profitable cotton mill, the best in the land, I am told. Your Institute is a most stimulating and enjoyable school for the little ones, is this not enough? We have this lovely home,' she waved towards the colourful herbaceous borders and riotous rose arbours, 'the grounds are as lush as even Lady Mary's at Bonnington. We must thank God for all we have, be satisfied to have our healthy family and a good business to provide jobs for those less fortunate. May the Lord have mercy on us that we should wish for more when others crave a fraction of our happiness.'

Her arm was tucked under his and he squeezed it against him, affectionately, softening what he was about to say.

'I do not wish for more for myself or for you and our family. We have made our contented state ourselves, through our own hard work. It is the plight of those who do not have a say in their fate which drives me to do more.'

'Oh my dearest, if you would only allow God into your heart! I have prayed for so long for you to accept the Word of Our Father as the Truth. It is your hard line against the Church which wounds and alienates others, do you not see? Please, my dear, can you not believe, as I do ... as you did when you were young? I know you were a devout Christian many years ago, let Him soothe your soul again?'

'You speak of God as others speak of Mohammed or the Pagan's speak of the Spirit of the Earth. I have no tolerance of blind faith, for they all require *faith*. I sincerely believe there is some creator or supreme being but who that might be or where or when such an entity will be revealed is not known; neither to you or me.'

'If you acknowledged the presence of God, surely you would find peace and those who attack you so viciously would have no fuel.'

'Oh, Caroline, what you ask is impossible. I cannot give lip service to something which I simply do not believe.'

They walked on in silence, just the gentle swish of her hem on the grass and daisies underfoot and a blackbird's melodious song from his perch on the summer house roof.

After a while, Owen said, 'A minister said much the same thing to me, ye know. He told me the village of New Lanark and my Plan were perfect but for one thing, I had not founded them on Christian beliefs. I asked him if he knew of any other such happy community run by the Church and he admitted that, no, he did not. And there, my dear, lies your answer.'

Anne Caroline did not pursue the subject. She was watching her husband receive blow after blow, being held up to ridicule and his work picked apart and smashed. Her prayers became more fervent,

409

asking God to save him from himself and let the family live quietly, pleasantly doing their good work at their mills.

Towards the end of the year, Dr Gibson was called to one of the rooms in Double Row.

The superintendent for the stairs, a blousy widow with five children in the mills, met him at the street door holding a flannel to her nose.

'It's Dougie Maxwell, doctor, taken bad, he has. Ah can hear him moanin', terrible it is.'

It did not take long to make a diagnosis: typhoid fever.

'Are you *sure*,' Owen asked, 'typhoid is spread amongst the filthy and unwashed, as I understand? It is one of the many reasons why I insist on a high standard of hygiene and regular inspections.'

'There's no doubt, sir,' Gibson said firmly. 'Complaining of a headache, severe stomach pain and showing confusion. In Dougie's case, more than usual. There are a few livid pink spots on his chest, once seen, never forgotten; the tell tale marks of typhoid fever. The whole tenement must be scrubbed with hot water and sand, every article of clothing, cooking utensil, the water buckets ... the handle of the water pumps ... everything that the infected person may have touched must be thoroughly scoured.'

'I will give instructions immediately. Is Mr Maxwell the only victim?'

'So far. If this dirty disease was to be found anywhere here, I am not surprised it is at Maxwell's door. The rest of the residents are more diligent in their cleaning habits so we can be hopeful of containment.'

'It cannot only be spread by slovenly hygiene. My good friend, John Quincy Adams, lost his mother to this foul disease just a few years ago. What are the chances of survival?'

'Not good. Maybe one in five succumb but we are learning to flush the body with plenty of water, the patient must be encouraged to drink at every opportunity. I shall make sure they are nursed adequately and hope this is not another epidemic.'

Having prided himself on the cleanliness of his village, Owen's critics were delighted to throw this latest piece of bad luck in his face. He took it as he took all their insults, by giving them the response he felt they deserved; none. He was not going to waste

410

time explaining the possible causes or trying to mitigate his responsibility. It had happened; he was dealing with it.

Along with the other housewives in the village, Sarah, Cathy and Rosie set to work with boiled water, sand and scrubbing brushes. It was a nervous, harrowing time but in the end there were only three cases, all in the same stairwell.

The mild autumn moved into freezing winter mornings when the window panes were decorated with icy fern patterns, lasting until after midday. The old folk relaxed, mumbling wisely that the cold would kill the disease, cleanse the evil humours from the air.

Sitting in his study with the muffled sounds of New Year merriment beyond the closed oak door, Owen forced himself to sign a letter of agreement with his partners. This laid out their requested changes at the school, as raised by Allen in his visit.

The present teacher was to be replaced with one trained in the Lancastrian system, more religious teaching must be included in the curriculum and less dancing, in fact no dancing was to be taught at the company's expense. There was to be no singing, except psalms and all the boys over six years old were to wear trousers.

It was not what he wished to have happen, not at all, and he paused after dipping his quill in the ink. This was a major setback to his New System. His methods worked, they brought immense benefits along with the dancing and singing and combined with the practical, engaging lessons in geography, history, mathematics. He felt the oppressive shadow of religious bias from his Quaker partners blocking his vital basis of giving useful knowledge and social tolerance to the rising generation.

His Vision was losing ground.

As soon as the worst of the winter weather passed, Owen and Robert Dale travelled to London. Owen was rallying again and felt the desire to be amongst like-minded colleagues.

Ironically, given the changes which were being forced upon the village school, Robert Dale's little book on New Lanark's education system was newly published and provoking a lot of interest. To the young man's surprise, Jeremy Bentham read the book and asked Owen if his son would care to join his *symposium*, meaning his seven o'clock meal, that evening. This was a rare honour because, beyond a small circle of close friends, few people were asked to call at his home.

Owen was already committed that evening so, nervous and excited, Robert Dale crossed the dark London streets alone and duly turned up at the respected philosopher's door.

There was a gathering of four or five others invited that evening and Bentham kept them entertained with his views on principles and morals. When the manservant informed them dinner was served, Robert was taken aback by what he found in the large, high ceilinged dining room.

A sturdy platform ran down the centre of the room, raised two feet above the floor, allowing a passageway three or feet wide all round the outside. On top of the platform stood a dining table, laden with filled platters and lit by several elaborate candelabras. The table was surrounded by chairs and at the furthest end stood a large screen, shielding Bentham's seat from any draughts.

Nonplussed, and taking his lead from the others, Robert Dale stepped up to take his seat. The meal was delicious and the wine flowed freely, all accompanied by lively debates and fascinating insights into utilitarianism from the great man. Eventually, when the cloth was drawn, they relaxed with recharged glasses, sharing the use of engraved nut crackers to enjoy walnuts and hazelnuts.

In mid sentence, Bentham reached for the bell cord dangling at his side, summoning his butler.

'John, my marmalade!' he then smiled to the company, 'that Scotch marmalade is an excellent digester. I always take a little after dinner.'

From the hallway, a clock chimed the hour and Robert Dale became aware it was growing late. He did not wish to outstay his welcome, knowing at least one of the other guests, an American author, John Neal of Maine, was staying for the night.

Bentham tugged the bell pull again, this time calling, 'John, my night cap!'

Robert Dale folded his napkin and made to stand up.

'Ah!' Bentham drew a black silk cap over his head, his long grey hair lying limp around his shoulders. 'You think that's a hint to go? Not a bit of it, sit down! I'll tell you when I'm tired.' He grasped the arms of his chair and stood, 'I'm going to vibrate a little, that assists digestion too.'

412

For a full half hour he proceeded to walk briskly back and forth on the lower dining room floor, his head at a level with the seated young men. Earnestly, Robert Dale and the others twisted and swung in their seats to keep their eyes respectfully on the curious, black capped figure. All the time, Bentham regaled them with a very witty and erudite story of kings, priests and their retainers. Even when his 'vibrating' was completed, the party continued until midnight.

'Sir, I cannot thank you enough for such an enlightening and entertaining evening,' Robert Dale bowed as he took his leave at the door.

'God bless you ... if there is such a being.' Bentham raised a hand in farewell. 'And at all events, my young friend, take care of yourself.'

Chapter Twenty One

"Man is the creature of circumstances." Robert Owen

The Scotts were finally enjoying a contented period in their lives. Fiona had received several letters from Gideon relating news of her brother and she, Rosie and Sarah kept up a regular correspondence with Sam. Their far flung family seemed closer and in being able to share their lives through writing, they found a new peace. Even Stephen was now sending messages to his mother, causing her tears of relief.

In late May, in the warm peace of Anne Caroline's little upstairs morning room, Sarah knelt on the floor pinning up the hem of her employer's new day dress. The latest designs required a corset to nip in the waist, even on someone as slender as Mrs Owen but the overall effect was very becoming.

Miss Ramsay was sitting on the window seat using the bright daylight to sort through varying shades of ivory kid gloves. A breath of air filtered through the open window bringing with it the clicking, chattering of nesting swallows and distant hammering from the farrier in the stable yard.

Sarah pushed herself up from the rug, 'There now, Mrs Owen, whit dae ye think? A little shorter? or are ye happy wi' that?'

Anne Caroline was about to answer when the sound of hurrying footsteps caught her attention. Men's voices floated up from the hallway. She recognised her husband and elder sons', Clegg's and another, indistinct but with the rapid flow of urgency.

'It will be perfect,' she murmured to Sarah, troubled by the sudden commotion. 'The fashion for showing too much stocking at the ankle is not one I wish to entertain, I shall leave that to the younger set.'

Sarah knew she was referring to the high spirited Irish girls staying with Lady Mary Ross at Bonnington. The youngsters from the two big houses were on very friendly terms and she saw their frequent comings and goings from her workroom window.

As soon as Ramsay assisted her into her clothes for the day, Anne Caroline turned to Sarah.

'That will be the last fitting?' she asked.

'Aye.' Sarah dipped a curtsey, seeing the distracted look on Mrs Owen's face. 'It'll be finished an' brought up tae ye t'morra.'

'That will do nicely ...' fussing with the gold cross and chain at her neck, Anne Caroline hurried downstairs, knocked gently on Owen's study door and entered.

He was standing with his back to her, looking out over the garden.

'Is something amiss, my dear?' she asked, concerned when he didn't turn to see who entered the room.

'I have received bad news.' He remained facing away from her, 'my dear friend John Walker has died.'

She laid a hand on his shoulder, searching for words of comfort. She knew prayers would mean nothing to him in this time of grief.

'John understood what I was doing.' he said, gruffly. 'He was as much a devoted Quaker as Allen, yet he knew my wishes for the children's happiness ... supported me in my work. Of all my partners, dear John did me the honour of showing respect to my methods. Oh, what a joy it was to spend those weeks in Europe in his company; his expertise with the German language in Frankfurt was invaluable. And such warm hospitality in his house by the lake ... and walking in the woods at Arnos Grove. What treasured times we shared.'

Anne Caroline's own, brief, acquaintance with Mr Walker was enough to cause a wrench in her heart on hearing the news. How dreadful for his wife, Sarah: widowed just a year after losing a dear son.

'How terribly sad. I will write immediately. Poor Charles,' she had grown fond of the young man during his months in her home while learning the cotton trade, 'to lose his father and brother.'

Owen nodded, realising other implications to the business; after himself, John was the largest shareholder.

All that could wait, for now. He was stricken with the heavy sadness of knowing he could never see nor speak to his close friend again.

***

415

'Whit's he like?' Sarah asked Fiona on entering the Institute to prepare for her sewing class.

'The new teacher? John Daniel?' Fiona waggled her head from side to side. 'He's no' as friendly as Buchanan an' no' as quick witted as Murray but, och, he's nae sae bad.'

'Ah heard tell he wisnae gaun tae be havin' the dancin' in the mornin', but the last few days Ah've seen it as usual frae ma windae.'

'Aye, Ah ken Mr Owen has had a wurd wi' him. There's tae be less dancin' through the day, but, if yesterday wis onythin' tae gae by, things are just aboot the same.'

Along with several dozen tourists, there was another new face in the school room that day.

The important visitor was being given a personal tour by Robert Owen. He was a strongly built gentleman, past his fiftieth year, with a round cheeked avuncular face, rolling Ayrshire accent and deeply tanned skin.

Known internationally as a leading geologist, William Maclure had just returned to Britain after several years in Spain. He was very wealthy, having made the bulk of his money in his early years by trading goods to and from America and now indulged his personal interests and travelled the world as he pleased.

His most recent project was to set up an agricultural college near Alicante, but the establishment failed and he was heading back to America, his adopted home.

'Your school is superb!' Maclure enthused when he and Owen walked back up the hill to Braxfield. 'I see many similarities to the methods prescribed by my friend Johann Pestalozzi.'

'You know Pestalozzi?' Owen laughed, pleased with the connection. 'I had the pleasure of meeting him a few years ago at his school in Switzerland.'

'Aha! A splendid fellow.'

'I have always been of the view that children should be treated kindly and with respect from their earliest years, views I was delighted to find are also held by Pestalozzi.'

'Learning through doing, actually *applying* knowledge, teaching in a way that is tailored to the rate of each child's ability to learn, that is the answer!' Mclure glanced at Owen, catching his eye and seeing the same spark of understanding he felt himself. 'I must

416

have visited Yverdun half a dozen times! Fascinating results. I put finance into a school in my own home town of Philadelphia to bring this method of education to America.'

'Sir, you consider Philadelphia your home? I believed you Scottish!'

'Oh, aye, I'm Scottish. Ayrshire born and bred but back in the late 90s I made America my home. I'm a citizen, ye know? An American!'

'And your school in Philadelphia?'

'I brought a brilliant teacher over from Paris, Professor Neef who put the methods in place. There is also a delightful young lady, Madame Fretageot, who is a member of the Owenite Society over there. She is a strong advocate of your Essays.'

Owen knew of the society but was, nevertheless, very gratified to hear of it from the mouth of this eminent traveller.

Maclure paused, 'I am fascinated by the new ways of educating our young. You have thriving cotton mills, Owen, and having read your radical papers on communities, it is heart warming to see their embodiment in a living, working village.'

After dining, Robert Dale and William were included in the men's discussions in Owen's study where laughter and loud, genial exclamations could be heard.

Anne Caroline saw little of their house guest over the three days he was staying. On his arrival, a Friday, Owen whisked him away to show off the mills and school rooms. On the Saturday, although it was raining heavily, they left the house before she was dressed and returned just before dinner, leaving little time for social niceties in the drawing room before Sheddon rang the gong. The next day being a Sunday, she declined her husband's eager invitation to take a drive over to Bonnington House and walk to see the Falls of Clyde.

'It is the Sabbath, Robert,' she reminded him, 'I shall be attending church with the household and then spending the day in devotions.'

'Caroline, the Falls will be spectacular! It rained all of yesterday and most of the night. Imagine how wondrous they will appear?'

'Go, if you must.' She hid her displeasure in the pretence of looking for something in her dressing table drawer. 'I trust you will not be disturbing Lady Mary? You may not hold the Lord's day in high regard but there are many who do.'

In the end, Robert Dale and William joined Mclure and their father, proudly showing off the newly washed Clydesdale countryside from Owen's carriage. Mindful of leaving the Lockhart Rosses undisturbed, the coachman drove them to the back of Bonnington's walled garden, just a few hundred yards from the gorge.

'My word, would you smell that perfume!' whispered Maclure, climbing out the carriage and breathing deeply. 'Takes me back to my childhood in Ayr and walks with my parents. Elderflowers! Meadowsweet! Oh, the sweet Scottish air! I have spent too long in Alicante where it is burnt out and prickly by the end of May.'

'Listen,' said Owen, 'apart from the noisy family of woodpeckers above us, what do you hear?'

The roar of the river crashing over Corra Linn was already loud and, on approaching the little Pavilion, the party were forced to raise their voices to be heard.

'Well, I never!' Maclure exclaimed, hands on hips, surveying the foaming mass of water cascading down the cliff into the swirling pool below.

'Forty years ago ... this is the sight which inspired my father in law to build the mills!' Owen shouted over the tumult, droplets of spray settling on his hat and shoulders, glistening on his eyelashes. 'A brave and fine decision!'

His sons exchanged glances, leaning close together to agree the enormous impact which that one decision had made on their lives. They spoke in German, as they often did between themselves since their time in Hofwyl.

That evening, Anne Caroline heard Maclure's vivid descriptions of the waterfalls at the dinner table. She was pleased to find him so impressed with every aspect of New Lanark, including the villagers' allotments and woodland paths, but it still rankled that this frivolous sightseeing took place on a Sunday.

When the meal was finished, she excused herself and went upstairs to her own sitting room. Taking her Bible, she sat by the window. It was at times like these when she missed her dear father the most.

Down in Owen's study, the French doors were open to the terrace and Maclure was enjoying a lively debate on community living.

'Thinking of your Plan,' Maclure slid down comfortably in the armchair and stretched his legs, 'for the Villages of Mutual Co-operation? Do you know of the Shaker settlements in America?'

'Certainly. They are immensely successful, as are the Moravians.'

'And the Harmonists, Father Rapp's community on the Wabash River.'

'Oh yes, I have enjoyed a correspondence of views with Reverend Rapp. Indeed, an agent of Rapp's is coming to visit me next month. After ten years in the one place, the community is thinking of moving on, many hundred of them, I believe.'

Robert Dale was listening attentively and put in, 'Although, I understand they are against the, er, natural laws of reproduction. I would have thought that by its very nature, to encourage celibacy can only lead to a dwindling population amongst their followers.'

'I read somewhere that children are adopted into the community,' William said, 'or they would not last long.'

'The Amish have large families,' Robert Dale mentioned, remembering facts from a pamphlet he read in Hofwyl.

'Oh yes, the Amish.' Maclure mused. 'Living in Philadelphia and travelling throughout Pennsylvania, one sees a lot of Mennonites and Amish trotting about the place in their little black buggies. Extremely successful groups, they are too.'

It was dark when they left the fireside and bid each other goodnight, disappearing off to their rooms with candles. The house was sleeping, apart from Sheddon and Lily who stayed to attend to any requests.

'Straight up to your bed, now,' Sheddon told the housemaid, covering a yawn. 'Miss Wilson will be needing you at six, Mr Mclure will be leaving tomorrow and the Mistress wants an early breakfast laid out for them and a fire set in the diningroom. I know, it may be July, but she felt it was too cold this morning.'

Lily pattered up the stone back stairs and then, grasping the hand rails, on up the steep wooden ladder to her attic room. There was no need for a candle, the moon was nearly full, shining its white, ebbing and flowing beams through the skylights.

419

Being careful not to wake the other girls, she pulled the covers tight up around her chin, murmured the prayers her mother taught her and fell asleep.

***

Less than a month after William Maclure drove away from Braxfield House, Owen watched the fluttering manes and bobbing heads of a pair of horses drawing a bright yellow post chaise up the driveway to deliver another house guest.

This was Richard Flower, the agent sent by Father Rapp to speak with Owen, all the way from the United States.

The house was already busy with visitors, including another American, an aspiring portrait artist, Chester Harding. Owen introduced them as the two passed in the hallway, mentioning they were both a long way from their homeland.

'And a pleasure it is too,' the exceedingly tall young artist beamed, 'especially visiting your mills on this fine summer day, Mr Owen.'

Flower responded more curtly, 'Perhaps I should say, England is my homeland.'

An awkward silence followed and Owen showed the traveller through to the study.

Assessing the stocky middle aged man, he put him as being a little younger than himself, educated, but although well dressed with a fine wool jacket, silk cravat and quality leather boots, there was the roughness of a farmer about him

'You are English?' Owen asked, he had been expecting an American.

'I am, sir, but I left these shores to find a better life six years ago.'

'And have you found it?' Owen took his seat on one side of the empty hearth and indicated to Flower to sit opposite.

'It is certainly a different life, with abundant possibilities, unlike here.'

'You have come from Harmonie on Father Rapp's behalf but am I right in believing that you are not from that settlement?'

'Oh, no, indeed, I am not from Harmonie, I am not a Rappite.'
Flower gave a half smile, showing obvious gaps in his discoloured
teeth.

'You must be on close terms with Rapp to travel abroad on his
business?'

At first, Flower was reticent, weighing up the calm, collected
cotton baron and his elegant home with servants and luxuriant
gardens. As he talked, he began to relax, recounting the fortunes
and misfortunes which brought him to Owen's door.

In Sheddon's unobtrusive way, he arranged refreshments to be
served, hovering behind the footman assessing the needs of his
master. Platters of cold cuts, fruit and cheese, with a jug of
lemonade were laid at their side, later, as the sun dropped lower
and long shadows spread across the lawn beyond the window, a
tray of coffee and shortbread.

After the war, when Britain was plunging ever lower into a
financial depression, Richard Flower's son, George, had decided to
sail to America. Although not rich, he was educated and fortunate
to have useful contacts, carrying with him letters of introduction to
many influential Americans. His own forceful personality and
desire to settle in their country led to him staying at Thomas
Jefferson's residence at Poplar Forest, with Dr Priestly on the
Sasquahana, General Andrew Jackson in Nashville and many other
leading men.

While in Philadelphia, young George heard his friend, Morris
Birbeck, was in also in America, widowed and bringing his two
sons, two daughters and servants to make a new start.

The two men met up and decided, together, to 'go west' and
form a community. There was land to be had cheaply in Illinois so
they headed up the river and eventually settled at Boultenhouse
Prairie.

Richard Flower was keen to impress on Owen the trials his son
endured and how desperately hard frontier life was for new
settlers.

'In the winter the ground is hard as iron and can be buried deep
with snow for weeks on end, the river solid and clogged with ice.
In the summer the heat is fierce! One hundred degrees at times!
The air so damp and hot your shirt is soaked with sweat within

moments of putting it on your back. These extremes take their toll, especially on the women and elderly.'

He went on to tell how Birbeck and his son argued over a lady, which although Owen was too polite to press for details, was obviously, now, his visitor's daughter in law. In due course, Birkett moved away and began his own community, Wanborough.

Four years earlier, Father Rapp had formed Harmonie, just twenty five miles away across the Wabash river from where Flower started his settlement.

'It took two years of back breaking labour for George to build housing for us and sow a decent crop, but then he returned to England and we all went back to what is now called Albion.

As he spoke, Flower was scrutinising Owen's unruffled manner and became apprehensive that he was not describing the difficulties in adequate terms.

He leaned forward, jaw jutting out, 'The western frontier settlements have been literally *hacked out* of the forest.' He used his large, calloused hands expressively. 'Doctors, medicines of any description are just ... not there! We found a great deal of practical help from the Rappites, they are a resourceful and very hard working group.'

Owen stood up and wandered round the room, listening to Flower and acknowledging, posing questions and gathering information.

'And now,' Owen stopped beside the fireplace, one arm on the mantelshelf, 'Father Rapp wishes to move on, to build a new town and transfer his entire population to this new location?'

'He does,' Richard Flower took a deep breath and stood up, looking eye to eye with Owen. 'He has expressly sent me here to offer you the opportunity to buy the whole township. The buildings along with thousands of acres, including forests of good timber and five hundred acres of cleared, cultivated arable land with vineyards. Also, working mills and a substantial granary. He wishes to sell it *all* and believes it would be a proposition you would take seriously.'

When Owen and Flower finally emerged from the study Captain MacDonald was in the drawing room with the older Owen sons and more than a dozen visitors. Immediately, another intense discussion on the sale of Harmonie ensued, with even Harding, although a virtual stranger, imploring Owen not to be hasty.

That evening, Anne Caroline watched and listened as if caught in a nightmare. Her husband could not seriously be thinking of leaving their beautiful home and their hard won security to venture into the wild west of the New World?

By the following morning, the topic was still burning brightly. Owen, Robert Dale, William and Flower spent several hours in deep, concentrated conversation.

'Well, Robert?' Owen suddenly asked, 'what is it to be? New Lanark or Harmonie?'

Without a moment's hesitation, his eldest son replied, 'Harmonie.'

***

'Ye'll ne'er guess, no' in a million years!' Rosie shouted, rushing up to Sarah in the shop. 'Ah've jist heard, Mr Owen's gaun tae America!'

'Naw! All that way? Whitiver fae?' Sarah carried on pinning a paper pattern to a large square of red velvet.

'Tae buy a new toun! Wurd has it, he's gaun tae set up business o'er there!'

'As if he's no' busy enough here,' Sarah tut-tutted, her spectacles slipping down her nose when she leaned forward. 'Ah'll need tae ask Andy tae bend the legs o' these sae they hook roond ma ears better.' She pushed them firmly into place and bent to her work, her mind on the recent news from Cathy: a baby was on the way.

Disappointed by the cool reaction, Rosie hurried off to find someone else to tell.

Murdoch was dismayed by the news of Owen's plans to travel to north America. Emily would not be pleased to hear he would be away, perhaps for months, on the other side of the Atlantic Ocean. She was already making noises about not being happy, wanting to leave Braxfield and find positions for them both in a smaller, simpler household. Perhaps run an inn together?

As expected, Emily flew off the handle.

Crying and thumping her way about the tiny cottage, she accused him of not caring for his family, selfishly seeking adventure on the high seas and leaving them to fend for themselves. Witnessing their mother's rage, his little daughters joined the din and Murdoch retreated.

Knocking tentatively on the butler's door, he enquired, 'Mr Sheddon, sir, may I ha'e a wurd?'

When he heard the valet's problem, Sheddon could only, reluctantly, accept his resignation.

'You leave me and your master in a very precarious position.'

'Ah ken that sir, but Ah ha'e nae choice.'

'Before you married Mrs Murdoch, you told me your loyalty lay with Mr Owen. Now that appears *not* to be the case.'

'It's mair the bairns, sir. Ah cannae tell ye how it grieves me ...'

Sheddon could see his distress. 'Very well. I will inform Mr Owen. Unless you would like to do that yourself?'

'Ah'd be gratefu' if ye could dae it?'

'You will stay until a replacement is found, is that understood?'

'Aye, sir, thank ye, sir.'

Murdoch left the room and wandered miserably outside.

He loved Braxfield, he loved working for Mr Owen. What was he doing? Leaving such a position to go, where?

He went back to Emily and in an expressionless voice, told her that they would be leaving Braxfield as soon as a new valet was secured. For a moment, there was a victorious spark in her grey eyes then it changed to an altogether different emotion, reflecting his own: fear.

In the weeks before Owen was due to leave, Captain MacDonald and Archibald Hamilton were his close companions. They saw this move to America as the dawning of a new age, taking Owenism away from the rural backwaters of Scotland and placing it on the world stage.

Inspired by this enormous change, Hamilton renewed his contact with everyone who previously subscribed to building a Village of Co-operation on the banks of the Clyde.

'It is going well, Owen,' he told him, suddenly vivacious. 'I have a purpose, a true, good purpose! We shall build a Village at Orbiston as outlined years ago in your Report to Lanark. It was so well supported and my father was amenable to supply the land.

When you come back, you will see buildings in place ... your Vision brought to life!'

Captain MacDonald was also thrilled by the prospect of actually putting into practice a complete, populated Village of Cooperation.

'Come with me, Donald?' Owen suggested, brimming with enthusiasm. 'We worked well together on our last adventure around Ireland. What say you to joining me on this voyage?'

'Oh, most certainly!' MacDonald cried, 'Capital idea! Absolutely capital!'

Early, on a clear sunny morning a few days after making the momentous decision, Owen sought out Robert Dale and asked him to take a walk with him in the garden.

'Robert, this trip I am making, it is to test the water.' He gave a rueful, lop-sided smile, 'even I am not mad enough to buy a place unseen. If it is as Mr Flower has stated, then, yes, it is a tempting proposition, *but*, of course, I am not committing myself until I have inspected it myself.'

'Of course not, Father, I am sure no one thinks you would do that.'

Their footsteps left a path among the dewy petals of red and white clover as they made their way towards a bench.

Owen flicked away some fallen petals and sat down; his son joined him.

'New Lanark is a shining example of what my methods can achieve,' Owen said slowly, 'but now, I want to do more than run a business. I want to show the tremendous benefit to Man my methods can produce. You have seen the mill's accounts yourself, this is a thriving factory. Robert, I need you to stay here.' He saw the disappointment widening his son's eyes, the pupils dilating in disbelief.

He continued, talking to him as an adult, imbuing his words with the emotion he felt rising within him. 'I will take William with me.'

Robert's eyes flickered up to make contact then dropped.

Owen placed a hand on his son's back, 'You are my eldest son, I need you here to oversee the mills, oversee the school and, please, look after your mother and younger brothers and sisters while I am away.'

Rooks circling overhead and passing bumble bees replaced their words, filling the uncomfortable silence between them. Robert Dale leaned forward, holding his head in his hands, his fingers rubbing at his temples.

'You are old enough to know what needs to be done,' Owen said simply. 'The voyage alone is weeks long and goodness knows how easily I can be contacted over there?

'How long will you be away?'

'Truthfully, I have no idea. If Harmonie is not what I want, then, I may return almost straight away. If I *do* want to acquire it, maybe four ... six months?' he turned on the seat and looked directly at his son. 'Robert, if this is all I hope it is, I will return and we will *all* go back. It will be our new home. One way or another, we will all be together again soon.'

Robert straightened his back, suddenly resigned to his position and realising the trust his father was placing in him.

Breaking the news to his sons was one thing, dealing with his wife's emotional outpourings was quite another.

Anne Caroline became very distressed. No matter how many times she told herself that this voyage to America would be the same as her husband's other trips, she remained filled with terrible apprehension.

Praying zealously for him to reconsider, she spent hours on her knees beseeching God's help to save her husband's soul and allow him to be content with his current life.

In the days before his departure, Braxfield was busy with visitors eager for an appointment with Owen before he left and friends wishing him a safe journey. There never seemed a quiet moment for husband and wife to be alone until late at night.

Weary from entertaining strangers and organising the household, this was when she was at her lowest ebb; teary and fearful.

'Caroline, my dearest wife,' he cajoled, putting his arm around her and cuddling her against him as they lay in bed. 'There is no need for you to be so distraught. In no time, I shall be home again.'

'Will you? And then what will happen? You are searching for your Utopian dream and yet, for me, it is *here*, now. This home with our children around us ... I want for nothing more.'

'We have always been honest with one another, Caroline, that is why we are so close. We do not need to be physically side by side to know the strength of our bond. I cannot *unknow* what I know, and I have complete faith in my conviction of raising the next generations to form rational, kind individuals to bring an end to the war and greed we see in the world today.'

She was calmer, listening, watching every minute change in his expressive eyes.

He rearranged his position, looking directly at her, 'If there is the opportunity to free the world from continuous suffering, I cannot and will not stop pursuing my New System. Please understand, when I travel it is from no lack of love for you or the children, it is simply to progress my work.'

'Dearest Robert, I have been foolish wishing to keep you here in our country idyll. I see it now, clearly. Yes, you must do whatever is necessary to spread your vision and I shall pray it brings the relief you desire to those less fortunate.'

He held her close, 'I will come back, my dear, you know I will. If I *do* buy Harmonie, I will come back and take you over there, just as soon as I can. You and the children and Albga ... the servants too, if you would like?' He tried to make her smile, 'and perhaps the horses? There are many who take their horses and carriages across the sea, why not us, eh?'

'Your brother, William,' she murmured, 'he went to America and we never heard from him again.'

'We did not part on the best of terms which may explain his lack of contact. I am sure he is safe and well, living the life he wished to have with his new wife.'

Drained from weeks of anxiety, exhaustion eventually claimed her and she fell asleep in his arms.

Lying in the quiet, dark bedroom, Owen realised he was now older than his brother had been on their last meeting. Strange. He recalled thinking it brave for a man of nearly fifty years to venture across the Atlantic in search of a new life. Yet, here he was, at fifty three years of age, considering the same prospect.

On the banks of the Delaware river in the Catskill Mountains, William Owen had indeed created a new, satisfying life for himself. It was very different from London or even Newtown, but there were lush pastures for grazing livestock, rich soil for crops on the flood plains and mills along the waterside giving abundant opportunity to settlers. As well as his wife Dinah, with her two

427

boys from her first marriage, and their own son, William, two more children had been born, Thomas and Mary.

Risking the great adventure to the United States had served William Owen well, now it was for his younger brother to cross the ocean.

***

On a wet September morning, Owen departed for London. He had business to attend to and friends to see before heading up to Liverpool where they would board the packet ship to New York.

The weather did little to raise Anne Caroline's spirits. Praying to God for strength, she donned a brave face and placed her fate in the hands of the Lord to bring him safely home.

Sheddon was pleased to have procured a new valet at such short notice, a clean cut young Prussian by the name of Charles Schmidt. He came with excellent references, although, Sheddon confided in Miss Wilson, only time would tell whether the engagement was permanent.

The servants gathered in the hall, Miss Wilson and Ramsay standing stiffly, side by side. Both were aware of their mistress's unease and had tried their own ways to soothe her through the morning.

In varying degrees of excitement and sadness, Ann, Jane and Mary clung to their father, Margaret standing quietly at his side, eyes as wide as an owl. They were scared of the thought of the sea voyage and recalled stories of the wilderness of the inner states of America.

'Come now!' Owen told the assembly, 'we shall not be gone long. Let us leave on a happy note, with smiles and excitement for what the future will bring.'

Richard and David, urged by Robert Dale, gave a resounding cheer which was half-heartedly echoed by their sisters.

'Look after yourselves!' Owen's flushed face radiated goodwill, his gaze lingering on the faces of his loved ones. 'I will think of you fondly and often! Until we return ... farewell!'

Swiftly, aware of her barely concealed anguish, he kissed Anne Caroline's cheek and hurried out to the waiting carriage, William striding behind him.

Chapter Twenty Two

"But deep this truth impress'd my mind:
Thro' all His works abroad,
The heart benevolent and kind
The most resembles God"
Robert Burns

On a cold afternoon in early November, Robert Owen, William and Captain MacDonald braced themselves against the wind to stand on the deck of the packet vessel.

'New York!' William whistled, his hair blowing this way and that, gripping the icy rails for balance.

Land was looming up from either side and in the distance spiky outlines of sails and rigging stood out, showing where ships swayed at the quayside. William dashed a hand over his eyes and licked salty droplets from his lips. It was difficult to make out the scene drawing nearer. Slowly, staggering slightly on the heaving deck, he began to make out movement on the shoreline below a mass of buildings, misty with smoking chimneys.

'America!' Donald cried, 'a welcome sight after weeks on end of nothing but water!'

Seagulls screeched over their heads, joining the tapping and clattering of the sails on the three great masts and the shouts from sailors hauling on ropes.

'We have arrived,' Owen grinned, lashes lowered against the rush of air: savouring his first sight. 'Now, let us go below and allow these men to take us safely to the wharf.'

To their delight and amazement, the party discovered Owen's fame had preceded him. From the moment they walked down the gangplank onto the dock, they were greeted by the Mayor and journalists and agents for leading members of society, showering him with invitations.

Businessmen, bankers and private individuals from many walks of life were keen to meet the well known philanthropist. Over the last six or seven years, vivid descriptions of his cotton mill village had often been printed in newspapers and journals. New Lanark was held up as an example of financial success, humane conditions and revolutionary educational methods in a spectacularly beautiful setting. For the coming days they were wined and dined, attracting great attention as word spread of Owen's charismatic personality and enlightened views; not to mention the fact that he was an exceedingly wealthy man.

When Owen declared a desire to visit other communities and cotton mills before setting off for Indiana, arrangements were made to sail up the Hudson River on the steamboat, the *Hudson*. From Albany, a carriage took them to Niskayuna, a Shaker settlement, where Owen alighted with a bounce to his step: his first opportunity to see this kind of self sufficient township for himself.

Low clouds allowed little warmth to reach the men standing in the chilly air, but they were cordially greeted by a young man, a Shaker. When Owen explained his interest in the town, they were offered a tour. It soon became clear that their guide's simply fashioned attire of a warm brown wool knee-length jacket, dark breeches and a wide brimmed felt hat, was typical of almost all the other male residents.

William was intrigued by what they called the 'family' houses. These large timber or brick buildings, called North, South and West each held a self contained group, using three floors for living space, a basement with the kitchen and an attic.

'It seems a bit of a rum do,' Donald murmured to William as they left the North house and headed towards the white painted Meeting House, 'keeping men and women apart like that? A wing for each sex, with separate staircases? Even eating at separate tables?'

William raised an eyebrow and grimaced before assuming a bland smile, ramming his hands in his pockets and following his father across the muddy village square.

After being shown a small tannery and a broom making workroom, they entered another long, low ceilinged workshop where the highly commercial seed packaging business took place. Signalling the end of their experience, they were led into the cemetery where they came to a halt beside an engraved headstone.

'Here lies our Mother Ann,' the young guide said, solemnly. 'She came from your country, from Manchester. It was Mother Ann who started this town and the United Society of Believers in

Christ's Second Appearing. She taught us the true, pure way of celebrating the Glory of God and preparing for His reappearance.'

Politely, Owen thanked their guide for his time. He expressed how interesting they found the town but there was little time to linger in the freezing temperatures and the whirlwind tour must continue.

Due to Owen's profession, American contacts insisted he visit cotton mills at Watleswan and the Glanham wool factory before boarding the *Chancellor Livingston* steam boat back to New York.

As they chugged downstream, Owen and MacDonald discussed the Shaker settlement.

'Although it was a small place, there were upwards of two hundred and eighty people living there,' Owen said thoughtfully. 'As we saw, they can build houses and feed and clothe themselves adequately from their two and a half thousand acres.'

'And run small industries, covering many skills. I was impressed by the sacks of seeds!' Donald agreed. 'It was a thriving community.'

'Why do they call them Shakers?' William asked.

'It is a rather derogatory term, in my opinion.' Owen sipped his coffee, pleased to find it luke warm. 'You remember the Meeting House, their Church? The large space at the front without pews? That is for them to stand and sing and dance during services. They become quite carried, swaying and apparently moving their arms a great deal, shaking, if ye will. I have not seen it myself.'

William listened as the conversation turned to the need for similar settlements but without any religious restrictions; open to all. He watched the winter landscape drifting past the portholes, warm in his seat in the large public cabin off the lower deck. His toes and hands were tingling with feeling again, his stomach full with roasted pork and mashed potatoes. He was enjoying the experience, especially travelling by water. In order to reach the city in good time, the party were forced to take several different boats, William's favourite being the *Keat*, a large double-decked vessel.

He thought of New Lanark and it seemed very far away. Would there be snow on the ground? Would the Clyde be running high and all the mill wheels spraying water from below the village? Images played in his mind: his mother reading her bible by the fire in her little study, his sisters playing the piano or helping in the

431

school, Sheddon decanting the wine in the pantry, perhaps taking a surreptitious sip? Cook huffing and puffing over the range, Robert running the mills.

He did not envy his brother that chore. He shuddered, what a responsibility.

A fortunate aspect of his fame allowed Owen to receive letters wherever he was staying, merely addressed to Mr Robert Owen, New York. In this way, correspondence arrived daily, begging a meeting or inviting him and his party to dine or join them in their box at the theatre. It was not long before Mr Flower wrote to him, wishing to meet them in Philadelphia as soon as was practicable.

Within days, they were with Mr Flower who brought the news that Reverend Rapp was determined to sell Harmonie at the New Year, even if Owen did not wish to buy it.

This spurred them on, but Owen wanted to visit William Mclure's school in the city and wished to introduce himself to Madam Fretageot. He recalled that it was this lady who first drew Mclure's attention to his essays and that she was also trained in the teaching methods of Pestalozzi.

In the event, he did not need to seek her out. No sooner were they in Philadelphia than he received a letter from Marie Duclos Fretageot inviting him to a meeting of the city's Owenite Society.

'Monsieur Owen!' a vivacious young woman ran towards him as they entered the meeting, her brown eyes shining, 'Oh, how I have wished to make your acquaintance ...' the soft French accent caught his attention, 'and now you are here!'

Owen bowed, realising this must be Madame Fretageot.

'And there are so many others who wish to meet you!' she continued, nonchalantly flicking back dark curls escaping from her neatly pinned hairstyle. 'Come! Now, where is Monsieur Troost, he is an ardent follower and is planning to create his own Owenite community...' she ushered him into the throng.

Before making the journey to America, Owen had known of this Owenite Society and the encouraging response to his views, but suddenly he was among enthusiastic, highly intelligent young people. Many were also members of the Academy of Natural Sciences of which Mclure was the President.

Owen took a moment to absorb the scene around him.

The men, some loud and expansive others shy and thoughtful, with their colourful waistcoats and loose cravats, fashionable dark trousers looped under their shining shoes. He saw the perfumed ladies, young and old, in their rich jewel-coloured satins and silks, fur stoles draped over their shoulders, hair swept up with ribbons. They were more forthright in manner than in Britain, with their adornments of jauntily placed, decorated combs and silk turbans, their intense, questioning expressions, the spontaneous bursts of laughter and rapid, confident exchanges.

These were the people who actually *grasped* what he was trying to do: this vibrant society could be his hope for the future.

Five days after arriving, the Owen party was away again, rattling and bouncing along pot holed roads in the stage coach from Baltimore to Washington.

When they entered the capital city, William was astounded at the lack of buildings. The fellow occupants in the carriage were residents of the United States and were unconcerned, having visited before, but the Scottish contingent wiped the mist from the windows and peered out in disbelief.

Streets and buildings were only shown merely as markers in the grass across acres of open land dotted here and there with clusters of trees. Houses, great sprawling mansions and neater, symmetrically designed brick buildings, were set a quarter of a mile apart with hardly a horseman or carriage to be seen.

At least, William observed, the elegant Capitol building was complete, repaired and renovated since the damage wrought by the British during the war.

Owen's old friend John Quincy Adams, now Secretary of State, was delighted to see him, introducing him to Crawford, the Treasury Secretary and ensuring he attended an hour long private meeting with the President, James Monroe.

Having been the Secretary of War whilst Britain and America were engaged in battles, Owen had read a good deal about William Crawford and found him to be a pleasant, if reserved, gentleman.

The President gave an imperious first impression. James Monroe was tall and suave, his dark hair slicked back from a high forehead, his chin slightly raised over the starched white cravat. However, within minutes, he was more forthcoming, establishing an easy

433

rapport and expressing his interest in Owen's essays, several of which he had read.

'I am Scottish by descent,' Monroe laughed, 'with a little French thrown in! I have heard very encouraging reports about your mills in Scotland and your methods of teaching. Your concept of a New Moral World is exciting, Mr Owen, please keep me up to date with your plans on this side of the Atlantic!'

Finding a great deal in common, not least a detectable, but unspoken, leaning towards Deism rather than restrictions of an established Church, Owen left the President's company in high spirits.

Mindful of their mission, it was soon time to leave the refined society of Washington and journey on to Pittsburg.

In company with Mr Flower, they hired three hackney carriages, one for the Flowers, one for the Owens and one to carry the luggage. They set off over rough, muddy tracks, at times dangerously narrow and cut into the sloping hillside. Wearily, they drove through Pittsburg and arrived at Economy, the half built settlement where the Rappites intended to move their entire Harmonie population.

At last, with Mr Flower making the introductions, Owen met Father George Rapp.

In appearance alone, the self-styled prophet stood out from the other men in the room. Tall and straight backed, his black garbed figure belied his advancing three score and ten years. The top of his head was covered by a close fitting black cap, from under which flowed white hair and, growing beneath the line of his chin, a long white beard.

In recalling that first meeting, William and Donald agreed it was not so much the black robe or comparatively startling white hair which remained vivid in their mind, it was Rapp's eyes: pale, icy blue.

Father Rapp immediately drew Owen away from the main company and they sat at a small table set aside from the dining table. There, they fell into a long conversation.

Flower, with William and Donald, were pressed to take dinner with Rapp's friends. The evening passed well, sampling and enjoying Harmonie wine and helping themselves to the array of tasty, filling food.

Surprisingly, given their completely different backgrounds, Owen and Rapp got on very well. They stayed at Economy the following night as well, allowing a full day for the two leaders to discuss common points in their differing philosophies and share like minded views on communal living.

Now, to sail to Harmonie and see the place for themselves.

After the luxury of hotels and comfortable hospitality in private homes, the party was thrown into cramped conditions. Climbing on board a little steam boat, they found themselves closely confined with other travellers, including women and fractious young children.

It was bitterly cold on deck, although those who purchased a cheaper ticket had no choice but to sleep beneath the stars. Owen and his group were housed in the low ceilinged space below deck. A wood stove inside the canvas roofed cabin made the atmosphere stuffy and uncomfortable. Adding to the discomfort, from time to time dense clouds of steam escaped into the boat, alarming all on board. Berths were few and the mattresses laid down each night in every space were soon occupied. While Owen was offered, and accepted, a berth, William and the younger men were forced to sleep under their great coats.

With heads and joints aching, they steamed steadily at 9 or 10 knots deeper into America: past Cincinnatti, past Louisville and, with a change of vessel at Shippingport, on up the river. To William's utter disgust, he mistakenly opened a wrong door and discovered by chance that this boat also contained a hold filled with forty seven black slaves. Chained together, their soulful white eyes glowed from the darkness: they were being taken to be sold

On 15th December, they watched Evansville pass by and later, as darkness fell, they moored at Mount Vernon and spent the night at the James Hotel.

Now so close to Harmonie, they were eager to make the last few miles to their final destination and rose early to indulge in a hearty breakfast. Owen procured two wagons, each drawn by four horses, and all the trunks and belongings were loaded and arranged to form seats.

When the entourage was setting out, a woman was riding the same route and Owen, preferring to walk than ride in the jolting wagon, accompanied her for a few miles. She knew Harmonie and told him she often bought provisions from the Rappites but didn't like the place because 'they did not allow marriage'.

After a clear start, clouds began to spread across the sky, but they took away none of the enjoyment of admiring the foreign undulating countryside. It was not an arduous drive, with only a few steep hills for the wagons to negotiate. Flashes of brightly coloured woodpeckers caught their eye, soft calls of turtle doves and melodic whistles of unknown species rang out from patches of woodland.

Owen and William, both knowledgeable in the native plants and wildlife of their homeland, pointed out new species to one another. Small furry animals with bushy tails scampered in the bare branches of beech and ironwood trees, running up and down the trunks with ease. These were obviously squirrels but larger than the red ones in Braxfield's woods and their coats were a soft grey, their ears without tufts. Even the golden, fallen leaves beneath oak trees, although confirmed to be oak by Mr Flower, were formed differently, with sharper points.

'What a strange, wonderful new world,' William mused, humming to himself with pleasure and pointing out a group of sheep grazing nearby.

It started to rain as they approached the township of Harmonie; heavy drops in the still December air. Shelter was required so, seeing a sign stating 'Private Entertainment' on a large house on the main street, Captain MacDonald made enquiries and discovered it to be a lodging house.

'We only put that up on the sign so we can turn people away if we don't like the looks of them!' the owner said cheerily. 'You seem all right to me, come in out the rain. There's veal to eat if you are hungry?'

The dinner was plentiful and to Owen's liking: simple and nourishing. News of their arrival spread quickly and they were no sooner finishing the food than Reverend Rapp's adopted son, Frederick, came to greet them.

It soon became clear that Frederick, a man of Owen's generation, took charge of the business side of Reverend Rapp's ventures.

The rain clouds were passing, leaving a dull but fair afternoon and when Frederick offered to give them a tour of the town, they readily accepted. The streets were laid out in a grid pattern, lined with log cabins and painted timber or brick houses of differing sizes, each surrounded by a garden space with fruit trees. There were also two large churches, built back to back. One was of timber construction, painted white, the other, a much bulkier building, stood wide and solid in brick and mortar.

Frederick was an attentive guide, explaining enough without burdening them with too much information in their first hours in the settlement.

Unlike New Lanark's steep cobbled streets, the ground was almost flat, taking little effort to walk the entire circumference of the town. There was a small cotton mill, a wool mill, and a flour mill all driven by a steam engine with a large brick granary close by. Being accustomed to the energy of the river Clyde to drive all the machinery, another point which caused much laughter was to find the cotton spinning jennie were driven by a horse and a cow walking on an inclined plane.

In the south east part of the town, he showed them a distillery, the water being pumped by two dogs. Both William and Owen were pleased to hear that the dogs took it in turns, never working for more than an hour at a time and then, of course, only during the day.

They ended their walk by negotiating their way down a short grassy bank to a path beside the Wabash river. Here, they admired and discussed the Rappites' keel boats lying tethered at their moorings, waiting to be filled with goods for market.

Noting the growing dusk, Frederick took them back into the town, pausing between two large brick houses facing each other across the wide street.

'This is my father's house,' he said, pointing behind him, 'and the one across the road is occupied by about forty people, living as one family.'

William looked quizzically at his father. Surely, he thought, this is taking communal living to an extreme? Like the North House in Niskayuna?

Owen's attention had moved on, following Frederick into Father Rapp's home. Here, they were shown up several flights of stairs and out on to a balcony.

'You can see the whole town, yes?' Frederick stepped to one side, making a wide sweep of the panorama with his arm.

'This is Harmonie.' Owen's voice was barely audible, his attention transfixed on the view.

William came to his side, gazing out over the winter scene.

For a long time there was silence.

'It is *very* different from New Lanark,' William murmured, his breath floating like smoke on the cold evening air. 'The river slides past the town, unlike the rushing, cascading Clyde. The land is flat, even the surrounding hills are no more than mounds compared to Scotland. And the houses are small, just two stories as far as I can see,' he squinted against rays of low evening sun. 'It is strange to see all the timber or brick and the rough log cabins, whereas ours are tall and solid stone ... '

'It is the people who make a community,' Owen said, quietly, turning towards Frederick, 'not the material they use to build their houses.'

For the next week, Owen took himself off on his own and immersed himself in Harmonie. William and Donald rode and walked around the surrounding countryside, galloping across the prairies and wandering through the woods. Day after day, they awoke to clear blue skies and frost in the air; glorious, invigorating weather. By midday, the thermometer outside their lodging house showed a reasonable sixty degrees, the sun hot on their backs as they explored.

Christmas was coming up and Mr Flower extended an invitation to Owen and his party to come to Albion and spend the festival with his family. William and Donald were happy to accept and rode over, following detailed directions. However, Owen preferred to remain in Harmonie, waving them away and saying he would follow.

Owen needed this reflective time of solitude.

The last years of struggling with bigoted, narrow-minded politicians, legal dealings, writing and pushing for urgently required reforms, battling with his wits to try and bring the established church to understand they must *act* in a truly religious manner, not give lip service while pandering to tradition and greed.

Now, he was free, for a few days at least, to contemplate the past, enjoy the present and plan for the future.

By the time he joined William at Albion, his mind was made up and when they rode back, together, he shared his decision. William was suddenly overwhelmed with the enormity of what was to happen but he was also delighted.

On the frosty morning of Monday, 3rd January 1825, with the sun gleaming down from the clear sky, Robert Owen and Mr Rapp both signed the particulars of sale for Harmonie, declaring the sale to be agreed.

***

In New Lanark, four thousand miles away from Harmonie, the workrooms in the mills roared and hummed with production. It was the first week of January, cold and damp, but the Hogmanay ceilidh was already a memory.

Joe and four other men with measuring sticks and notebooks clambered between the blackened footings and the exposed iron water wheel in the gap between Mill Two and Mill Four. At last, they were surveying it for quotes to rebuild. Standing at the side, his face alive with interest, Robert Dale answered questions and called requests, laughing at shared jokes.

The short day pulled darkness around it and lamps and stoves were lit, throwing out lines of glowing, moving light reflecting down from the mills. Joe talked over figures with Robert Dale and senior managers in the office then wandered over to the shop.

'We'll be closin' soon, sir,' Andrew Dudley called through from the back, then saw the customer. 'Och, it's yersel'! Are ye stayin' in the village until the bell rings?'

'Aye, Ah thocht as much, nae point gaun up the hill, jist tae come back doon! The Lodge is closed the noo, can Ah wait here?'

'Come through by,' Dudley ushered him into a small back room, made even smaller by stacked shelves lining the walls. 'Ye can tak a seat by the coals, it'll no' be lang noo. Sarah and Fiona are fair excited, an' Ah ha'e tae say, Ah'm pleased as punch mesel'.'

'It's grand news.'

When the mill bell peeled across the dark village, the streets were suddenly flowing with lanterns and people.

Joe waited for Andrew to lock up and then they walked to the Institute. It was a slow, hampered process against the flood of rushing children and workers charging up the hill to their homes.

'Joe!' Fiona appeared, waving to him over the swarm of heads, 'ye made it! Och, Ah'm glad!'

Sarah was at her side, hurrying along, skirts kicking out round her boots, trying to tie her bonnet ribbons.

'An' wid Ah miss it!' Joe greeted both of them, smiling.

They made their way past New Buildings and on along the Row. Rosie was waiting for them in the street.

'Where ha'e ye bin? Ah didnae want tae gae up afore ye but it's freezin' ma taes aff oot here after the warmth at the mules!'

'Let's gae up then,' Joe put his arm around her, hugging her to him in a rough, brotherly embrace, smiling at her pretence to push him away.

'The times Ah've walked up these stairs!' Sarah laughed, pushing open the tenement door.

'We all ha'e,' Fiona reminded her. 'Ye see the wear on the stanes up yon steps, that's frae the feet o' the Scotts!'

On the second floor, Sarah opened her door with a flourish, revealing Cathy sitting by the fire, a shawl around her shoulders and her new baby in her arms.

'Come in!' Sarah chivvied her family into the room. Having orchestrated the gathering, she was bursting with pride, 'come in and meet the new member o' the Scott family, ma wee grandson.'

'The wee soul ... och, he's awfy bonnie ... a halo of golden hair,' Fiona kissed Cathy. 'Whit are ye callin' him?'

It was Sarah who answered, a note of defiance in her voice.

'It's fae baith their Grandfaithers, Cameron Sean.'

Fiona noticed the glance passing between Cathy and her mother.

'Bless him!' Rosie whispered, tucking a shining coin in the baby's blanket.

Sarah had tears on her cheeks and a crumpled handkerchief clutched in her hand.

'Yer alis greetin'' Rosie teased, smiling despite her words, 'can ye no' be happy wi'oot ballin' yer eyes oot?'

Ross and his parents arrived, then neighbours bearing posies of snowdrops and scented witch hazel, black bun, shortbread and ale, adding to the spread of food on the table. When the room became too crowded with well wishers, Joe and Fiona took their leave, telling Sarah what a fine idea it was to hold a party, 'a wee welcome' as she called it, for the new baby.

'Whit a wonderful wiy tae stairt the year,' Fiona said, dreamily, laying her head against Joe's shoulder as they walked along the dark, empty street towards the steps to Lanark. 'It wis awfy nice tae see them sae happy, an' see every yin in oor auld room. It gave me a warm, happy feelin'.'

'Aye, this is a happy time, ma darlin'.'

She raised her head and glanced up at him, suddenly concerned; 'An' whit happens if Mr Owen ups and sells the mills?'

Joe looked around at the bulky black tenements, lights glinting behind shutters, plumes of smoke rising over the tiled roofs.

'This place, the mills ... oor happiness, they dinnae depend on Mr Owen bein' here, no' oany mair. New Lanark will be here fur a lang time tae come. Mr Owen's taught us how guid life can be if ye just treat every yin with kindness and respect. Take the time tae unnerstaun those who are different, an' cooperate wi' each ither. Treat ithers as ye wish tae be treated yersel', but *truly*, no jist when it suits ye.'

He kissed her firmly on the lips, 'He's gi'en us the chance tae learn, tae better oorsels ... think fur oorsels. The rest is up tae us.'

By the light of the waning gibbous moon, they began climbing the steps: a breeze stirring the bare branches, owls calling, a fox's eerie bark sounding from the woodland across the river.

Fiona's thoughts were on Tom. He was coming home to see them, one of his fleeting visits before returning to the life he now knew in Glasgow. Within a year he would be qualified and tending patients beside an experienced doctor. Remembering how slender he looked when he was last at home, she wondered if he was eating properly. Alex, on the other hand, was growing quite plump, despite spending his days labouring and learning the trade beside his brothers.

At the top of the hill, Joe stopped and looked thoughtfully down at the village. He was proud of the fact that he and his family had played a part in the building and legacy of New Lanark. Whatever happened, they were privileged to have known the great David Dale and his visionary son in law. If Robert Owen could spread his New System far and wide, the world would be a much happier, more peaceful place.

He wished him luck.

The New Lanark Trilogy by C A Hope

Based on the true story of the New Lanark Cotton Mills.

These meticulously researched novels bring alive historical characters and actual events during the first forty years of the Scottish mill village under David Dale and Robert Owen.

New Lanark
Spinning New Lives
The First Book 1788-1799

The lives of a young labourer, Joe Scott, Fiona, a Highland orphan and Anne Caroline, David Dale's little daughter, are bound together by Dale's pioneering community. Set against the turbulent backdrop of the French Revolution, Highland Clearances and the dawning of the Scottish Enlightenment.

New Lanark
Living With A Visionary
The Second Book 1800-1814

When Robert Owen and his wife take up residence in the mill village, he immediately makes sweeping changes ... not all of them welcomed.

New Lanark
In Search Of Utopia
The Third Book 1814-1825

Watched by society and the Church, the villagers of New Lanark learn how to live their lives under Robert Owen's philosophy. Owen soon looks beyond the Scottish mills and seeks to influence government policy and world leaders, determined to bring happiness to society.

Real Life Characters

British Prime Minister: Lord Liverpool
On the throne: George III and George IV
Albga, the Owens' pet dog
Allen, William, chemist, Quaker, partner of Owen
Armadale, Lord Justice. Sir William Honyman m Mary McQueen
Astley, Philip (and son, John) circus entertainers/proprietors
Bayley, Thomas
Bentham, Jeremy 1748-1832
Braxfield, Lord, Lord Justice Clerk, Robert MacQueen 1722-1799
Brown, John, banker
Brougham, Henry, lawyer, 1778-1868
Buchanan, John, teacher at New Lanark
Burns, Robert, poet 1759 – 1796
Campbell, Alexander of Hallyards, Glasgow businessman
Campbell, Colin, businessman
Campbell, John, of Jura, Edinburgh
Carrick, Robert, banker, Ship Bank
Clegg, Mr, Owen's clerk
Cleland, James
Combe, Abram
Craig, Mr, manager of Stanley Mills
Crichton, Sir Alexander (1763-1856)
Currie, Dr, friend of David Dale
Cuvier, Jean Léopold 'Georges', French zoologist 1769-1832
Dale, Anne Caroline, (1778- 1831) Margaret, Jean (Jane) and Julia
Dale, David 1739 - 1806
Dale, David, nephew of David Dale
Dale, James, half brother of David 1753-1819 (m.Marion Haddow)
Dale, William, 1784-1790 son of David Dale
Dalglish, Robert
Daniel, John, teacher at New Lanark
Dennistoun, Robert, Glasgow business man
Dodge, Mr, dancing teacher
Drinkwater, Peter
Dunn, the one-armed postman
Fellenberg, Philipp Emanuel von, educator, Hofwyl 1771-1844
Finlay, Kirkman, mill owner and businessman
Fitzgerald, Augustus 3rd Duke of Leinster 1791-1874
Flower, Richard,
Fretageot, Mdme Marie Duclos, educator
Fry, Elizabeth
Gibbs, Michael, businessman
Gibson, William, Doctor at New Lanark

Godwin, William 1756-1836
Griscom, John 1774-1852
Hamilton, Alexander, of Dalzell
Houldsworth, Henry, cotton mill manager, Glasgow
Humboldt, Alexander von, naturalist 1769-1859
Humphreys, Robert
Kelly, William, clockmaker, engineer and mill manager
Lancaster, Joseph, educationalist 1778-1838
Laplace, Pierre Simon, French scholar, 1749-1827
Lavasseur, Monsieur, French prisoner of war, tutor.
Logan, Willie, Freemason of Lanark
Macaulay, Zecheriah
MacDonald, Captain Donald
Macgregor, Alexander, lawyer (for Owen)
MacIntosh, Charles, chemist 1766-1843 (m.Mary Fisher)
MacIntosh George, businessman 1739 – 1807
Mclure, William, educator
Menzies, Reverend William, Minister in Lanark
Mill, James political philosopher 1773-1836
More, John
Murray, Matt, Freemason of Lanark
Neef, Professor, teacher
Nicolas, Grand Duke of Russia (brother of Tsar)
Lawson, Bob, Freemason of Lanark
Owen, William, brother of Robert, children: William, Thomas, Mary
Owen, Anne, sister of Robert
Peel, Sir Robert, mill owner, Member of Parliament.
Pestalozzi, Johan Heinrich 1746-1827, educator
Pictet, de Rochemont, Charles 1755-1824
Place, Francis 1771-1854
Rapp, Reverend George and Frederick (Reichert) his adopted son.
Ross, Lady Mary Lockhart (of Bonnington)
Schmidt, Charles, Robert Owen's Prussian manservant
Scott, Robert, artist
Scott Moncrieff, Robert, banker businessman 1738-1814
Sheddon, William, Owen's butler
Smith, Benjamin
Stuart, Rev James Haldane, m Mary Dale, sons David Dale, James
Tennant, Charles, chemist 1768-1838 (m. Margaret Wilson)
Vansittart, Nicolas, Chancellor of the Exchequer
Walker, John (father) partner of Owen, Charles, son
Whitwell, Miss, teacher at New Lanark
Wilson, Miss, Owen's housekeeper at Braxfield House
Winning, John, artist at New Lanark and his daughter, Janet

Guide to the Dialect used in this Novel

aye – yes (or, in context, aye means all)
auld lang syne – old, long days ago: days now in the past
bairns – children
bàn – blonde / fair skinned (Scottish Gaelic)
besom – a naughty, cheeky or bad girl/woman
bin – been
brèagha – beautiful (Scottish Gaelic)
brither – brother
buildseach – witch (Scottish Gaelic)
cannae – cannot
caunel - candle
chap – knock (chap ma door – knock on my door)
cheerio – goodbye
chiel - child
cla'es – clothes
cludgie - toilet
crabbit – bad tempered, snappy
cry him – call him (his name)
cuddies – horse, pony or donkey
dinnae fash yersel' – don't upset yourself
dinnae ken – don't know
donder – a little walk, meander
dour – glum
douth – depressed, gloomy
driech – dreary, wet or depressing
drookit – soaked
dwam - dream
efter – after
Feasgar math – Good evening (Scottish Gaelic)
gae – go
gaun – going
gowd – gold
gowping – giving pain, hurting
greetin' – crying (tae greet – to cry)
grun - ground
guid - good
haud – hold
haun – hand (gi'e me a haun – give me a hand, help me)
havering and footering – prevaricating
heid – head
jennies – engines (spinning jennies, engines for spinning)

kens – knows (ye ken – you know)
lang may yer lum reek – long may your chimney smoke (traditional wish
    for someone moving into a new home)
lummock – clumsy, lumbering
mair – more (onymair – anymore)
mind – remember
mon – man
mony – money or (in context) many
muckle oota a mickle – (making) much out of a little
neb - nose
neeps – turnips
neònach – strange, weird (Scottish Gaelic)
nicht – night
noo - now
nuthin' or nuchin' - nothing
ony – any
oot - out
richt – right
scratcher – bed (from the scratchy mattresses)
sgriosail – dreadful, damnable (Scottish Gaelic)
sich - such
skelpit erse – smacked bottom
slitter – untidy, dirty person
stoater – great, brilliant
tae – to
tatties - potatoes
thocht – thought
thole – bear pain, cannae thole it – cannot bear it.
t'morra – tomorrow (tomorra)
trauchled- tired out, exhausted
vennel – narrow lane, close
weans – small children
wee - small
whaur – where
wheesht – shush, be quiet
wid – would
yin – one
yon – that or there

Bibliography

Owen, Robert Dale, *Threading My Way,*
Owen Robert, *A New View of Society,*
Donnachie, Ian and Hewitt, George (*1993*) *Historic New Lanark,* Edinburgh University Press, Edinburgh
Pitzer, Donald E, Darryl D Jones, *New Harmony Then & Now,* Quarry Books, Indiana University Press
Whatley, Christopher A (*2000*), *Scottish Society 1707-1830,* Manchester University Press, Manchester
New Lanark Trust, *The Story of New Lanark: Living in New Lanark: The Story of Robert Owen*
McLaren, David J (*1990*) *David Dale of New Lanark,* CWS Scottish CO-OP
Griffiths, Trevor and Morton, Graeme (2010) *A History of Everyday Life in Scotland 1800 to 1900,* Edinburgh University Press
RCAHMS *Falls of Clyde, Artists and Monuments* Broadsheet 14
Podmore, Frank, (repro of pre 1923 book) *Robert Owen: A Biography*
Sinclair, John, *"Old" Statistical Account of Scotland*
Author Note: and many other sources, especially access to the wonderful 'Look to the Distaff' and other Owen family papers.

Grateful thanks to:
Clifford Owen
Lorna Davidson
Docey Lewis
Professor Donald E Pitzer
Pat Brandwood and the Robert Owen Museum, Newtown, Wales
New Lanark Trust
Cooperative Archives, Manchester
Pioneers Museum, Rochdale

You can visit: Robert Owen Museum, Newtown, Wales; New Harmony, Indiana, USA; New Lanark Mills, South Lanarkshire, Scotland, now a UNESCO World Heritage Site.

Lightning Source UK Ltd.
Milton Keynes UK
UKOW06f0211280516

275152UK00012B/243/P